YOUNG HELLBOY
™

THE HIDDEN LAND

Created by
MIKE MIGNOLA

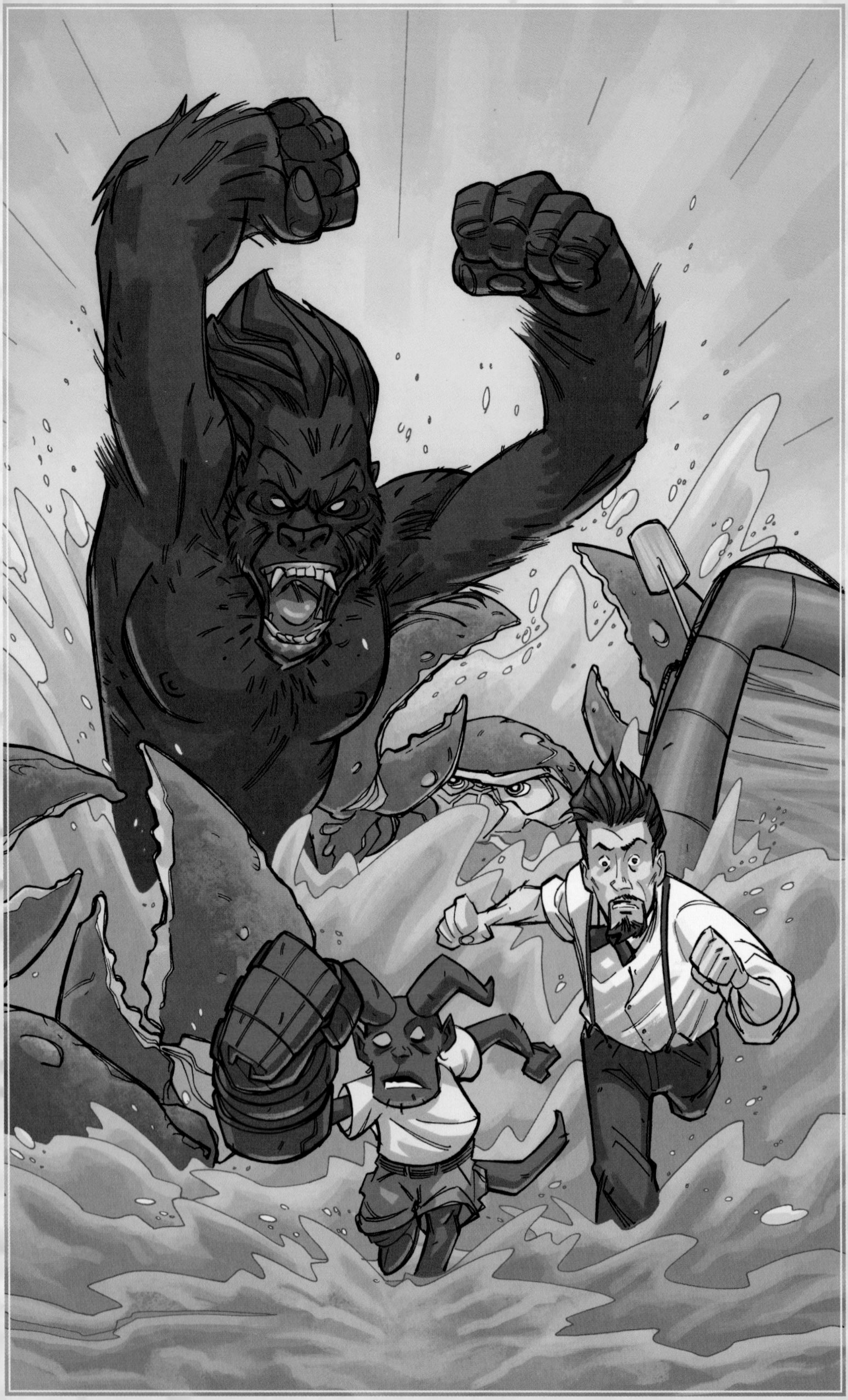

YOUNG HELLBOY™

THE HIDDEN LAND

Story by
MIKE MIGNOLA and **THOMAS SNIEGOSKI**

Art by
CRAIG ROUSSEAU

Colors by
DAVE STEWART

Letters by
CLEM ROBINS

Cover and Chapter Break Art by
MATT SMITH

◆

Publisher MIKE RICHARDSON

Editor KATII O'BRIEN

Associate Editor JENNY BLENK

Collection designer PATRICK SATTERFIELD

Digital Art Technician ANN GRAY

Dark Horse Books

◆

YOUNG HELLBOY: THE HIDDEN LAND

Young Hellboy™ © 2021 Mike Mignola. Hellboy™ and all other prominently featured characters are trademarks of Mike Mignola. Dark Horse Books ® and the Dark Horse logo are trademarks of Dark Horse Comics LLC, registered in various categories and countries. All rights reserved. No portion of this publication may be reproduced or transmitted, in any form or by any means, without the express written permission of Dark Horse Comics LLC. Names, characters, places, and incidents featured in this publication either are the product of the author's imagination or are used fictitiously. Any resemblance to actual persons (living or dead), events, institutions, or locales, without satiric intent, is coincidental.

This book collects *Young Hellboy: The Hidden Land* #1-#4.

Published by
DARK HORSE BOOKS
A division of Dark Horse Comics LLC
10956 SE Main Street • Milwaukie, OR 97222

DarkHorse.com
Facebook.com/DarkHorseComics • Twitter.com/DarkHorseComics

Advertising Sales: (503) 905-2315 • Comic shop locator service: comicshoplocator.com

First edition: September 2021
eBOOK ISBN: 978-1-50672-399-0
ISBN: 978-1-50672-398-3

1 3 5 7 9 10 8 6 4 2
Printed in China

Library of Congress Cataloging-in-Publication Data

Names: Mignola, Mike, author. | Sniegoski, Tom, author. | Rousseau, Craig, artist. | Stewart, Dave, colourist. | Robins, Clem, 1955- letterer. | Smith, Matt, cover artist.
Title: Young Hellboy : the hidden land / story by Mike Mignola and Thomas Sniegoski ; art by Craig Rousseau ; colors by Dave Stewart ; letters by Clem Robins ; cover and chapter break art by Matt Smith.
Description: First edition. | Milwaukie, OR : Dark Horse Books, 2021. | "This book collects Young Hellboy: The Hidden Land #1-#4." | Summary: "Stranded on a strange island after a mishap on their way to a South American dig site, Hellboy and Professor Bruttenholm are confronted by all manner of monsters on land, sea, and sky! A stranger who rescues them turns out to be one of Hellboy's heroes, but they still aren't as safe as they think they are! An old evil that the island protects is about to reawaken, drawing Hellboy and his new allies into a desperate battle!"-- Provided by publisher.
Identifiers: LCCN 2021010102 (print) | LCCN 2021010103 (ebook) | ISBN 9781506723983 (hardcover) | ISBN 9781506723990 (ebook)
Subjects: LCSH: Comic books, strips, etc.
Classification: LCC PN6728.H3838 M69 2021 (print) | LCC PN6728.H3838 (ebook) | DDC 741.5/973--dc23
LC record available at https://lccn.loc.gov/2021010102
LC ebook record available at https://lccn.loc.gov/2021010103

CHAPTER ONE

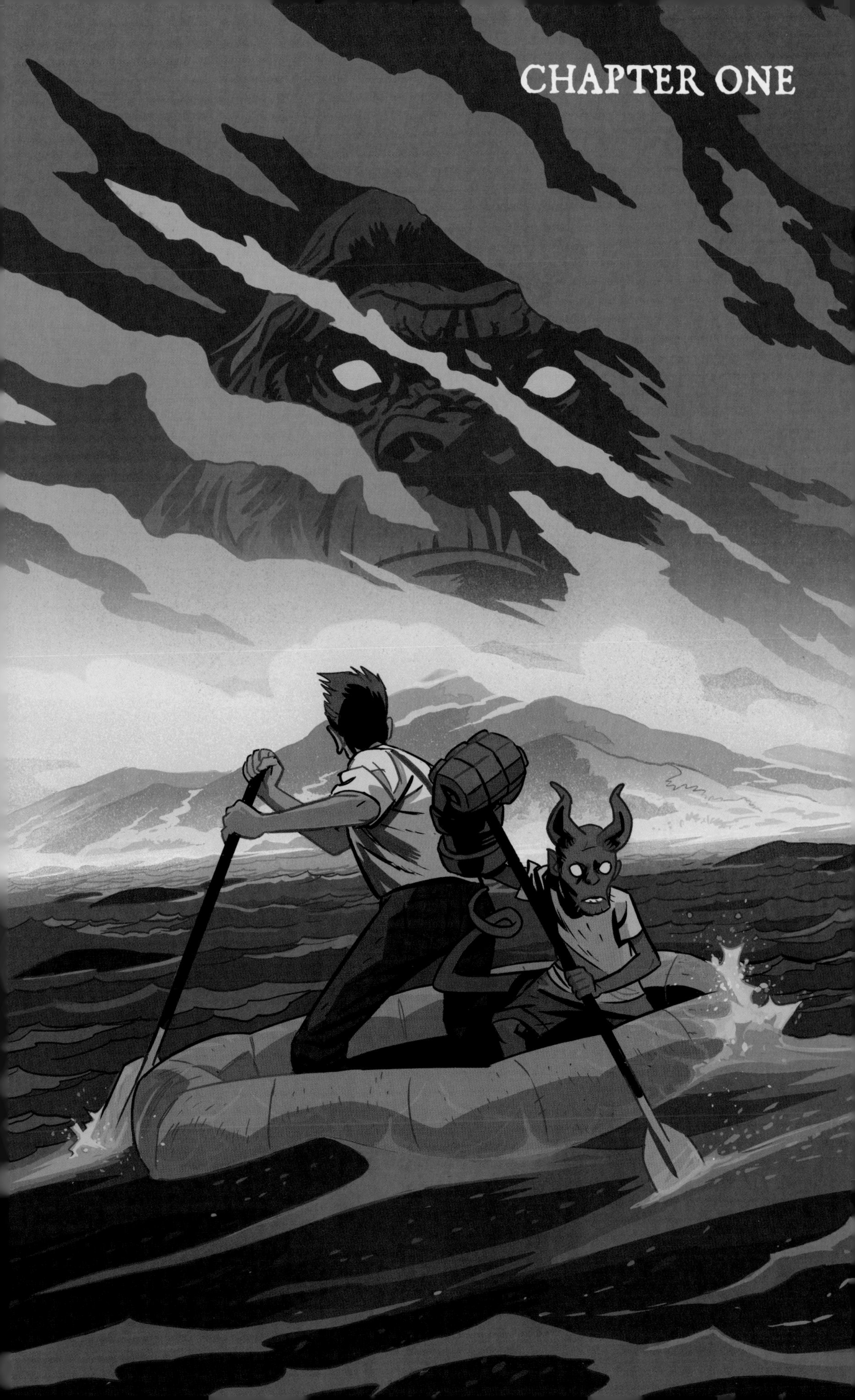

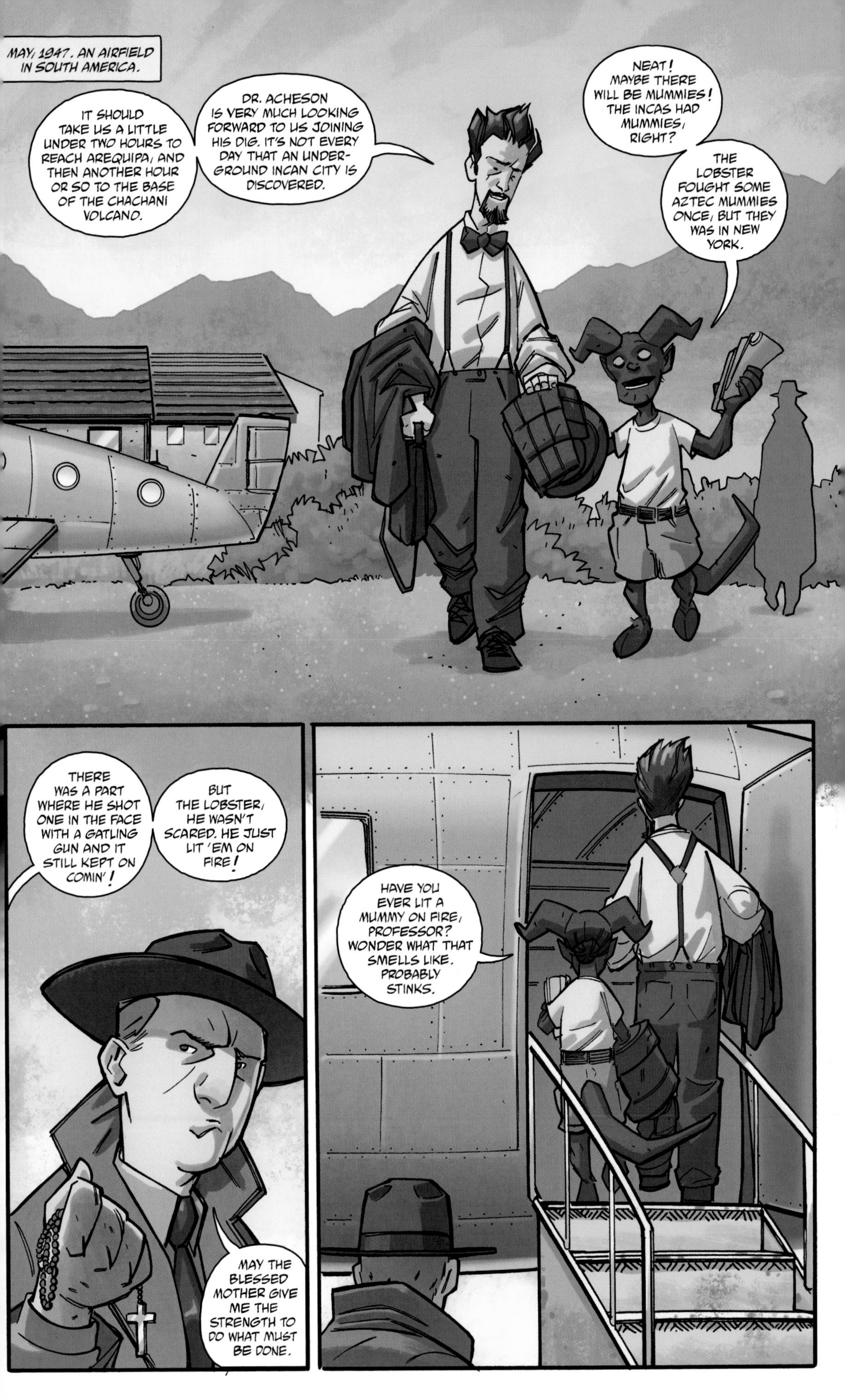
MAY, 1947. AN AIRFIELD IN SOUTH AMERICA.
IT SHOULD TAKE US A LITTLE UNDER TWO HOURS TO REACH AREQUIPA, AND THEN ANOTHER HOUR OR SO TO THE BASE OF THE CHACHANI VOLCANO.
DR. ACHESON IS VERY MUCH LOOKING FORWARD TO US JOINING HIS DIG. IT'S NOT EVERY DAY THAT AN UNDER-GROUND INCAN CITY IS DISCOVERED.
NEAT! MAYBE THERE WILL BE MUMMIES! THE INCAS HAD MUMMIES, RIGHT?
THE LOBSTER FOUGHT SOME AZTEC MUMMIES ONCE, BUT THEY WAS IN NEW YORK.
THERE WAS A PART WHERE HE SHOT ONE IN THE FACE WITH A GATLING GUN AND IT STILL KEPT ON COMIN'!
BUT THE LOBSTER, HE WASN'T SCARED. HE JUST LIT 'EM ON FIRE!
MAY THE BLESSED MOTHER GIVE ME THE STRENGTH TO DO WHAT MUST BE DONE.
HAVE YOU EVER LIT A MUMMY ON FIRE, PROFESSOR? WONDER WHAT THAT SMELLS LIKE. PROBABLY STINKS.

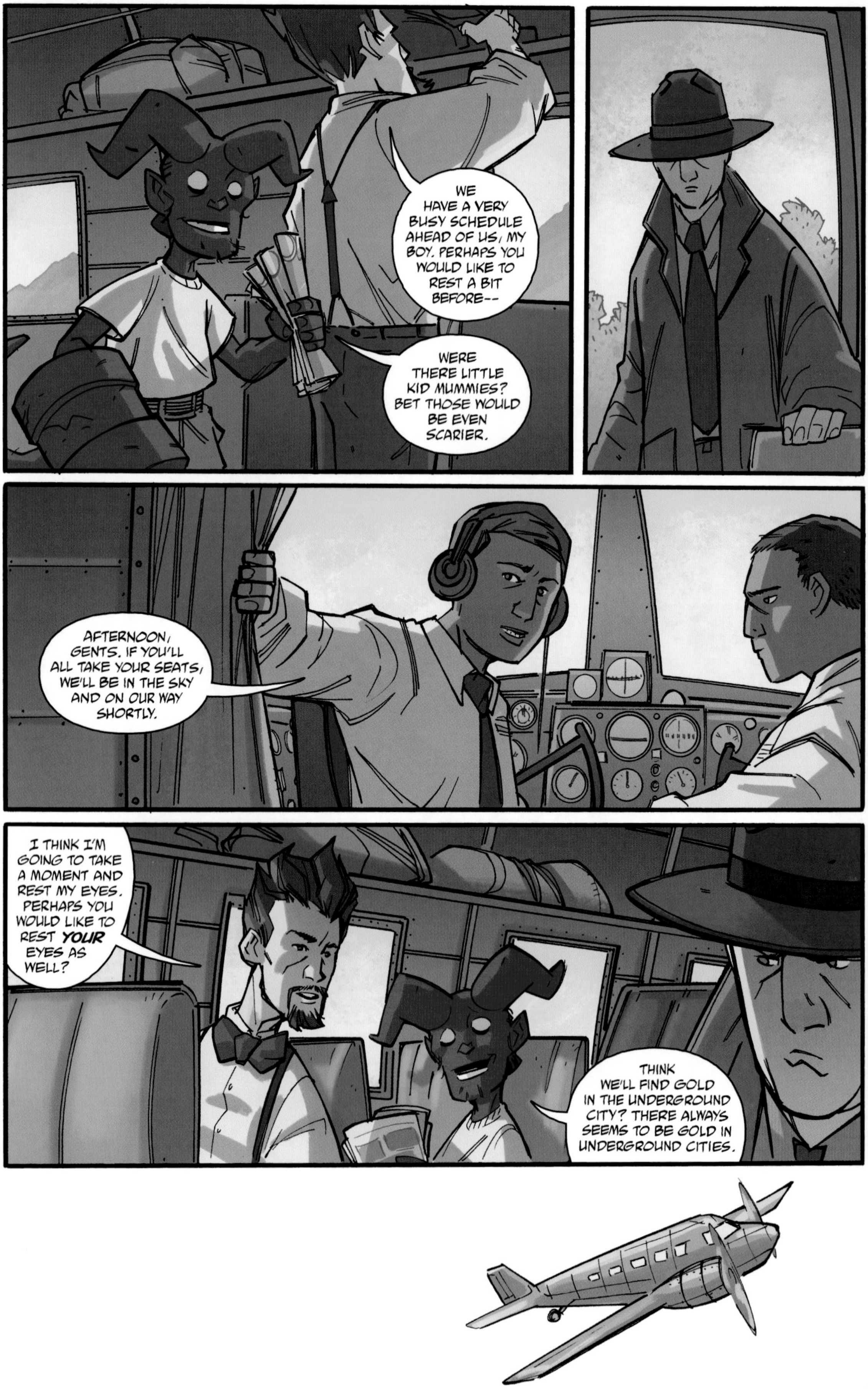
WE HAVE A VERY BUSY SCHEDULE AHEAD OF US, MY BOY. PERHAPS YOU WOULD LIKE TO REST A BIT BEFORE--
WERE THERE LITTLE KID MUMMIES? BET THOSE WOULD BE EVEN SCARIER.
AFTERNOON, GENTS. IF YOU'LL ALL TAKE YOUR SEATS, WE'LL BE IN THE SKY AND ON OUR WAY SHORTLY.
I THINK I'M GOING TO TAKE A MOMENT AND REST MY EYES. PERHAPS YOU WOULD LIKE TO REST **YOUR** EYES AS WELL?
THINK WE'LL FIND GOLD IN THE UNDERGROUND CITY? THERE ALWAYS SEEMS TO BE GOLD IN UNDERGROUND CITIES.

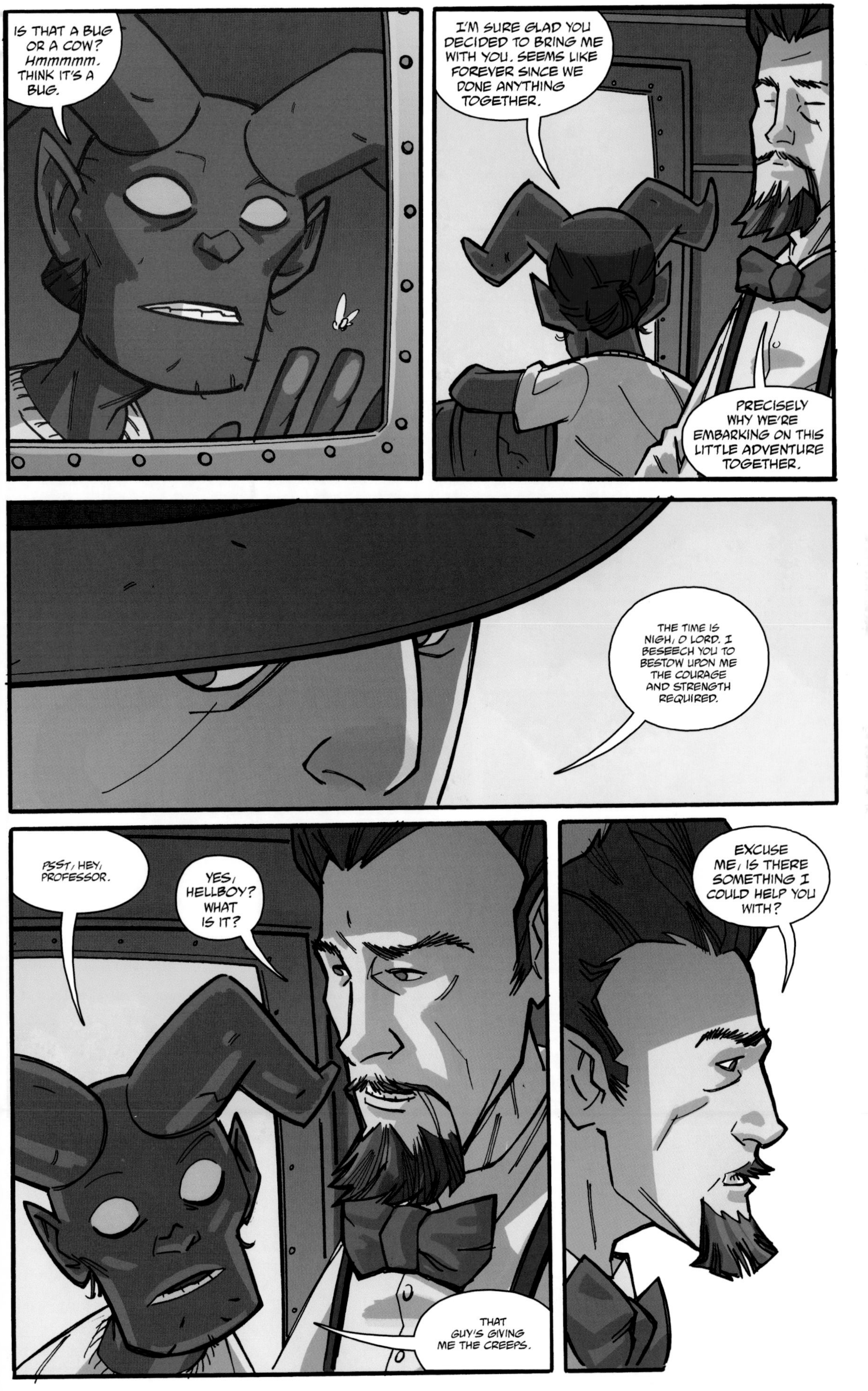
IS THAT A BUG OR A COW? Hmmmmm. THINK IT'S A BUG.
I'M SURE GLAD YOU DECIDED TO BRING ME WITH YOU. SEEMS LIKE FOREVER SINCE WE DONE ANYTHING TOGETHER.
PRECISELY WHY WE'RE EMBARKING ON THIS LITTLE ADVENTURE TOGETHER.
THE TIME IS NIGH, O LORD. I BESEECH YOU TO BESTOW UPON ME THE COURAGE AND STRENGTH REQUIRED.
PSST, HEY, PROFESSOR.
YES, HELLBOY? WHAT IS IT?
THAT GUY'S GIVING ME THE CREEPS.
EXCUSE ME, IS THERE SOMETHING I COULD HELP YOU WITH?

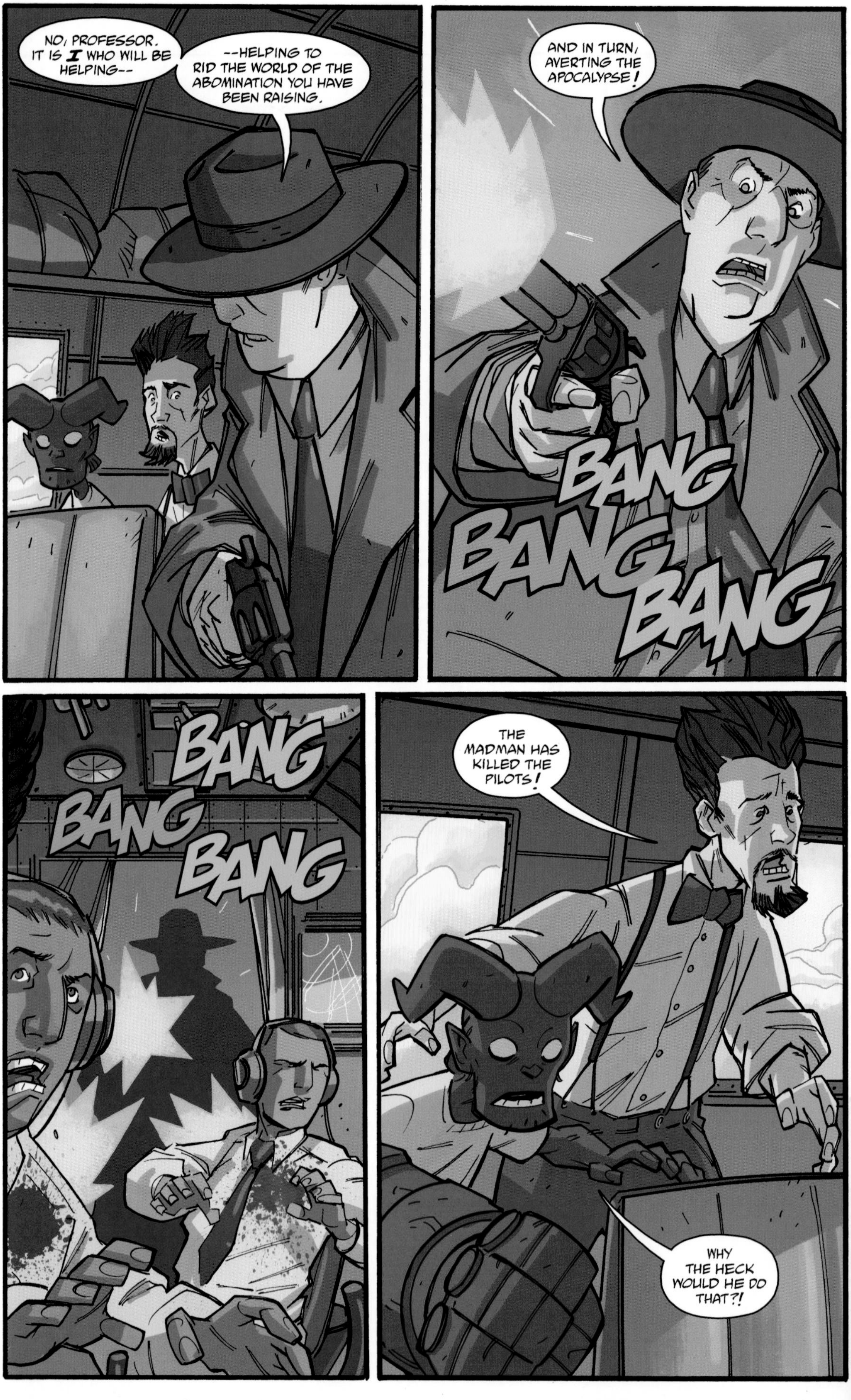

NO, PROFESSOR. IT IS I WHO WILL BE HELPING--
--HELPING TO RID THE WORLD OF THE ABOMINATION YOU HAVE BEEN RAISING.
AND IN TURN, AVERTING THE APOCALYPSE!
BANG BANG BANG
BANG BANG BANG
THE MADMAN HAS KILLED THE PILOTS!
WHY THE HECK WOULD HE DO THAT?!

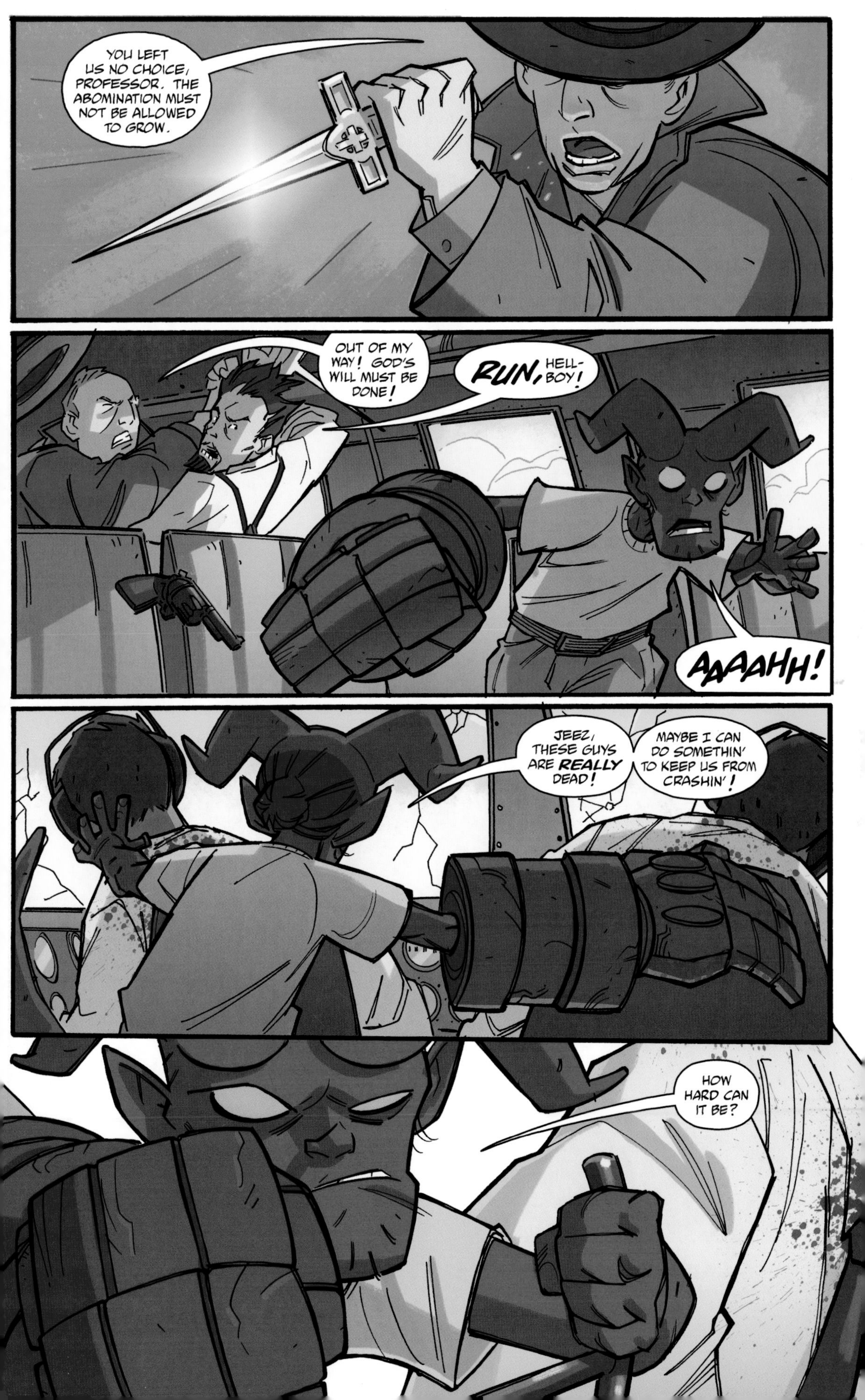
YOU LEFT US NO CHOICE, PROFESSOR. THE ABOMINATION MUST NOT BE ALLOWED TO GROW.
OUT OF MY WAY! GOD'S WILL MUST BE DONE!
RUN, HELL-BOY!
AAAAHH!
JEEZ, THESE GUYS ARE **REALLY** DEAD!
MAYBE I CAN DO SOMETHIN' TO KEEP US FROM CRASHIN'!
HOW HARD CAN IT BE?

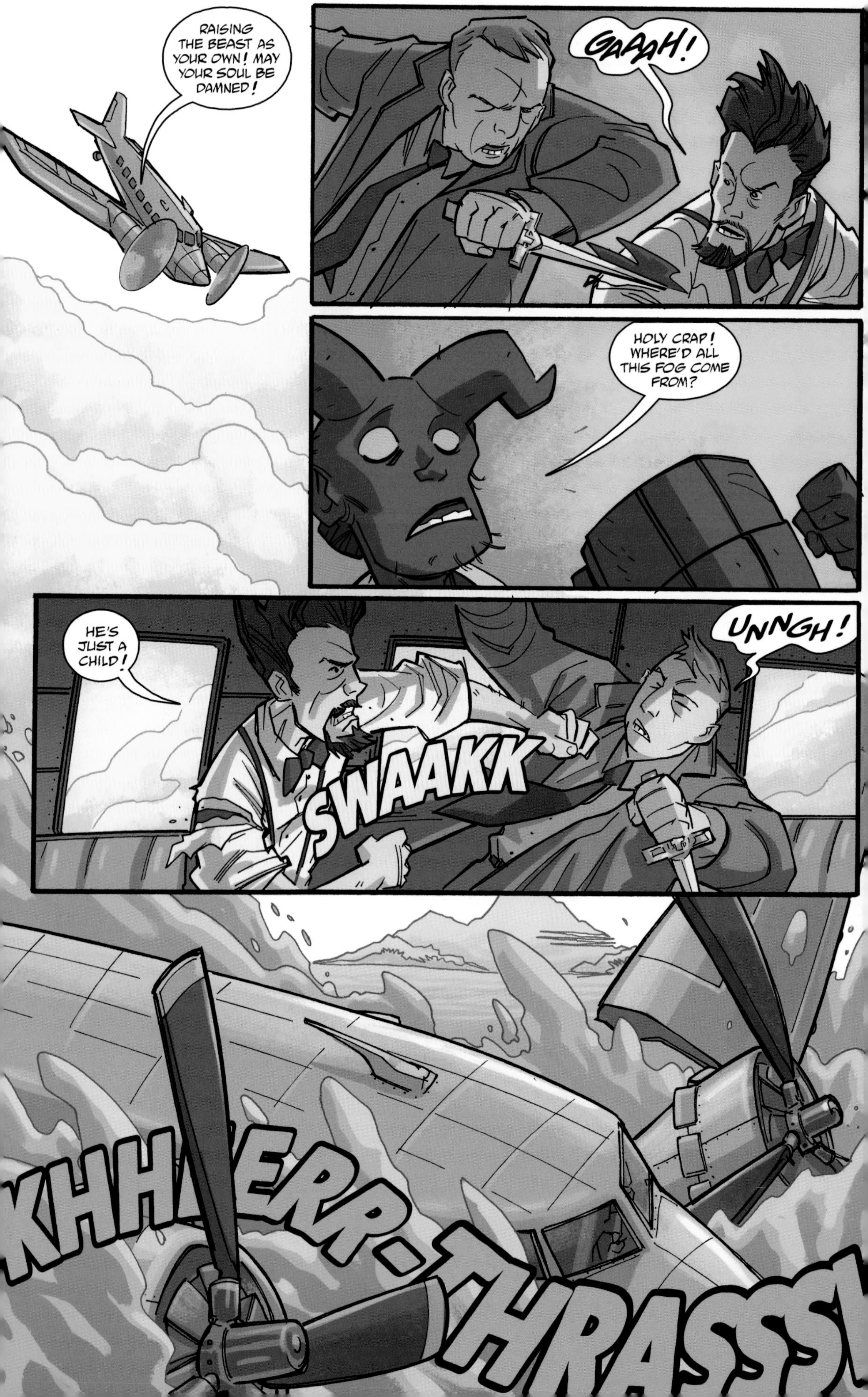
RAISING THE BEAST AS YOUR OWN! MAY YOUR SOUL BE DAMNED!
GAAAH!
HOLY CRAP! WHERE'D ALL THIS FOG COME FROM?
HE'S JUST A CHILD!
UNNGH!
SWAAKK
KHHHERR-THRASSS!

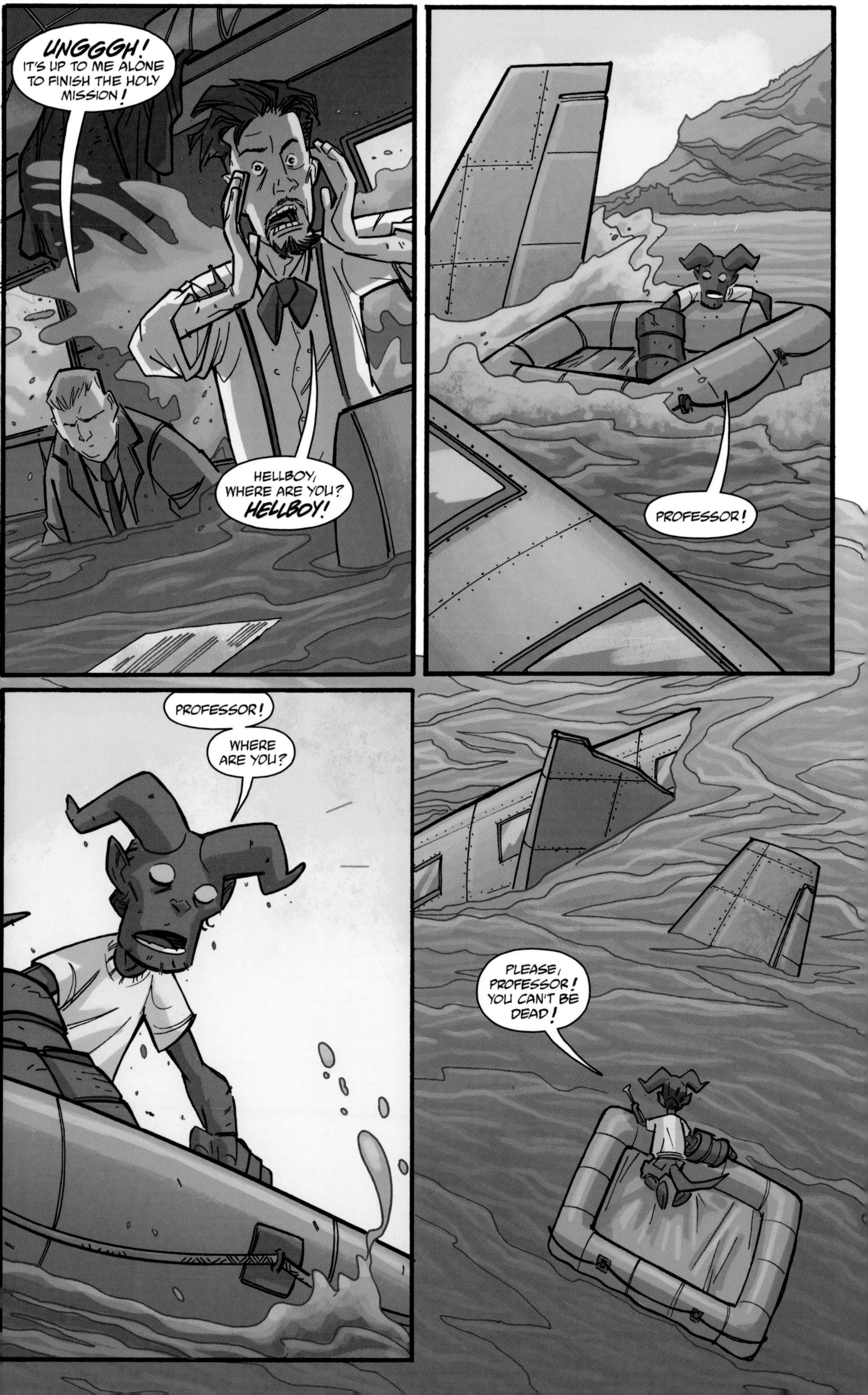
UNGGGH! IT'S UP TO ME ALONE TO FINISH THE HOLY MISSION!
HELLBOY, WHERE ARE YOU? HELLBOY!
PROFESSOR!
PROFESSOR!
WHERE ARE YOU?
PLEASE, PROFESSOR! YOU CAN'T BE DEAD!

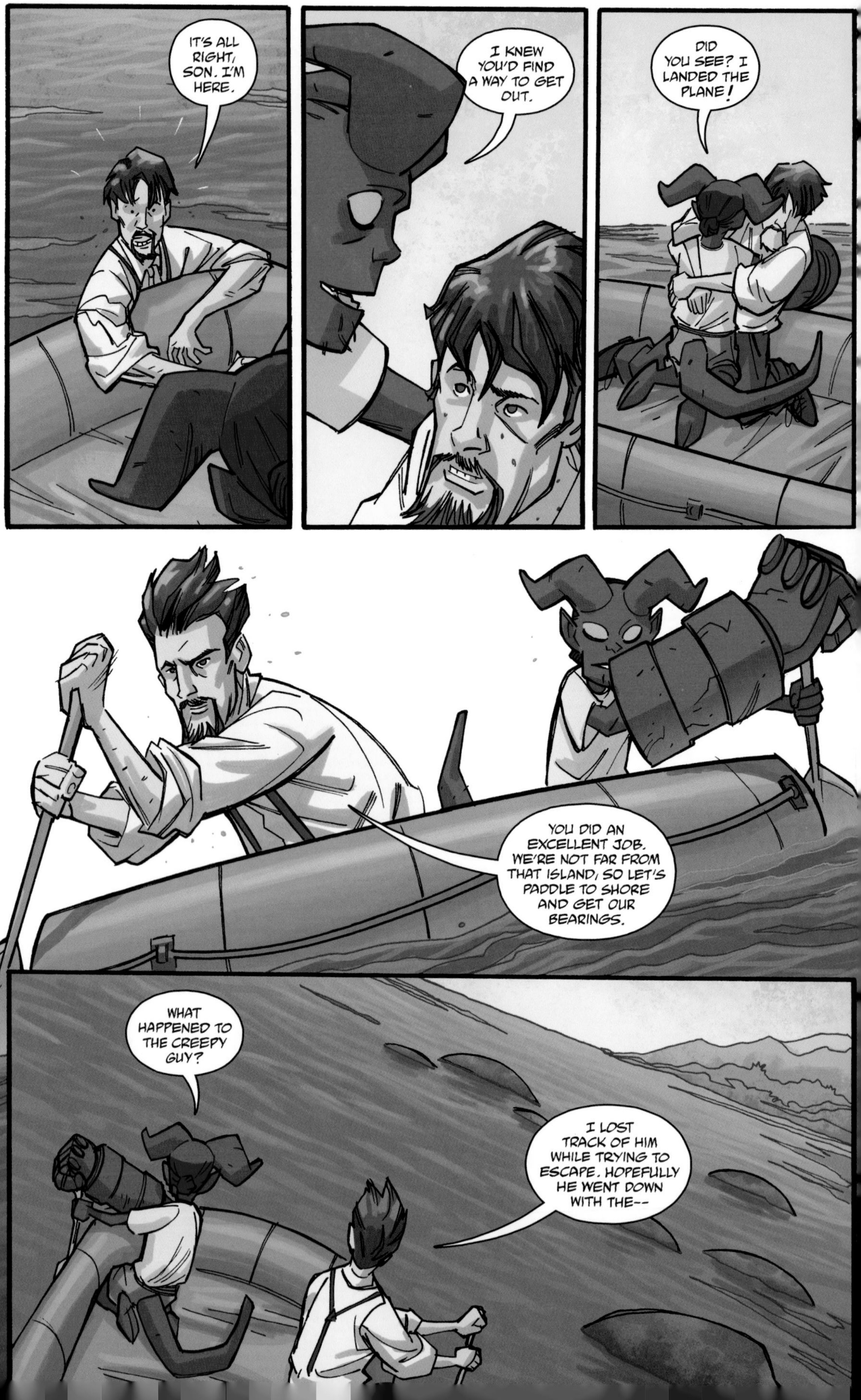
IT'S ALL RIGHT, SON. I'M HERE.
I KNEW YOU'D FIND A WAY TO GET OUT.
DID YOU SEE? I LANDED THE PLANE!
YOU DID AN EXCELLENT JOB. WE'RE NOT FAR FROM THAT ISLAND, SO LET'S PADDLE TO SHORE AND GET OUR BEARINGS.
WHAT HAPPENED TO THE CREEPY GUY?
I LOST TRACK OF HIM WHILE TRYING TO ESCAPE. HOPEFULLY HE WENT DOWN WITH THE--

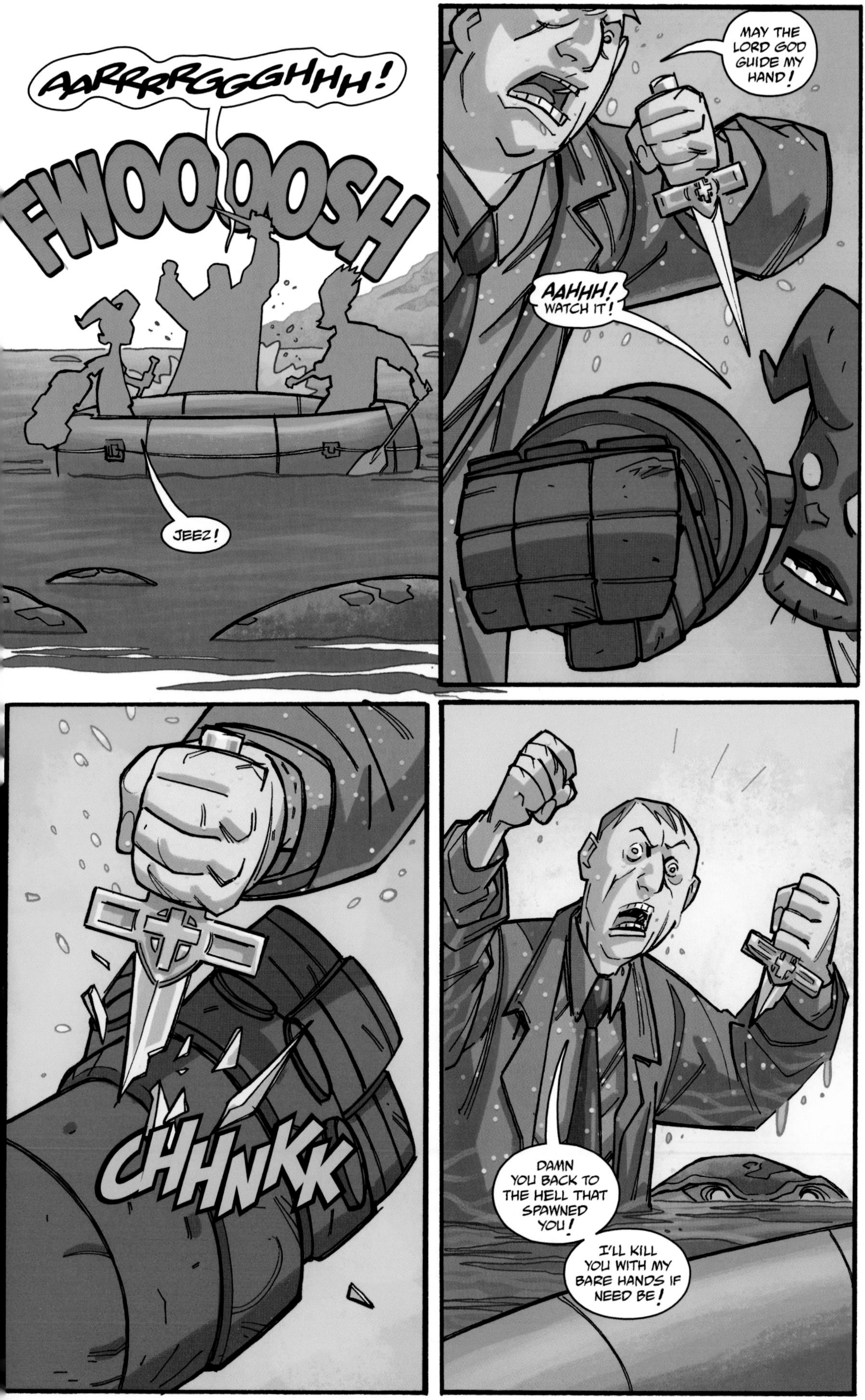
AARRRRGGGHHHH!
FWOOOOSH
JEEZ!
MAY THE LORD GOD GUIDE MY HAND!
AAHHH! WATCH IT!
CHHNKK
DAMN YOU BACK TO THE HELL THAT SPAWNED YOU!
I'LL KILL YOU WITH MY BARE HANDS IF NEED BE!

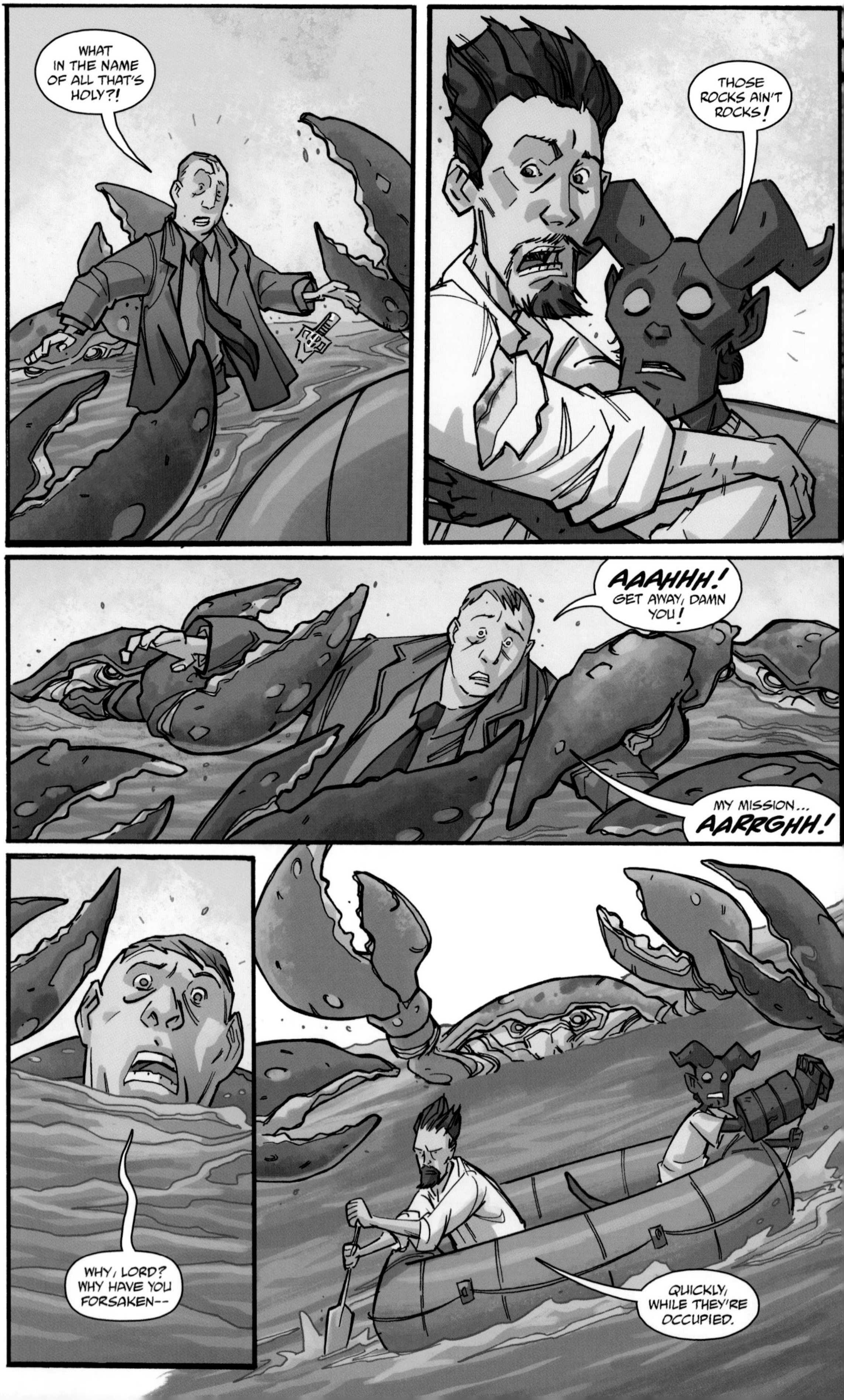

WHAT IN THE NAME OF ALL THAT'S HOLY?!
THOSE ROCKS AIN'T ROCKS!
AAAHHH! GET AWAY, DAMN YOU!
MY MISSION... AARRGHH!
WHY, LORD? WHY HAVE YOU FORSAKEN--
QUICKLY, WHILE THEY'RE OCCUPIED.

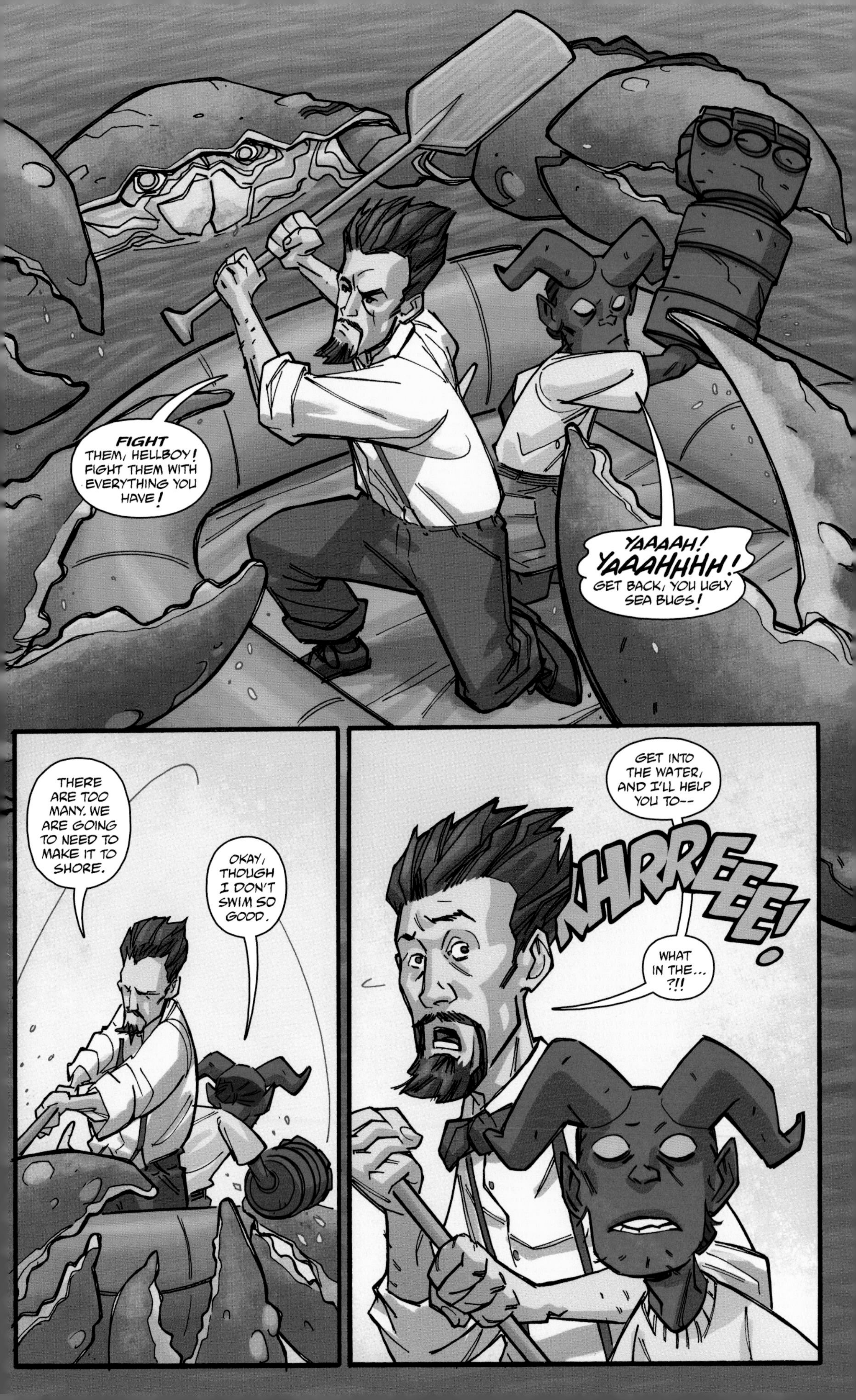
FIGHT THEM, HELLBOY! FIGHT THEM WITH EVERYTHING YOU HAVE!
YAAAAH! YAAAHHHH! GET BACK, YOU UGLY SEA BUGS!
THERE ARE TOO MANY. WE ARE GOING TO NEED TO MAKE IT TO SHORE.
OKAY, THOUGH I DON'T SWIM SO GOOD.
GET INTO THE WATER, AND I'LL HELP YOU TO--
KHRREEEE!
WHAT IN THE... ?!!

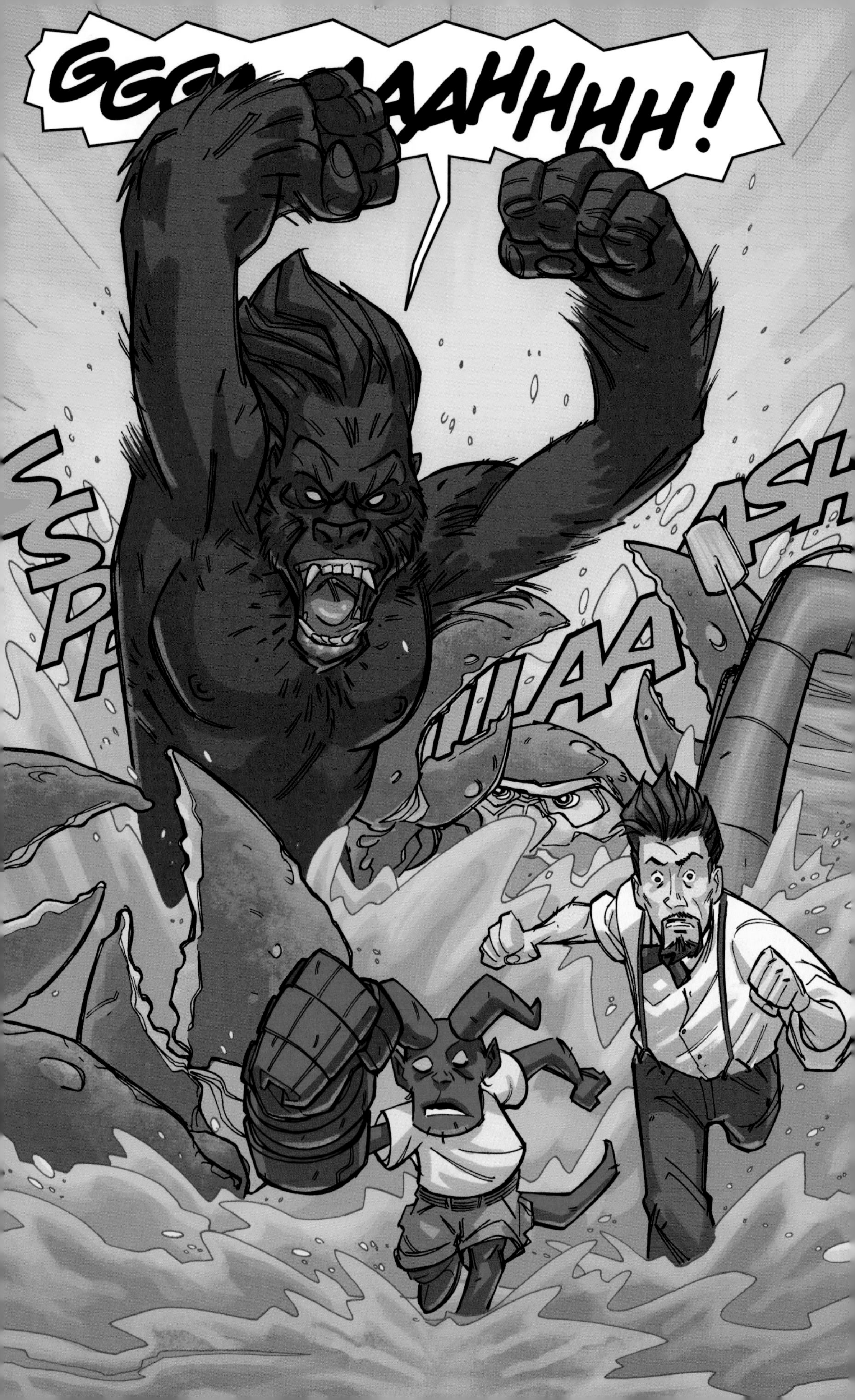
GGG
AAHHHH!

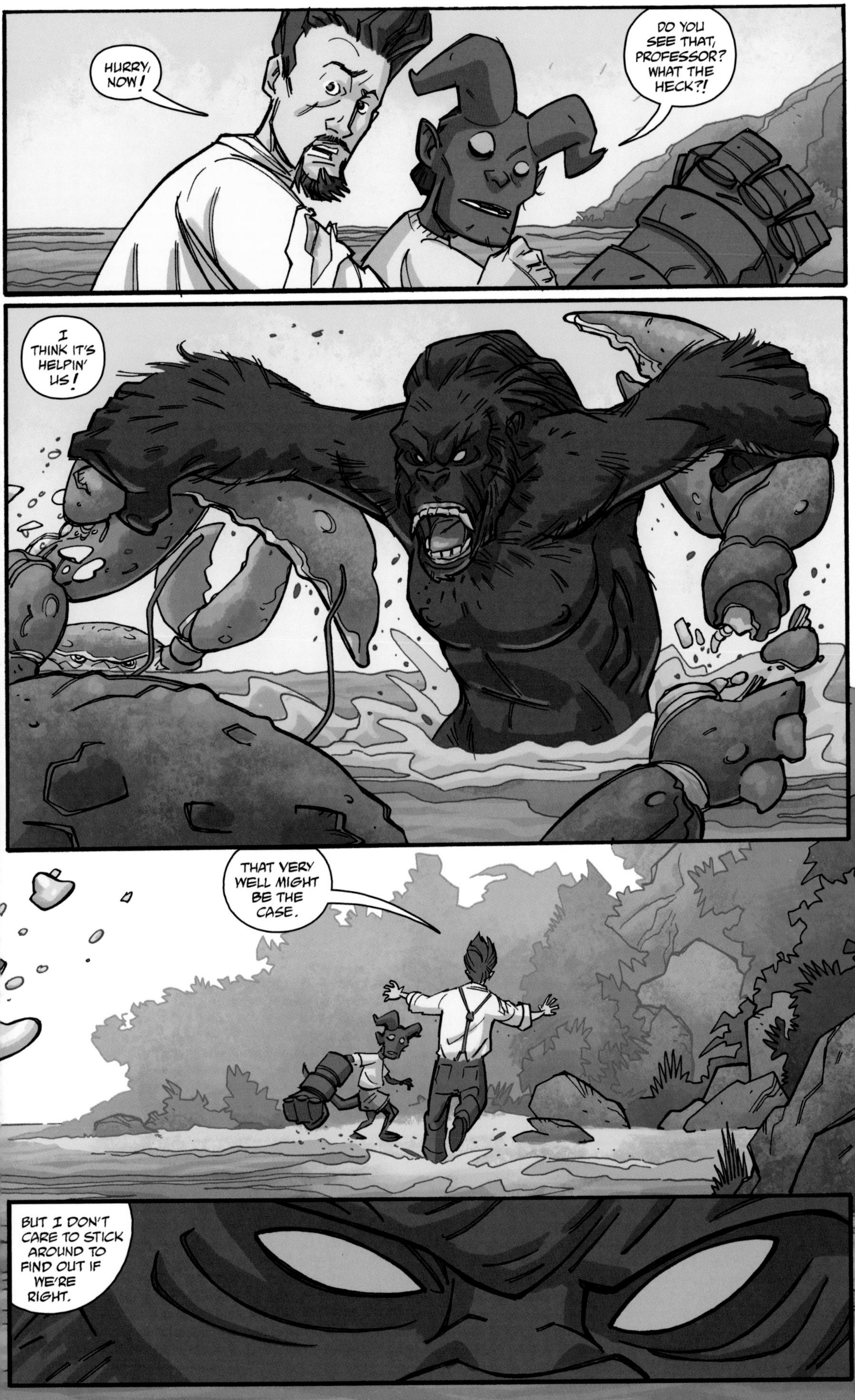
HURRY, NOW!
DO YOU SEE THAT, PROFESSOR? WHAT THE HECK?!
I THINK IT'S HELPIN' US!
THAT VERY WELL MIGHT BE THE CASE.
BUT I DON'T CARE TO STICK AROUND TO FIND OUT IF WE'RE RIGHT.

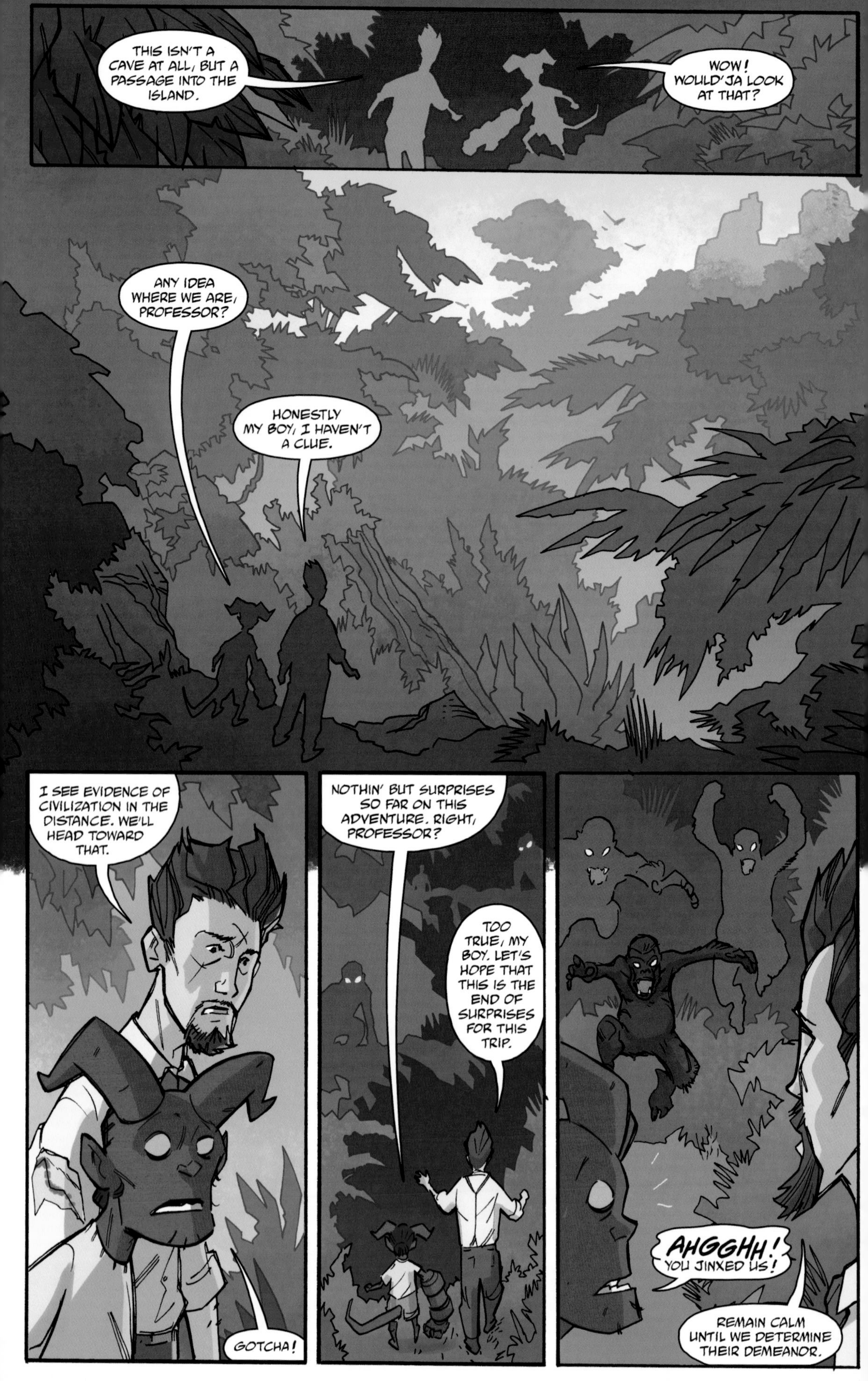
THIS ISN'T A CAVE AT ALL, BUT A PASSAGE INTO THE ISLAND.
WOW! WOULD'JA LOOK AT THAT?
ANY IDEA WHERE WE ARE, PROFESSOR?
HONESTLY MY BOY, I HAVEN'T A CLUE.
I SEE EVIDENCE OF CIVILIZATION IN THE DISTANCE. WE'LL HEAD TOWARD THAT.
GOTCHA!
NOTHIN' BUT SURPRISES SO FAR ON THIS ADVENTURE. RIGHT, PROFESSOR?
TOO TRUE, MY BOY. LET'S HOPE THAT THIS IS THE END OF SURPRISES FOR THIS TRIP.
AHGGHH! YOU JINXED US!
REMAIN CALM UNTIL WE DETERMINE THEIR DEMEANOR.

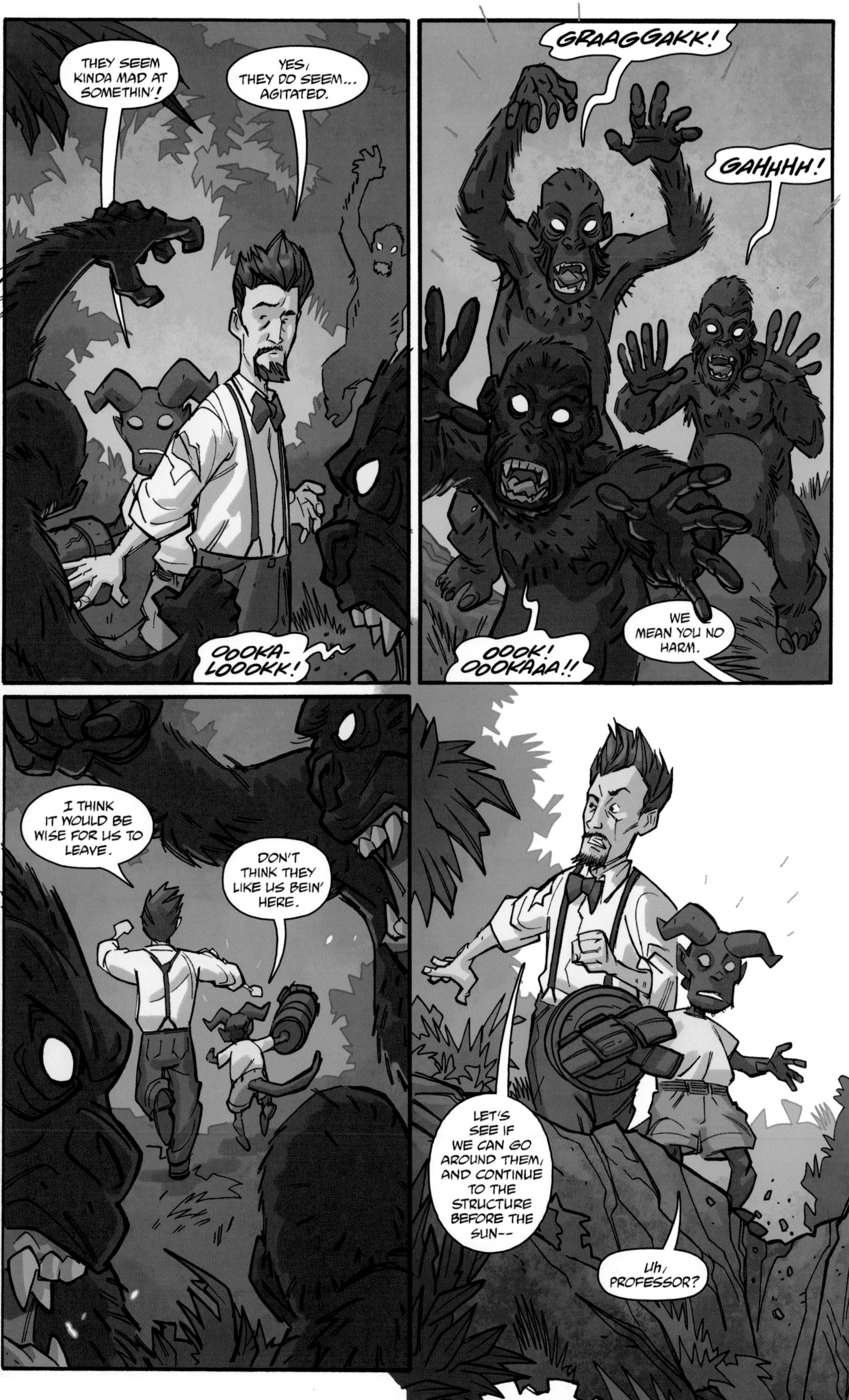
THEY SEEM KINDA MAD AT SOMETHIN'!
YES, THEY DO SEEM... AGITATED.
OOOKA-LOOOKK!
GRAAGGAKK!
GAHHHH!
OOOK! OOOKAAA!!
WE MEAN YOU NO HARM.
I THINK IT WOULD BE WISE FOR US TO LEAVE.
DON'T THINK THEY LIKE US BEIN' HERE.
LET'S SEE IF WE CAN GO AROUND THEM, AND CONTINUE TO THE STRUCTURE BEFORE THE SUN--
UH, PROFESSOR?

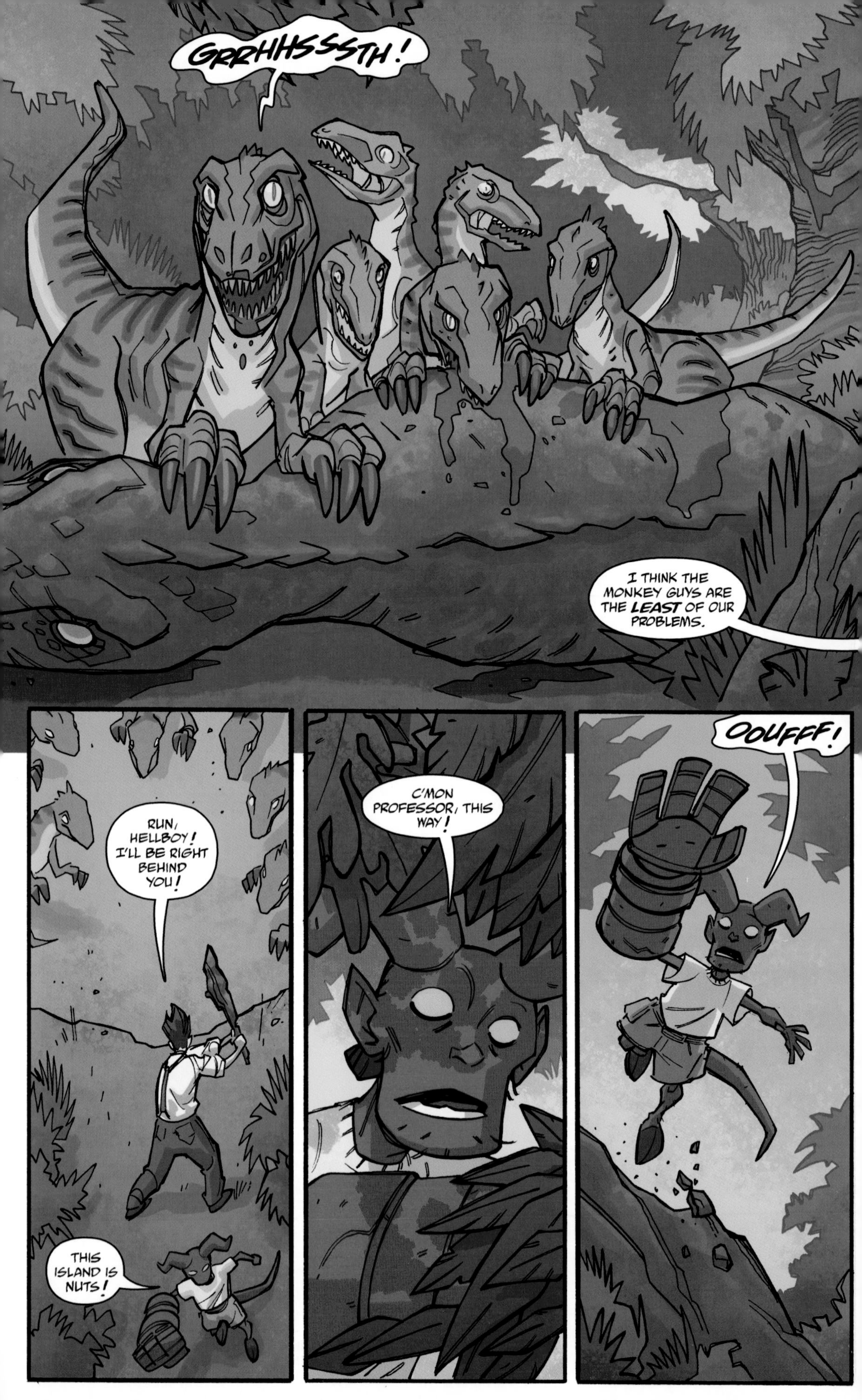
GRRHHSSSSTH!
I THINK THE MONKEY GUYS ARE THE LEAST OF OUR PROBLEMS.
RUN, HELLBOY! I'LL BE RIGHT BEHIND YOU!
THIS ISLAND IS NUTS!
C'MON PROFESSOR, THIS WAY!
OOUFFF!

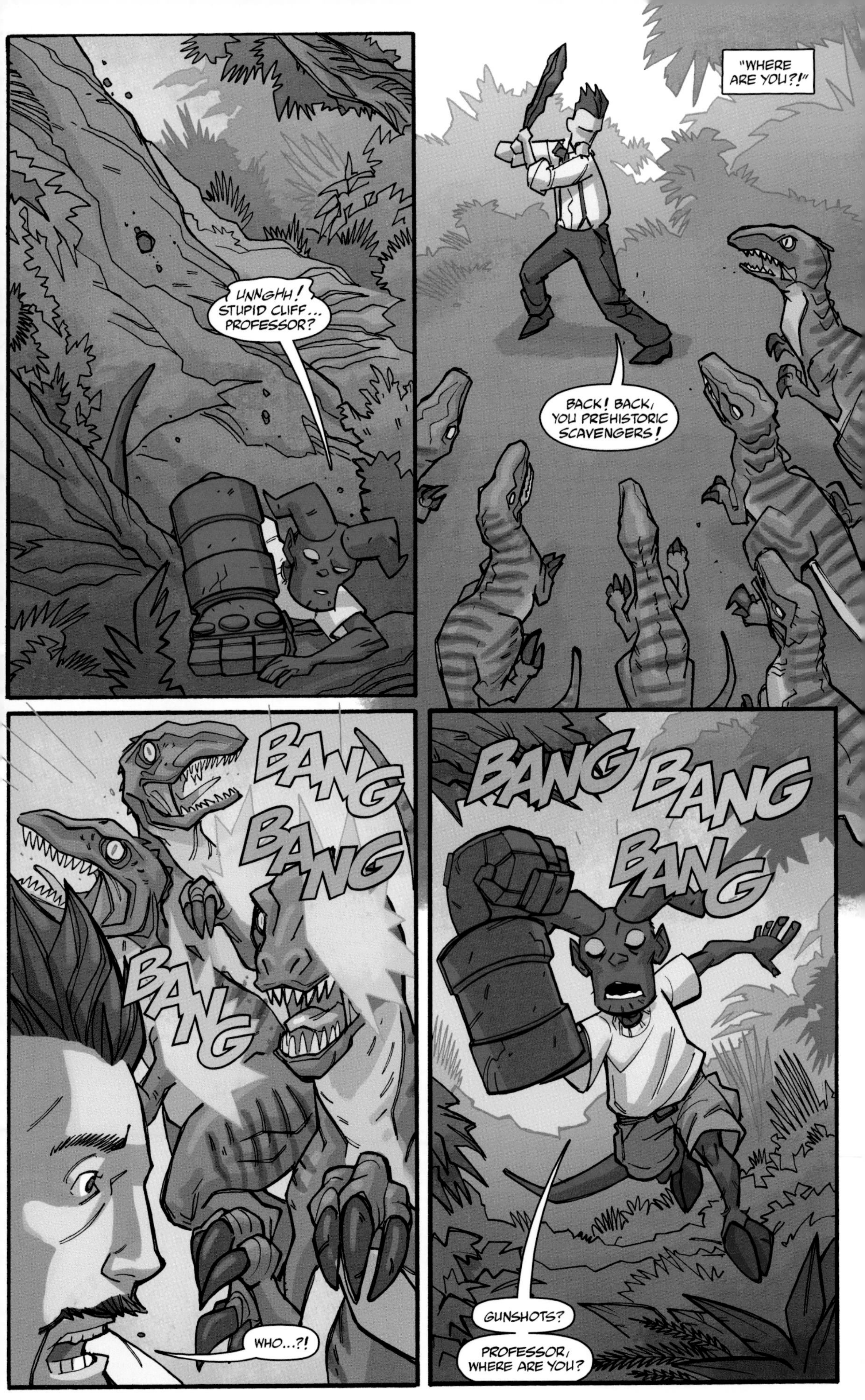
UNNGHH! STUPID CLIFF... PROFESSOR?
"WHERE ARE YOU?!"
BACK! BACK, YOU PREHISTORIC SCAVENGERS!
BANG
BANG
BANG
WHO...?!
BANG BANG
BANG
GUNSHOTS?
PROFESSOR, WHERE ARE YOU?

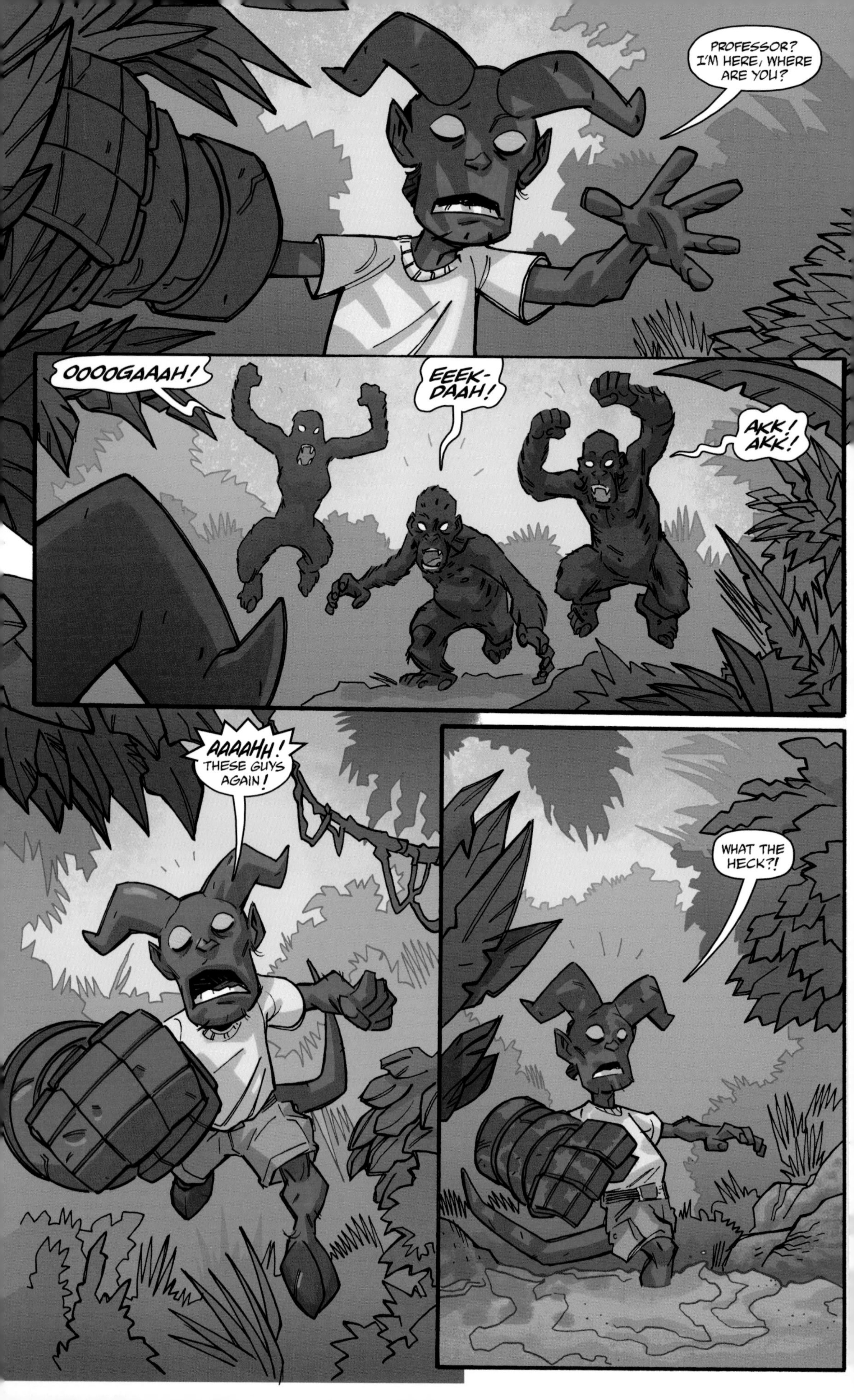
PROFESSOR? I'M HERE, WHERE ARE YOU?
OOOOGAAAH!
EEEK-DAAH!
AKK! AKK!
AAAAHH! THESE GUYS AGAIN!
WHAT THE HECK?!

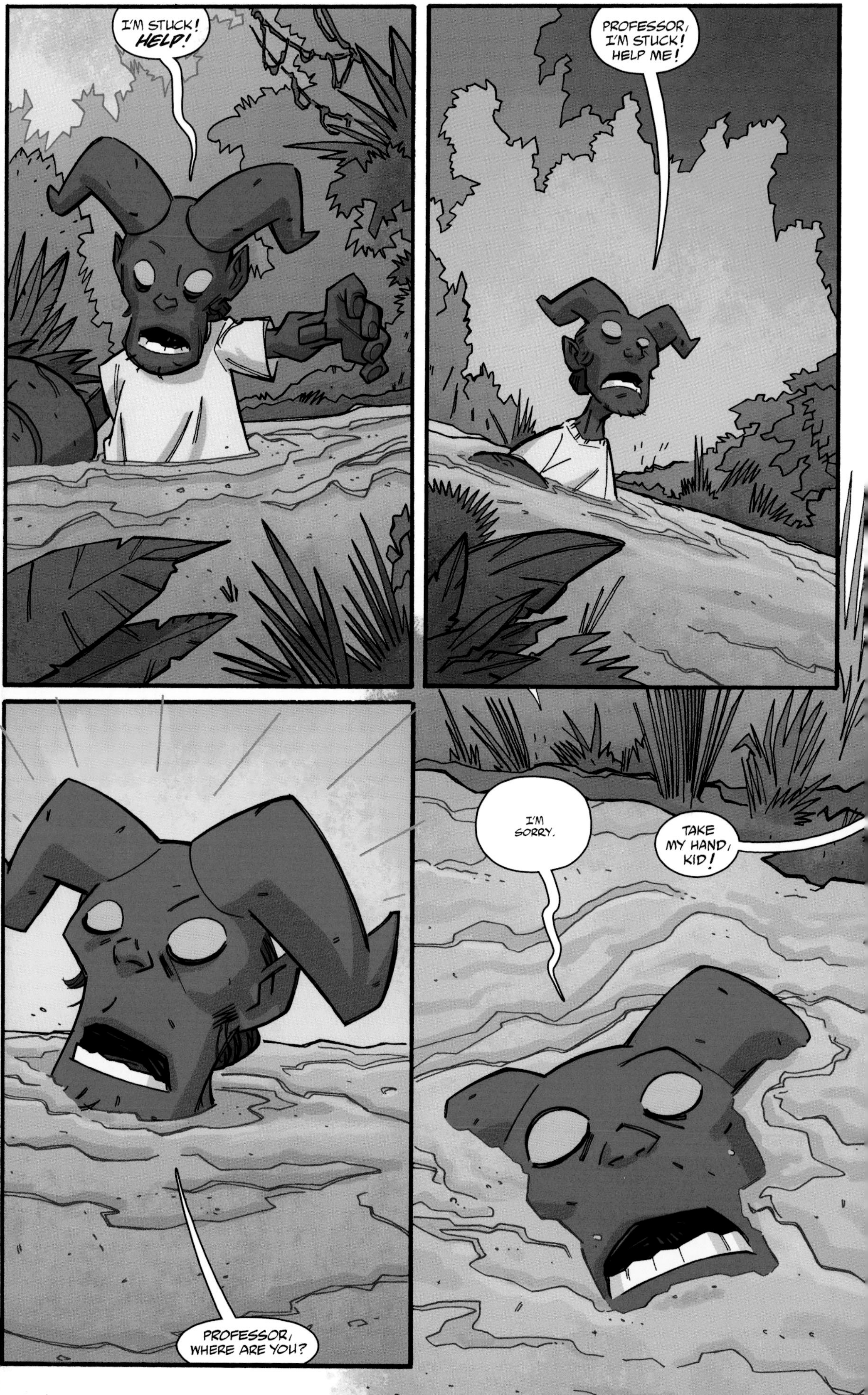
I'M STUCK! HELP!
PROFESSOR, I'M STUCK! HELP ME!
PROFESSOR, WHERE ARE YOU?
I'M SORRY.
TAKE MY HAND, KID!

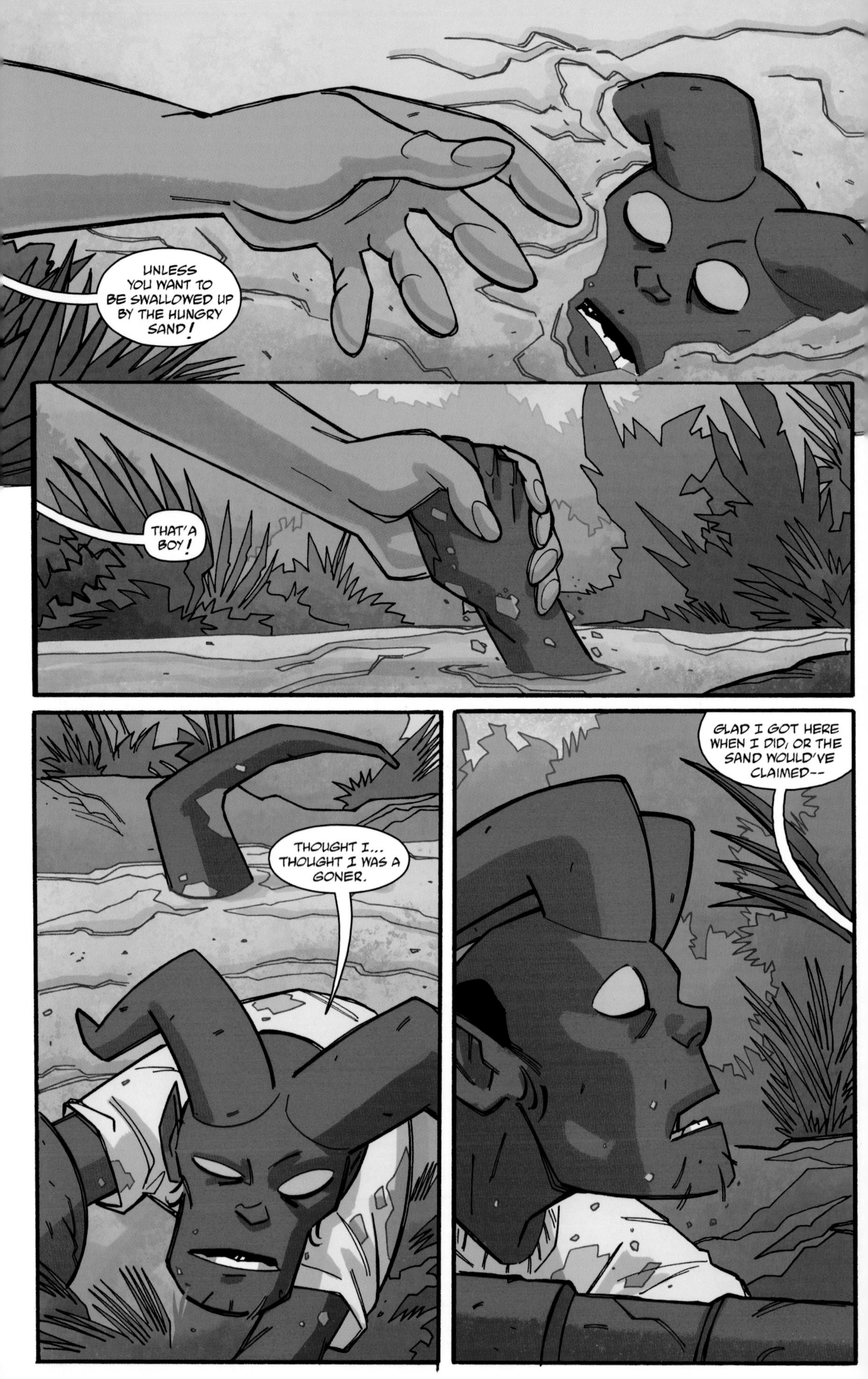
UNLESS YOU WANT TO BE SWALLOWED UP BY THE HUNGRY SAND!
THAT'A BOY!
THOUGHT I... THOUGHT I WAS A GONER.
GLAD I GOT HERE WHEN I DID, OR THE SAND WOULD'VE CLAIMED--

WHOA! *JUNGLE GIRL!*

YOU MIGHT SAY I'VE ADAPTED TO MY *SURROUNDIN'S.*

HEY, WAIT A MINUTE!

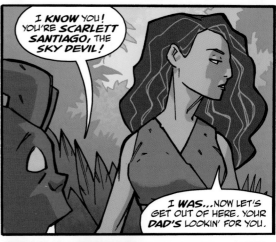

I *KNOW* YOU! YOU'RE *SCARLETT SANTIAGO,* THE *SKY DEVIL!*

I *WAS*...NOW LET'S GET OUT OF HERE. YOUR *DAD'S* LOOKIN' FOR YOU.

MISS *SKY DEVIL?* HOW'D YOU BECOME A *JUNGLE GIRL?*

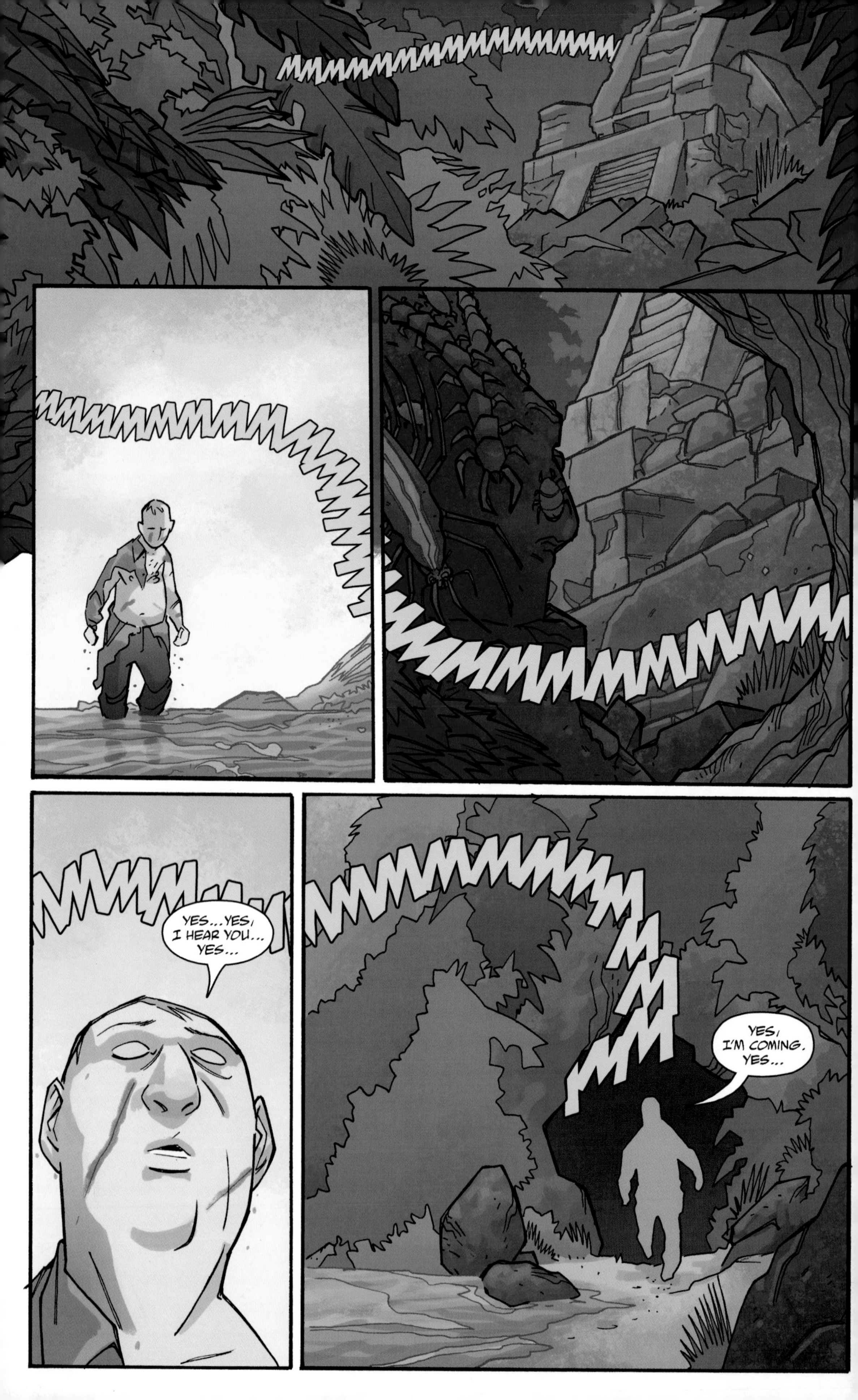
MMMMMMMMMMMMMMMMM
MMMMMMMMMMMMMM
MMMMMMMMMMMMMMMMMMMMMM
MMMMMMMMMMMMMMMMMMMM
YES...YES, I HEAR YOU... YES...
YES, I'M COMING. YES...

CHAPTER TWO

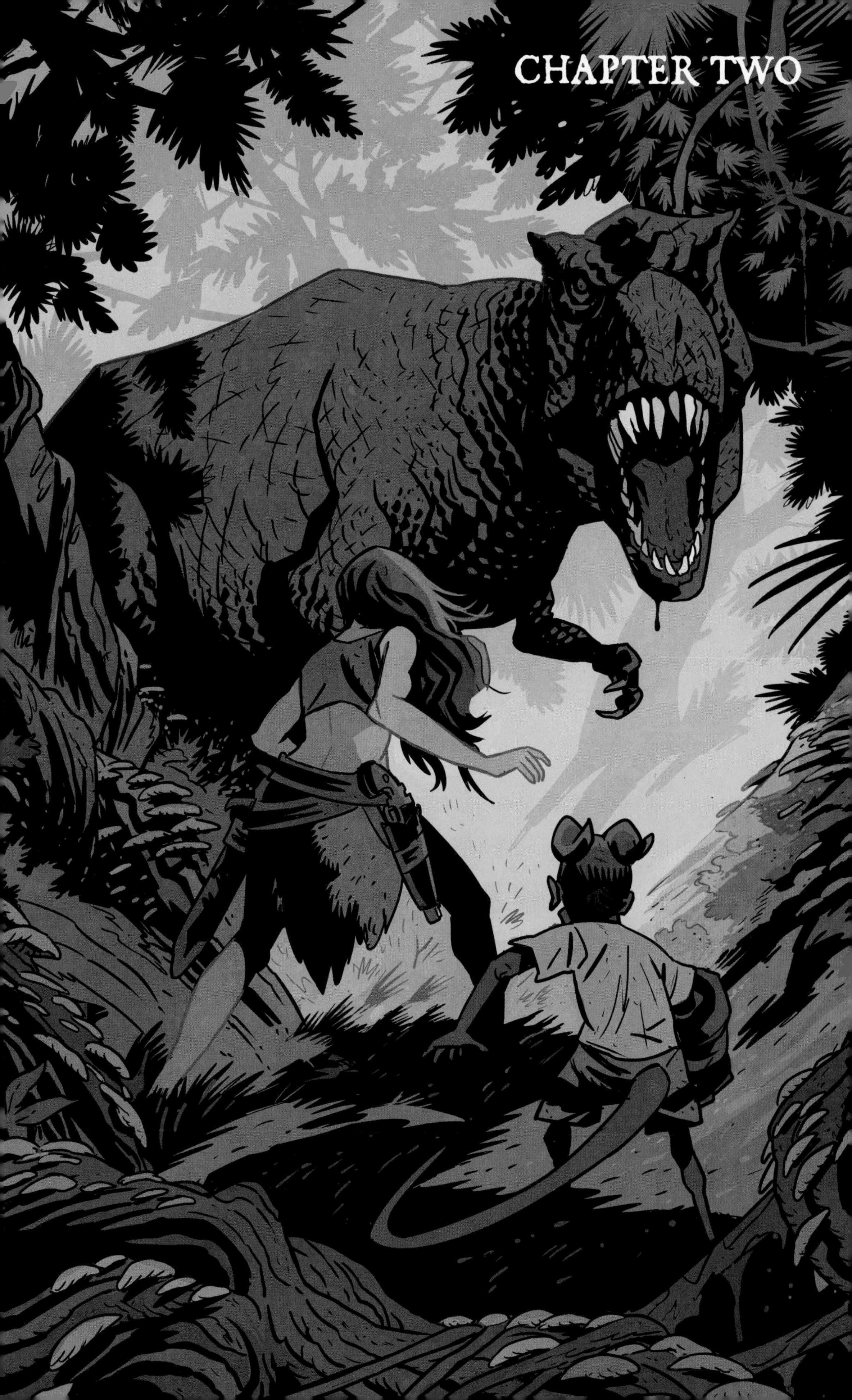

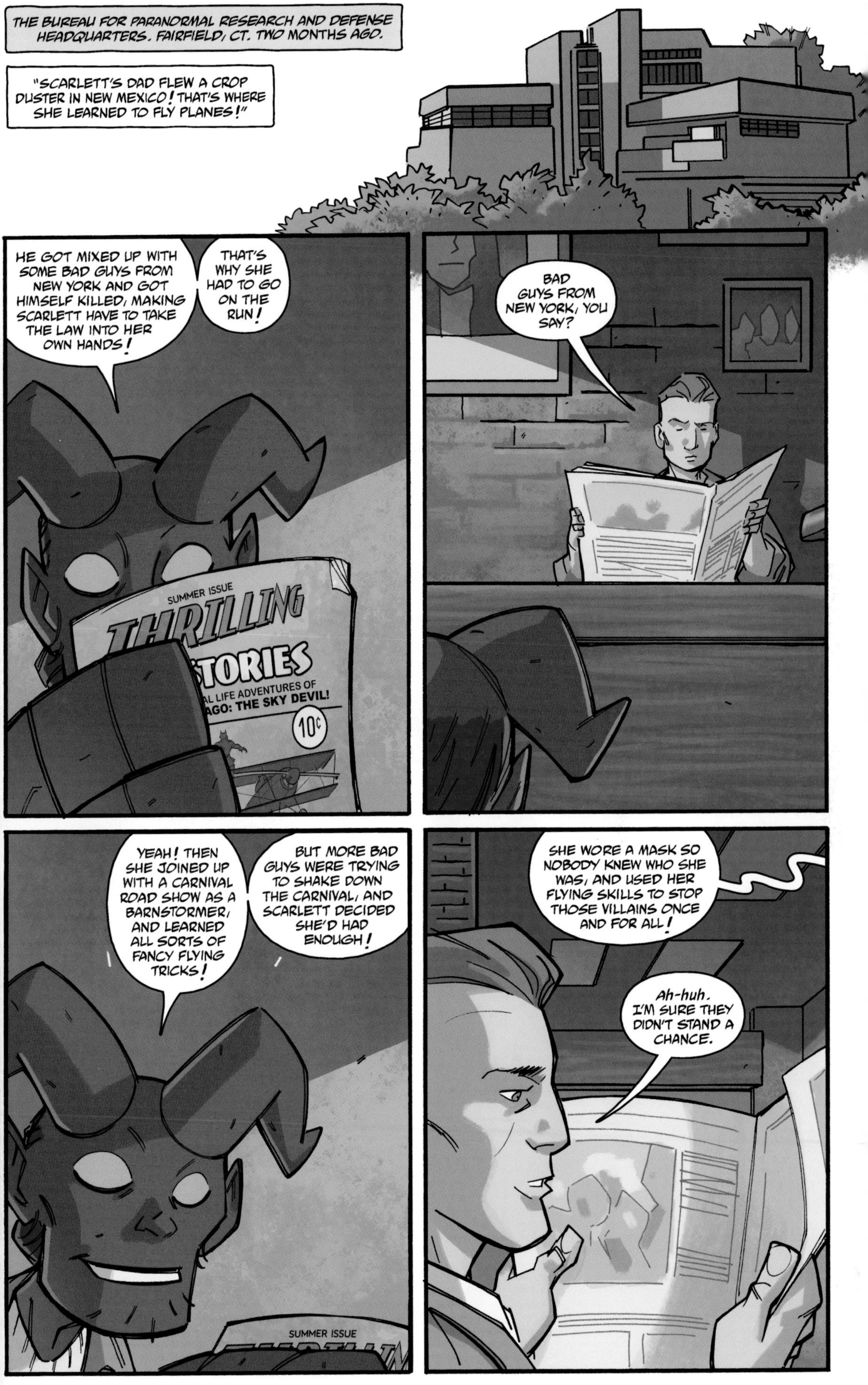
THE BUREAU FOR PARANORMAL RESEARCH AND DEFENSE HEADQUARTERS. FAIRFIELD, CT. TWO MONTHS AGO.
"SCARLETT'S DAD FLEW A CROP DUSTER IN NEW MEXICO! THAT'S WHERE SHE LEARNED TO FLY PLANES!"
HE GOT MIXED UP WITH SOME BAD GUYS FROM NEW YORK AND GOT HIMSELF KILLED, MAKING SCARLETT HAVE TO TAKE THE LAW INTO HER OWN HANDS!
THAT'S WHY SHE HAD TO GO ON THE RUN!
SUMMER ISSUE
THRILLING
STORIES
AL LIFE ADVENTURES OF
AGO: THE SKY DEVIL!
10¢
BAD GUYS FROM NEW YORK, YOU SAY?
YEAH! THEN SHE JOINED UP WITH A CARNIVAL ROAD SHOW AS A BARNSTORMER, AND LEARNED ALL SORTS OF FANCY FLYING TRICKS!
BUT MORE BAD GUYS WERE TRYING TO SHAKE DOWN THE CARNIVAL, AND SCARLETT DECIDED SHE'D HAD ENOUGH!
SUMMER ISSUE
SHE WORE A MASK SO NOBODY KNEW WHO SHE WAS, AND USED HER FLYING SKILLS TO STOP THOSE VILLAINS ONCE AND FOR ALL!
Ah-huh. I'M SURE THEY DIDN'T STAND A CHANCE.

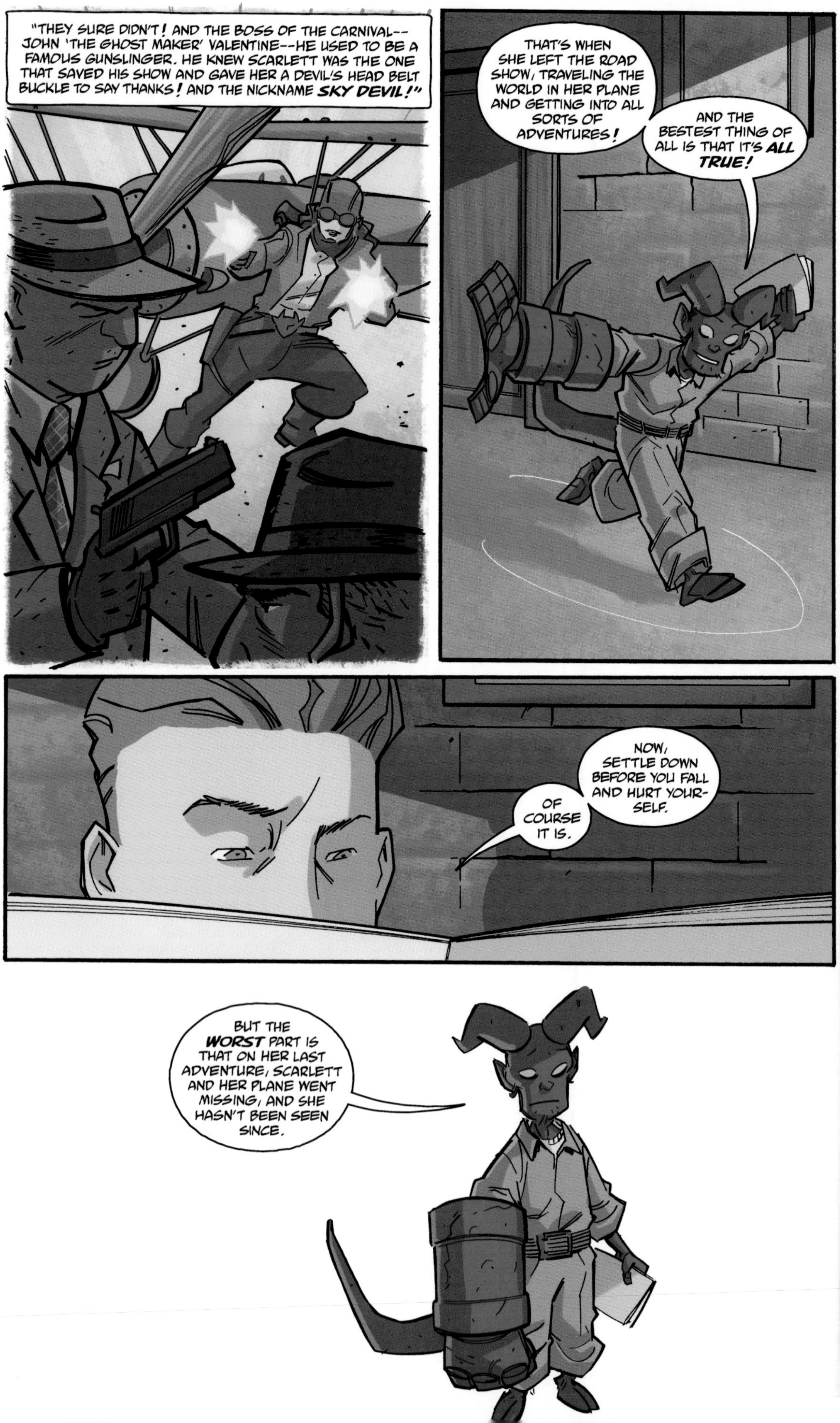
"THEY SURE DIDN'T! AND THE BOSS OF THE CARNIVAL--JOHN 'THE GHOST MAKER' VALENTINE--HE USED TO BE A FAMOUS GUNSLINGER. HE KNEW SCARLETT WAS THE ONE THAT SAVED HIS SHOW AND GAVE HER A DEVIL'S HEAD BELT BUCKLE TO SAY THANKS! AND THE NICKNAME SKY DEVIL!"
THAT'S WHEN SHE LEFT THE ROAD SHOW, TRAVELING THE WORLD IN HER PLANE AND GETTING INTO ALL SORTS OF ADVENTURES!
AND THE BESTEST THING OF ALL IS THAT IT'S ALL TRUE!
OF COURSE IT IS.
NOW, SETTLE DOWN BEFORE YOU FALL AND HURT YOURSELF.
BUT THE WORST PART IS THAT ON HER LAST ADVENTURE, SCARLETT AND HER PLANE WENT MISSING, AND SHE HASN'T BEEN SEEN SINCE.

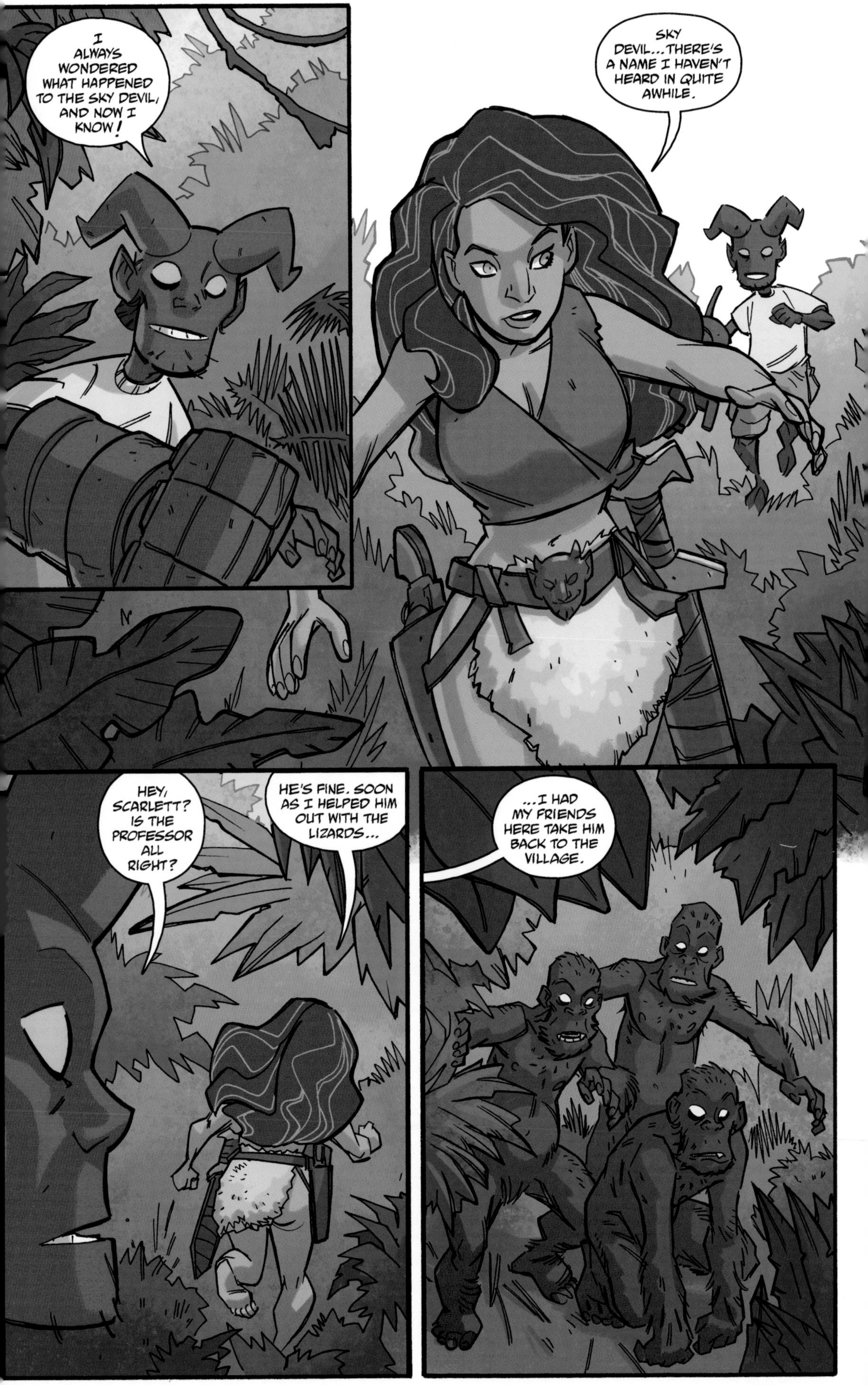
I ALWAYS WONDERED WHAT HAPPENED TO THE SKY DEVIL, AND NOW I KNOW!
SKY DEVIL... THERE'S A NAME I HAVEN'T HEARD IN QUITE AWHILE.
HEY, SCARLETT? IS THE PROFESSOR ALL RIGHT?
HE'S FINE. SOON AS I HELPED HIM OUT WITH THE LIZARDS...
...I HAD MY FRIENDS HERE TAKE HIM BACK TO THE VILLAGE.

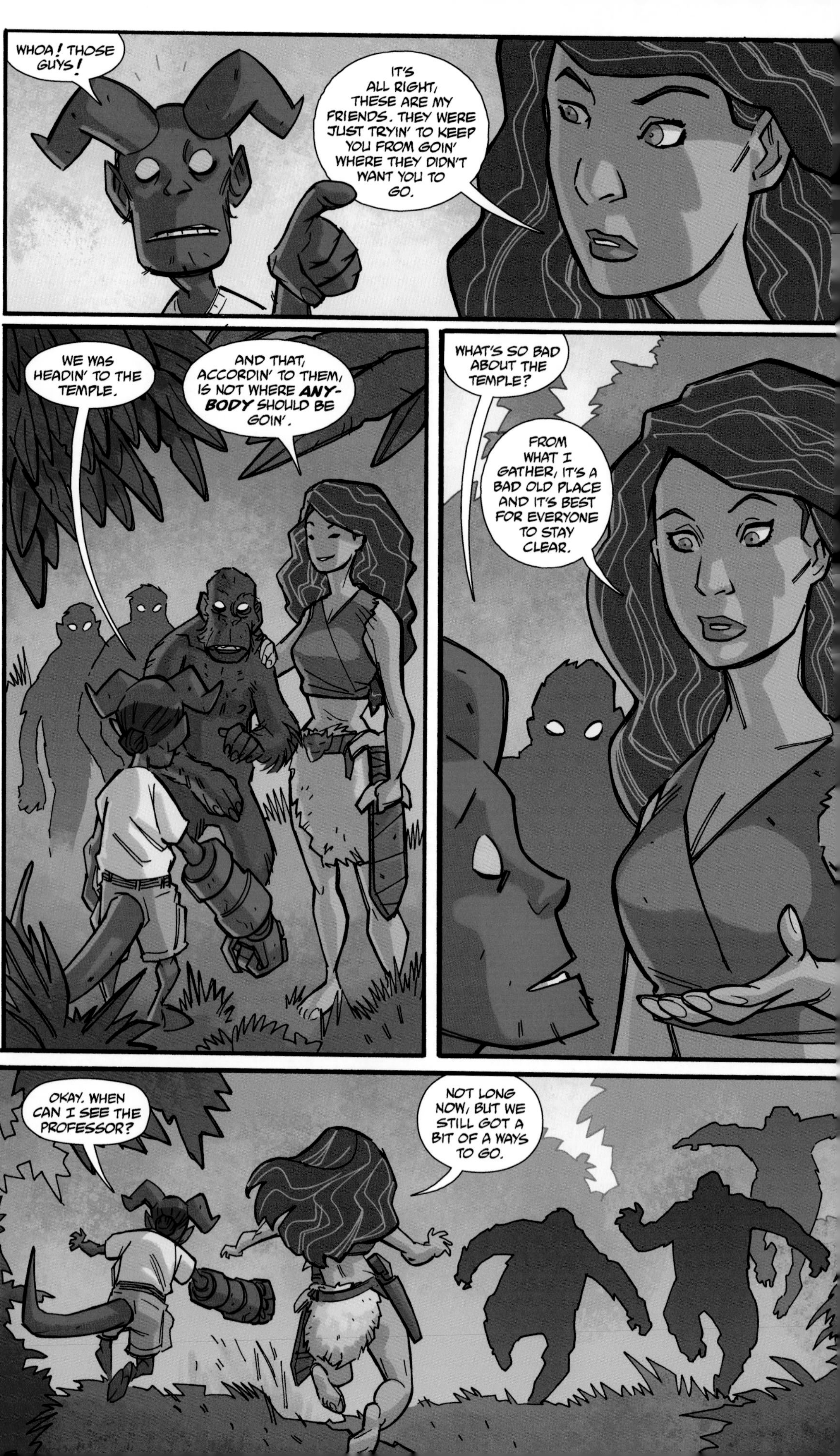
WHOA! THOSE GUYS!
IT'S ALL RIGHT, THESE ARE MY FRIENDS. THEY WERE JUST TRYIN' TO KEEP YOU FROM GOIN' WHERE THEY DIDN'T WANT YOU TO GO.
WE WAS HEADIN' TO THE TEMPLE.
AND THAT, ACCORDIN' TO THEM, IS NOT WHERE ANY-BODY SHOULD BE GOIN'.
WHAT'S SO BAD ABOUT THE TEMPLE?
FROM WHAT I GATHER, IT'S A BAD OLD PLACE AND IT'S BEST FOR EVERYONE TO STAY CLEAR.
OKAY. WHEN CAN I SEE THE PROFESSOR?
NOT LONG NOW, BUT WE STILL GOT A BIT OF A WAYS TO GO.

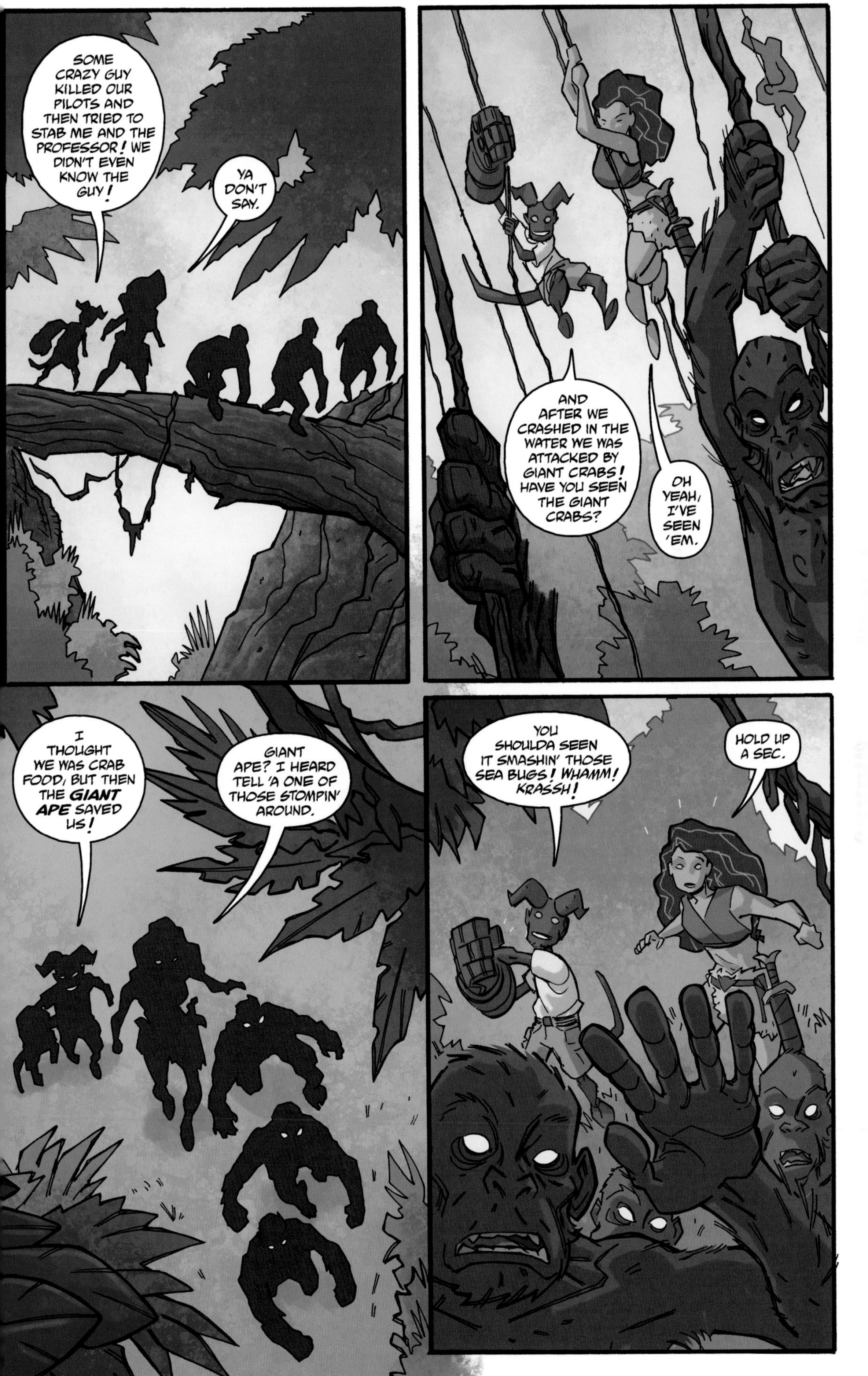
SOME CRAZY GUY KILLED OUR PILOTS AND THEN TRIED TO STAB ME AND THE PROFESSOR! WE DIDN'T EVEN KNOW THE GUY!
YA DON'T SAY.
AND AFTER WE CRASHED IN THE WATER WE WAS ATTACKED BY GIANT CRABS! HAVE YOU SEEN THE GIANT CRABS?
OH YEAH, I'VE SEEN 'EM.
I THOUGHT WE WAS CRAB FOOD, BUT THEN THE GIANT APE SAVED US!
GIANT APE? I HEARD TELL 'A ONE OF THOSE STOMPIN' AROUND.
YOU SHOULDA SEEN IT SMASHIN' THOSE SEA BUGS! WHAMM! KRASSH!
HOLD UP A SEC.

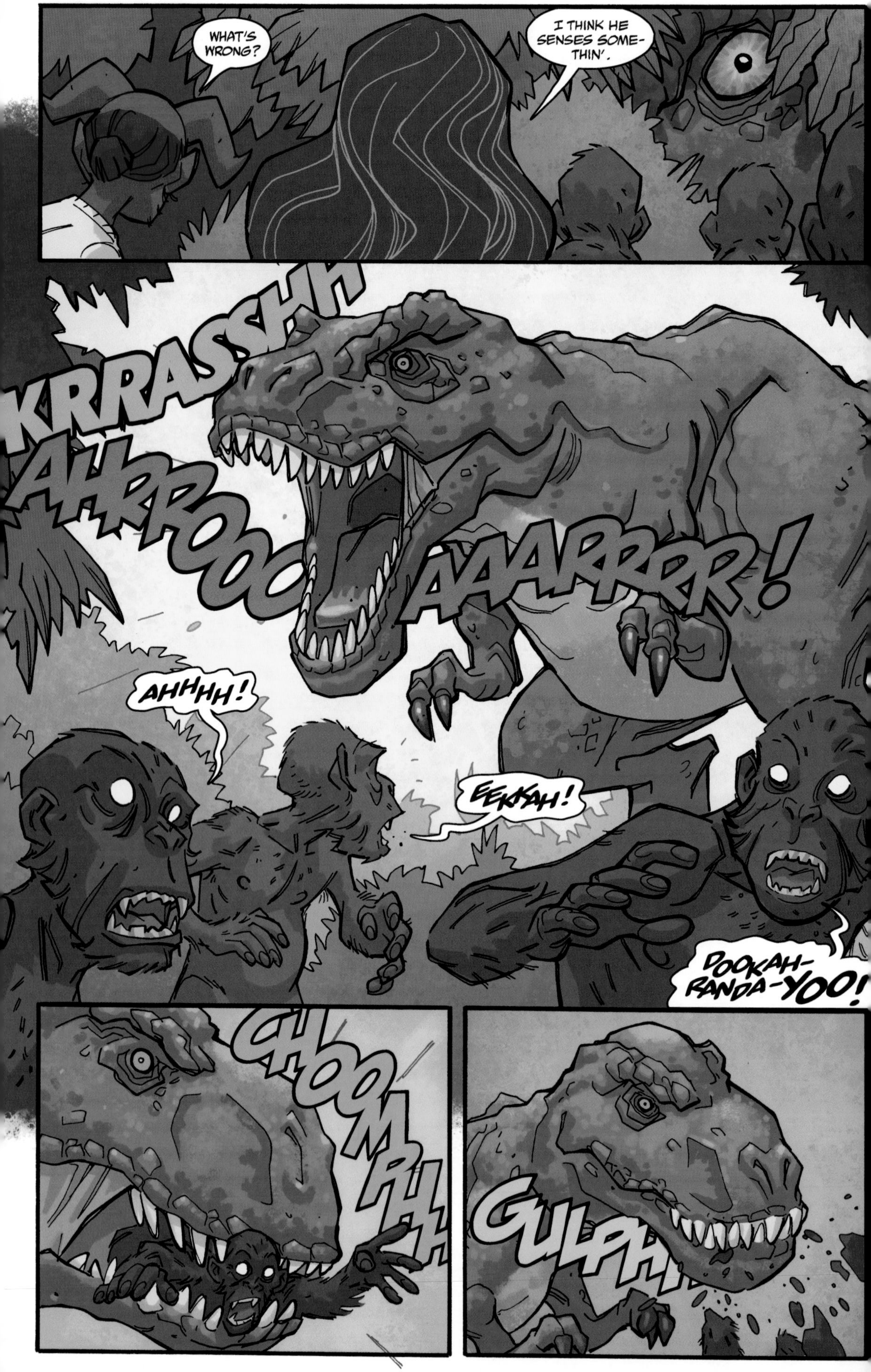

WHAT'S WRONG?
I THINK HE SENSES SOME-THIN'.
KRRASSHH
AHRROOOOAAAARRRR!
AHHHH!
EEKKAH!
DOOKAH-RANDA-YOO!
CHOOMPHH
GULPHH

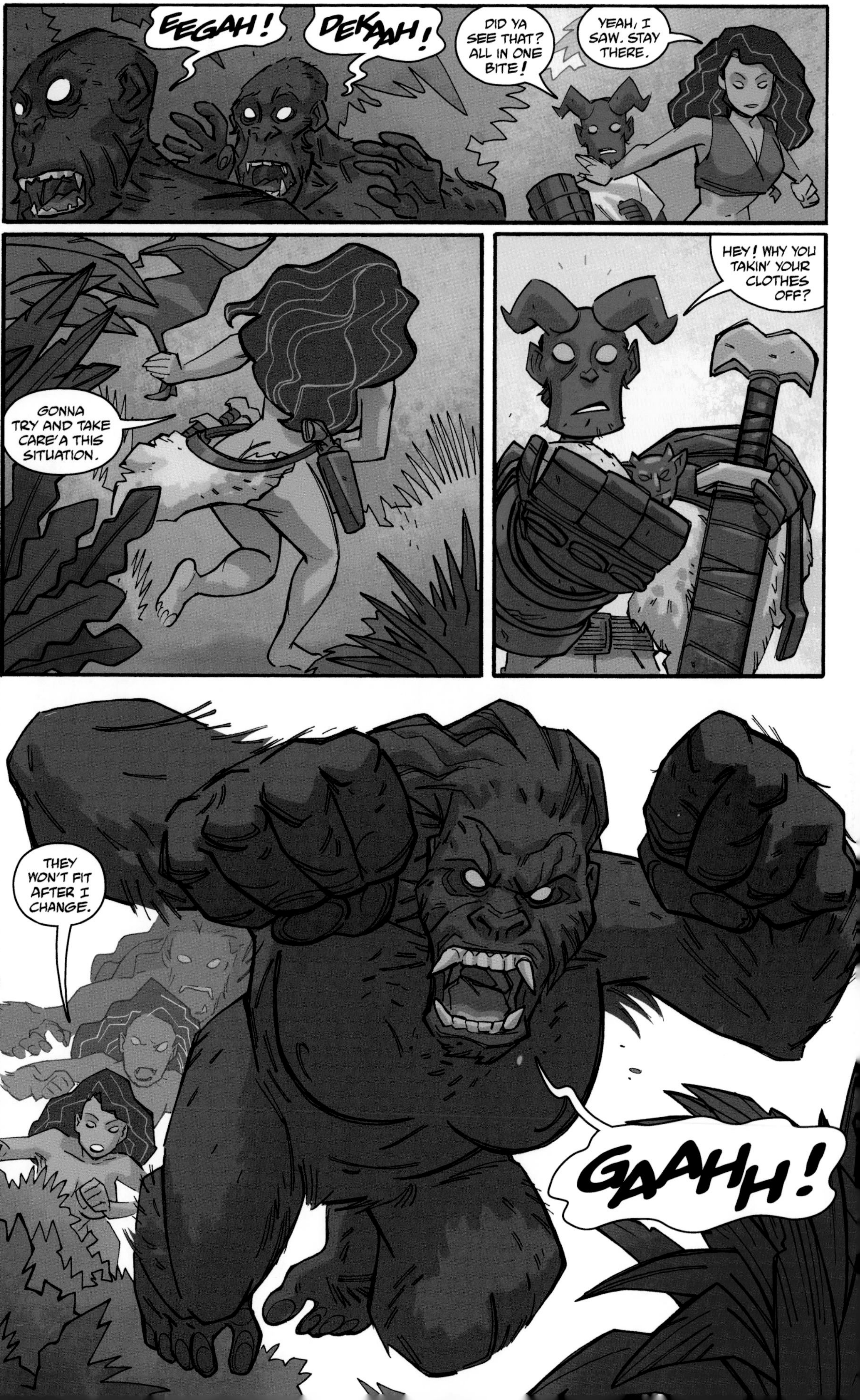
EEGAH!
DEKAAH!
DID YA SEE THAT? ALL IN ONE BITE!
YEAH, I SAW. STAY THERE.
GONNA TRY AND TAKE CARE'A THIS SITUATION.
HEY! WHY YOU TAKIN' YOUR CLOTHES OFF?
THEY WON'T FIT AFTER I CHANGE.
GAAHH!

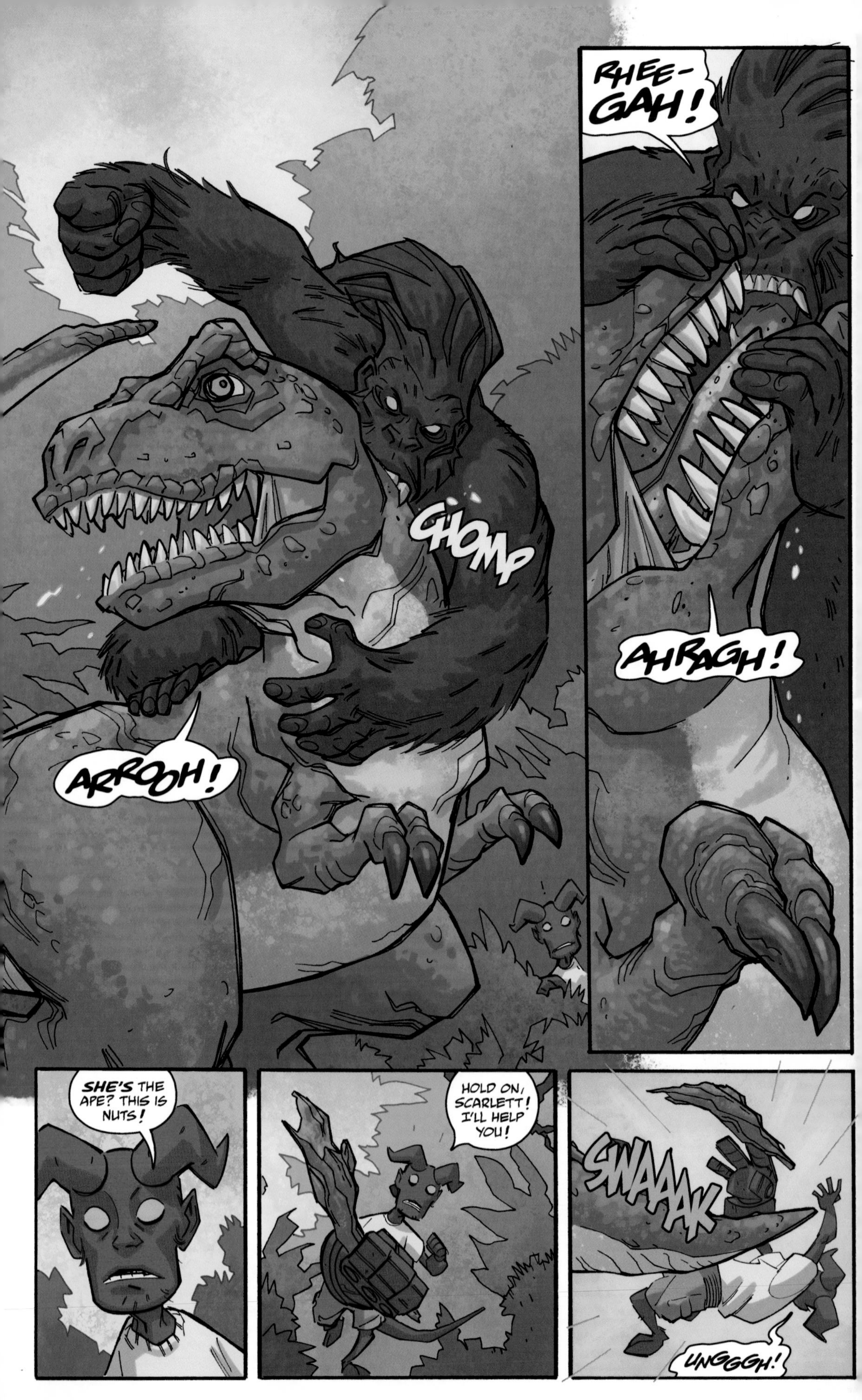
RHEE-GAH!
CHOMP
ARROOH!
AHRAGH!
SHE'S THE APE? THIS IS NUTS!
HOLD ON, SCARLETT! I'LL HELP YOU!
SWAAAK
UNGGGH!

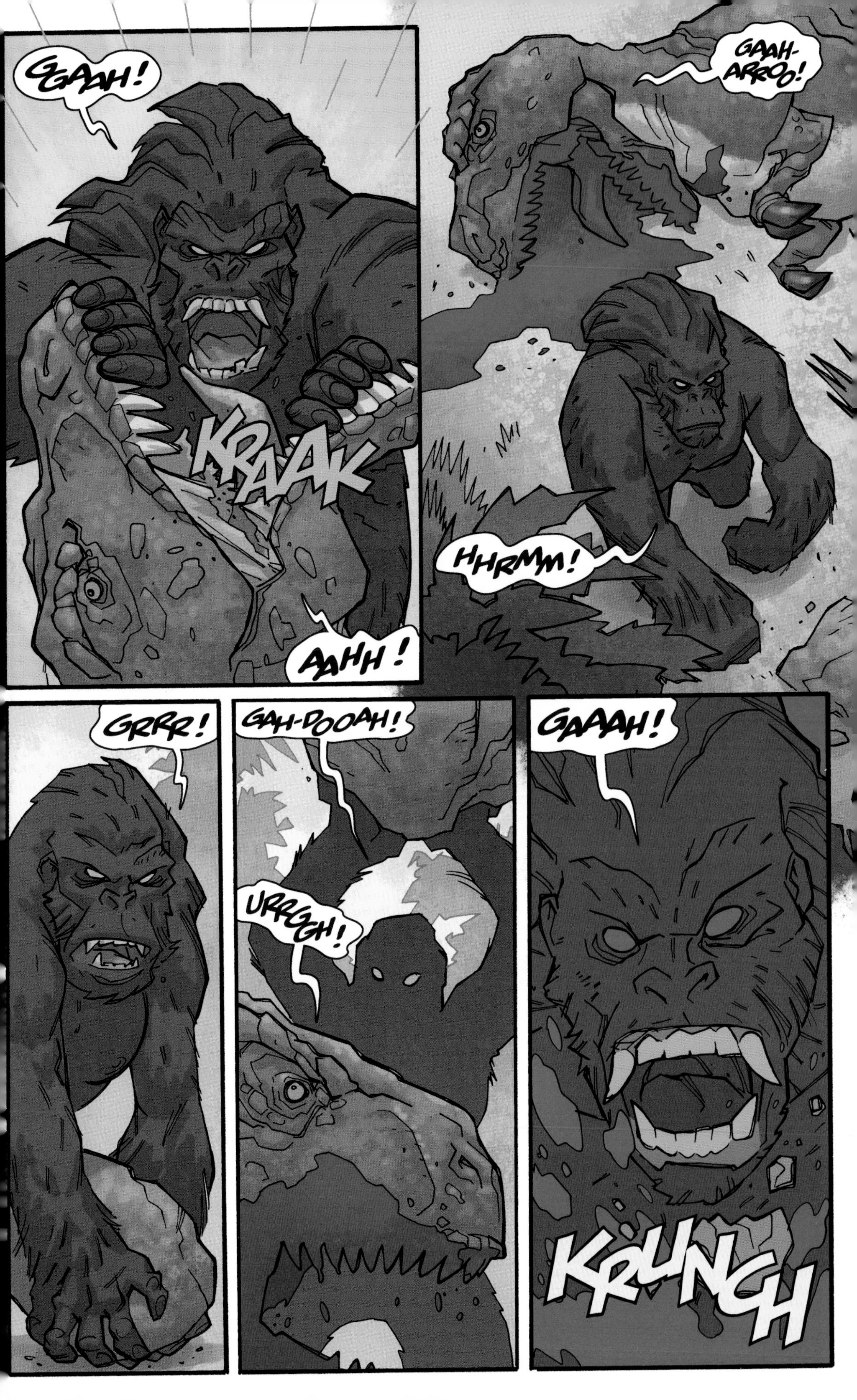
GGAAH!
KRAAAK
AAHH!
GAAH-ARROO!
HHRMM!
GRRR!
GAH-DOOAH!
URRGGH!
GAAAH!
KRUNCH

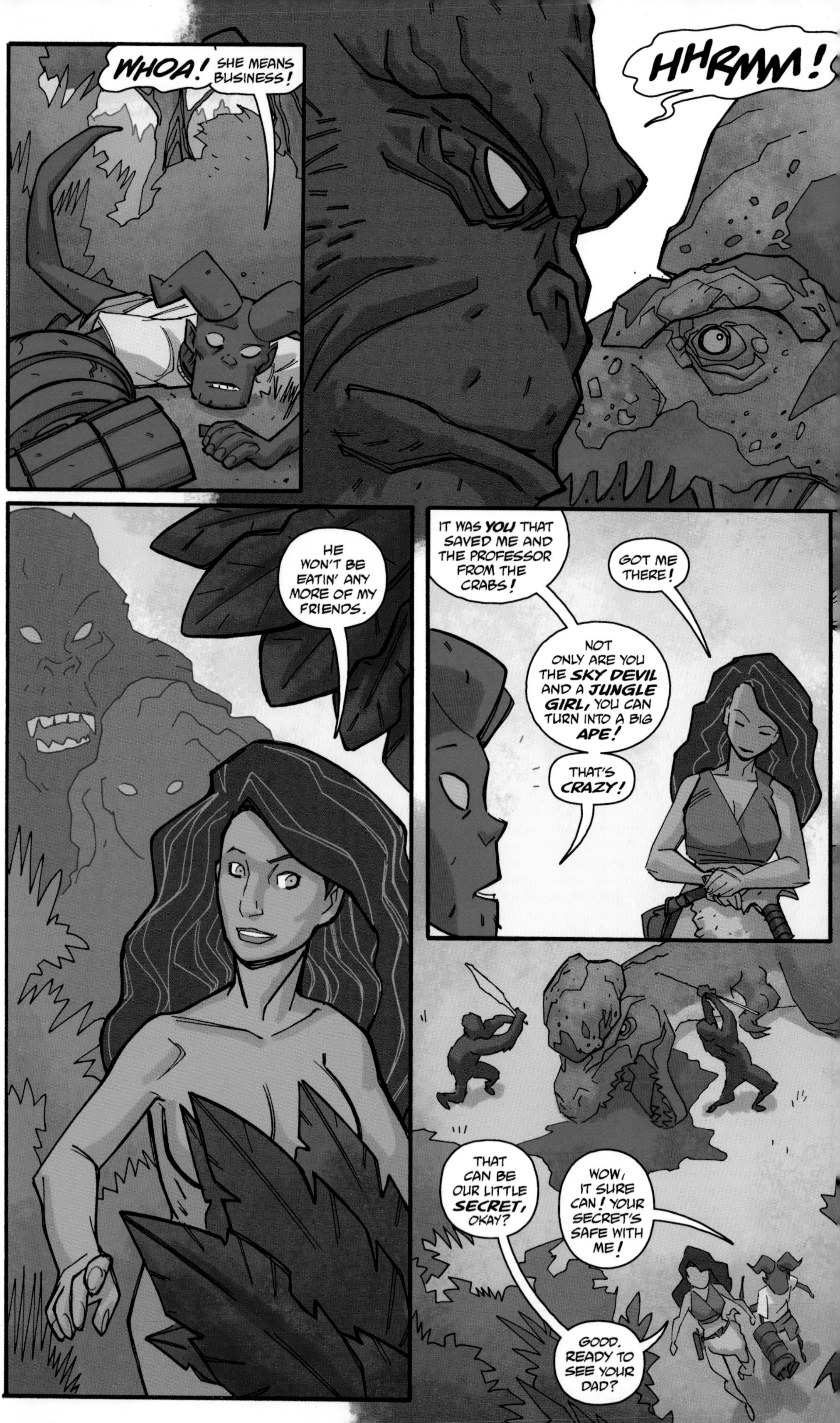
WHOA! SHE MEANS BUSINESS!
HHRMM!
HE WON'T BE EATIN' ANY MORE OF MY FRIENDS.
IT WAS YOU THAT SAVED ME AND THE PROFESSOR FROM THE CRABS!
GOT ME THERE!
NOT ONLY ARE YOU THE SKY DEVIL AND A JUNGLE GIRL, YOU CAN TURN INTO A BIG APE!
THAT'S CRAZY!
THAT CAN BE OUR LITTLE SECRET, OKAY?
WOW, IT SURE CAN! YOUR SECRET'S SAFE WITH ME!
GOOD. READY TO SEE YOUR DAD?

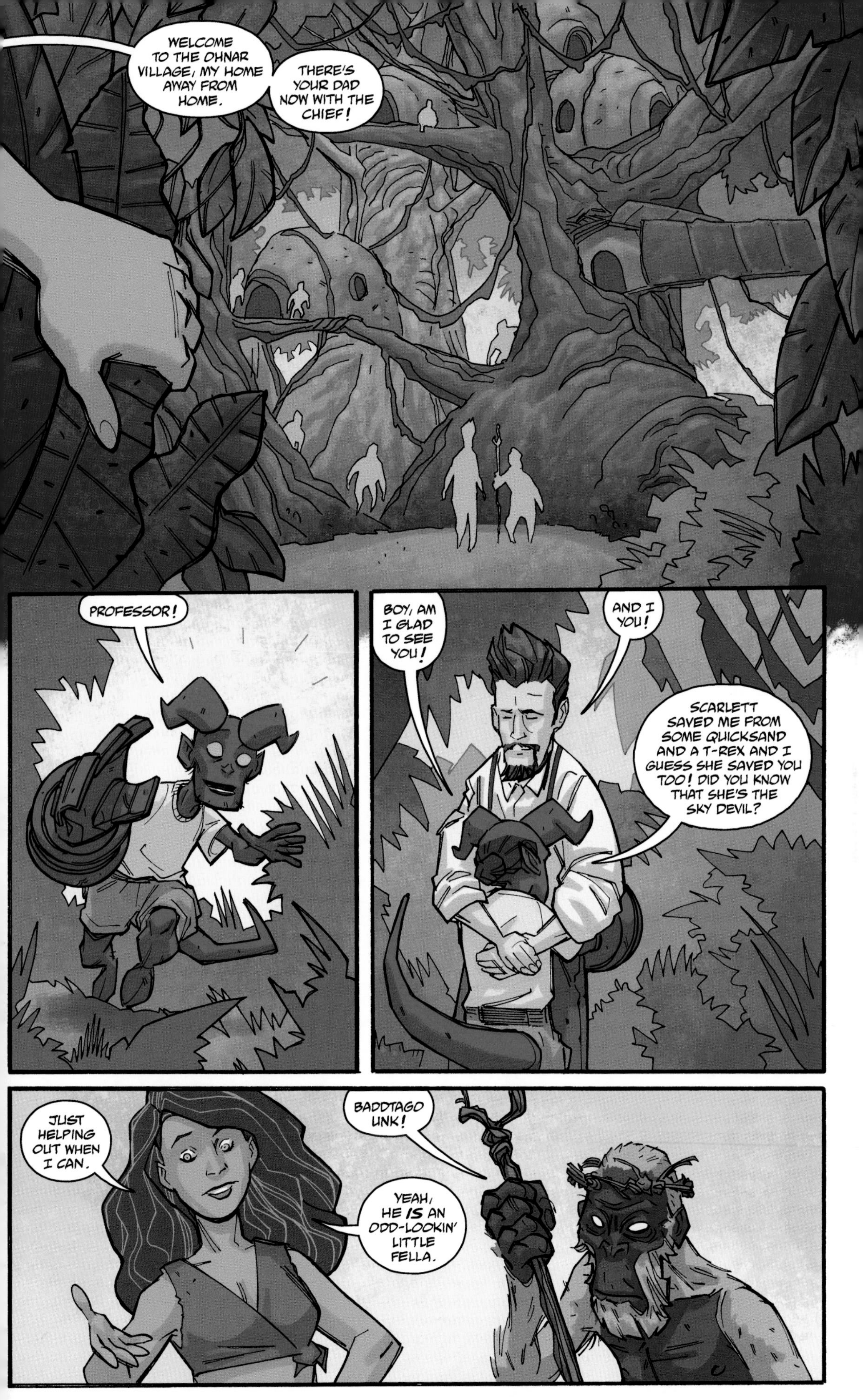
WELCOME TO THE OHNAR VILLAGE, MY HOME AWAY FROM HOME.
THERE'S YOUR DAD NOW WITH THE CHIEF!
PROFESSOR!
BOY, AM I GLAD TO SEE YOU!
AND I YOU!
SCARLETT SAVED ME FROM SOME QUICKSAND AND A T-REX AND I GUESS SHE SAVED YOU TOO! DID YOU KNOW THAT SHE'S THE SKY DEVIL?
JUST HELPING OUT WHEN I CAN.
BADDTAGO UNK!
YEAH, HE IS AN ODD-LOOKIN' LITTLE FELLA.

AFTER NIGHTFALL.

I CAN'T THANK YOU ENOUGH FOR LOOKING OUT FOR HIM--AND MYSELF, FOR THAT MATTER.

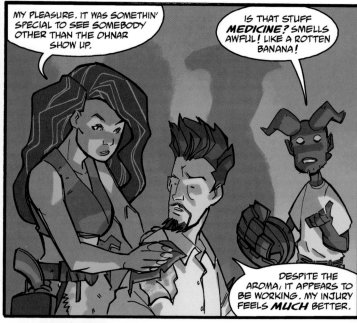

MY PLEASURE. IT WAS SOMETHIN' SPECIAL TO SEE SOMEBODY OTHER THAN THE OHNAR SHOW UP.

IS THAT STUFF **MEDICINE?** SMELLS AWFUL! LIKE A ROTTEN BANANA!

DESPITE THE AROMA, IT APPEARS TO BE WORKING. MY INJURY FEELS **MUCH** BETTER.

THE OHNAR HAVE SHARED A **LOT** OF THEIR SECRETS WITH ME. HECK, THEY SAVED MY LIFE, AND IN DOING SO, **CHANGED** ME.

HOPEFULLY FOR THE BETTER?

IS THAT HOW YOU CAN TURN INTO AN **APE?**

WHOOPS...

I MEAN...

AWW, CRAP. I SPILLED THE BEANS.

IT'S QUITE ALL RIGHT, MY BOY. I HAD MY SUSPICIONS AFTER SEEING OUR APE SAVIOR'S UNIQUELY COLORED **EYES,** AND MEETING OUR **NEW FRIEND.**

THEY USE'TA BE BROWN. A SIDE EFFECT OF WHAT THE OHNAR DONE TO SAVE MY LIFE.

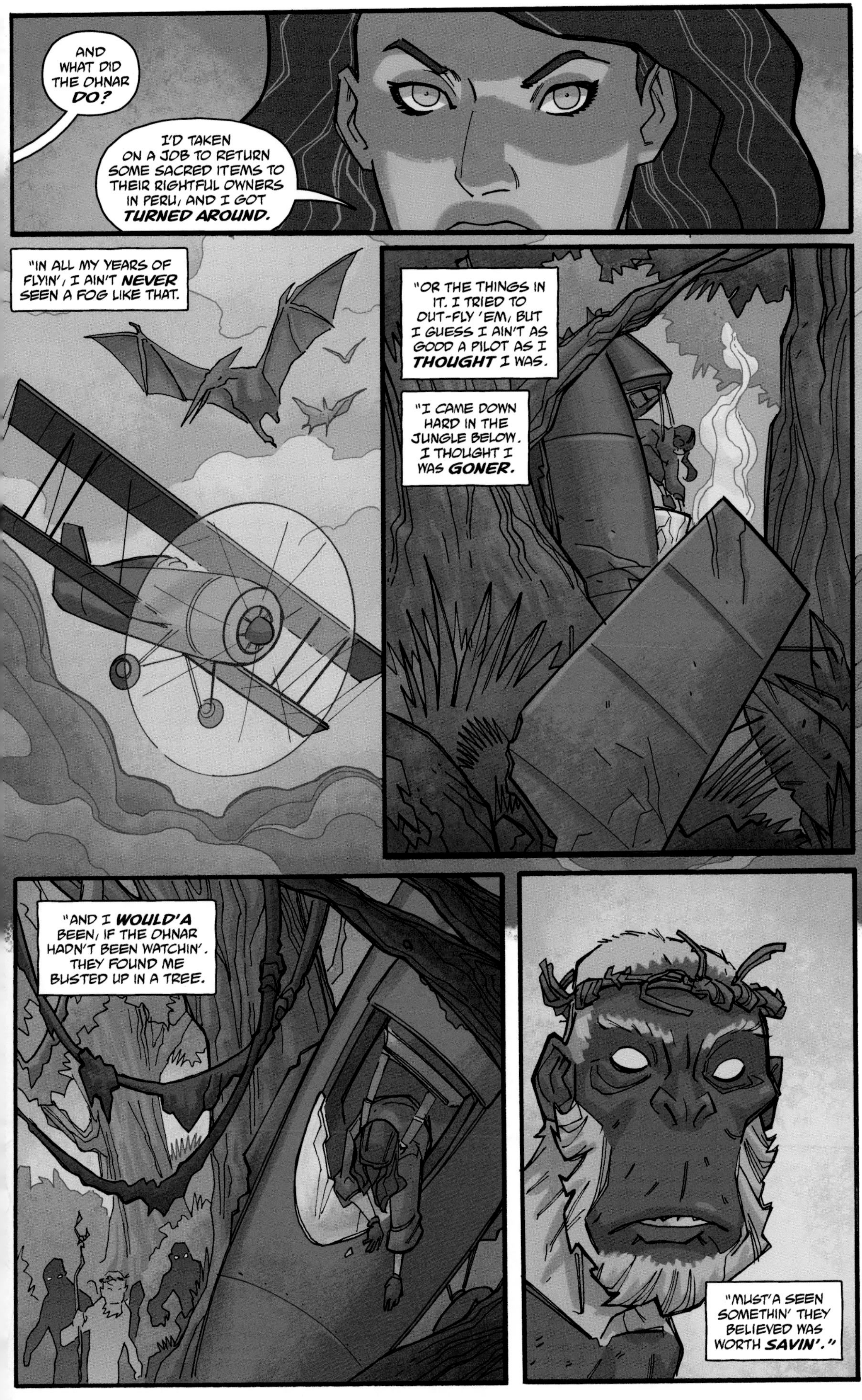
AND WHAT DID THE OHNAR DO?
I'D TAKEN ON A JOB TO RETURN SOME SACRED ITEMS TO THEIR RIGHTFUL OWNERS IN PERU, AND I GOT TURNED AROUND.
"IN ALL MY YEARS OF FLYIN', I AIN'T NEVER SEEN A FOG LIKE THAT.
"OR THE THINGS IN IT. I TRIED TO OUT-FLY 'EM, BUT I GUESS I AIN'T AS GOOD A PILOT AS I THOUGHT I WAS.
"I CAME DOWN HARD IN THE JUNGLE BELOW. I THOUGHT I WAS GONER.
"AND I WOULD'A BEEN, IF THE OHNAR HADN'T BEEN WATCHIN'. THEY FOUND ME BUSTED UP IN A TREE.
"MUST'A SEEN SOMETHIN' THEY BELIEVED WAS WORTH SAVIN'."

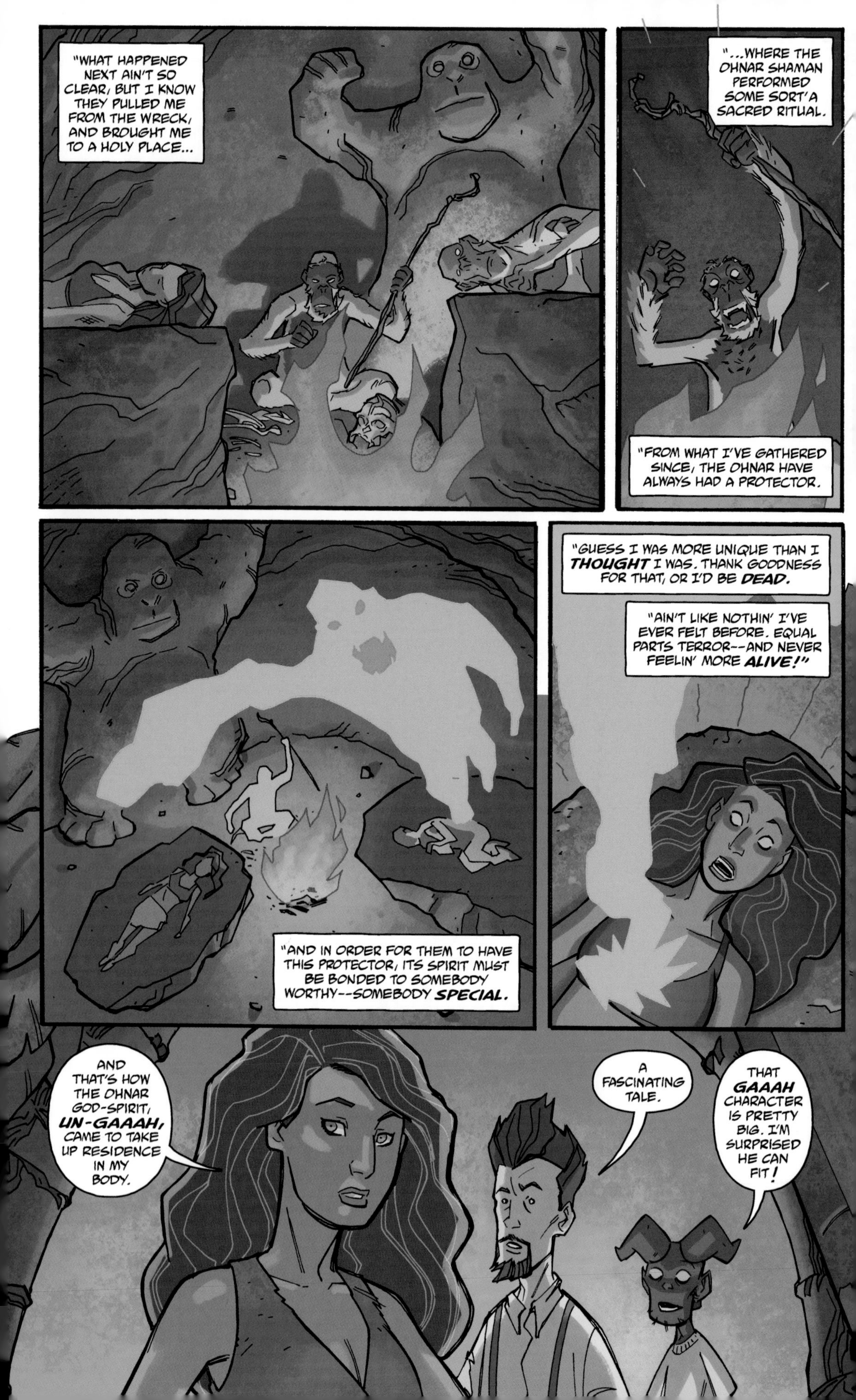
"WHAT HAPPENED NEXT AIN'T SO CLEAR, BUT I KNOW THEY PULLED ME FROM THE WRECK, AND BROUGHT ME TO A HOLY PLACE...
"...WHERE THE OHNAR SHAMAN PERFORMED SOME SORT'A SACRED RITUAL.
"FROM WHAT I'VE GATHERED SINCE, THE OHNAR HAVE ALWAYS HAD A PROTECTOR.
"AND IN ORDER FOR THEM TO HAVE THIS PROTECTOR, ITS SPIRIT MUST BE BONDED TO SOMEBODY WORTHY--SOMEBODY SPECIAL.
"GUESS I WAS MORE UNIQUE THAN I THOUGHT I WAS. THANK GOODNESS FOR THAT, OR I'D BE DEAD.
"AIN'T LIKE NOTHIN' I'VE EVER FELT BEFORE. EQUAL PARTS TERROR--AND NEVER FEELIN' MORE ALIVE!"
AND THAT'S HOW THE OHNAR GOD-SPIRIT, UN-GAAAH, CAME TO TAKE UP RESIDENCE IN MY BODY.
A FASCINATING TALE.
THAT GAAAH CHARACTER IS PRETTY BIG. I'M SURPRISED HE CAN FIT!

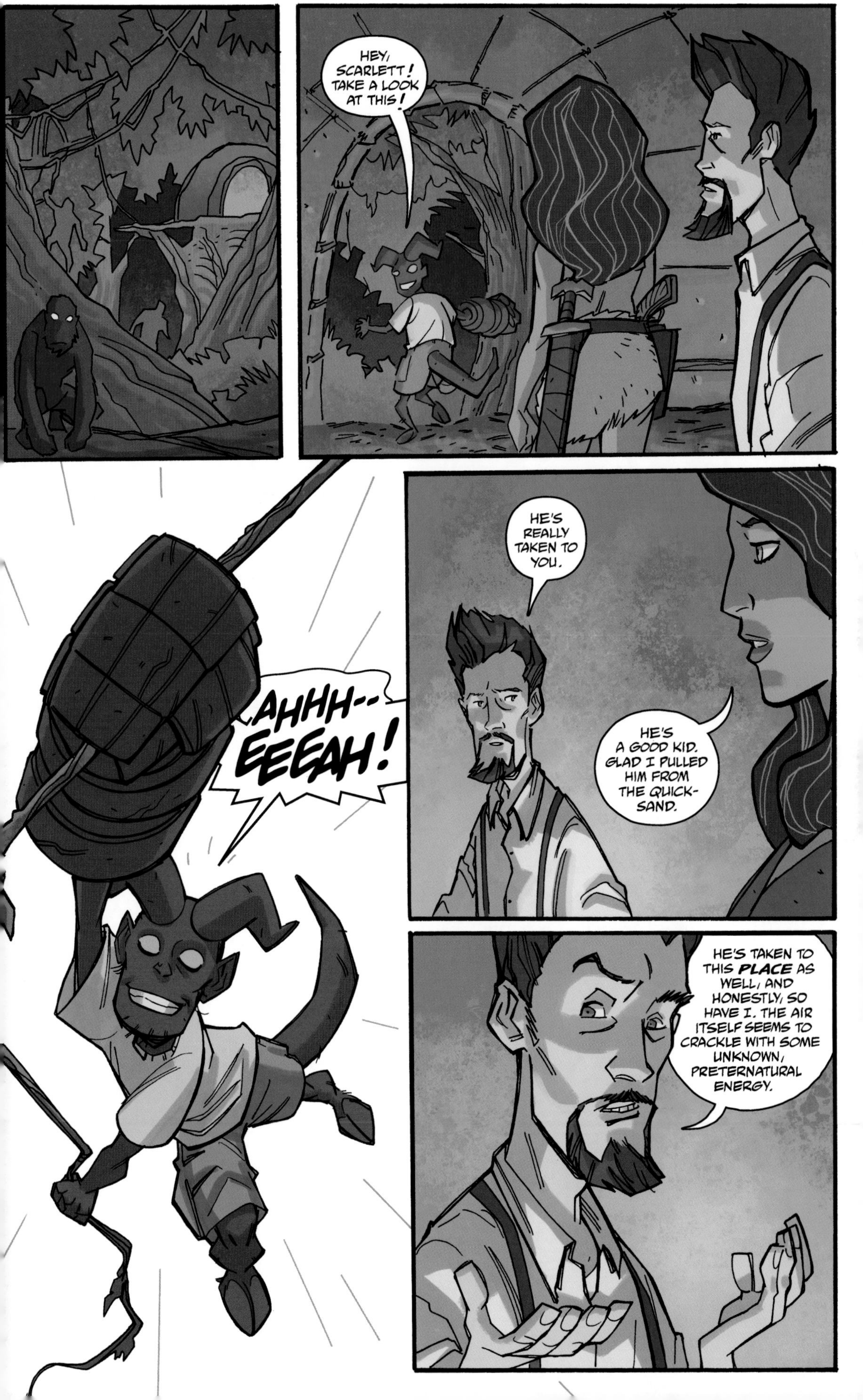
HEY, SCARLETT! TAKE A LOOK AT THIS!
AHHH-- EEEAH!
HE'S REALLY TAKEN TO YOU.
HE'S A GOOD KID. GLAD I PULLED HIM FROM THE QUICK-SAND.
HE'S TAKEN TO THIS PLACE AS WELL, AND HONESTLY, SO HAVE I. THE AIR ITSELF SEEMS TO CRACKLE WITH SOME UNKNOWN, PRETERNATURAL ENERGY.

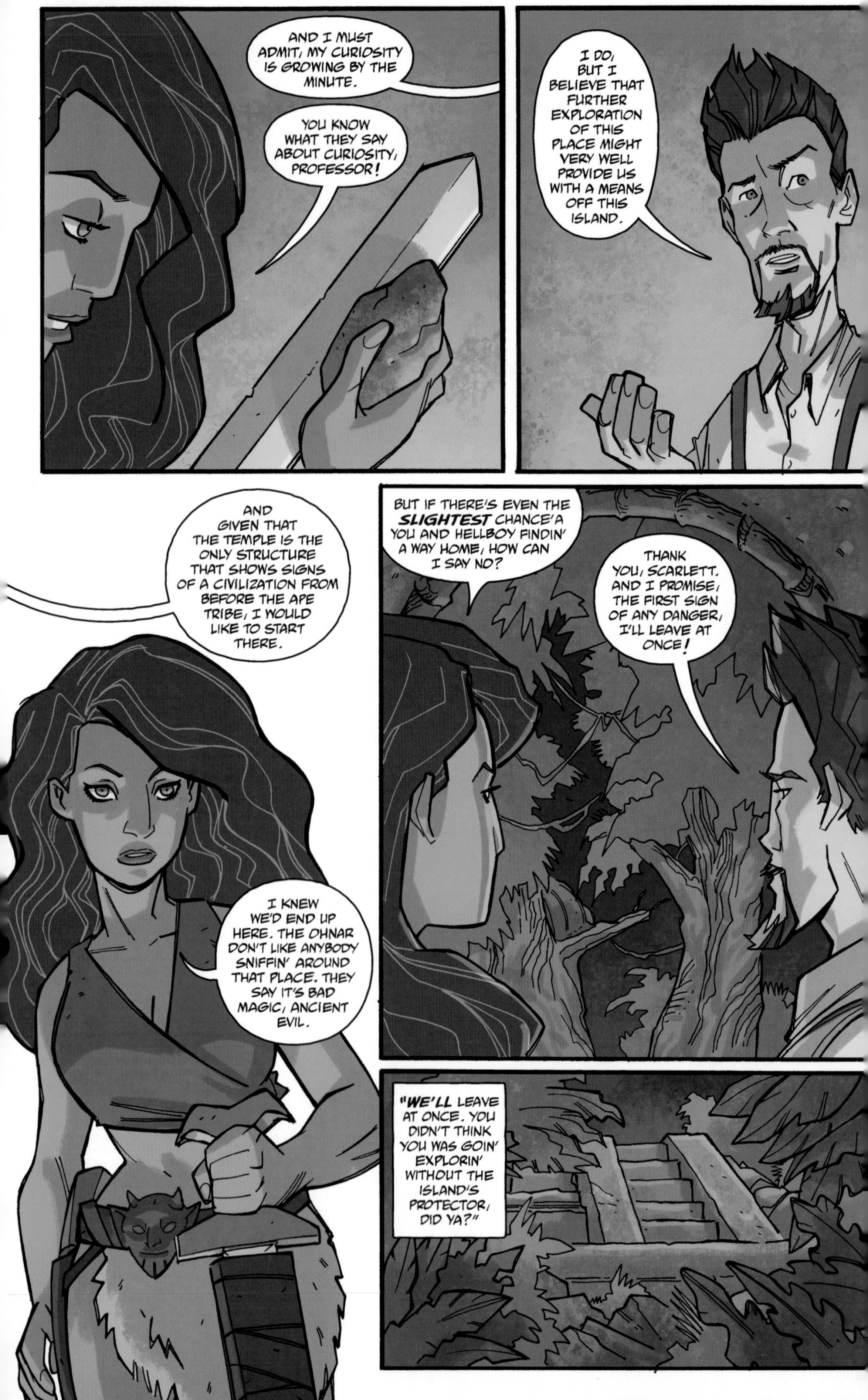
AND I MUST ADMIT, MY CURIOSITY IS GROWING BY THE MINUTE.
YOU KNOW WHAT THEY SAY ABOUT CURIOSITY, PROFESSOR!
I DO, BUT I BELIEVE THAT FURTHER EXPLORATION OF THIS PLACE MIGHT VERY WELL PROVIDE US WITH A MEANS OFF THIS ISLAND.
AND GIVEN THAT THE TEMPLE IS THE ONLY STRUCTURE THAT SHOWS SIGNS OF A CIVILIZATION FROM BEFORE THE APE TRIBE, I WOULD LIKE TO START THERE.
I KNEW WE'D END UP HERE. THE OHNAR DON'T LIKE ANYBODY SNIFFIN' AROUND THAT PLACE. THEY SAY IT'S BAD MAGIC, ANCIENT EVIL.
BUT IF THERE'S EVEN THE SLIGHTEST CHANCE'A YOU AND HELLBOY FINDIN' A WAY HOME, HOW CAN I SAY NO?
THANK YOU, SCARLETT. AND I PROMISE, THE FIRST SIGN OF ANY DANGER, I'LL LEAVE AT ONCE!
"WE'LL LEAVE AT ONCE. YOU DIDN'T THINK YOU WAS GOIN' EXPLORIN' WITHOUT THE ISLAND'S PROTECTOR, DID YA?"

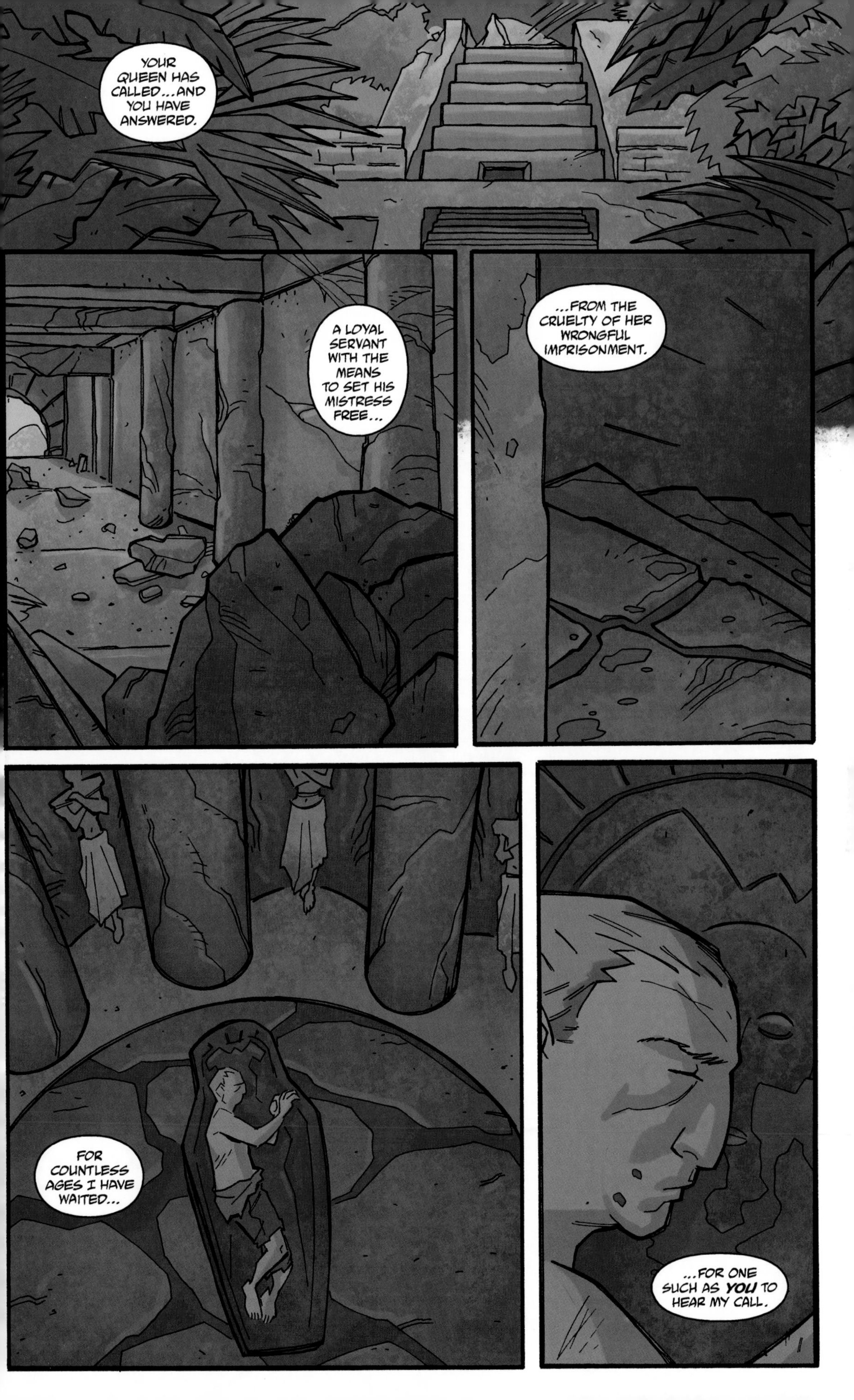
YOUR QUEEN HAS CALLED...AND YOU HAVE ANSWERED.
A LOYAL SERVANT WITH THE MEANS TO SET HIS MISTRESS FREE...
...FROM THE CRUELTY OF HER WRONGFUL IMPRISONMENT.
FOR COUNTLESS AGES I HAVE WAITED...
...FOR ONE SUCH AS *YOU* TO HEAR MY CALL.

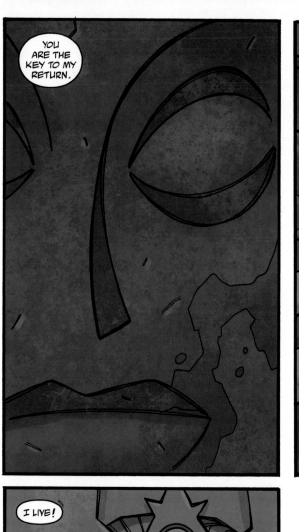

YOU ARE THE KEY TO MY RETURN.

THE FOUNT OF MY REBIRTH.

I LIVE!

AND THE WORLD WILL ONCE AGAIN KNOW OF MY MAGNIFICENCE.

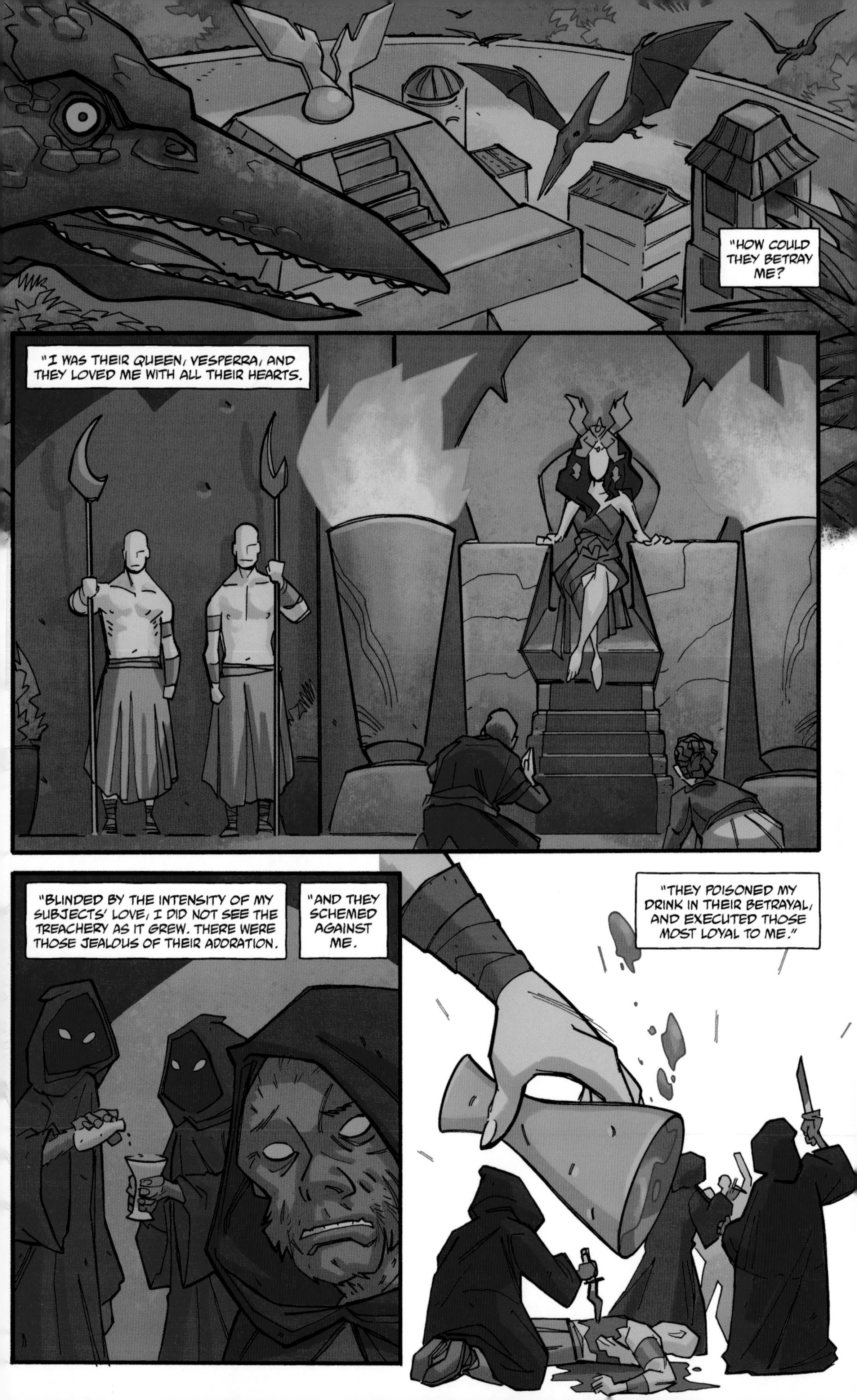
"HOW COULD THEY BETRAY ME?
"I WAS THEIR QUEEN, VESPERRA, AND THEY LOVED ME WITH ALL THEIR HEARTS.
"BLINDED BY THE INTENSITY OF MY SUBJECTS' LOVE, I DID NOT SEE THE TREACHERY AS IT GREW. THERE WERE THOSE JEALOUS OF THEIR ADORATION.
"AND THEY SCHEMED AGAINST ME.
"THEY POISONED MY DRINK IN THEIR BETRAYAL, AND EXECUTED THOSE MOST LOYAL TO ME."

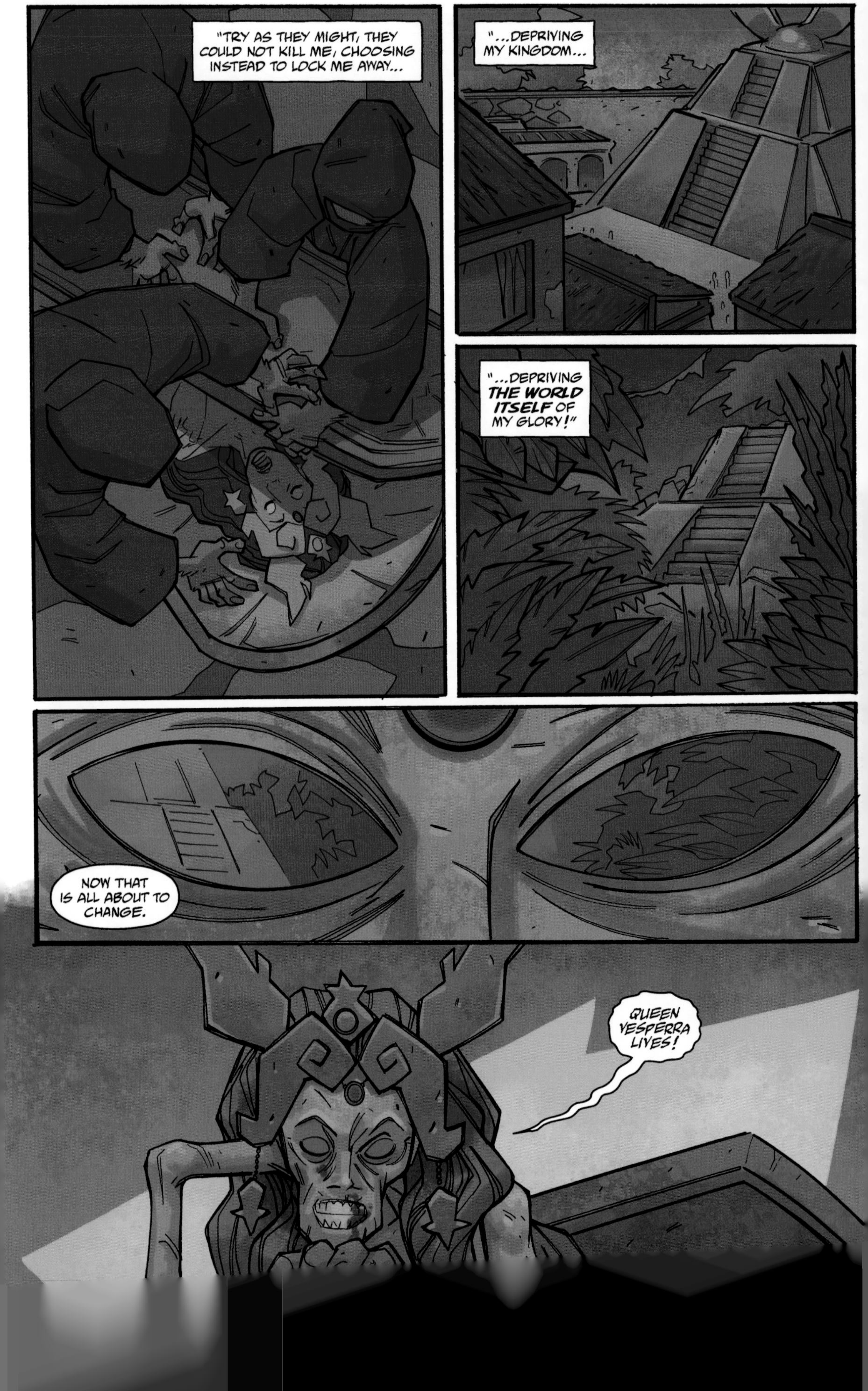
"TRY AS THEY MIGHT, THEY COULD NOT KILL ME, CHOOSING INSTEAD TO LOCK ME AWAY...
"...DEPRIVING MY KINGDOM...
"...DEPRIVING **THE WORLD ITSELF** OF MY GLORY!"
NOW THAT IS ALL ABOUT TO CHANGE.
QUEEN VESPERRA LIVES!

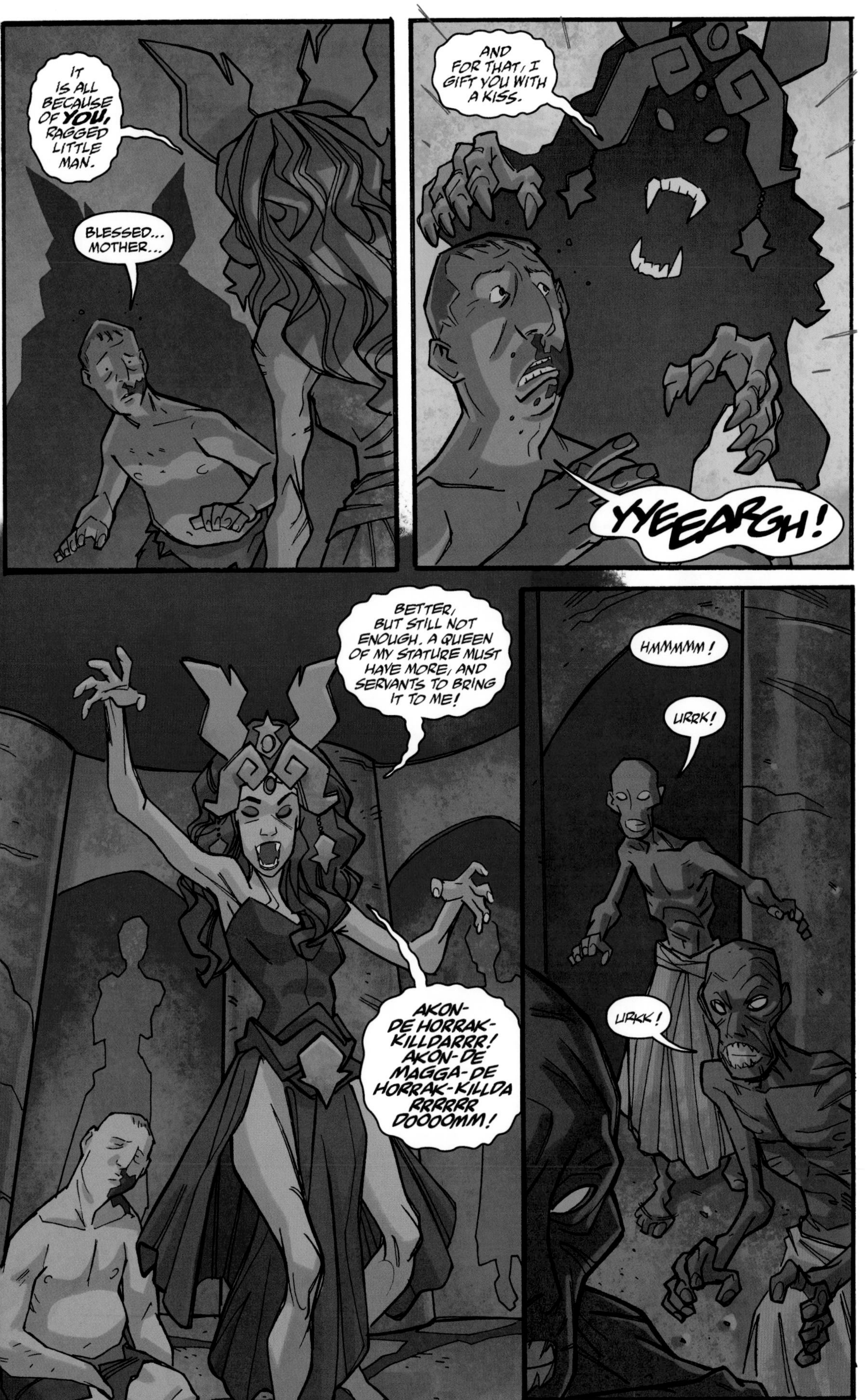
IT IS ALL BECAUSE OF YOU, RAGGED LITTLE MAN.
BLESSED... MOTHER...
AND FOR THAT, I GIFT YOU WITH A KISS.
YYEEARGH!
BETTER, BUT STILL NOT ENOUGH. A QUEEN OF MY STATURE MUST HAVE MORE, AND SERVANTS TO BRING IT TO ME!
AKON-DE HORRAK-KILLDARRR! AKON-DE MAGGA-DE HORRAK-KILLDA RRRRRR DOOOOMM!
HMMMMM!
URRK!
URKK!

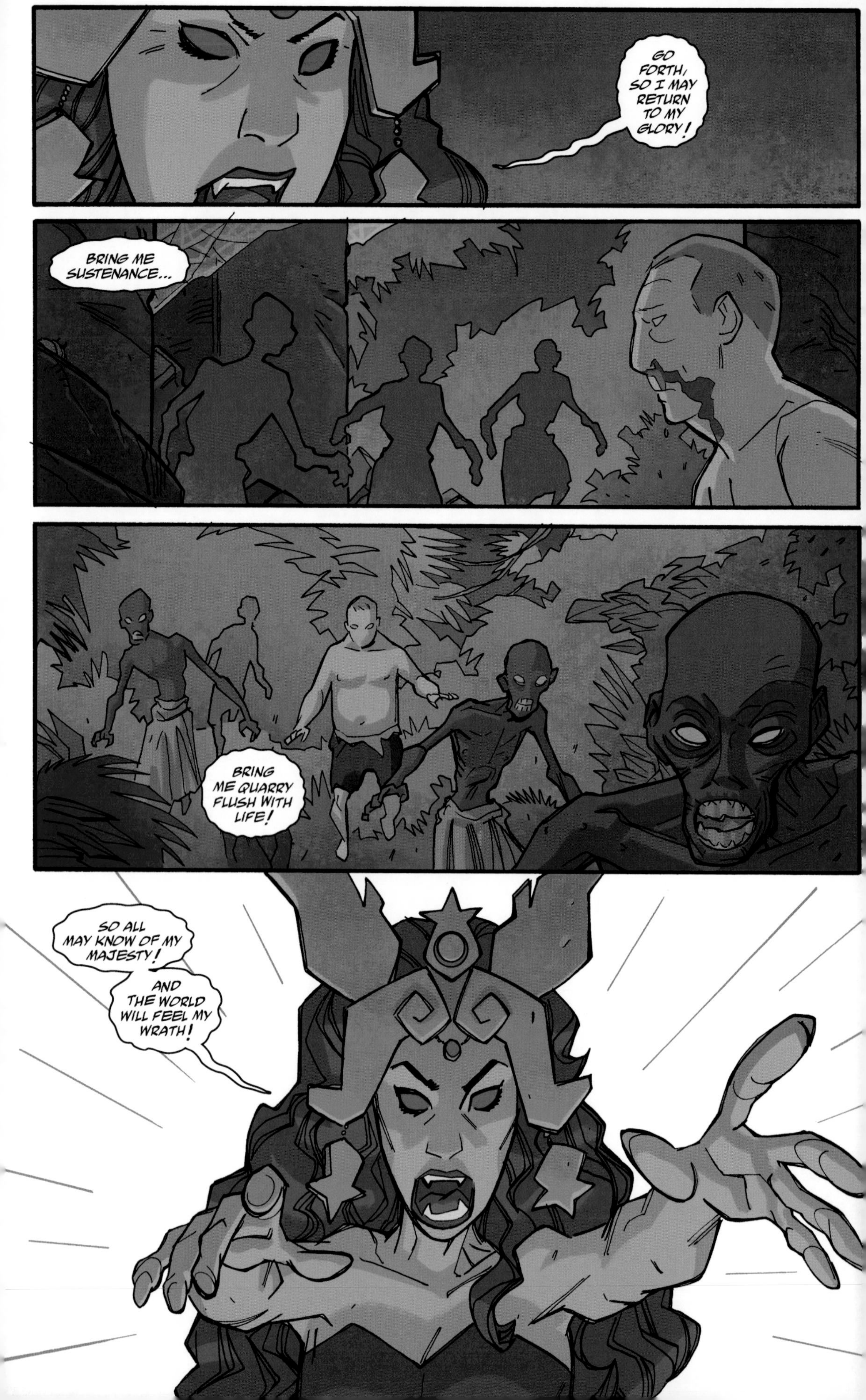
GO FORTH, SO I MAY RETURN TO MY GLORY!
BRING ME SUSTENANCE...
BRING ME QUARRY FLUSH WITH LIFE!
SO ALL MAY KNOW OF MY MAJESTY!
AND THE WORLD WILL FEEL MY WRATH!

CHAPTER THREE

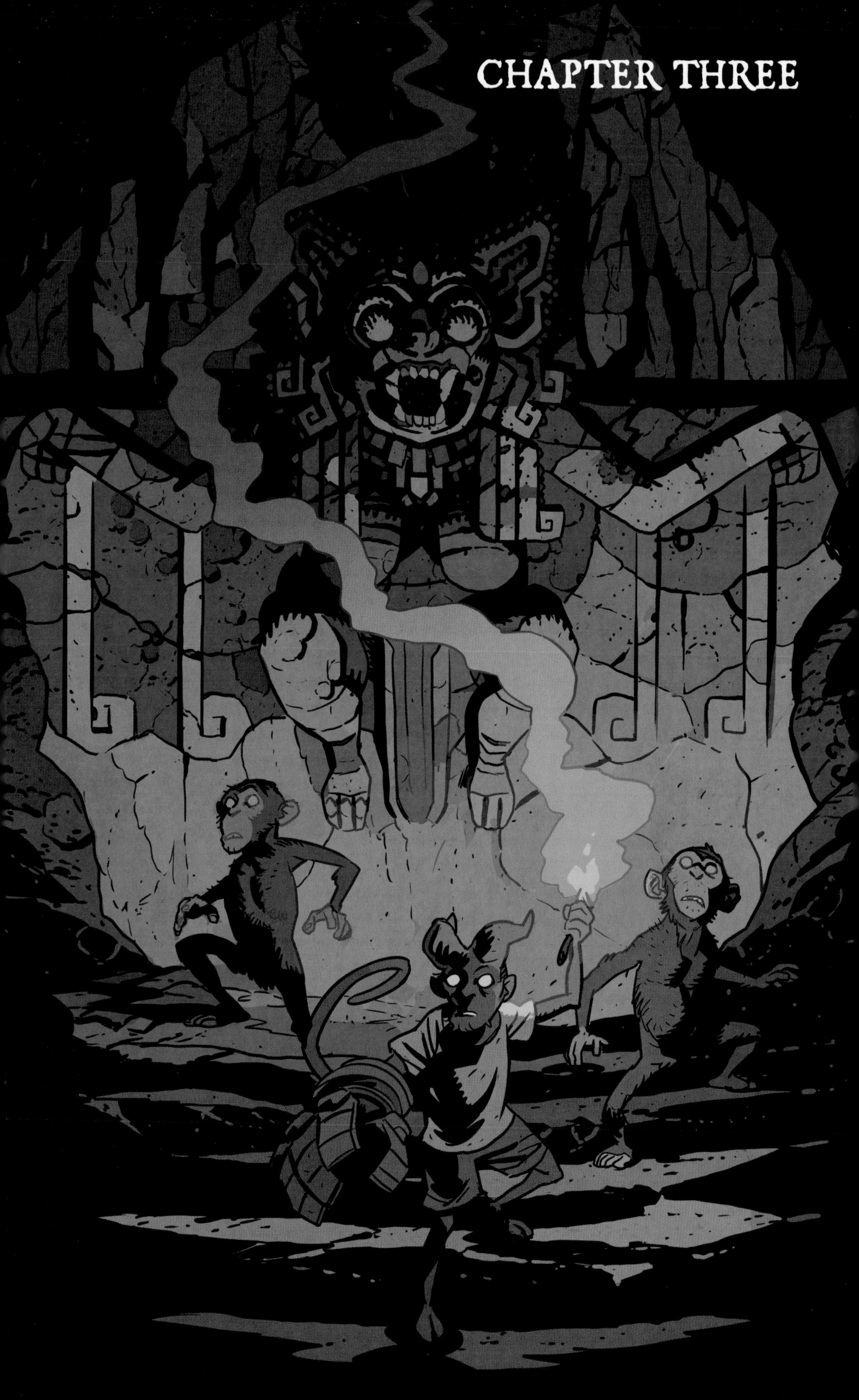

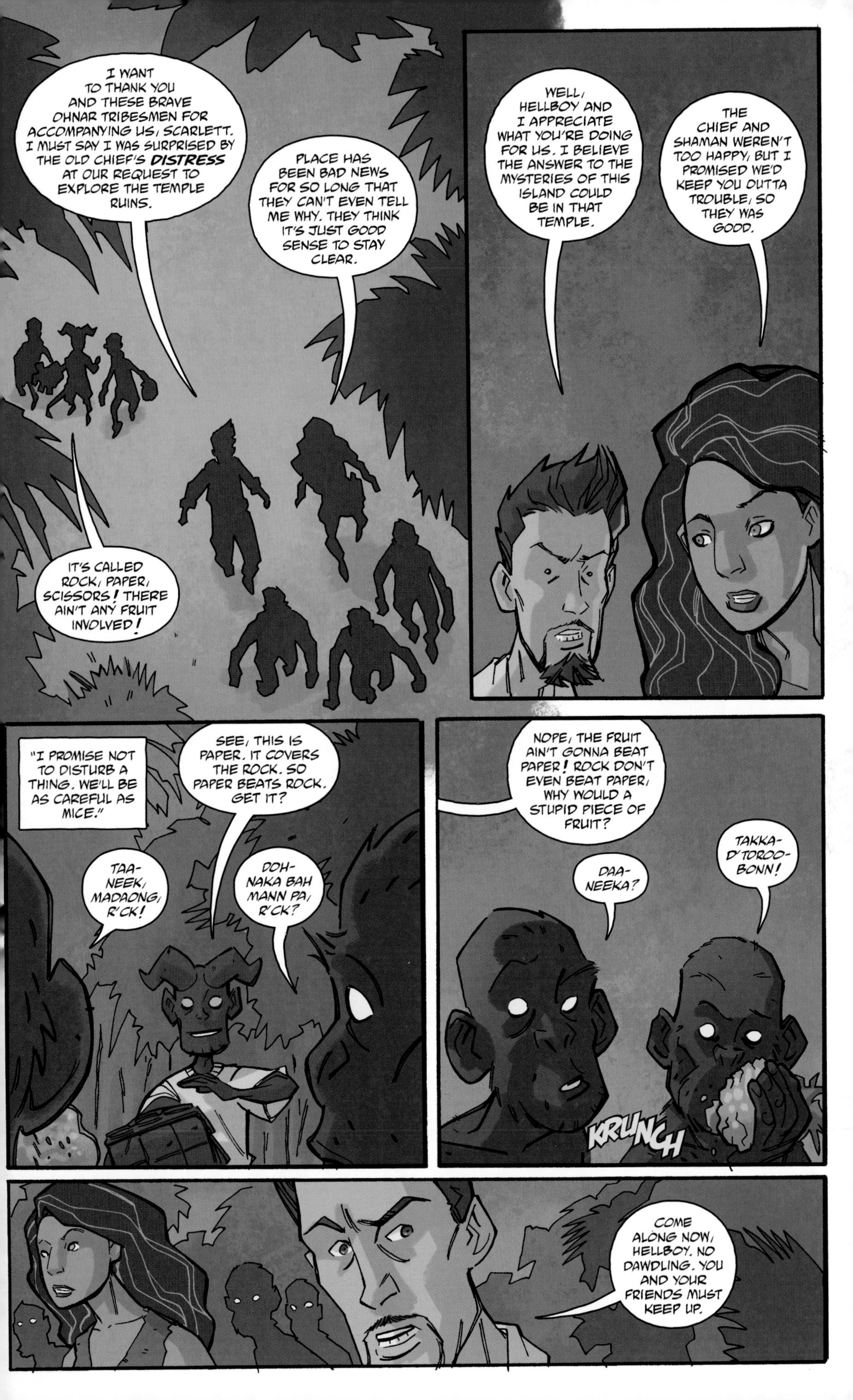
I WANT TO THANK YOU AND THESE BRAVE OHNAR TRIBESMEN FOR ACCOMPANYING US, SCARLETT. I MUST SAY I WAS SURPRISED BY THE OLD CHIEF'S DISTRESS AT OUR REQUEST TO EXPLORE THE TEMPLE RUINS.
PLACE HAS BEEN BAD NEWS FOR SO LONG THAT THEY CAN'T EVEN TELL ME WHY. THEY THINK IT'S JUST GOOD SENSE TO STAY CLEAR.
IT'S CALLED ROCK, PAPER, SCISSORS! THERE AIN'T ANY FRUIT INVOLVED!
WELL, HELLBOY AND I APPRECIATE WHAT YOU'RE DOING FOR US. I BELIEVE THE ANSWER TO THE MYSTERIES OF THIS ISLAND COULD BE IN THAT TEMPLE.
THE CHIEF AND SHAMAN WEREN'T TOO HAPPY, BUT I PROMISED WE'D KEEP YOU OUTTA TROUBLE, SO THEY WAS GOOD.
"I PROMISE NOT TO DISTURB A THING. WE'LL BE AS CAREFUL AS MICE."
SEE, THIS IS PAPER. IT COVERS THE ROCK. SO PAPER BEATS ROCK. GET IT?
TAA-NEEK, MADAONG, R'CK!
DOH-NAKA BAH MANN PA, R'CK?
NOPE, THE FRUIT AIN'T GONNA BEAT PAPER! ROCK DON'T EVEN BEAT PAPER, WHY WOULD A STUPID PIECE OF FRUIT?
DAA-NEEKA?
TAKKA-D'TOROO-BONN!
KRUNCH
COME ALONG NOW, HELLBOY. NO DAWDLING. YOU AND YOUR FRIENDS MUST KEEP UP.

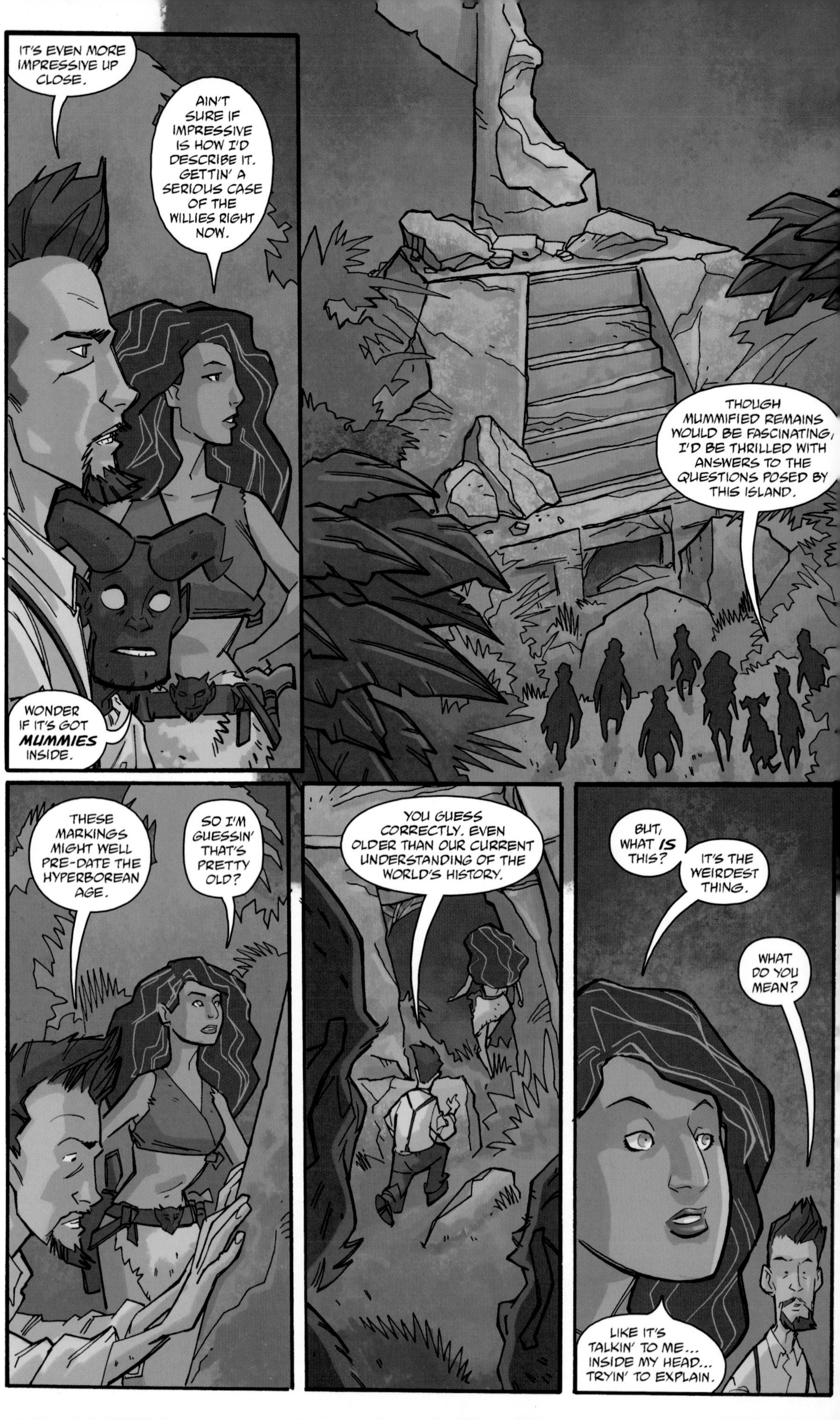
IT'S EVEN MORE IMPRESSIVE UP CLOSE.
AIN'T SURE IF IMPRESSIVE IS HOW I'D DESCRIBE IT. GETTIN' A SERIOUS CASE OF THE WILLIES RIGHT NOW.
WONDER IF IT'S GOT **MUMMIES** INSIDE.
THOUGH MUMMIFIED REMAINS WOULD BE FASCINATING, I'D BE THRILLED WITH ANSWERS TO THE QUESTIONS POSED BY THIS ISLAND.
THESE MARKINGS MIGHT WELL PRE-DATE THE HYPERBOREAN AGE.
SO I'M GUESSIN' THAT'S PRETTY OLD?
YOU GUESS CORRECTLY. EVEN OLDER THAN OUR CURRENT UNDERSTANDING OF THE WORLD'S HISTORY.
BUT, WHAT ***IS*** THIS?
IT'S THE WEIRDEST THING.
WHAT DO YOU MEAN?
LIKE IT'S TALKIN' TO ME... INSIDE MY HEAD... TRYIN' TO EXPLAIN.

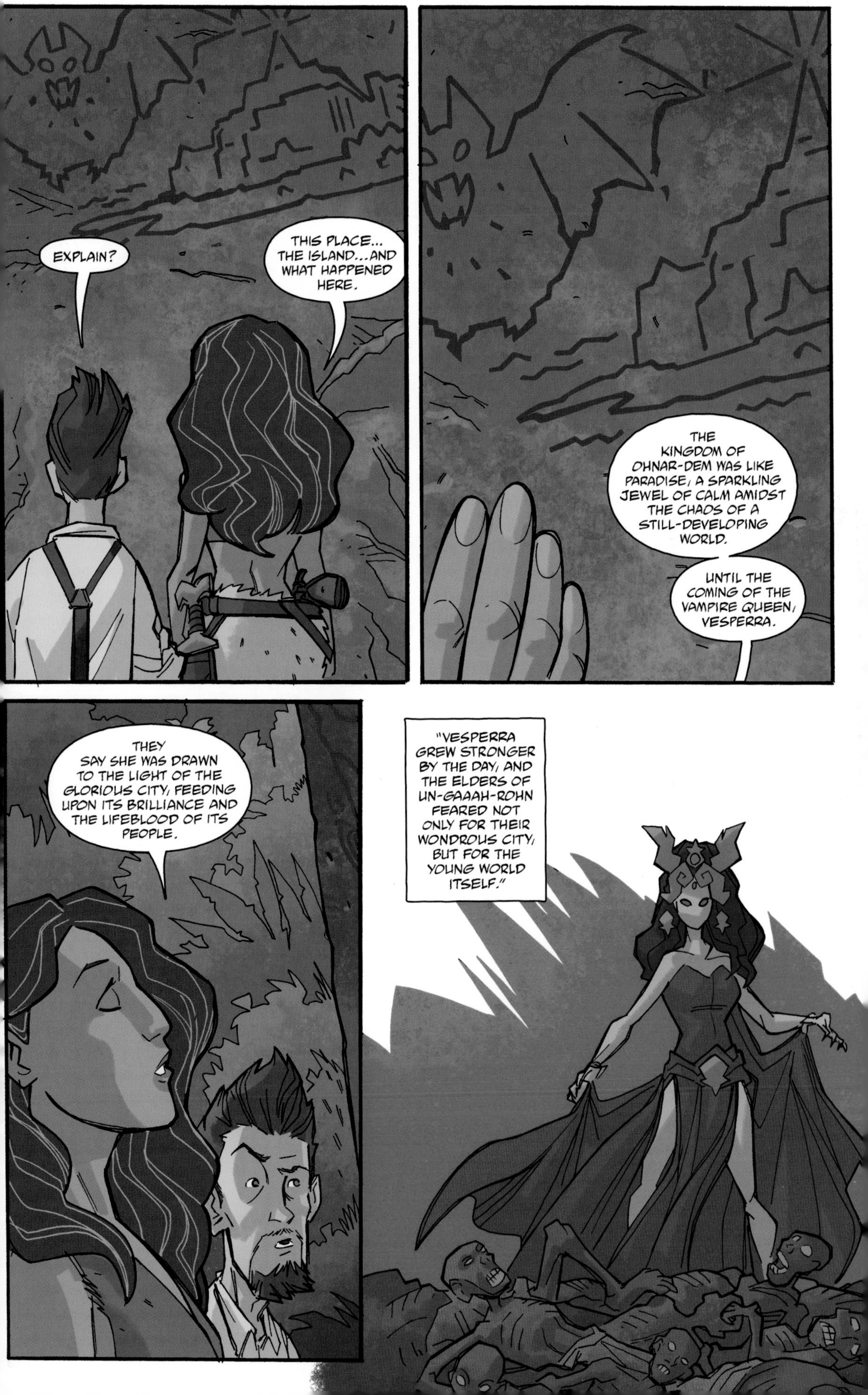
EXPLAIN?
THIS PLACE... THE ISLAND...AND WHAT HAPPENED HERE.
THE KINGDOM OF OHNAR-DEM WAS LIKE PARADISE, A SPARKLING JEWEL OF CALM AMIDST THE CHAOS OF A STILL-DEVELOPING WORLD.
UNTIL THE COMING OF THE VAMPIRE QUEEN, VESPERRA.
THEY SAY SHE WAS DRAWN TO THE LIGHT OF THE GLORIOUS CITY, FEEDING UPON ITS BRILLIANCE AND THE LIFEBLOOD OF ITS PEOPLE.
"VESPERRA GREW STRONGER BY THE DAY, AND THE ELDERS OF UN-GAAAH-ROHN FEARED NOT ONLY FOR THEIR WONDROUS CITY, BUT FOR THE YOUNG WORLD ITSELF."

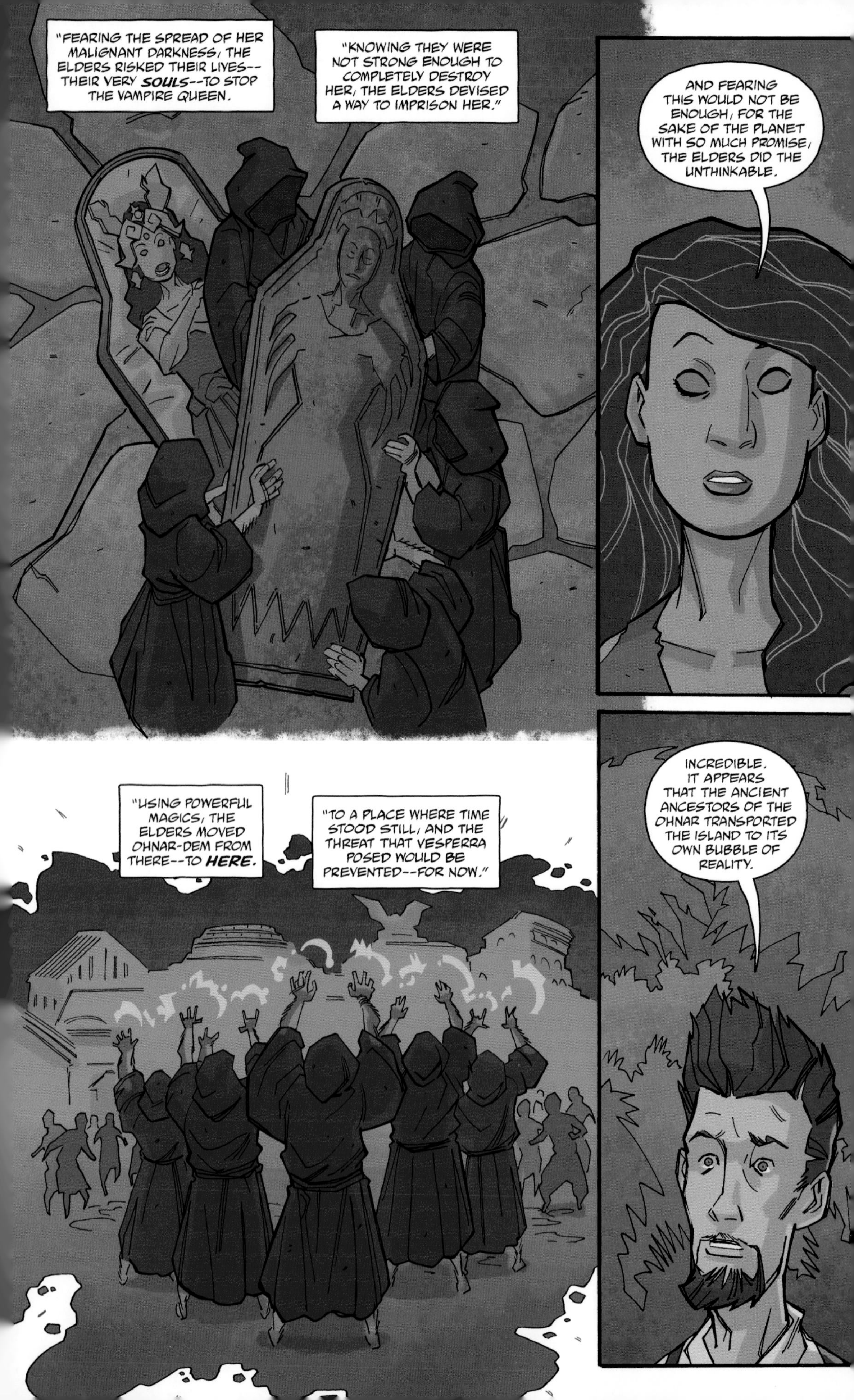
"FEARING THE SPREAD OF HER MALIGNANT DARKNESS, THE ELDERS RISKED THEIR LIVES--THEIR VERY SOULS--TO STOP THE VAMPIRE QUEEN.
"KNOWING THEY WERE NOT STRONG ENOUGH TO COMPLETELY DESTROY HER, THE ELDERS DEVISED A WAY TO IMPRISON HER."
AND FEARING THIS WOULD NOT BE ENOUGH, FOR THE SAKE OF THE PLANET WITH SO MUCH PROMISE, THE ELDERS DID THE UNTHINKABLE.
"USING POWERFUL MAGICS, THE ELDERS MOVED OHNAR-DEM FROM THERE--TO HERE.
"TO A PLACE WHERE TIME STOOD STILL, AND THE THREAT THAT VESPERRA POSED WOULD BE PREVENTED--FOR NOW."
INCREDIBLE. IT APPEARS THAT THE ANCIENT ANCESTORS OF THE OHNAR TRANSPORTED THE ISLAND TO ITS OWN BUBBLE OF REALITY.

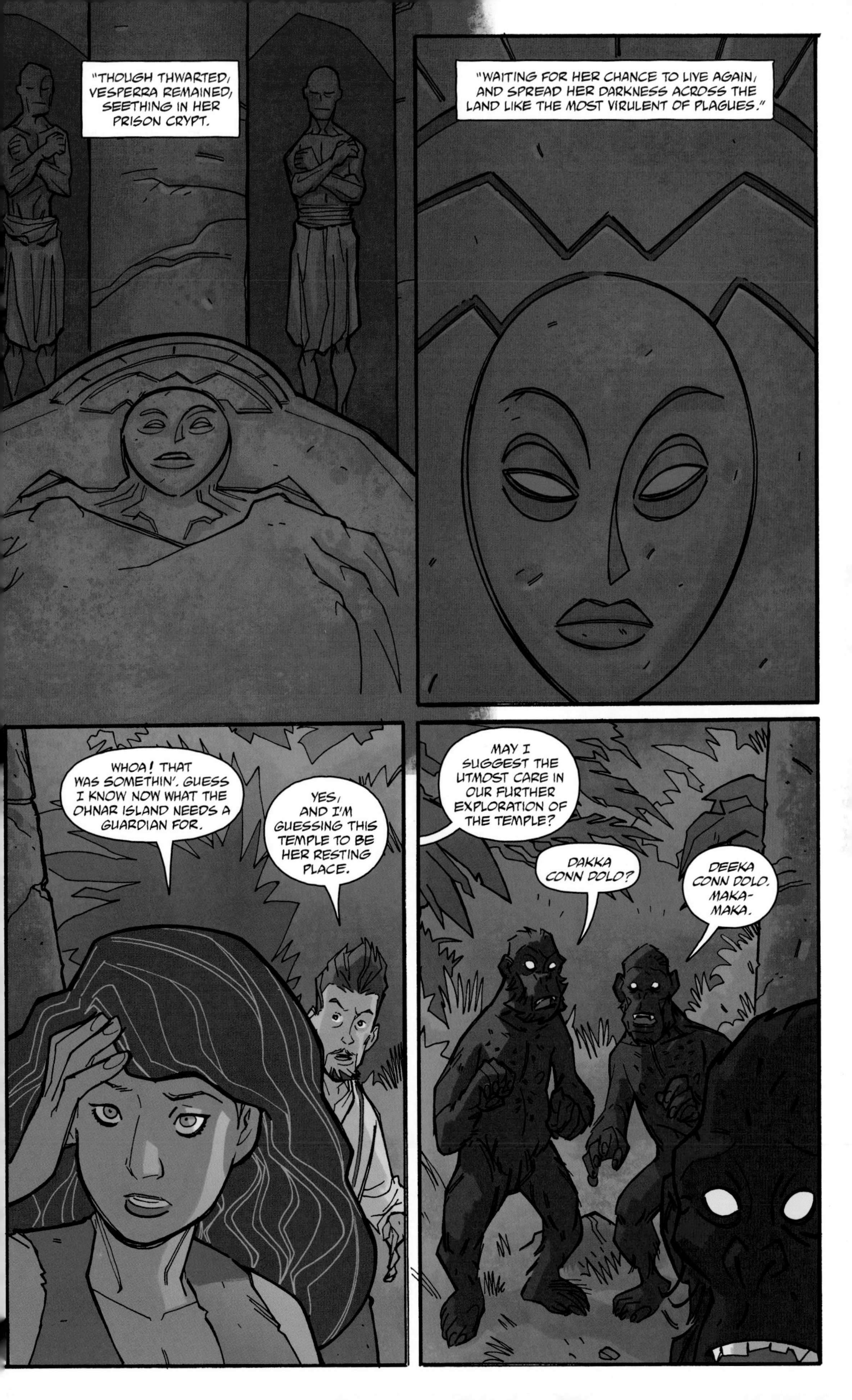
"THOUGH THWARTED, VESPERRA REMAINED, SEETHING IN HER PRISON CRYPT.
"WAITING FOR HER CHANCE TO LIVE AGAIN, AND SPREAD HER DARKNESS ACROSS THE LAND LIKE THE MOST VIRULENT OF PLAGUES."
WHOA! THAT WAS SOMETHIN'. GUESS I KNOW NOW WHAT THE OHNAR ISLAND NEEDS A GUARDIAN FOR.
YES, AND I'M GUESSING THIS TEMPLE TO BE HER RESTING PLACE.
MAY I SUGGEST THE UTMOST CARE IN OUR FURTHER EXPLORATION OF THE TEMPLE?
DAKKA CONN DOLO?
DEEKA CONN DOLO. MAKA-MAKA.

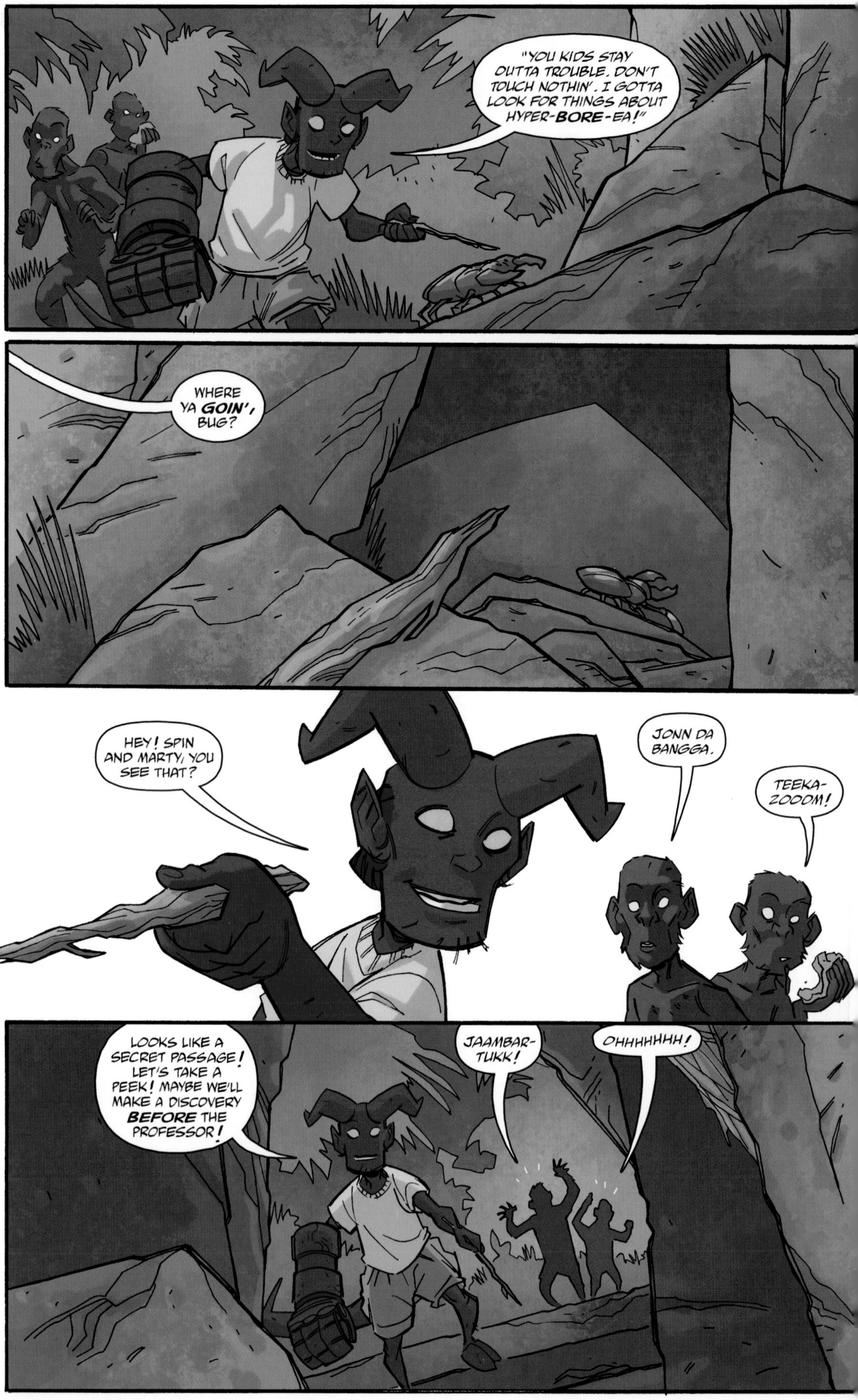
"YOU KIDS STAY OUTTA TROUBLE. DON'T TOUCH NOTHIN'. I GOTTA LOOK FOR THINGS ABOUT HYPER-BORE-EA!"
WHERE YA GOIN', BUG?
HEY! SPIN AND MARTY, YOU SEE THAT?
JONN DA BANGGA.
TEEKA-ZOOOM!
LOOKS LIKE A SECRET PASSAGE! LET'S TAKE A PEEK! MAYBE WE'LL MAKE A DISCOVERY BEFORE THE PROFESSOR!
JAAMBAR-TUKK!
OHHHHHHH!

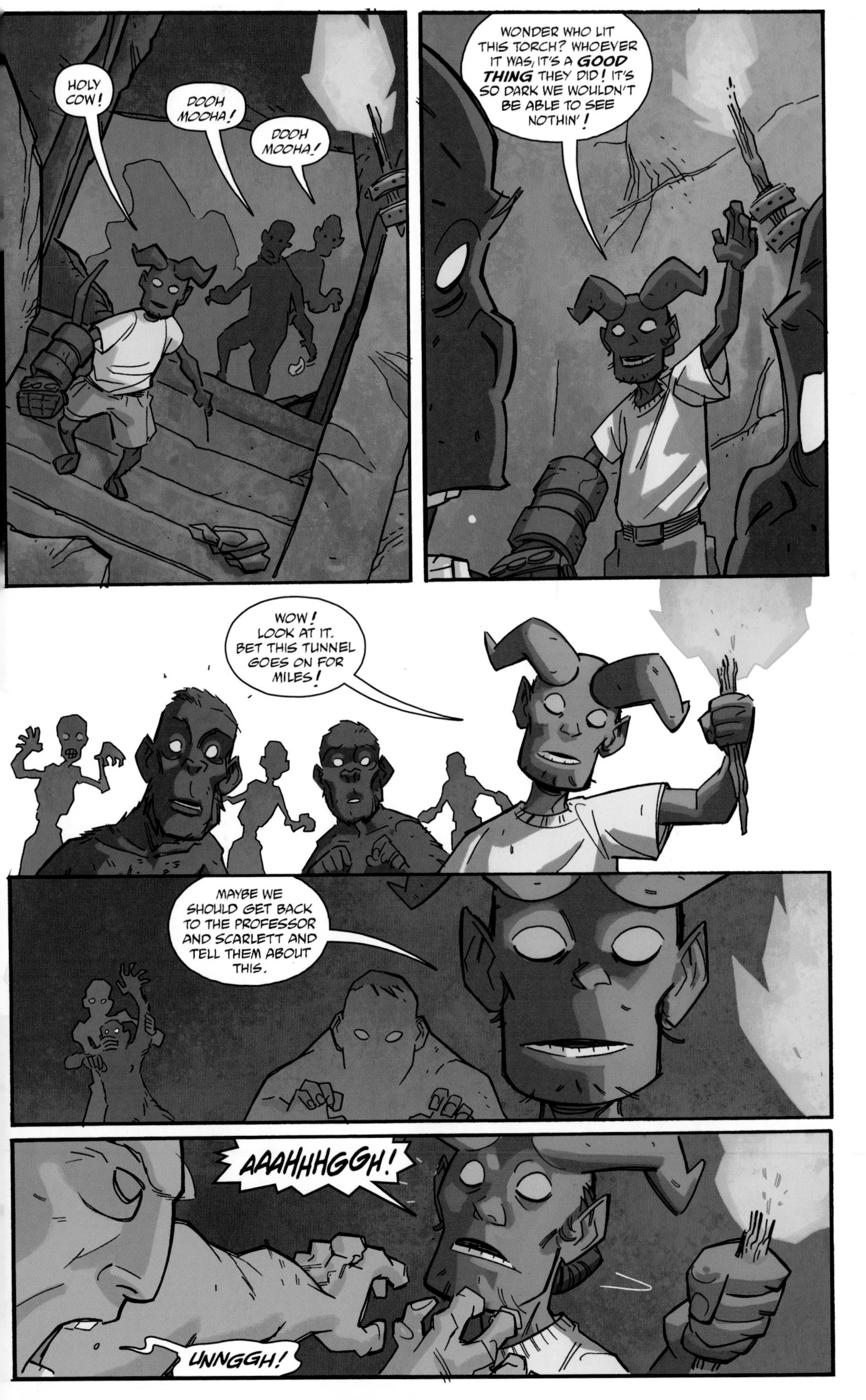
HOLY COW!
OOOH MOOHA!
OOOH MOOHA!
WONDER WHO LIT THIS TORCH? WHOEVER IT WAS, IT'S A GOOD THING THEY DID! IT'S SO DARK WE WOULDN'T BE ABLE TO SEE NOTHIN'!
WOW! LOOK AT IT. BET THIS TUNNEL GOES ON FOR MILES!
MAYBE WE SHOULD GET BACK TO THE PROFESSOR AND SCARLETT AND TELL THEM ABOUT THIS.
AAAHHHGGH!
UNNGGH!

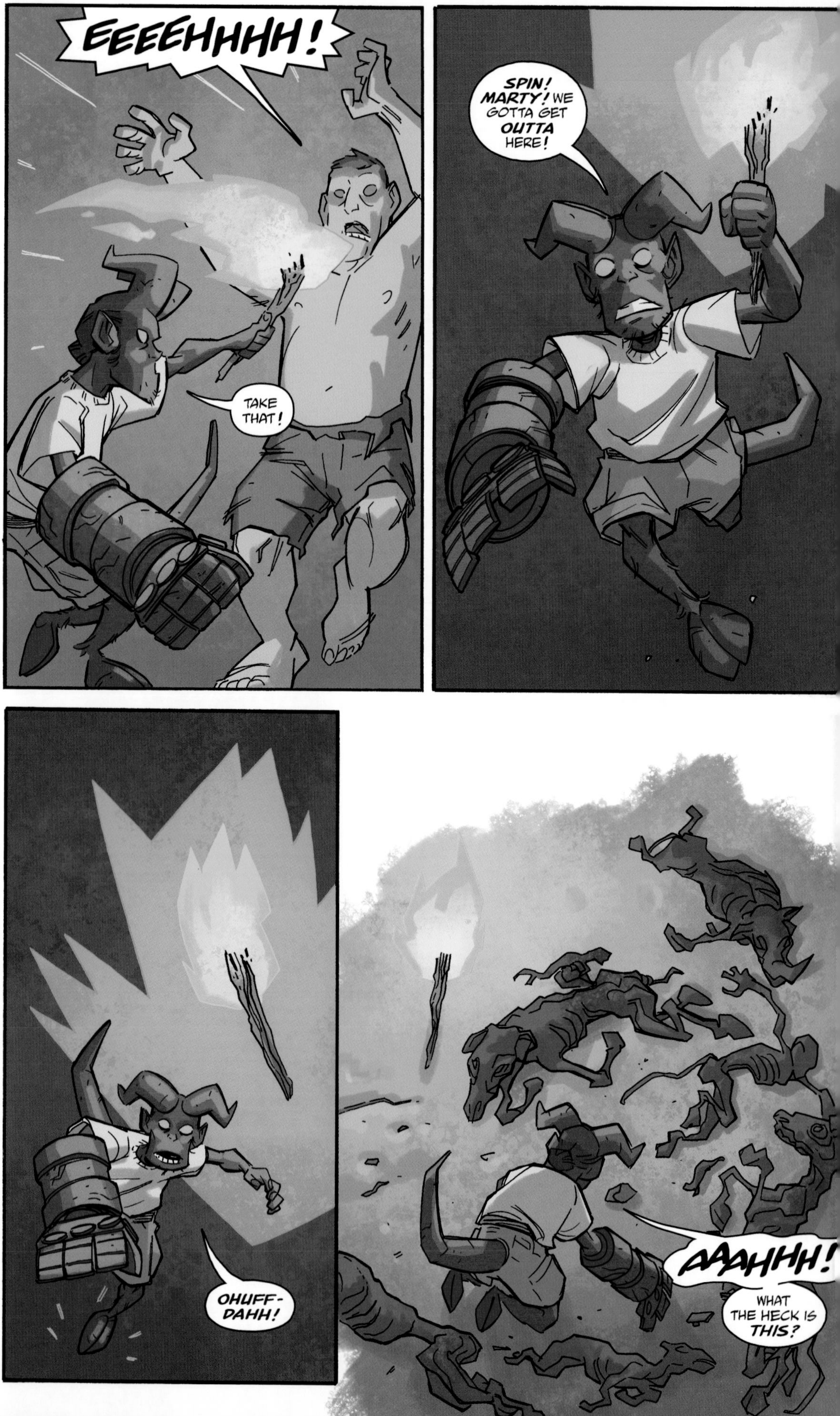
EEEEHHHH!
TAKE THAT!
SPIN! MARTY! WE GOTTA GET OUTTA HERE!
OHUFF-DAHH!
AAAHHH!
WHAT THE HECK IS THIS?

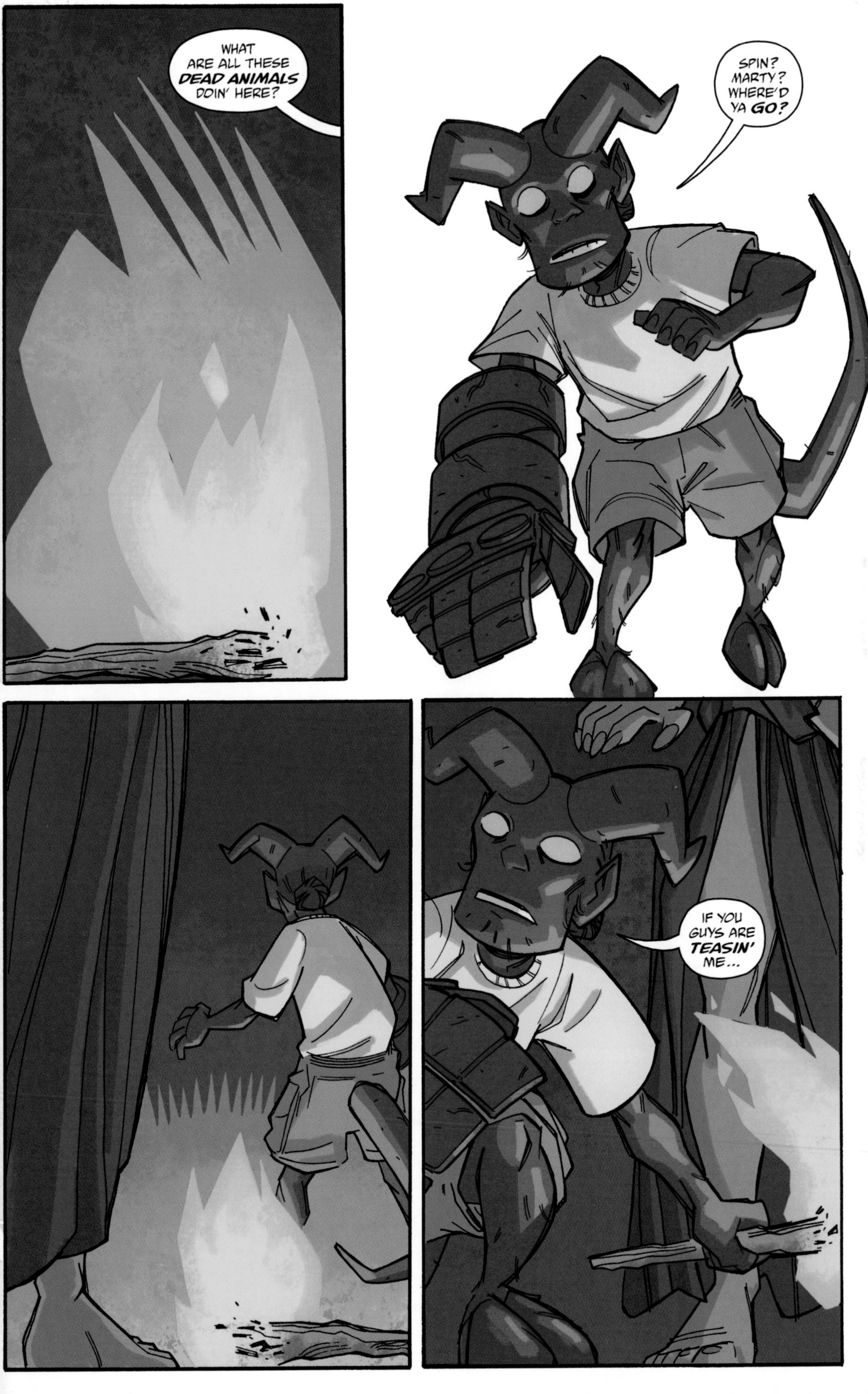
WHAT ARE ALL THESE DEAD ANIMALS DOIN' HERE?
SPIN? MARTY? WHERE'D YA GO?
IF YOU GUYS ARE TEASIN' ME...

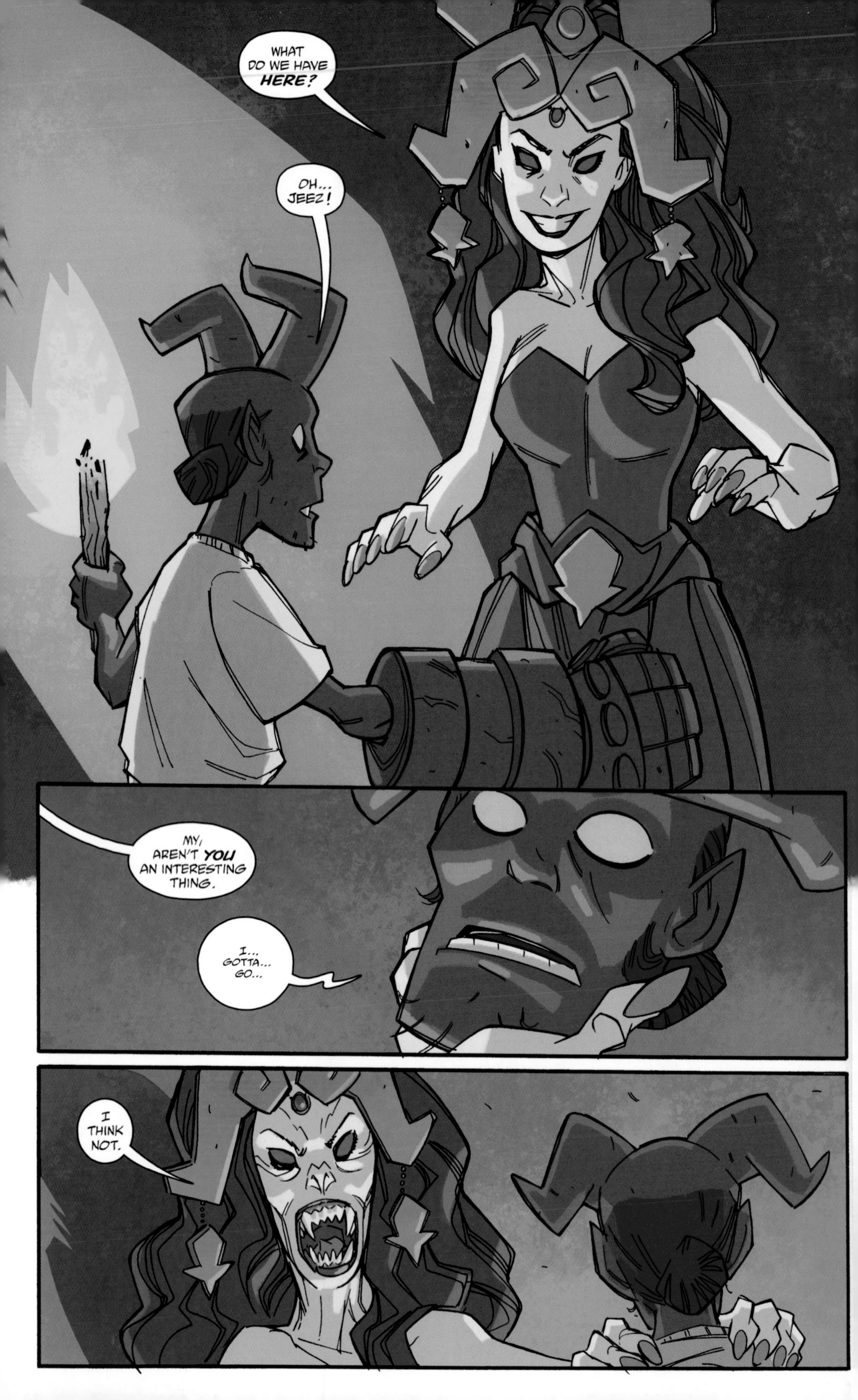
WHAT DO WE HAVE HERE?
OH... JEEZ!
MY, AREN'T YOU AN INTERESTING THING.
I... GOTTA... GO...
I THINK NOT.

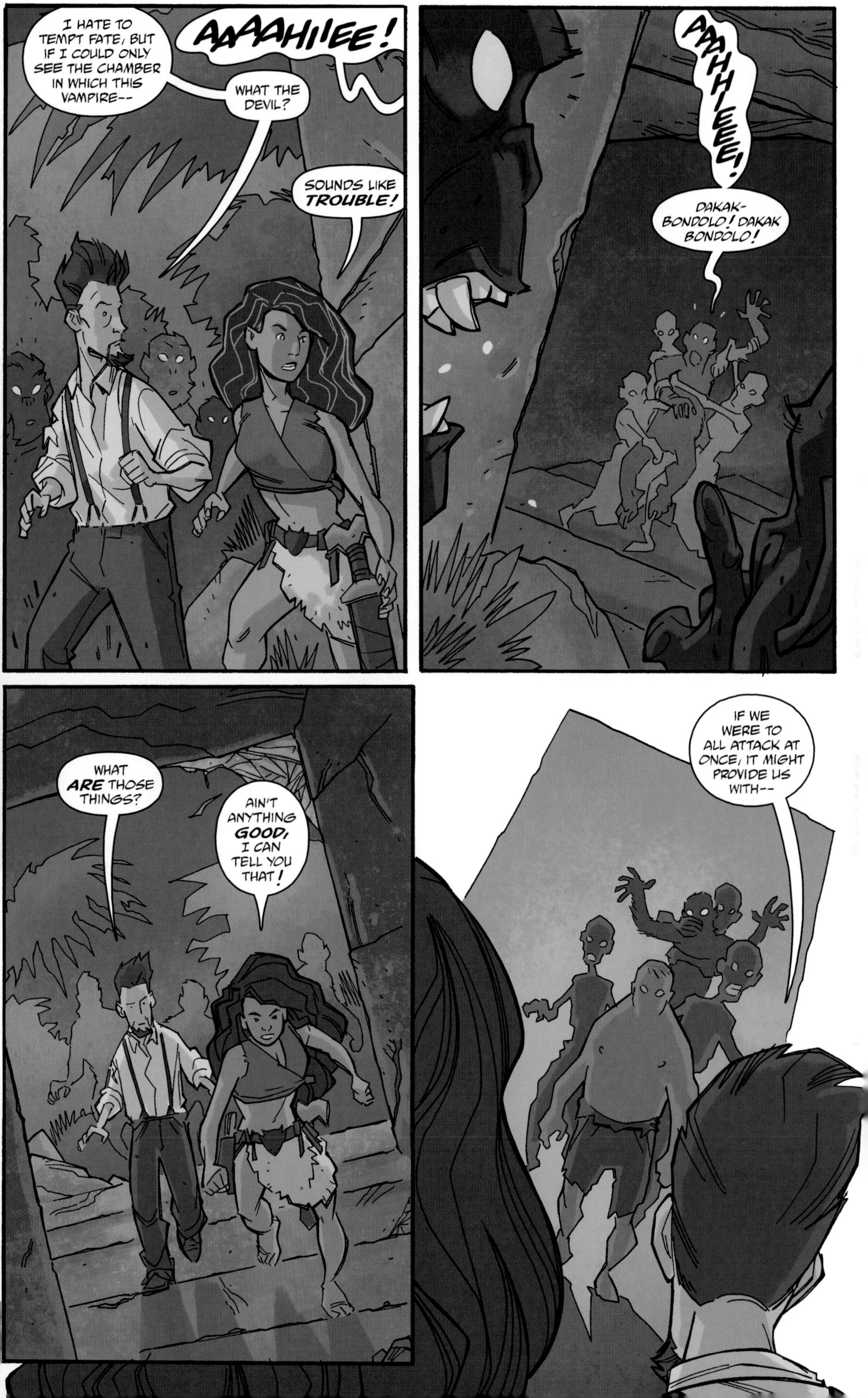
I HATE TO TEMPT FATE, BUT IF I COULD ONLY SEE THE CHAMBER IN WHICH THIS VAMPIRE--
AAAAHIIEE!
WHAT THE DEVIL?
SOUNDS LIKE TROUBLE!
AAAHHIEEE!
DAKAK-BONDOLO! DAKAK BONDOLO!
WHAT ARE THOSE THINGS?
AIN'T ANYTHING GOOD, I CAN TELL YOU THAT!
IF WE WERE TO ALL ATTACK AT ONCE, IT MIGHT PROVIDE US WITH--

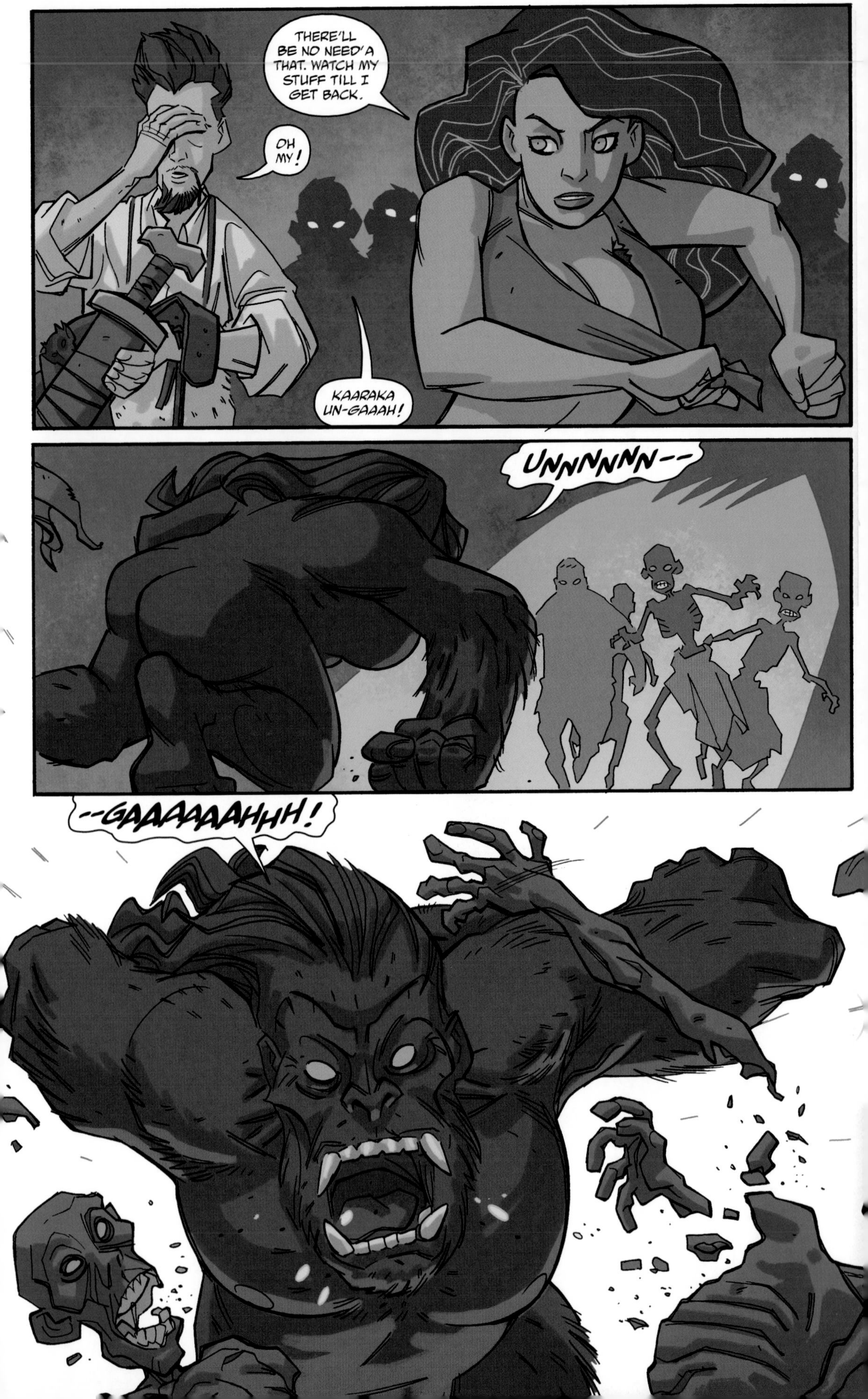
OH MY!
THERE'LL BE NO NEED'A THAT. WATCH MY STUFF TILL I GET BACK.
KAARAKA UN-GAAAH!
UNNNNNN--
--GAAAAAAAHHH!

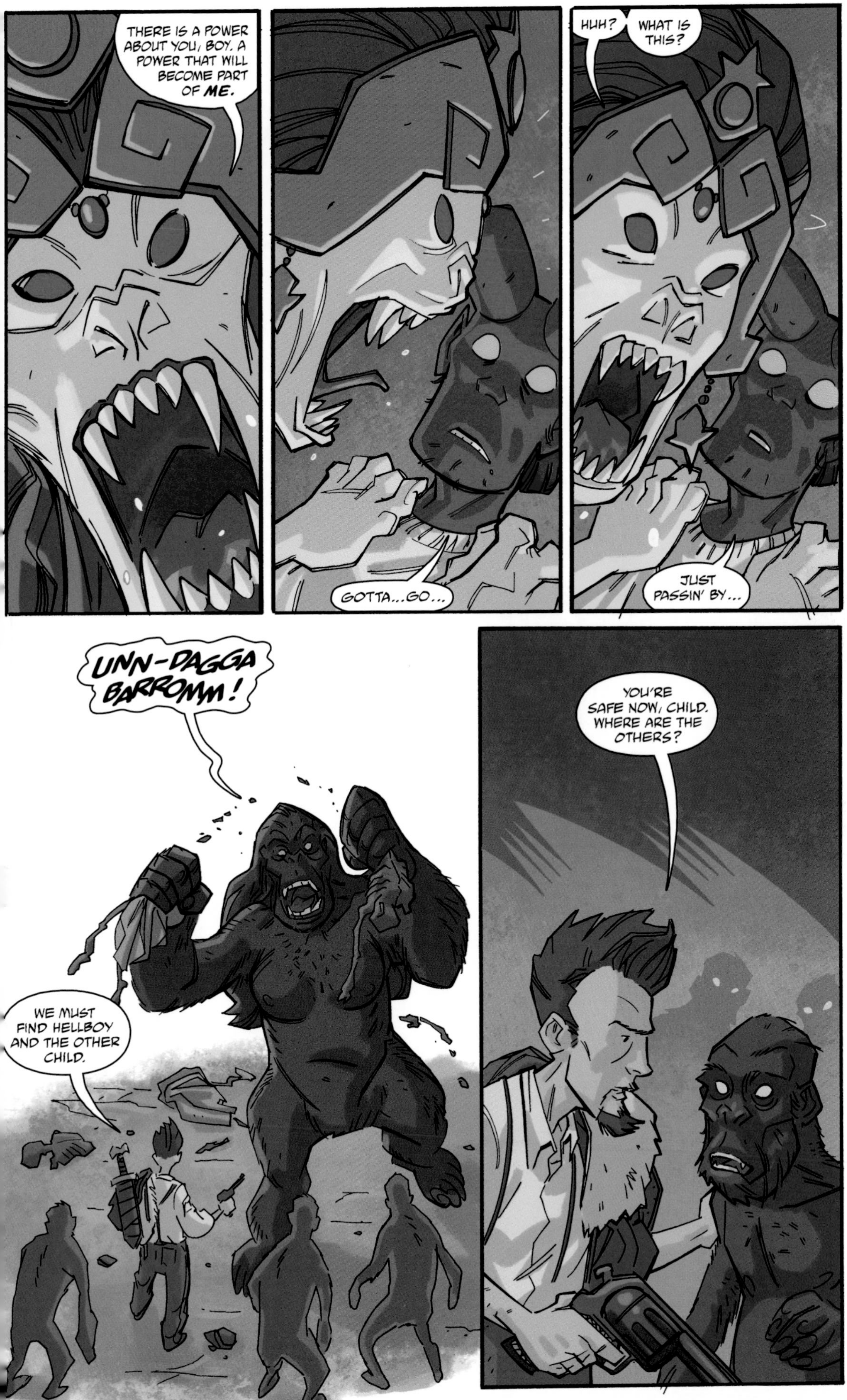
THERE IS A POWER ABOUT YOU, BOY. A POWER THAT WILL BECOME PART OF *ME.*
GOTTA...GO...
HUH?
WHAT IS THIS?
JUST PASSIN' BY...
UNN-DAGGA BARROMM!
WE MUST FIND HELLBOY AND THE OTHER CHILD.
YOU'RE SAFE NOW, CHILD. WHERE ARE THE OTHERS?

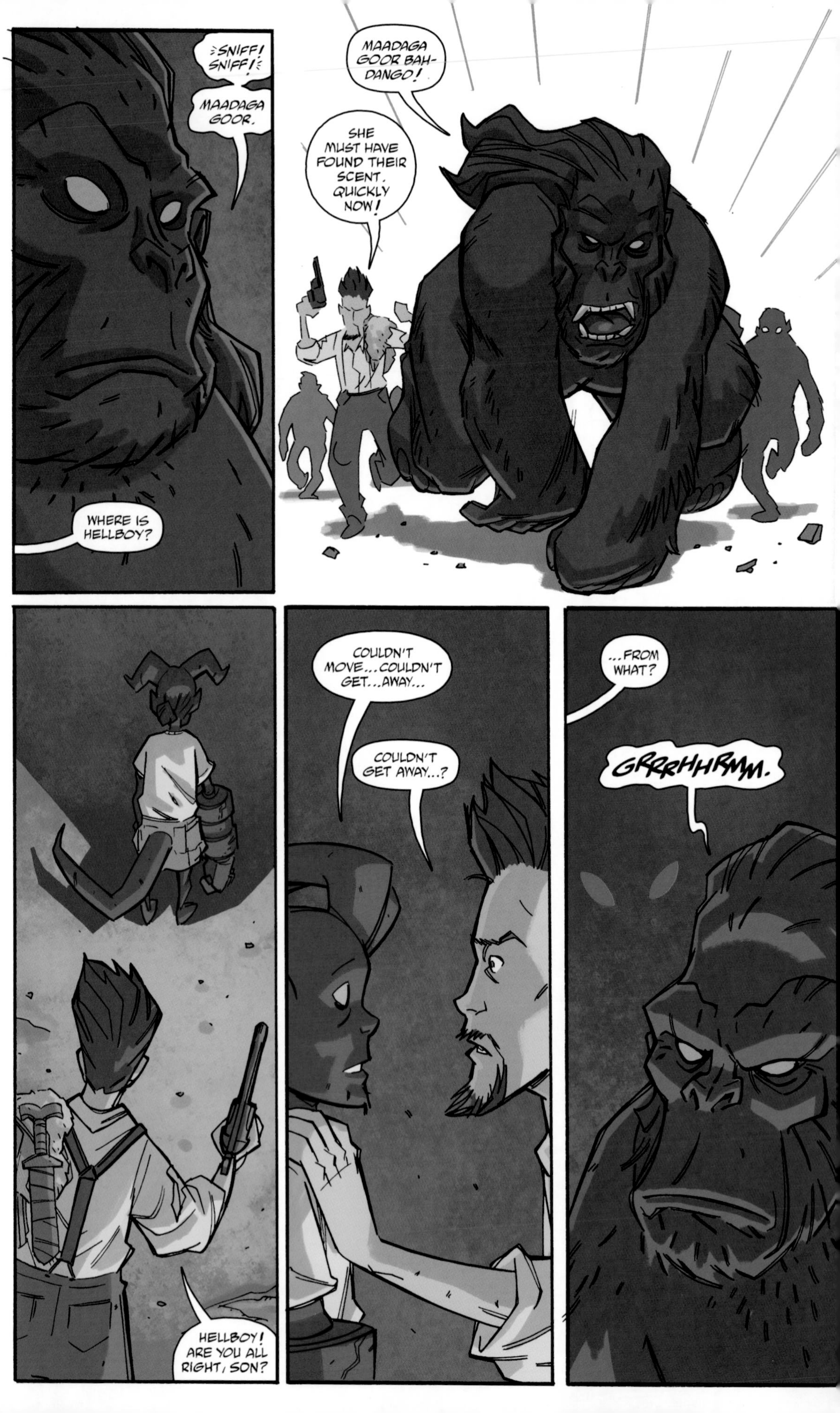
SNIFF! SNIFF!
MAADAGA GOOR.
WHERE IS HELLBOY?
MAADAGA GOOR BAH-DANGO!
SHE MUST HAVE FOUND THEIR SCENT. QUICKLY NOW!
HELLBOY! ARE YOU ALL RIGHT, SON?
COULDN'T MOVE...COULDN'T GET...AWAY...
COULDN'T GET AWAY...?
...FROM WHAT?
GRRRHHRMM.

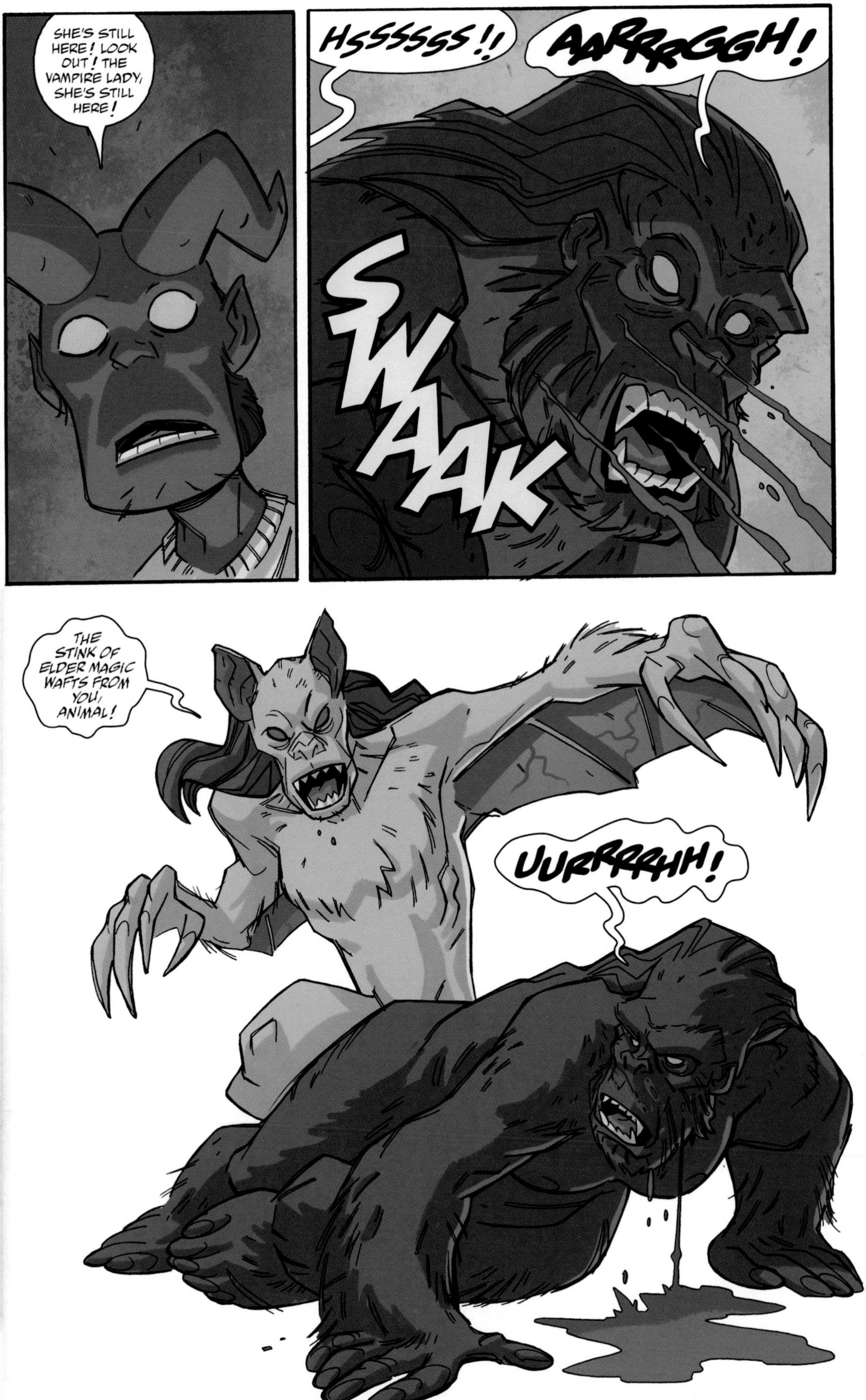
SHE'S STILL HERE! LOOK OUT! THE VAMPIRE LADY, SHE'S STILL HERE!
HSSSSSS!!
AARRRGGGH!
SWAAAK
THE STINK OF ELDER MAGIC WAFTS FROM YOU, ANIMAL!
UURRRRHH!

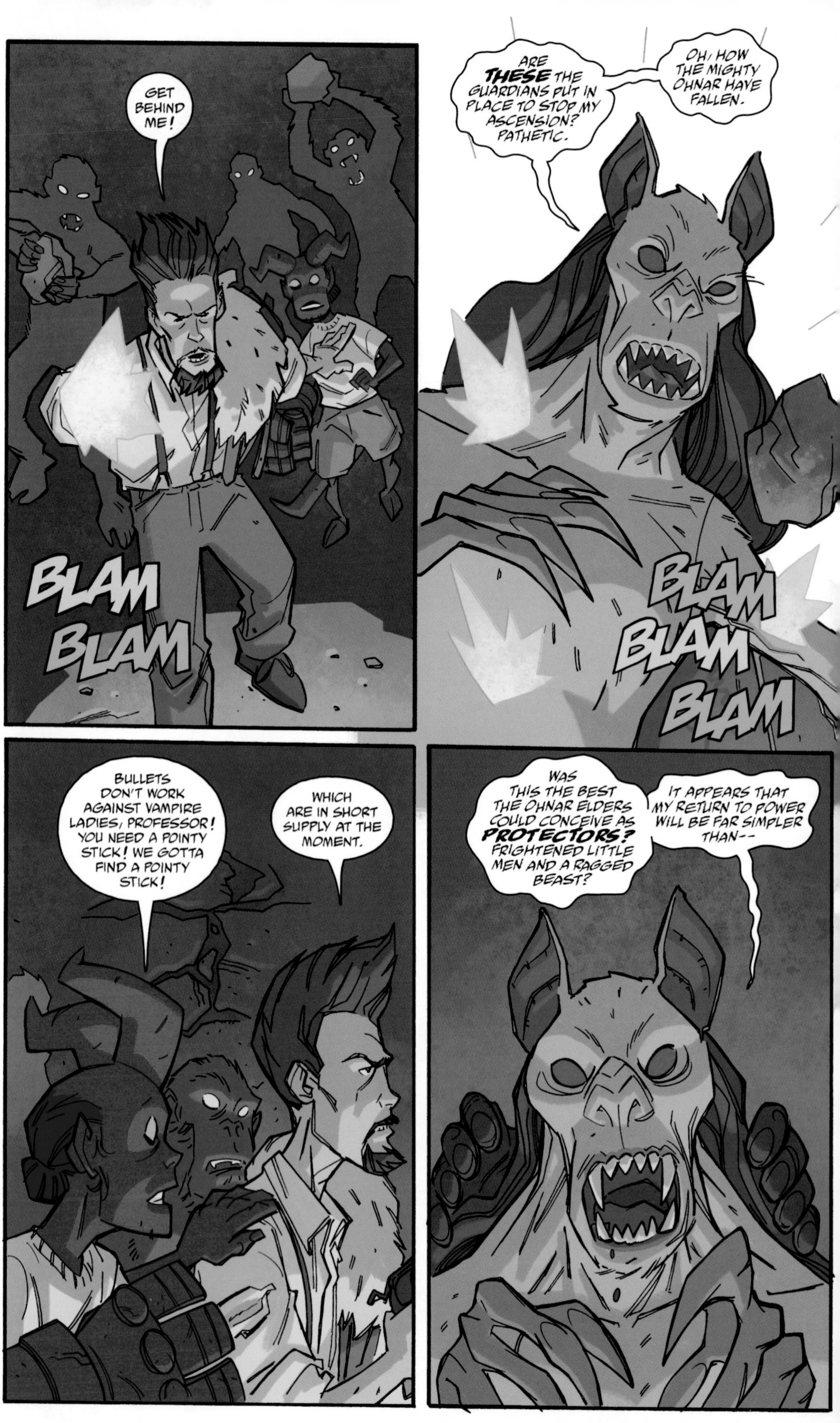
GET BEHIND ME!
BLAM BLAM
ARE THESE THE GUARDIANS PUT IN PLACE TO STOP MY ASCENSION? PATHETIC.
OH, HOW THE MIGHTY OHNAR HAVE FALLEN.
BLAM BLAM BLAM
BULLETS DON'T WORK AGAINST VAMPIRE LADIES, PROFESSOR! YOU NEED A POINTY STICK! WE GOTTA FIND A POINTY STICK!
WHICH ARE IN SHORT SUPPLY AT THE MOMENT.
WAS THIS THE BEST THE OHNAR ELDERS COULD CONCEIVE AS PROTECTORS? FRIGHTENED LITTLE MEN AND A RAGGED BEAST?
IT APPEARS THAT MY RETURN TO POWER WILL BE FAR SIMPLER THAN--

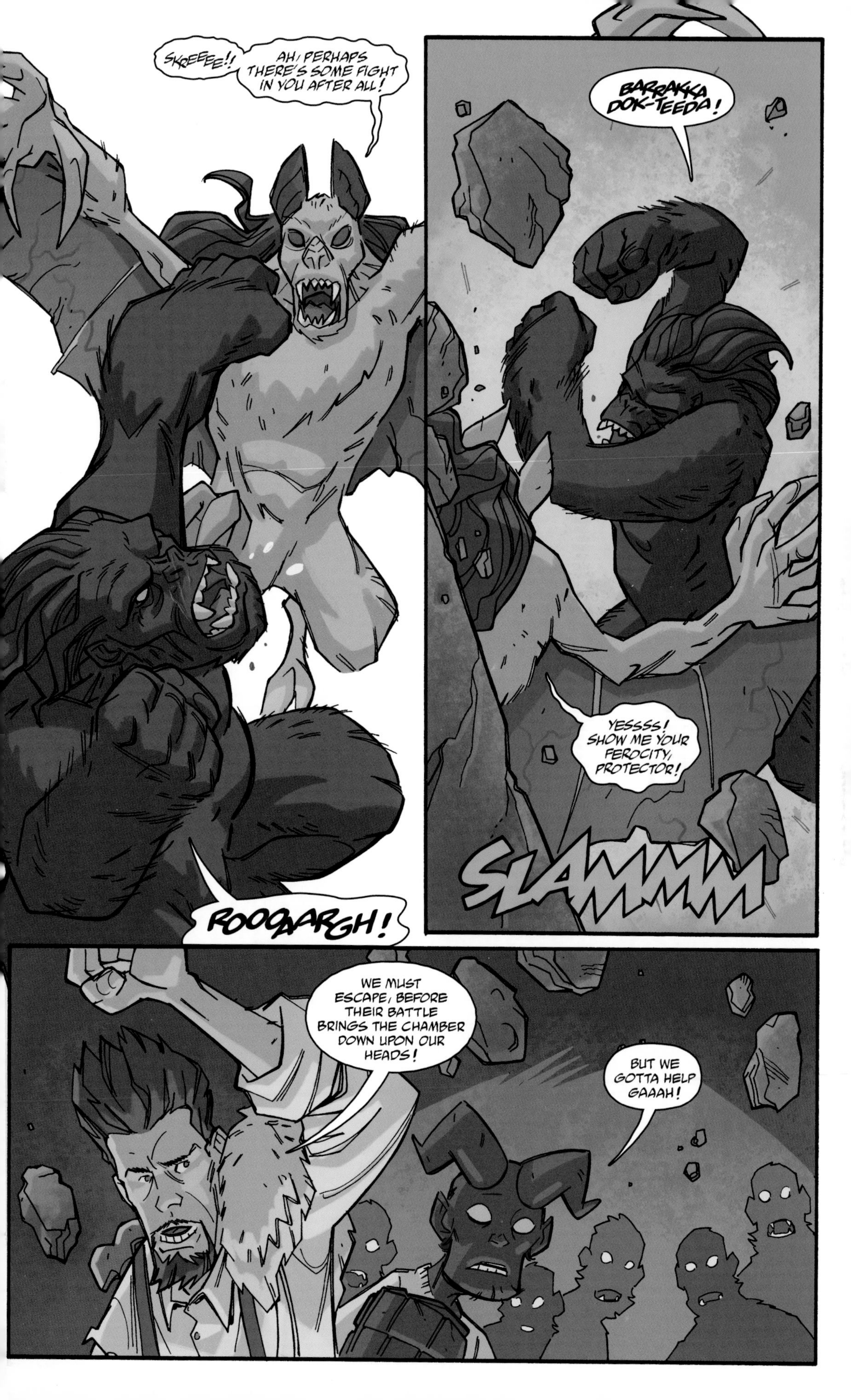
SKREEEEE!!
AH, PERHAPS THERE'S SOME FIGHT IN YOU AFTER ALL!
ROOOAARGH!
BARRAKKA DOK-TEEDA!
YESSSS! SHOW ME YOUR FEROCITY, PROTECTOR!
SLAMMM
WE MUST ESCAPE, BEFORE THEIR BATTLE BRINGS THE CHAMBER DOWN UPON OUR HEADS!
BUT WE GOTTA HELP GAAAH!

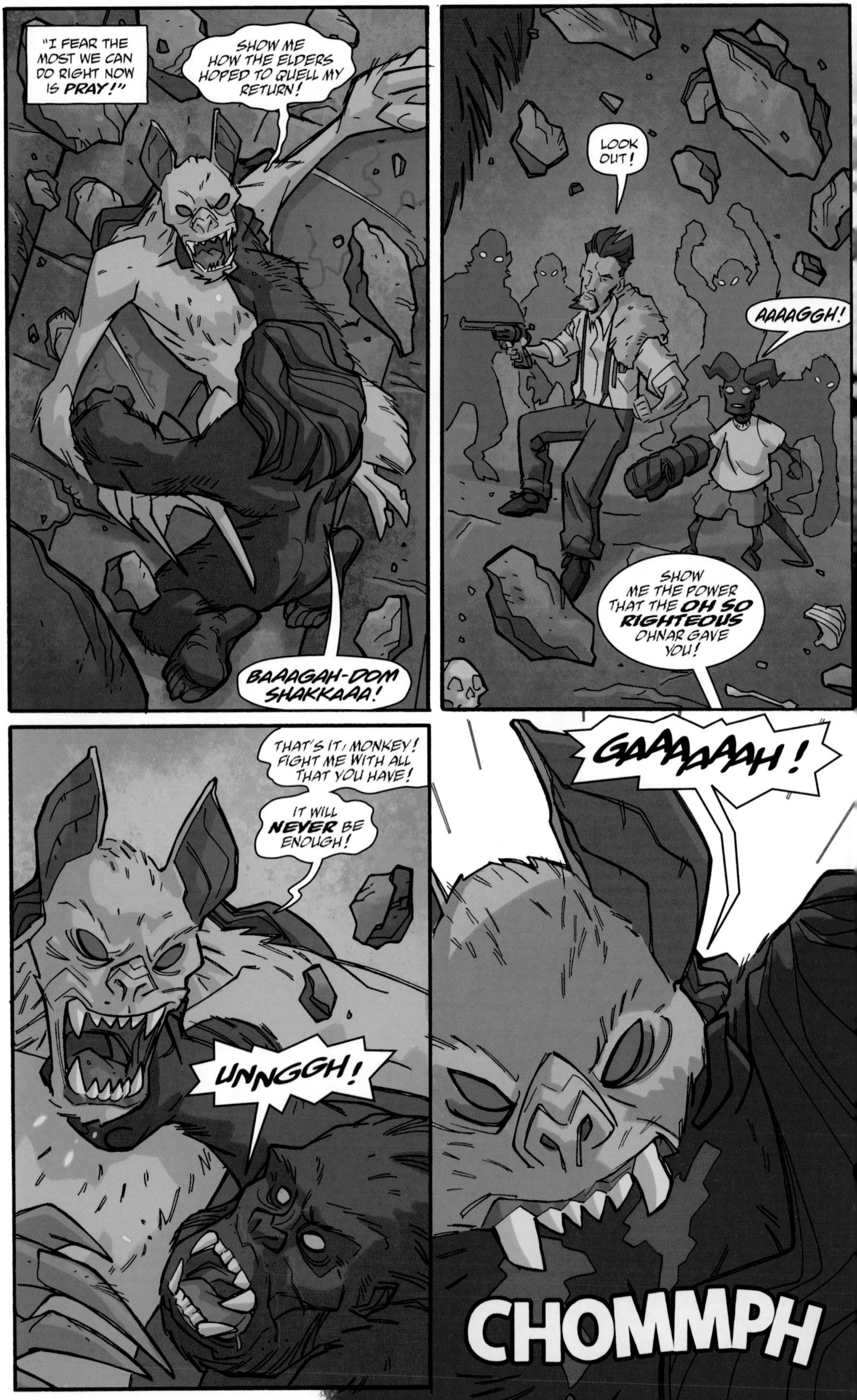
"I FEAR THE MOST WE CAN DO RIGHT NOW IS PRAY!"
SHOW ME HOW THE ELDERS HOPED TO QUELL MY RETURN!
BAAAGAH-DOM SHAKKAAA!
LOOK OUT!
AAAAGGH!
SHOW ME THE POWER THAT THE OH SO RIGHTEOUS OHNAR GAVE YOU!
THAT'S IT, MONKEY! FIGHT ME WITH ALL THAT YOU HAVE!
IT WILL NEVER BE ENOUGH!
UNNGGH!
GAAAAAAH!
CHOMMPH

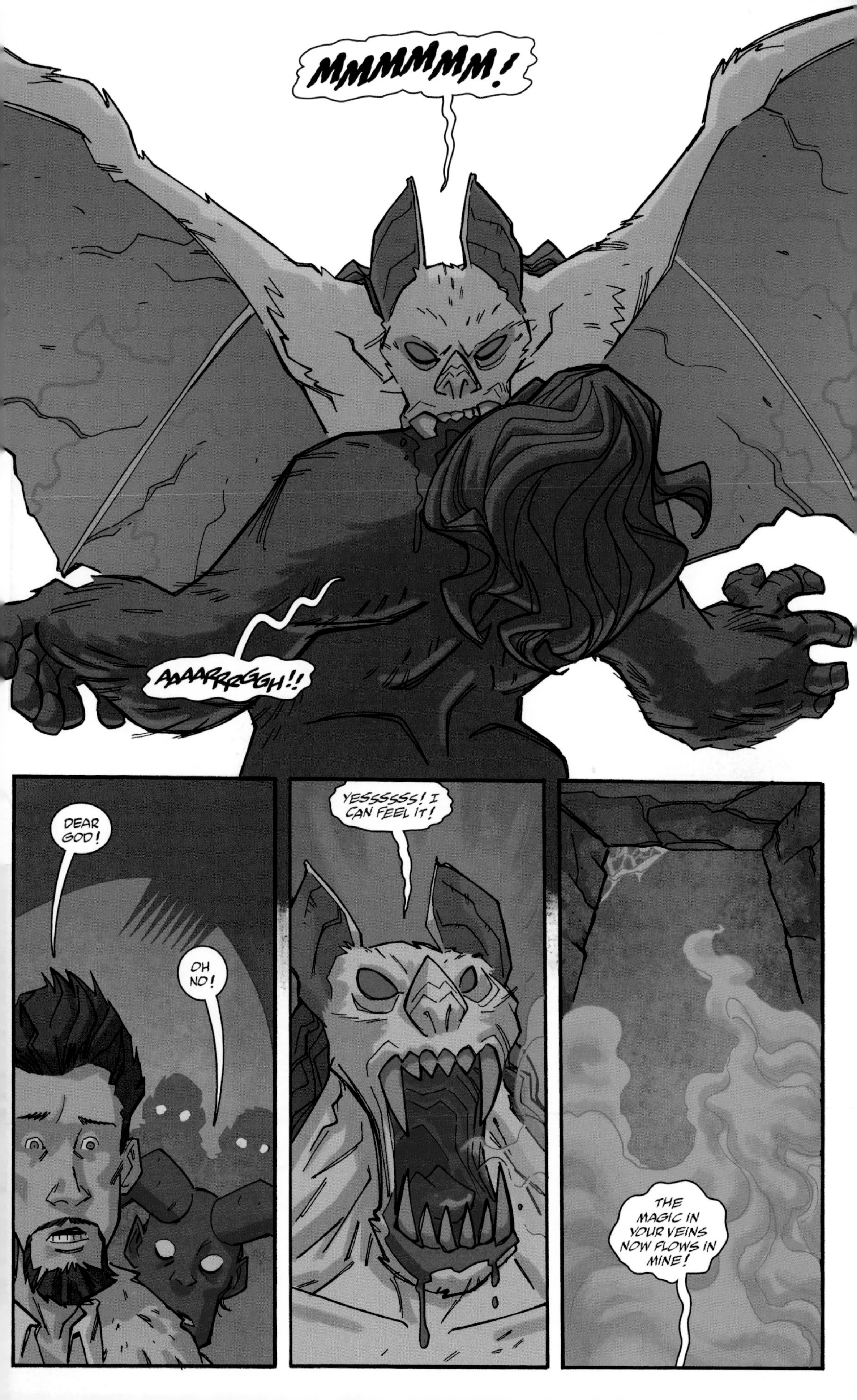
MMMMMM!
AAAARRRGGH!!
DEAR GOD!
OH NO!
YESSSSSS! I CAN FEEL IT!
THE MAGIC IN YOUR VEINS NOW FLOWS IN MINE!

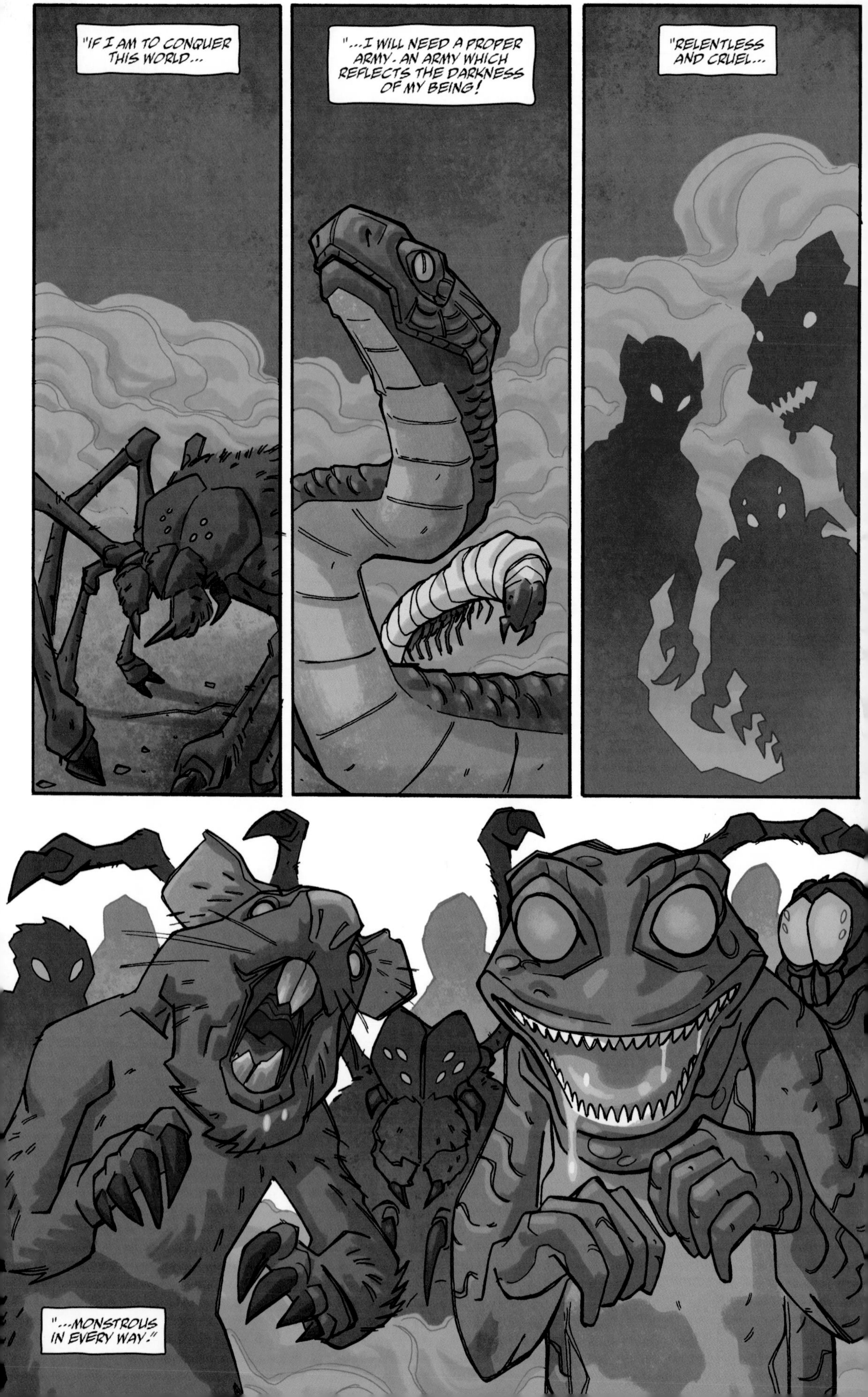
"IF I AM TO CONQUER THIS WORLD...
"...I WILL NEED A PROPER ARMY- AN ARMY WHICH REFLECTS THE DARKNESS OF MY BEING!
"RELENTLESS AND CRUEL...
"...MONSTROUS IN EVERY WAY."

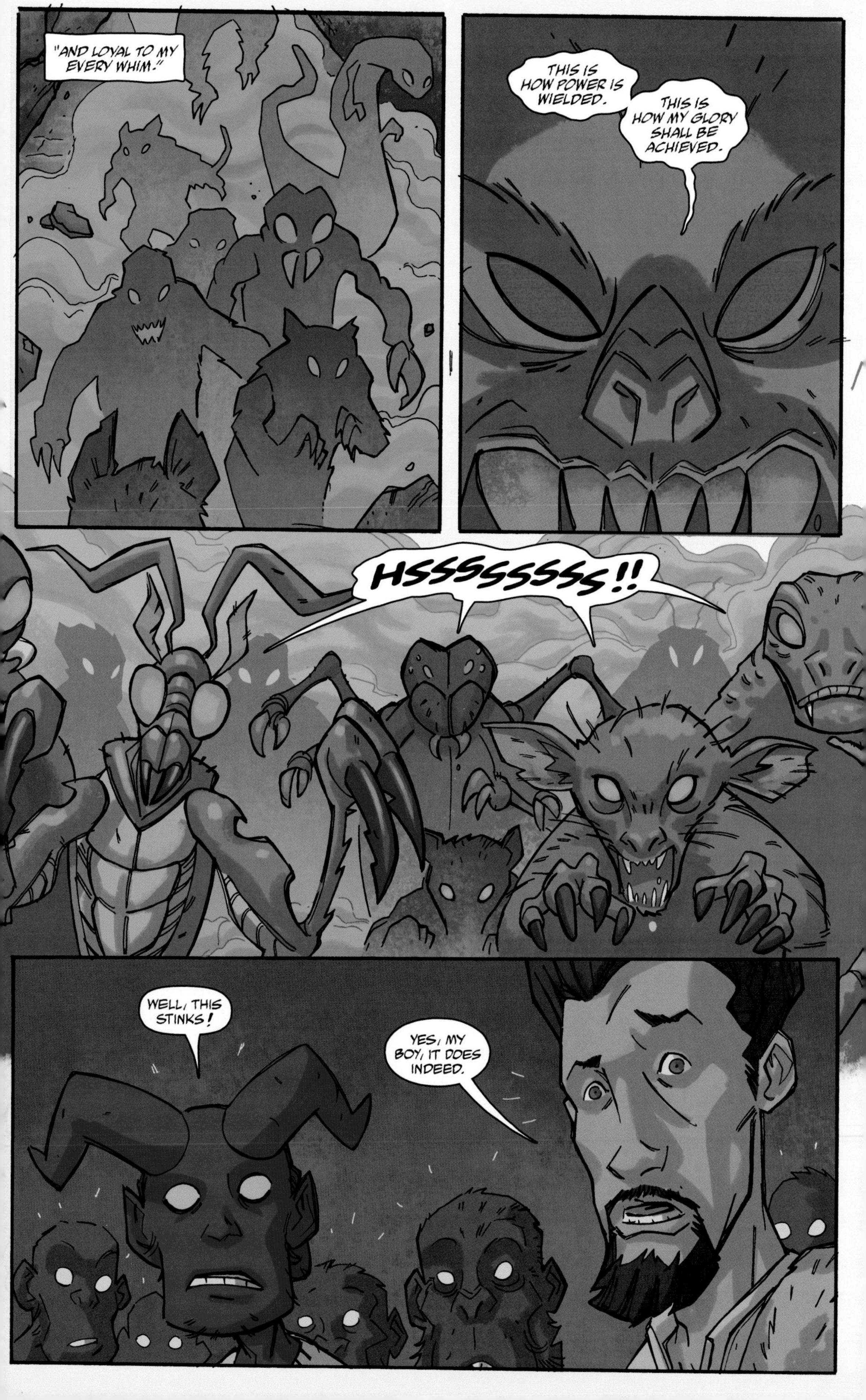
"AND LOYAL TO MY EVERY WHIM."
THIS IS HOW POWER IS WIELDED.
THIS IS HOW MY GLORY SHALL BE ACHIEVED.
HSSSSSSSS!!
WELL, THIS STINKS!
YES, MY BOY, IT DOES INDEED.

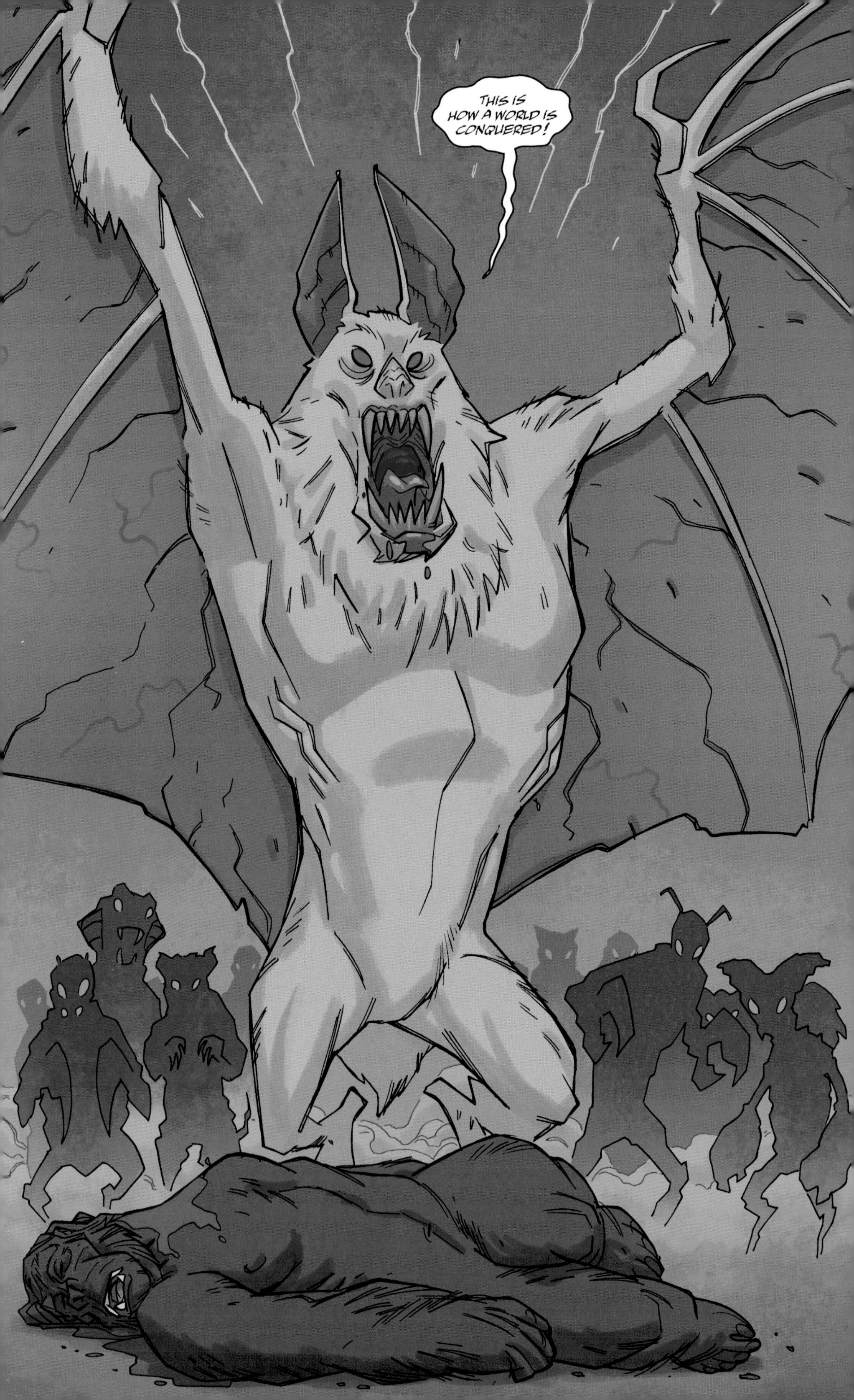
THIS IS HOW A WORLD IS CONQUERED!

CHAPTER FOUR

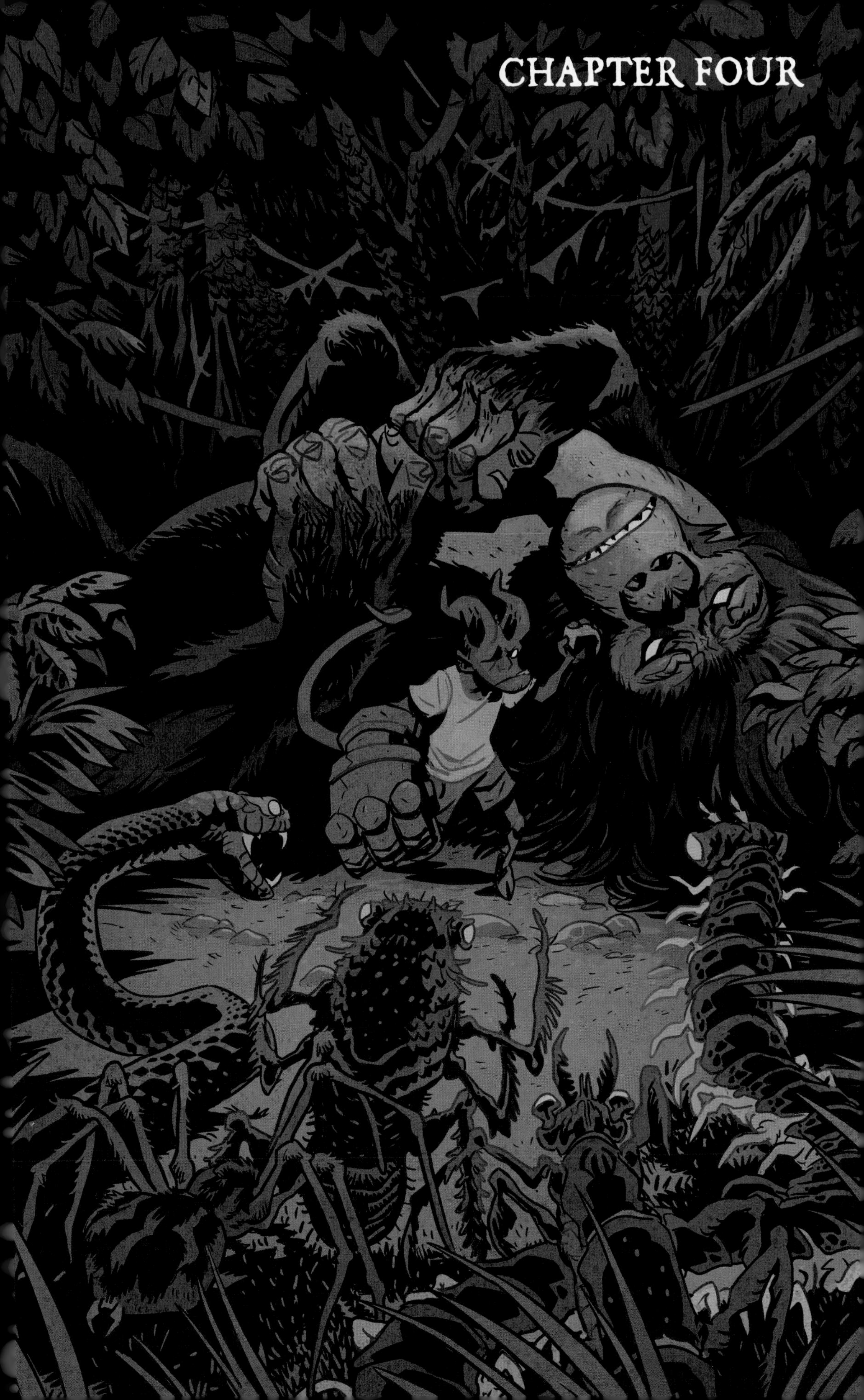

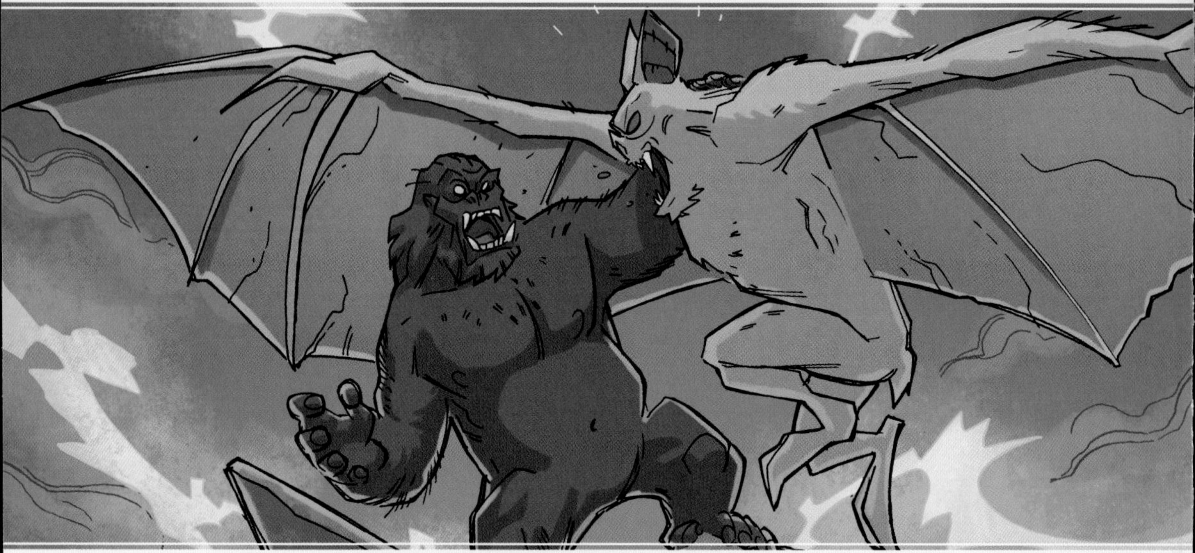

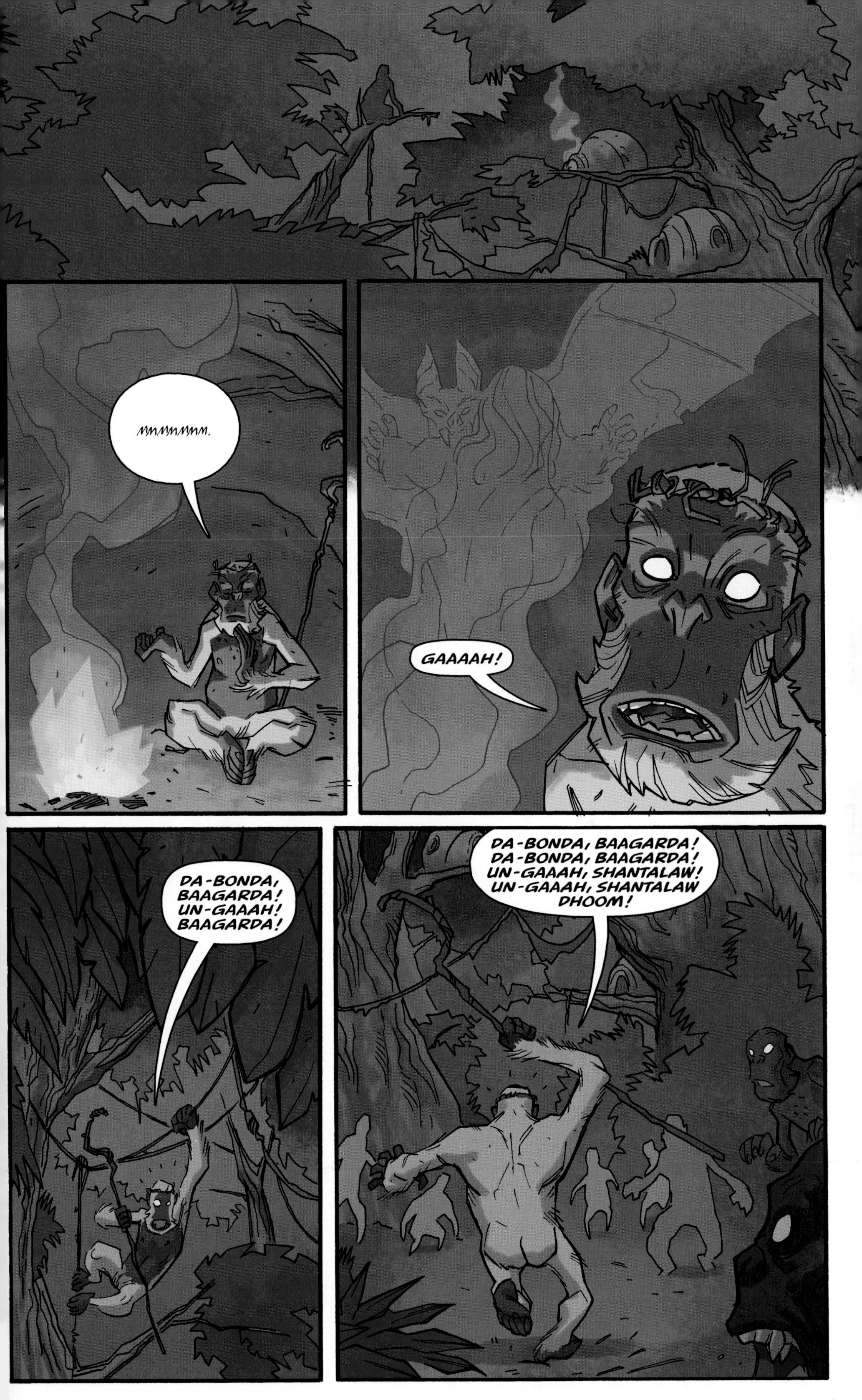
MMMMMMM.
GAAAAH!
DA-BONDA, BAAGARDA! UN-GAAAH! BAAGARDA!
DA-BONDA, BAAGARDA! DA-BONDA, BAAGARDA! UN-GAAAH, SHANTALAW! UN-GAAAH, SHANTALAW DHOOM!

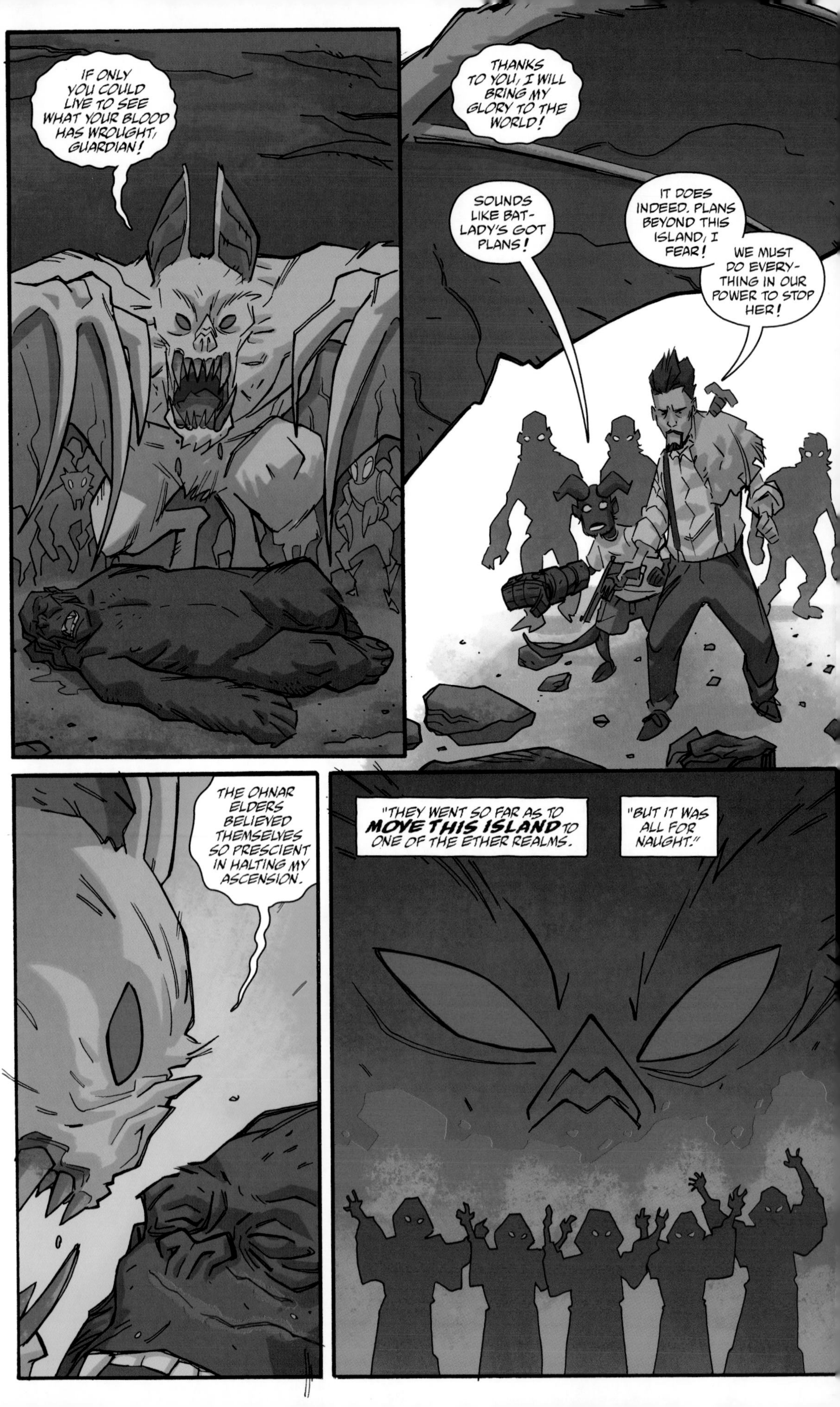
IF ONLY YOU COULD LIVE TO SEE WHAT YOUR BLOOD HAS WROUGHT, GUARDIAN!
THANKS TO YOU, I WILL BRING MY GLORY TO THE WORLD!
SOUNDS LIKE BAT-LADY'S GOT PLANS!
IT DOES INDEED. PLANS BEYOND THIS ISLAND, I FEAR!
WE MUST DO EVERY-THING IN OUR POWER TO STOP HER!
THE OHNAR ELDERS BELIEVED THEMSELVES SO PRESCIENT IN HALTING MY ASCENSION.
"THEY WENT SO FAR AS TO MOVE THIS ISLAND TO ONE OF THE ETHER REALMS.
"BUT IT WAS ALL FOR NAUGHT."

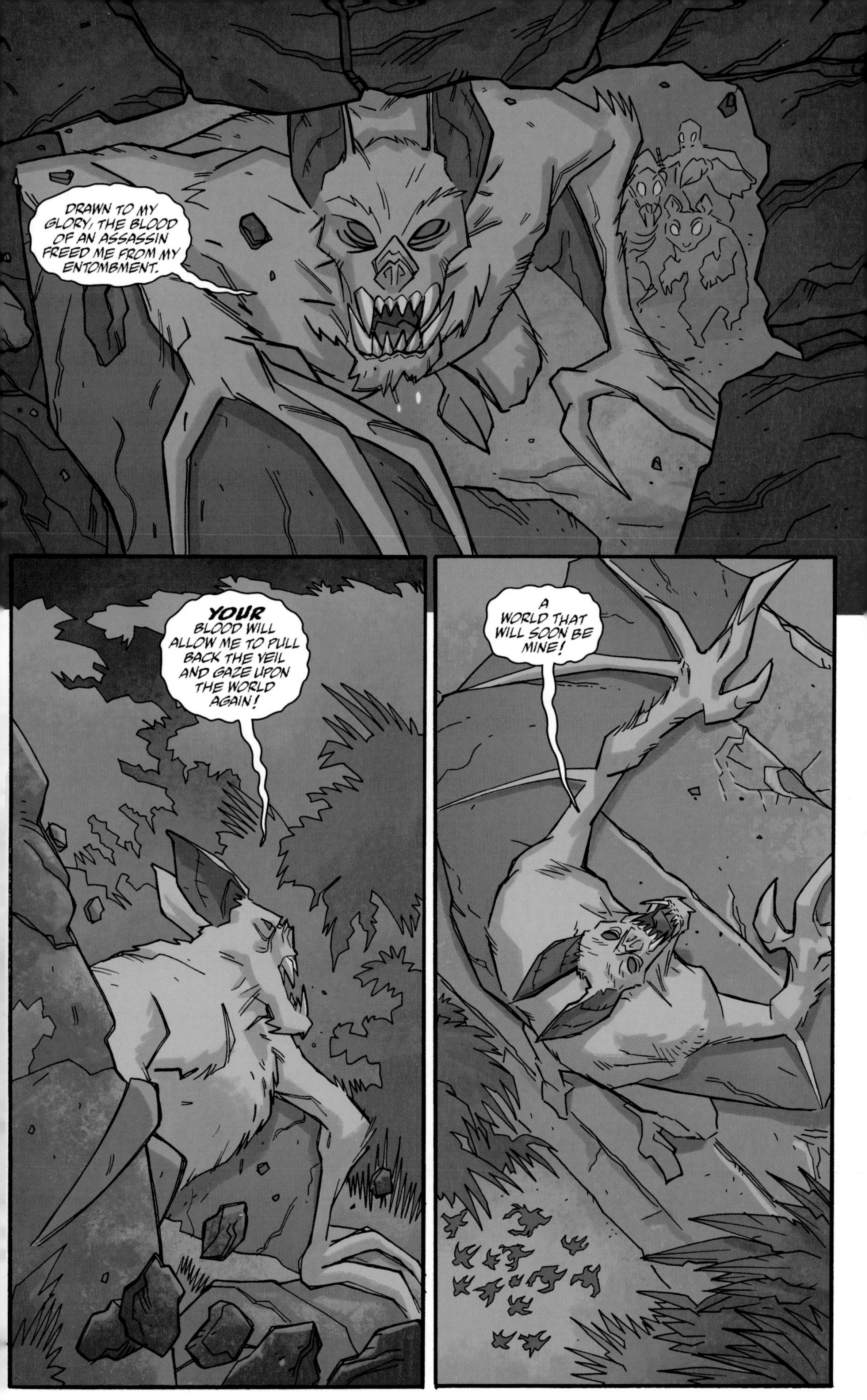
DRAWN TO MY GLORY; THE BLOOD OF AN ASSASSIN FREED ME FROM MY ENTOMBMENT.
YOUR BLOOD WILL ALLOW ME TO PULL BACK THE VEIL AND GAZE UPON THE WORLD AGAIN!
A WORLD THAT WILL SOON BE MINE!

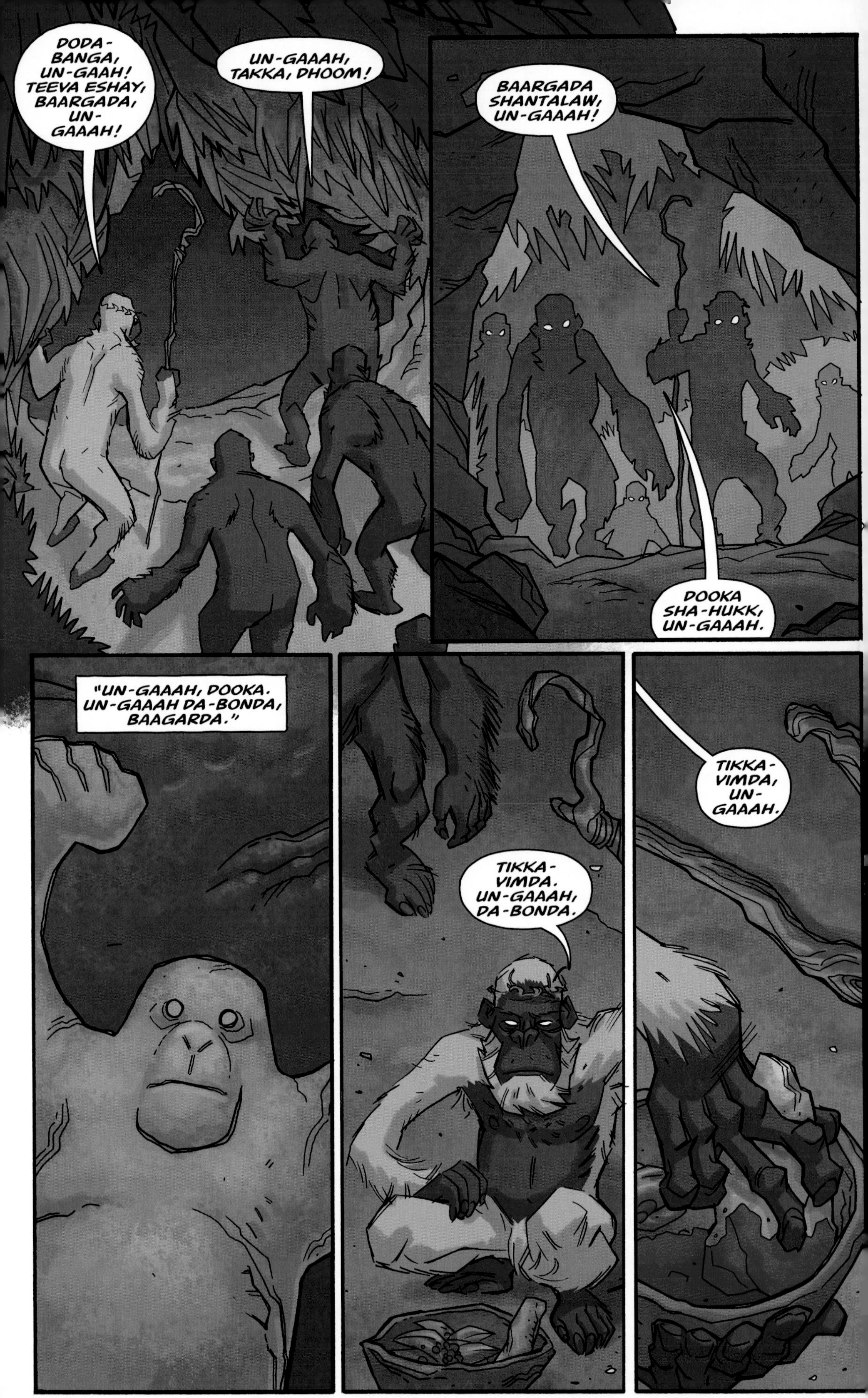
DODA-BANGA, UN-GAAH! TEEVA ESHAY, BAARGADA, UN-GAAAH!
UN-GAAAH, TAKKA, DHOOM!
BAARGADA SHANTALAW, UN-GAAAH!
DOOKA SHA-HUKK, UN-GAAAH.
"UN-GAAAH, DOOKA. UN-GAAAH DA-BONDA, BAAGARDA."
TIKKA-VIMDA. UN-GAAAH, DA-BONDA.
TIKKA-VIMDA, UN-GAAAH.

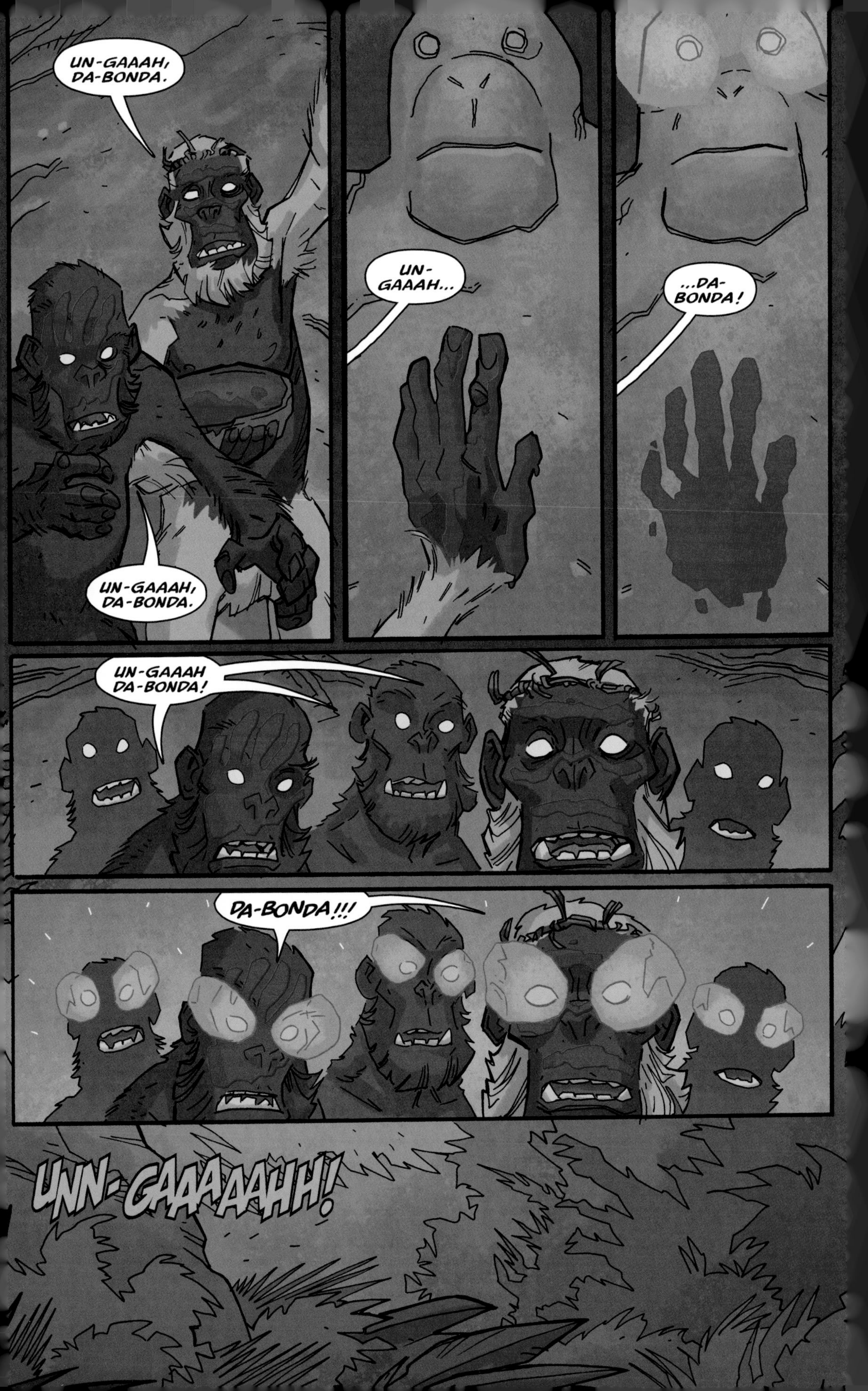
UN-GAAAH, DA-BONDA.
UN-GAAAH, DA-BONDA.
UN-GAAAH...
...DA-BONDA!
UN-GAAAH DA-BONDA!
DA-BONDA!!!
UNN-GAAAAAHH!

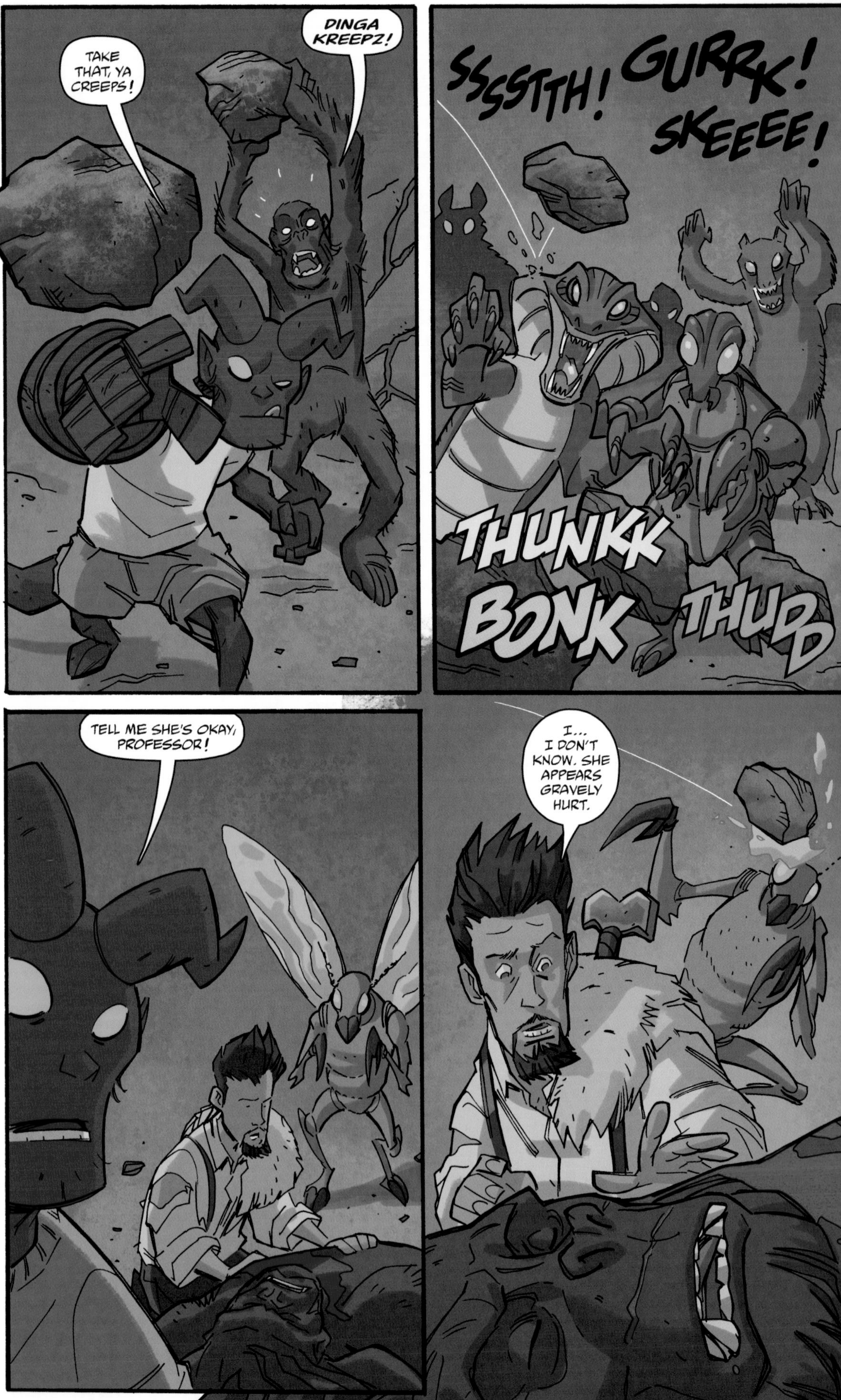
TAKE THAT, YA CREEPS!
DINGA KREEPZ!
SSSSTTH! GURRRK!
SKEEEEE!
THUNKK
BONK
THUDD
TELL ME SHE'S OKAY, PROFESSOR!
I... I DON'T KNOW. SHE APPEARS GRAVELY HURT.

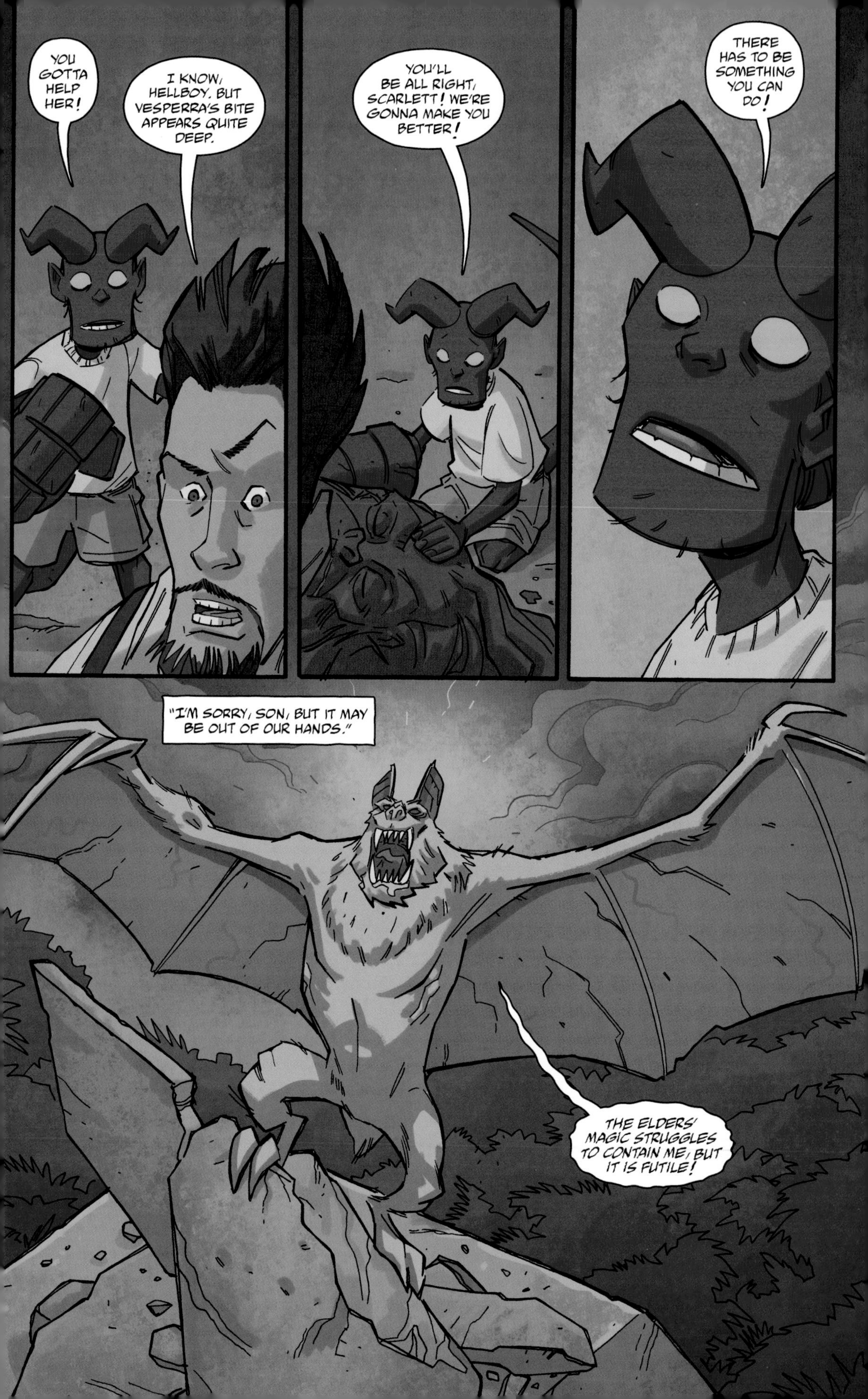
YOU GOTTA HELP HER!
I KNOW, HELLBOY, BUT VESPERRA'S BITE APPEARS QUITE DEEP.
YOU'LL BE ALL RIGHT, SCARLETT! WE'RE GONNA MAKE YOU BETTER!
THERE HAS TO BE SOMETHING YOU CAN DO!
"I'M SORRY, SON, BUT IT MAY BE OUT OF OUR HANDS."
THE ELDERS' MAGIC STRUGGLES TO CONTAIN ME, BUT IT IS FUTILE!

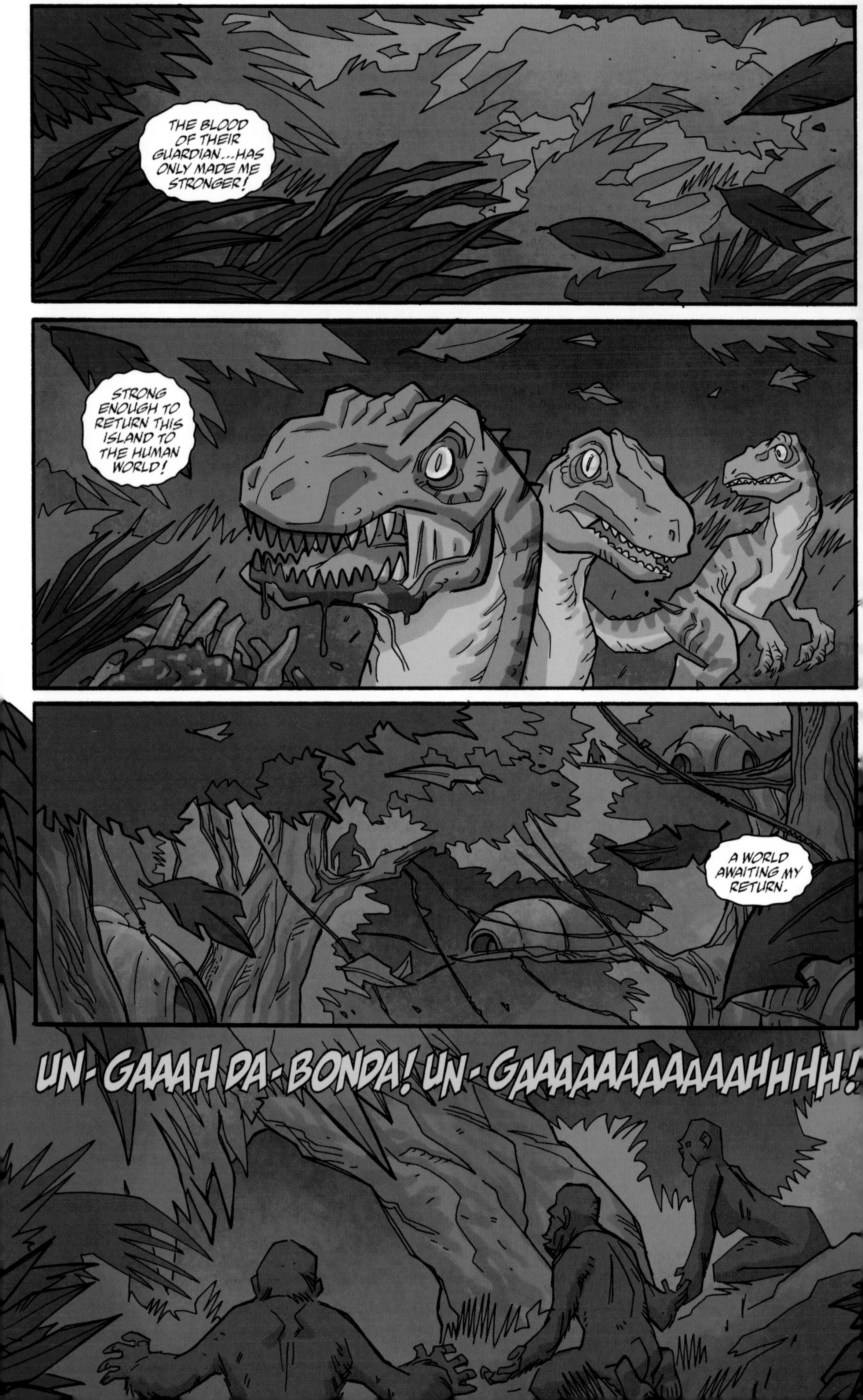
THE BLOOD OF THEIR GUARDIAN... HAS ONLY MADE ME STRONGER!
STRONG ENOUGH TO RETURN THIS ISLAND TO THE HUMAN WORLD!
A WORLD AWAITING MY RETURN.
UN-GAAAH DA-BONDA! UN-GAAAAAAAAAAAHHHH!

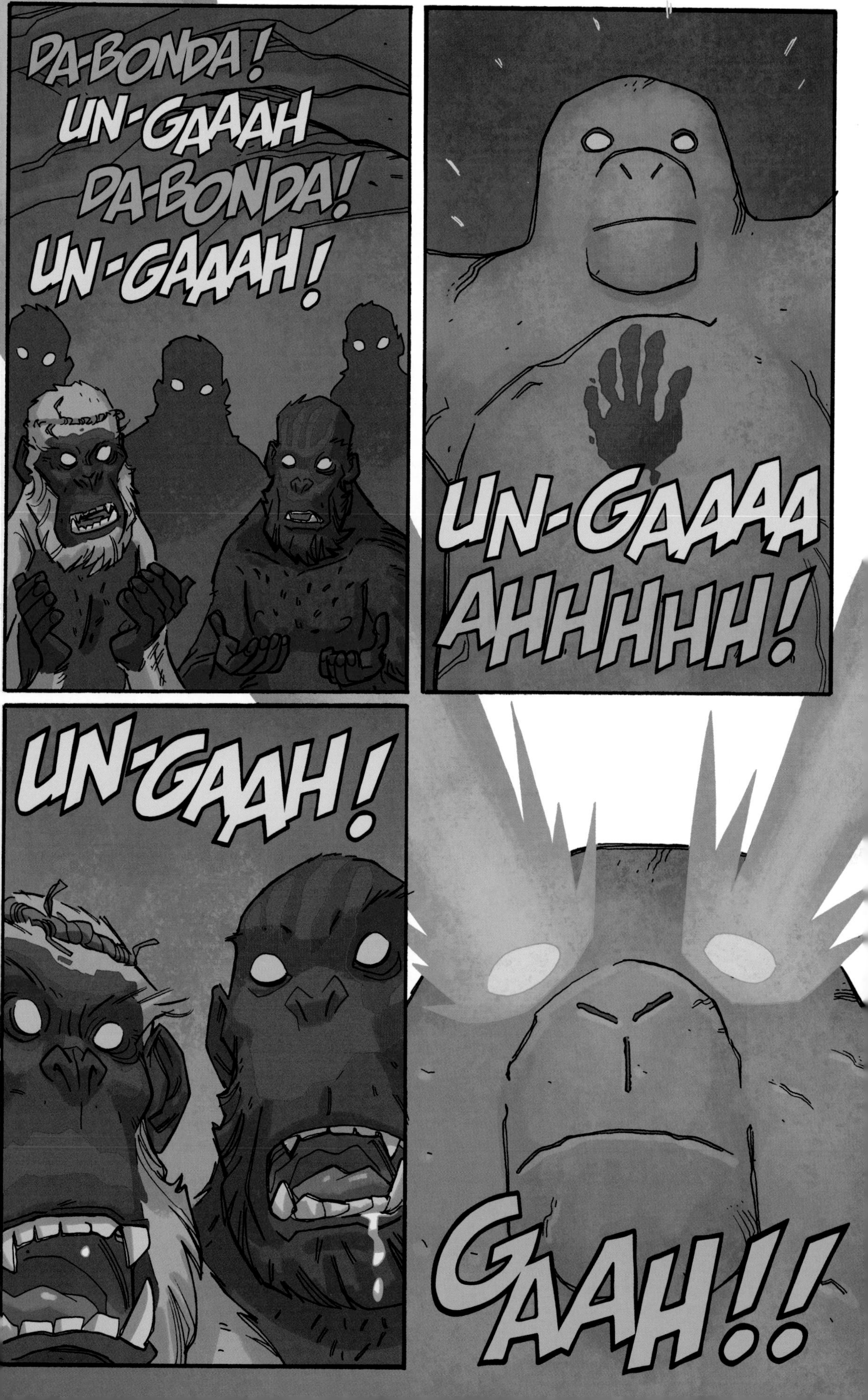
DA-BONDA!
UN-GAAAH
DA-BONDA!
UN-GAAAH!
UN-GAAAA AHHHHH!
UN-GAAH!
GAAH!!

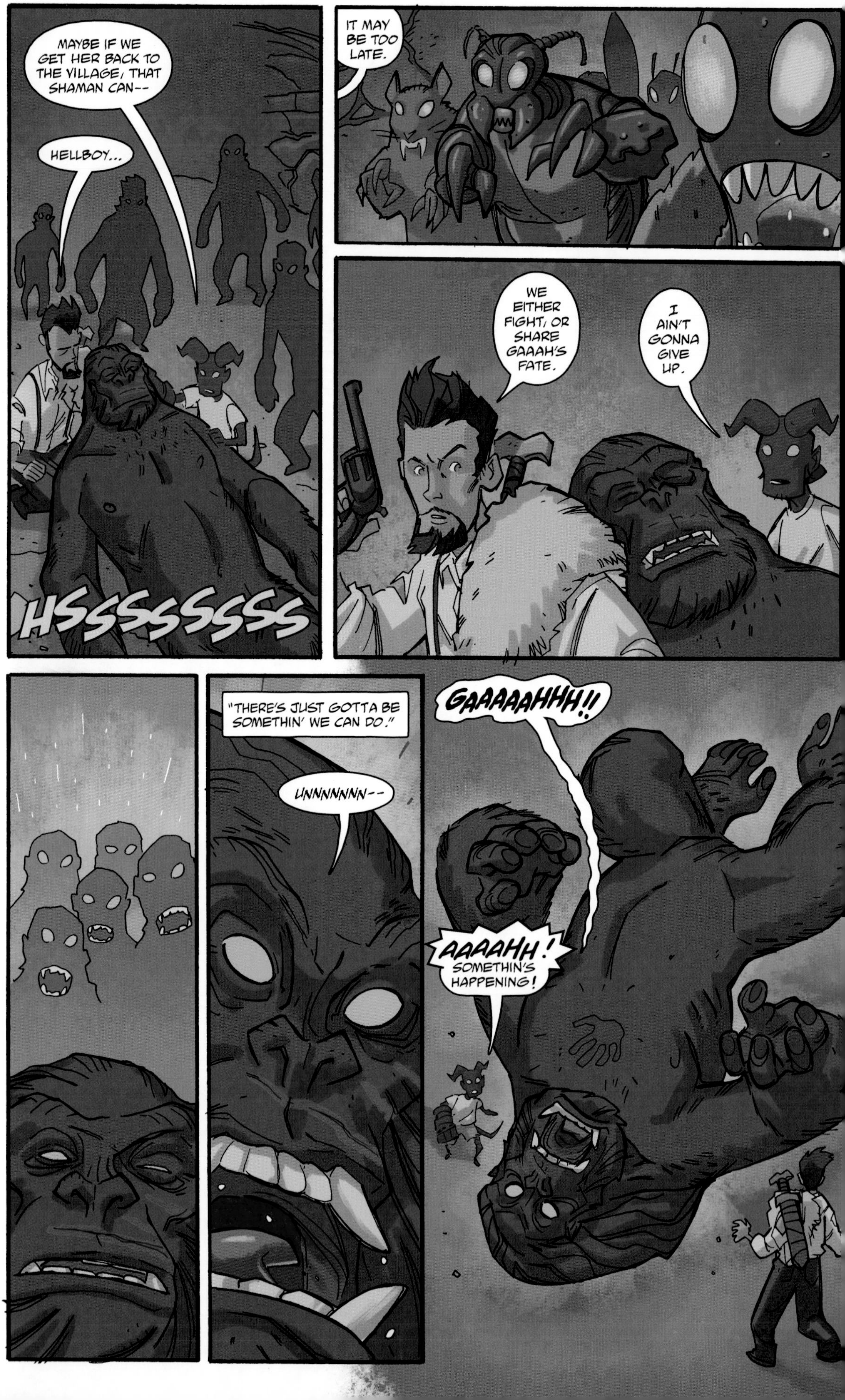
MAYBE IF WE GET HER BACK TO THE VILLAGE, THAT SHAMAN CAN--
HELLBOY...
HSSSSSSSS
IT MAY BE TOO LATE.
WE EITHER FIGHT, OR SHARE GAAAH'S FATE.
I AIN'T GONNA GIVE UP.
"THERE'S JUST GOTTA BE SOMETHIN' WE CAN DO."
UNNNNNNN--
GAAAAAHHH!!
AAAAHH! SOMETHIN'S HAPPENING!

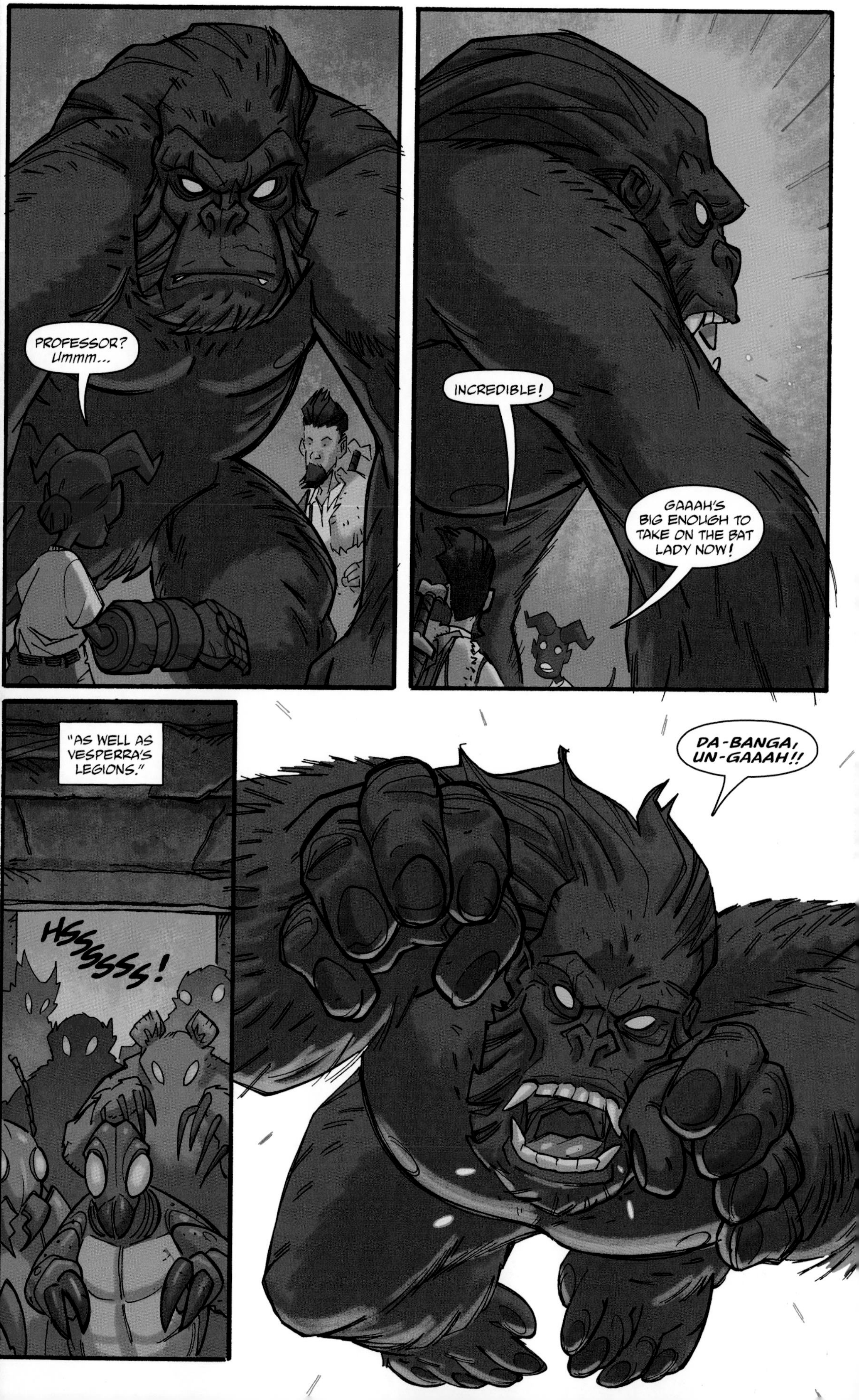
PROFESSOR? Ummm...
INCREDIBLE!
GAAAH'S BIG ENOUGH TO TAKE ON THE BAT LADY NOW!
"AS WELL AS VESPERRA'S LEGIONS."
HSSSSSS!
DA-BANGA, UN-GAAAH!!

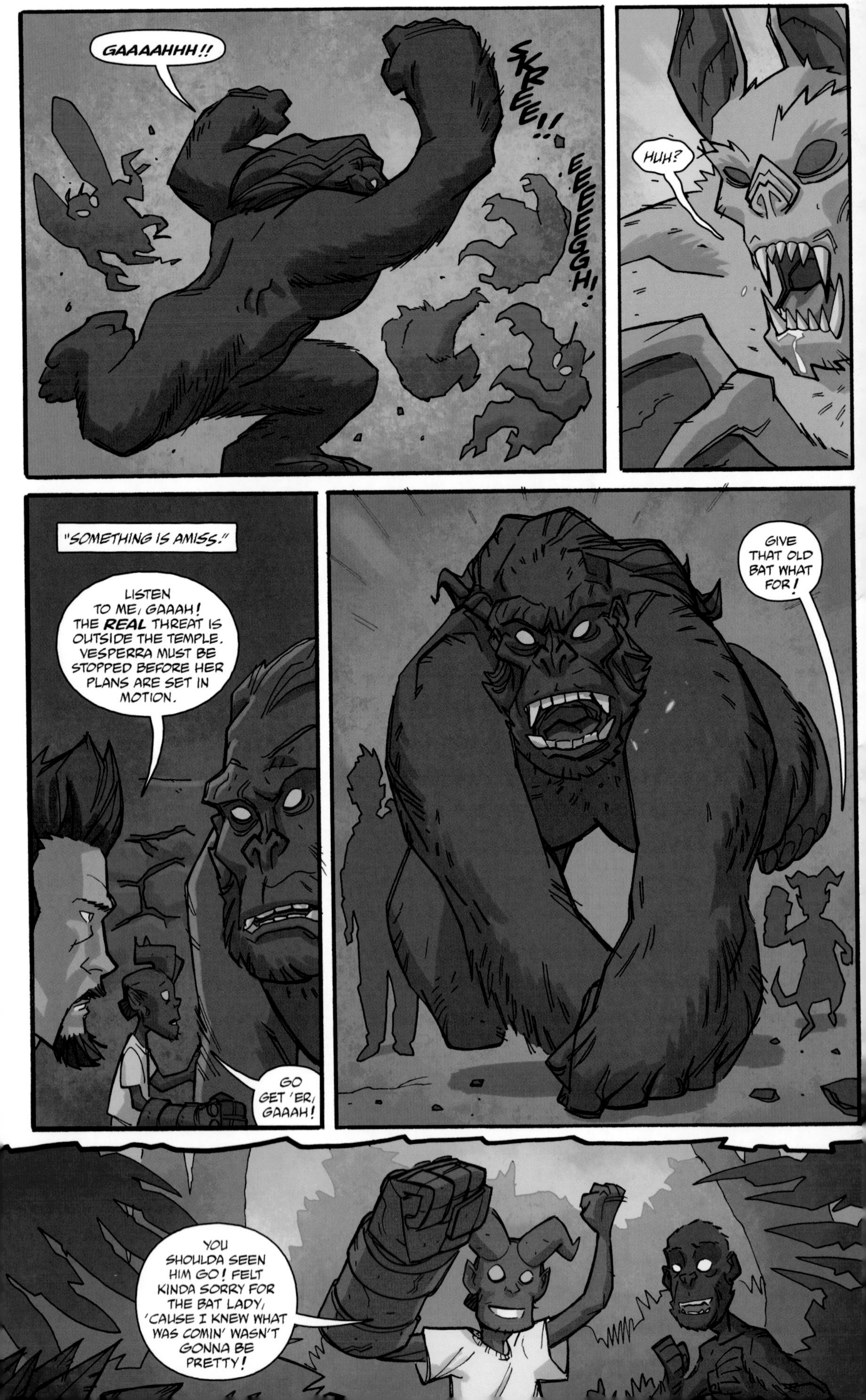

GAAAAHHH!!
SKREE!!
EEEEEGGH!
HUH?
"SOMETHING IS AMISS."
LISTEN TO ME, GAAAH! THE REAL THREAT IS OUTSIDE THE TEMPLE. VESPERRA MUST BE STOPPED BEFORE HER PLANS ARE SET IN MOTION.
GO GET 'ER, GAAAH!
GIVE THAT OLD BAT WHAT FOR!
YOU SHOULDA SEEN HIM GO! FELT KINDA SORRY FOR THE BAT LADY, 'CAUSE I KNEW WHAT WAS COMIN' WASN'T GONNA BE PRETTY!

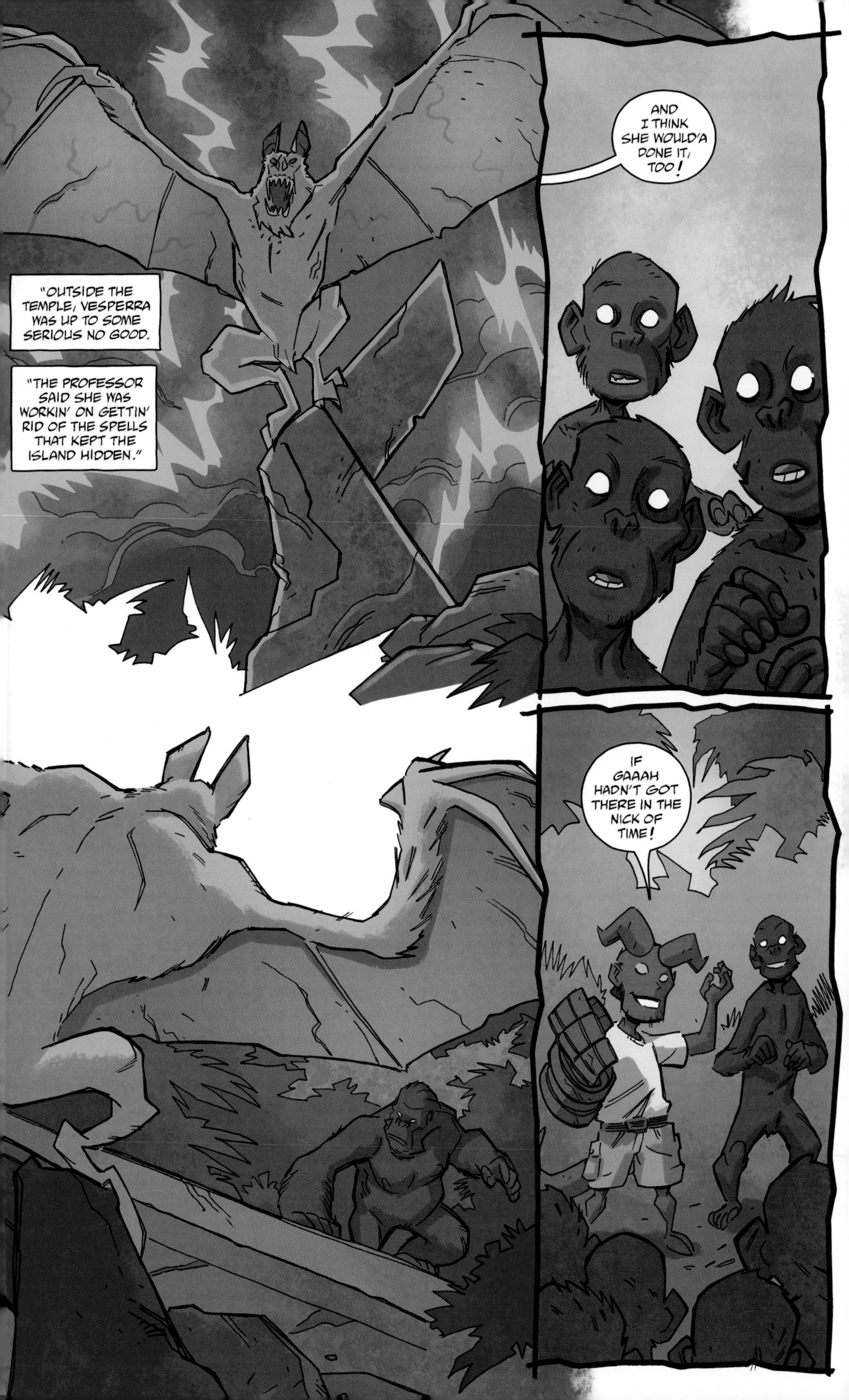
"OUTSIDE THE TEMPLE, VESPERRA WAS UP TO SOME SERIOUS NO GOOD.
"THE PROFESSOR SAID SHE WAS WORKIN' ON GETTIN' RID OF THE SPELLS THAT KEPT THE ISLAND HIDDEN."
AND I THINK SHE WOULD'A DONE IT, TOO!
IF GAAAH HADN'T GOT THERE IN THE NICK OF TIME!

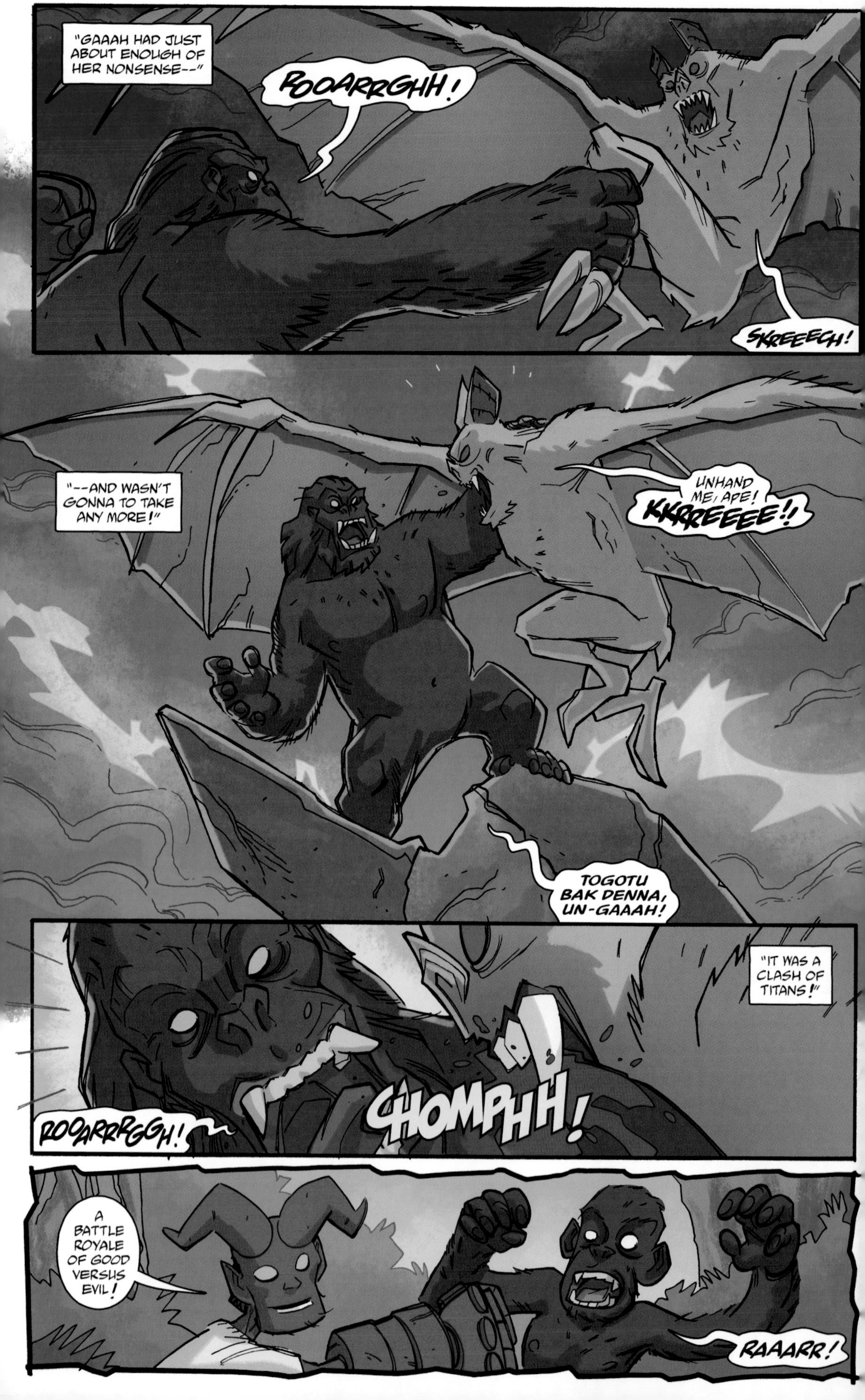
"GAAAH HAD JUST ABOUT ENOUGH OF HER NONSENSE--"
ROOARRGHH!
SKREEECH!
"--AND WASN'T GONNA TO TAKE ANY MORE!"
UNHAND ME, APE! KKRREEEE!!
TOGOTU BAK DENNA, UN-GAAAH!
"IT WAS A CLASH OF TITANS!"
ROOARRRGGH!
CHOMPHH!
A BATTLE ROYALE OF GOOD VERSUS EVIL!
RAAARR!

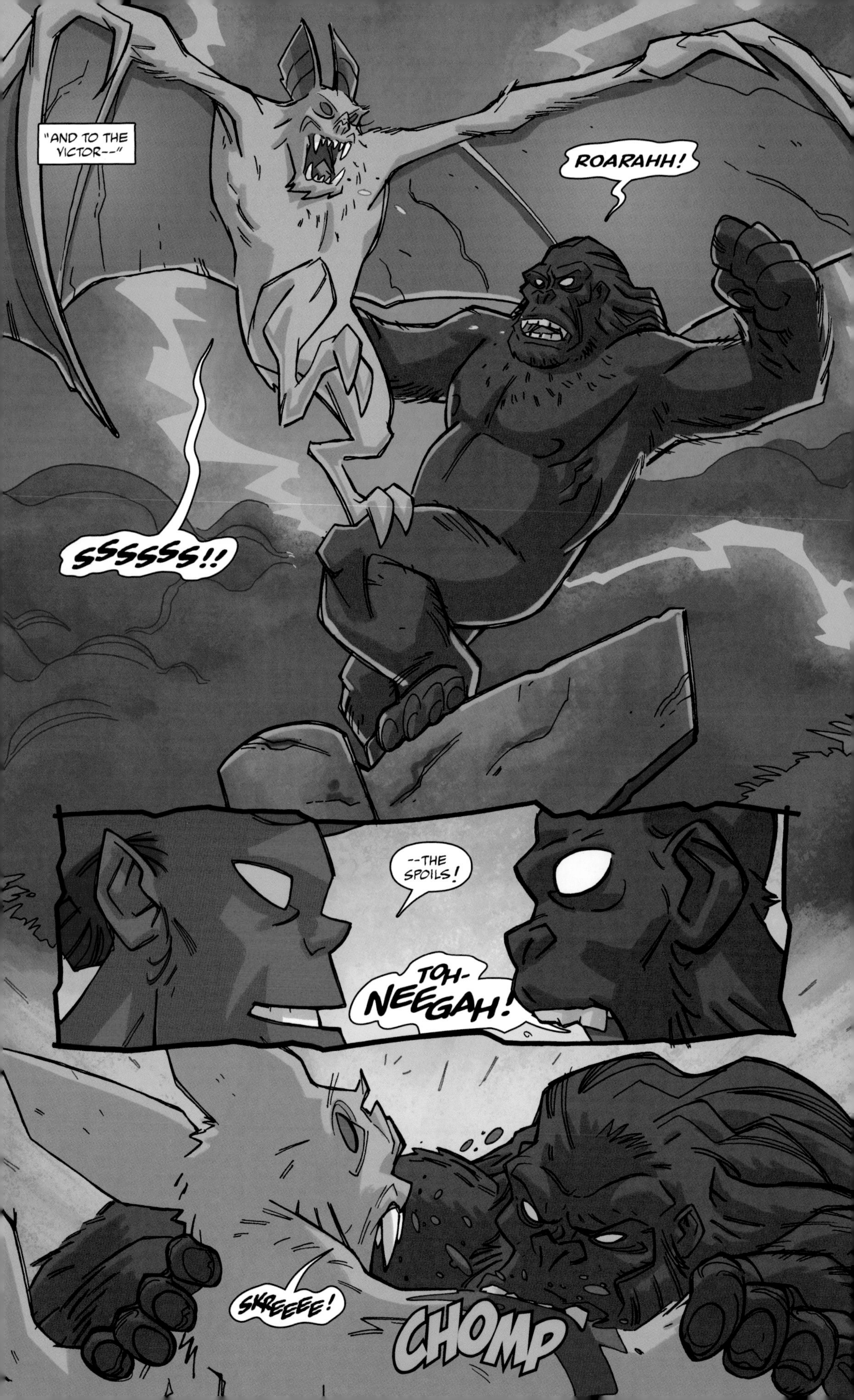
"AND TO THE VICTOR--"
ROARAHH!
SSSSSS!!
--THE SPOILS!
TOH-NEEGAH!
SKREEEEE!
CHOMP

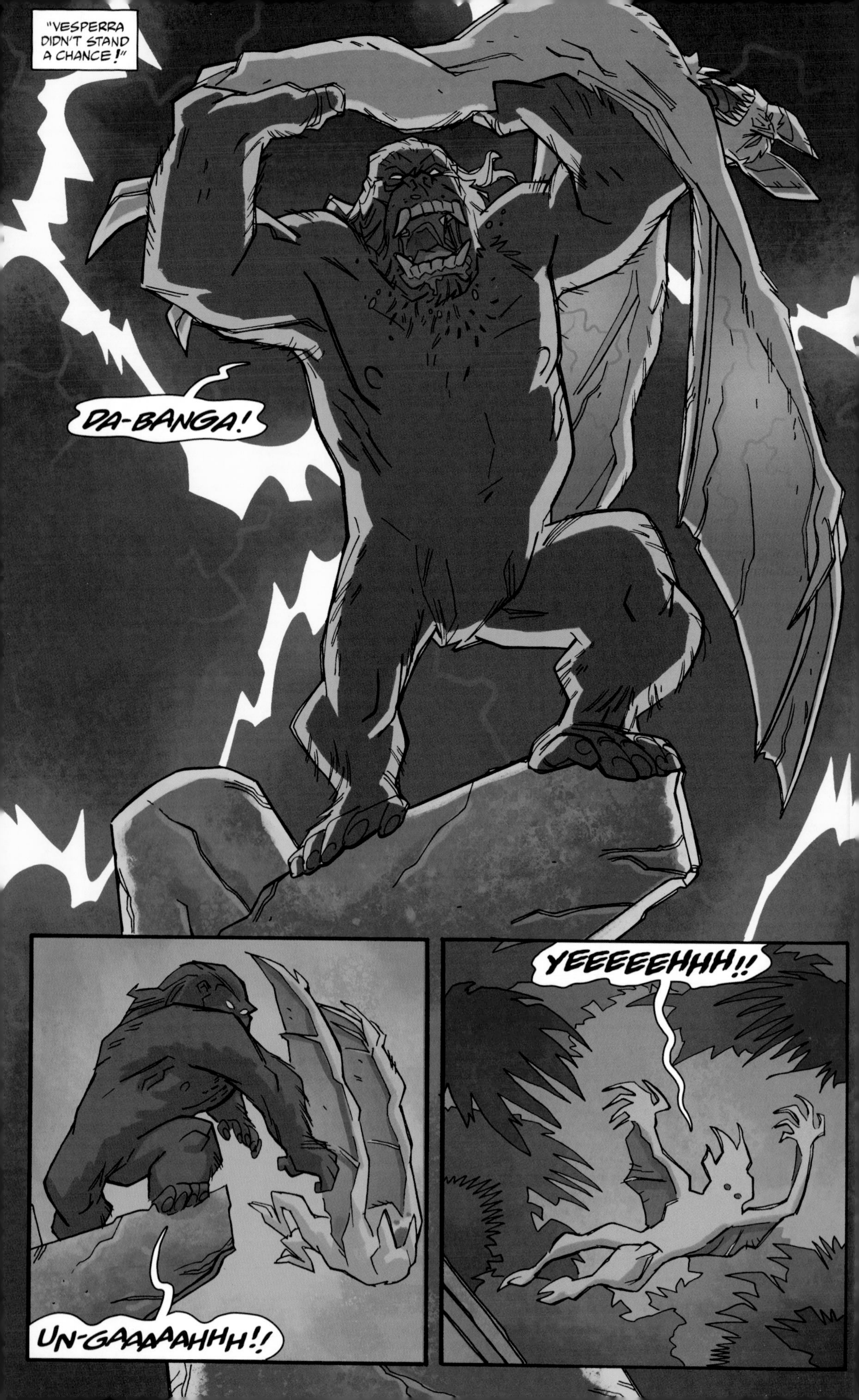
"VESPERRA DIDN'T STAND A CHANCE!"
DA-BANGA!
UN-GAAAAAHHH!!
YEEEEEEHHH!!

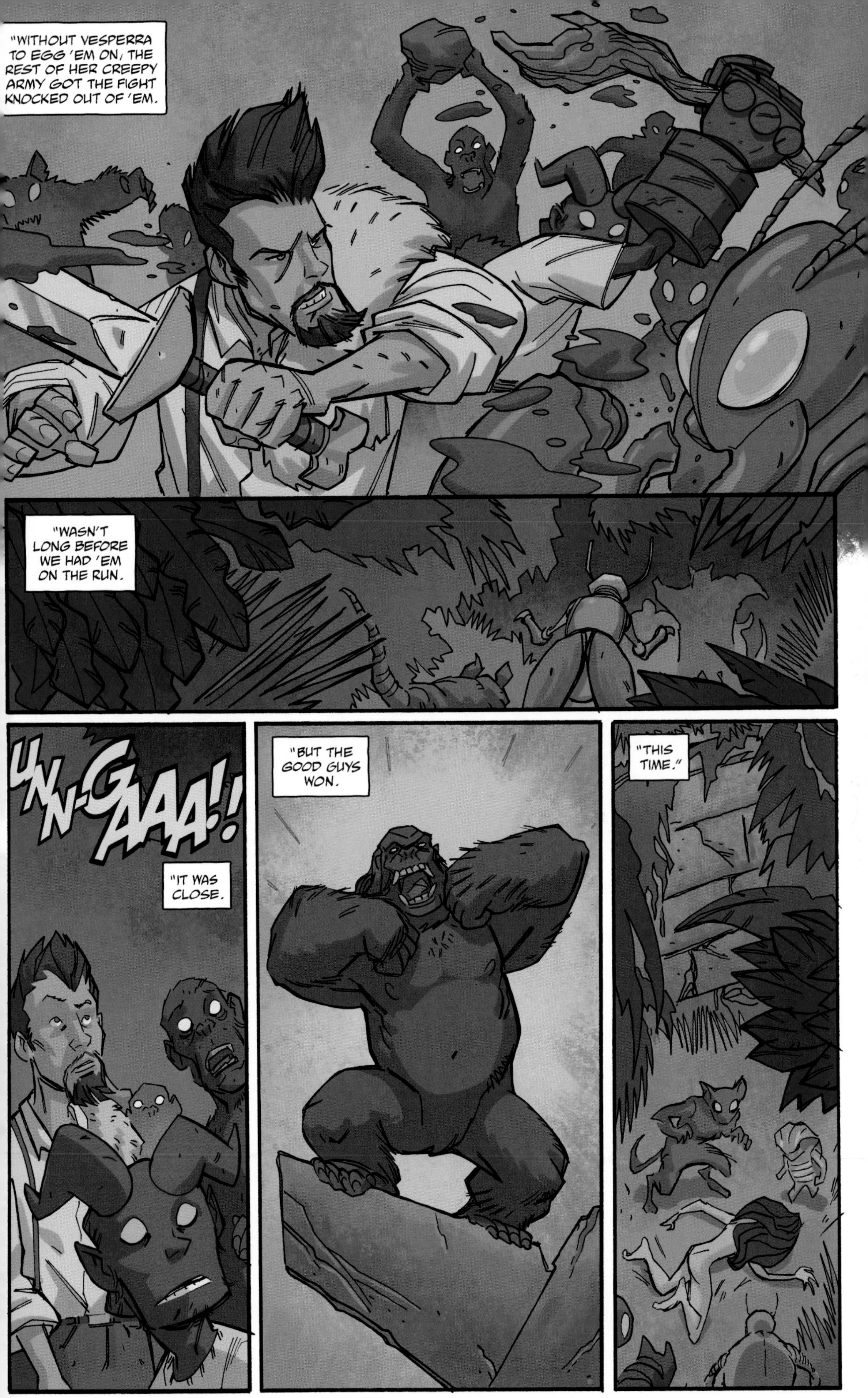
"WITHOUT VESPERRA TO EGG 'EM ON, THE REST OF HER CREEPY ARMY GOT THE FIGHT KNOCKED OUT OF 'EM.
"WASN'T LONG BEFORE WE HAD 'EM ON THE RUN.
UNN-GAAA!!
"IT WAS CLOSE.
"BUT THE GOOD GUYS WON.
"THIS TIME."

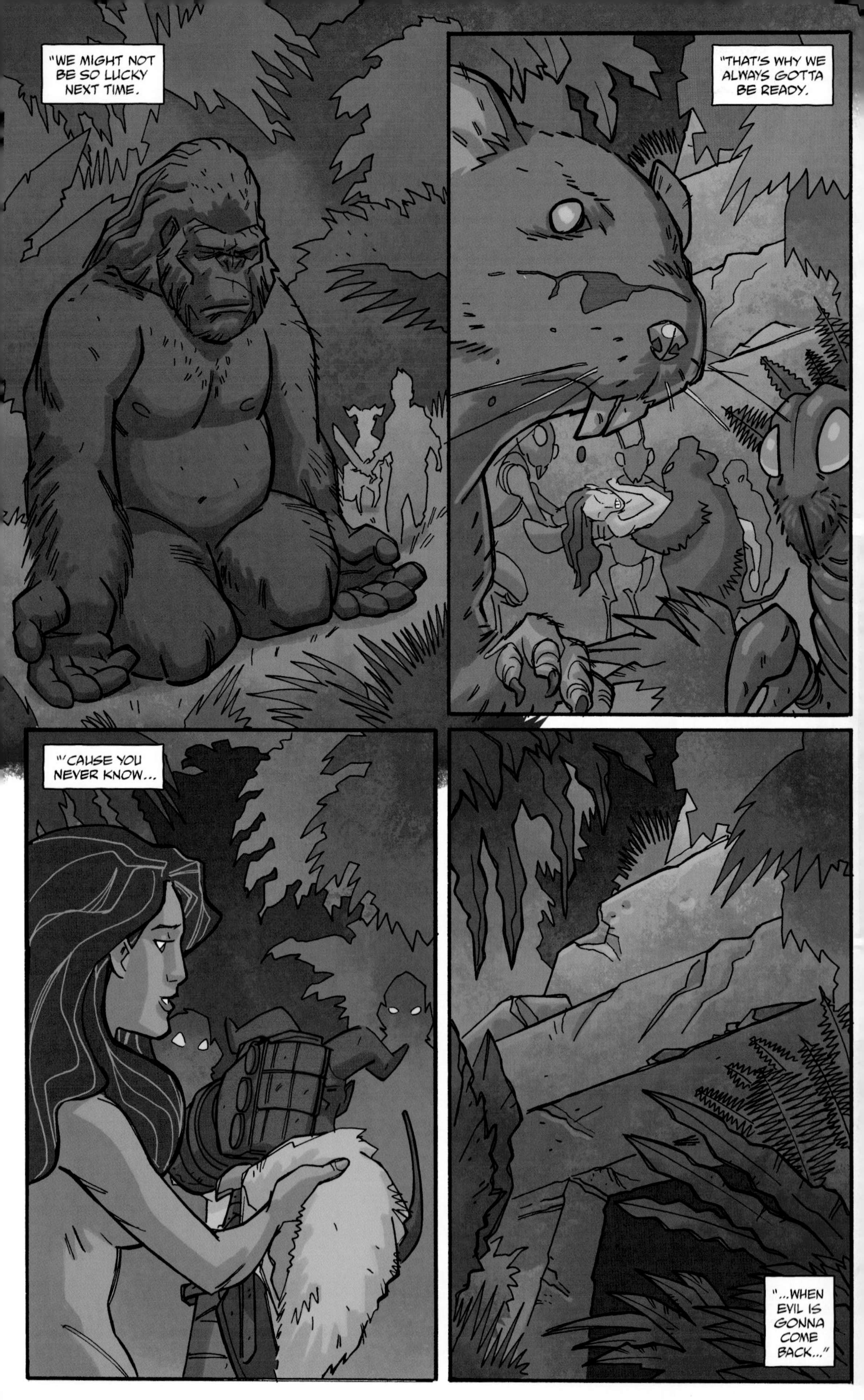
"WE MIGHT NOT BE SO LUCKY NEXT TIME.
"THAT'S WHY WE ALWAYS GOTTA BE READY.
"'CAUSE YOU NEVER KNOW...
"...WHEN EVIL IS GONNA COME BACK..."

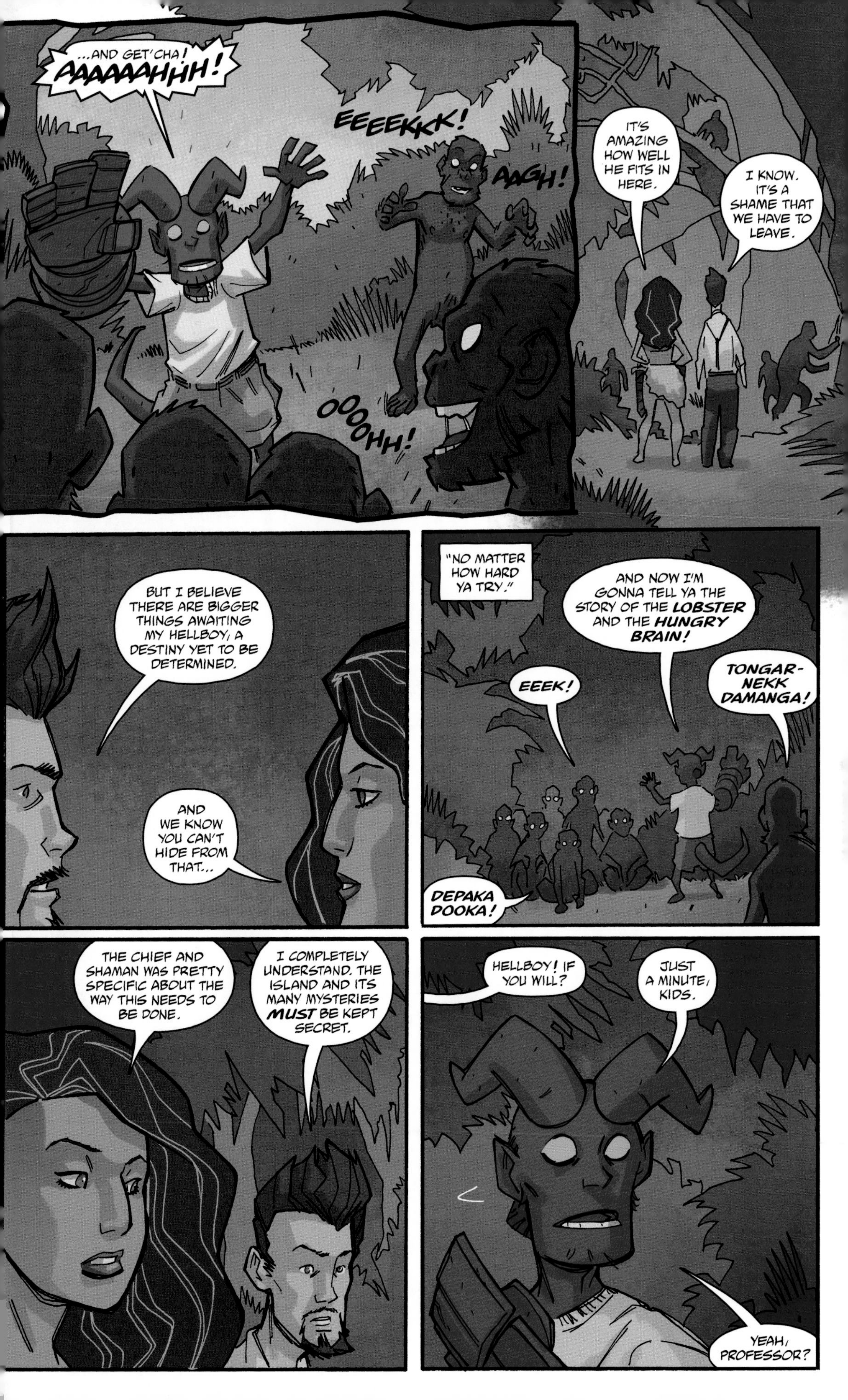

...AND GET'CHA! AAAAAAHHH!
EEEEKKK!
AAGH!
OOOOHH!
IT'S AMAZING HOW WELL HE FITS IN HERE.
I KNOW. IT'S A SHAME THAT WE HAVE TO LEAVE.
BUT I BELIEVE THERE ARE BIGGER THINGS AWAITING MY HELLBOY, A DESTINY YET TO BE DETERMINED.
AND WE KNOW YOU CAN'T HIDE FROM THAT...
"NO MATTER HOW HARD YA TRY."
AND NOW I'M GONNA TELL YA THE STORY OF THE LOBSTER AND THE HUNGRY BRAIN!
EEEK!
TONGAR-NEKK DAMANGA!
DEPAKA DOOKA!
THE CHIEF AND SHAMAN WAS PRETTY SPECIFIC ABOUT THE WAY THIS NEEDS TO BE DONE.
I COMPLETELY UNDERSTAND. THE ISLAND AND ITS MANY MYSTERIES MUST BE KEPT SECRET.
HELLBOY! IF YOU WILL?
JUST A MINUTE, KIDS.
YEAH, PROFESSOR?

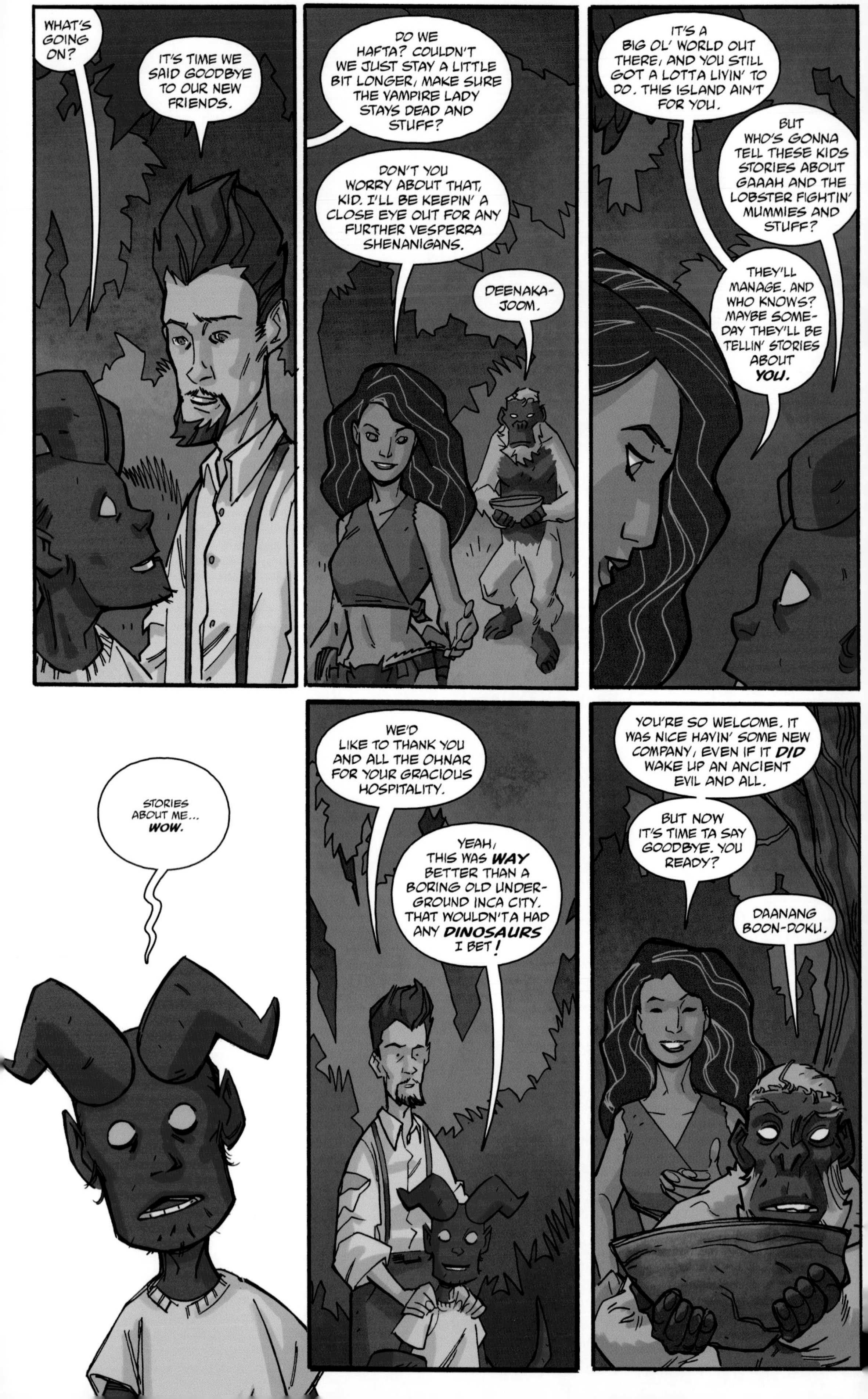
WHAT'S GOING ON?
IT'S TIME WE SAID GOODBYE TO OUR NEW FRIENDS.
DO WE HAFTA? COULDN'T WE JUST STAY A LITTLE BIT LONGER, MAKE SURE THE VAMPIRE LADY STAYS DEAD AND STUFF?
DON'T YOU WORRY ABOUT THAT, KID. I'LL BE KEEPIN' A CLOSE EYE OUT FOR ANY FURTHER VESPERRA SHENANIGANS.
DEENAKA-JOOM.
IT'S A BIG OL' WORLD OUT THERE, AND YOU STILL GOT A LOTTA LIVIN' TO DO. THIS ISLAND AIN'T FOR YOU.
BUT WHO'S GONNA TELL THESE KIDS STORIES ABOUT GAAAH AND THE LOBSTER FIGHTIN' MUMMIES AND STUFF?
THEY'LL MANAGE. AND WHO KNOWS? MAYBE SOME-DAY THEY'LL BE TELLIN' STORIES ABOUT **YOU.**
STORIES ABOUT ME... **WOW.**
WE'D LIKE TO THANK YOU AND ALL THE OHNAR FOR YOUR GRACIOUS HOSPITALITY.
YEAH, THIS WAS **WAY** BETTER THAN A BORING OLD UNDER-GROUND INCA CITY. THAT WOULDN'T'A HAD ANY **DINOSAURS** I BET!
YOU'RE SO WELCOME. IT WAS NICE HAVIN' SOME NEW COMPANY, EVEN IF IT **DID** WAKE UP AN ANCIENT EVIL AND ALL.
BUT NOW IT'S TIME TA SAY GOODBYE. YOU READY?
DAANANG BOON-DOKU.

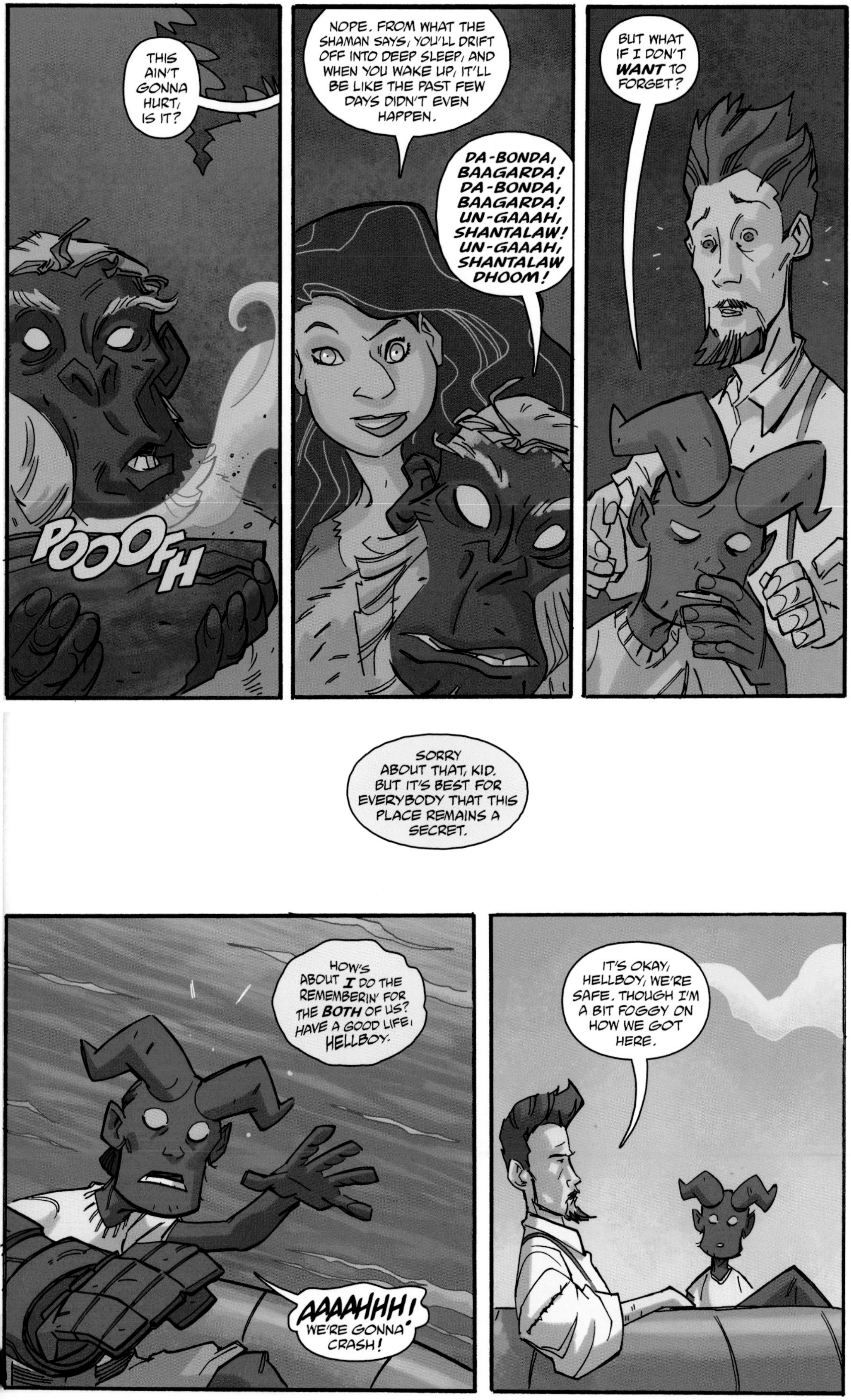
THIS AIN'T GONNA HURT, IS IT?
NOPE. FROM WHAT THE SHAMAN SAYS, YOU'LL DRIFT OFF INTO DEEP SLEEP, AND WHEN YOU WAKE UP, IT'LL BE LIKE THE PAST FEW DAYS DIDN'T EVEN HAPPEN.
DA-BONDA, BAAGARDA! DA-BONDA, BAAGARDA! UN-GAAAH, SHANTALAW! UN-GAAAH, SHANTALAW DHOOM!
BUT WHAT IF I DON'T WANT TO FORGET?
POOOFH
SORRY ABOUT THAT, KID. BUT IT'S BEST FOR EVERYBODY THAT THIS PLACE REMAINS A SECRET.
HOW'S ABOUT I DO THE REMEMBERIN' FOR THE BOTH OF US? HAVE A GOOD LIFE, HELLBOY.
AAAAHHH! WE'RE GONNA CRASH!
IT'S OKAY, HELLBOY, WE'RE SAFE. THOUGH I'M A BIT FOGGY ON HOW WE GOT HERE.

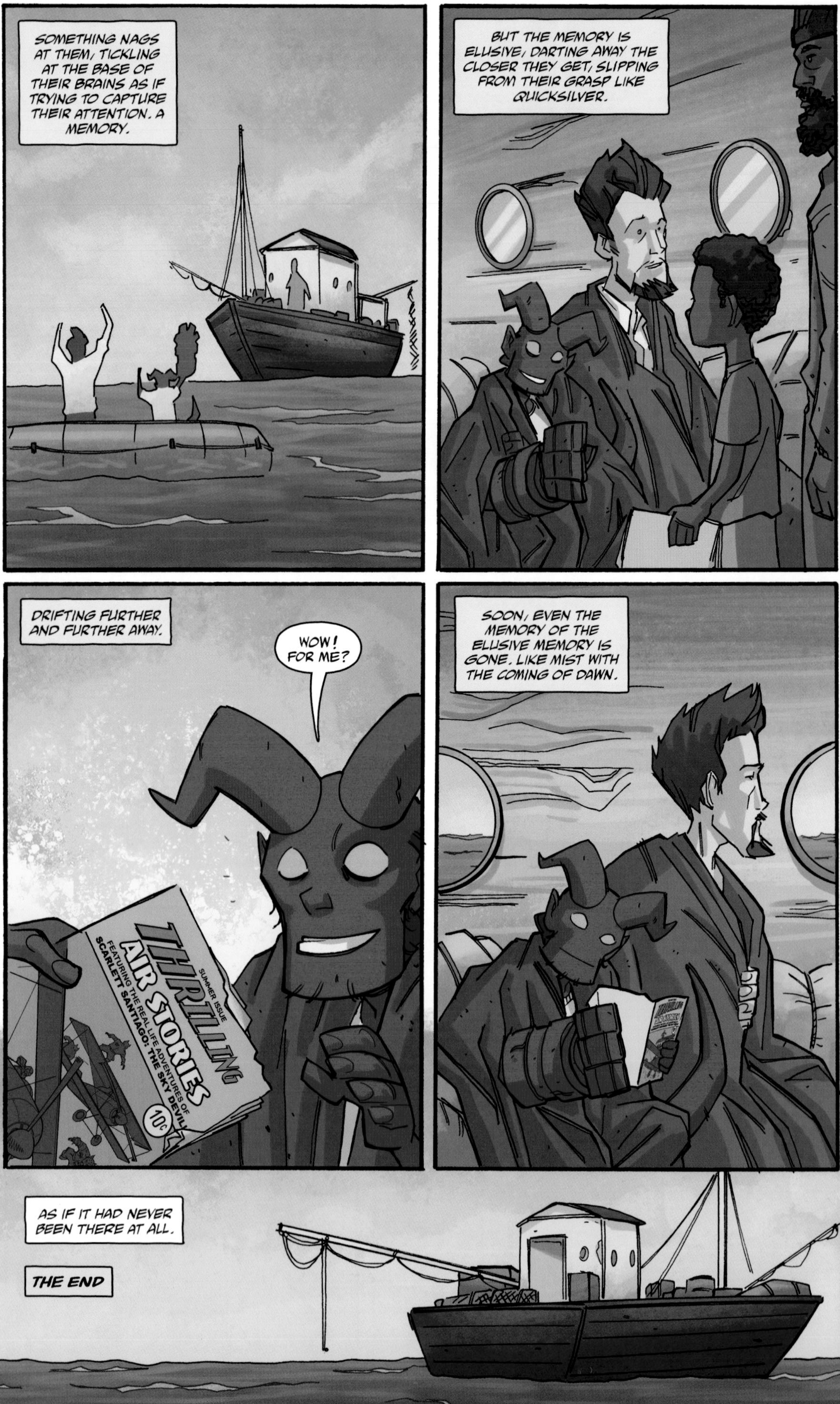
SOMETHING NAGS AT THEM, TICKLING AT THE BASE OF THEIR BRAINS AS IF TRYING TO CAPTURE THEIR ATTENTION. A MEMORY.
BUT THE MEMORY IS ELUSIVE, DARTING AWAY THE CLOSER THEY GET, SLIPPING FROM THEIR GRASP LIKE QUICKSILVER.
DRIFTING FURTHER AND FURTHER AWAY.
WOW! FOR ME?
SUMMER ISSUE
THRILLING
AIR STORIES
FEATURING THE REAL LIFE ADVENTURES OF
SCARLETT SANTIAGO: THE SKY DEVIL
10¢
SOON, EVEN THE MEMORY OF THE ELUSIVE MEMORY IS GONE. LIKE MIST WITH THE COMING OF DAWN.
AS IF IT HAD NEVER BEEN THERE AT ALL.
THE END

YOUNG HELLBOY ™

THE HIDDEN LAND

SKETCHBOOK

Notes by Katii O'Brien

Craig started sketches for Hellboy right away, with a few rounds of head and full-body studies. Hellboy has been drawn a few times as a kid, by several artists, but Craig's Hellboy is especially active and expressive because of the rollicking, action-adventure feeling of the story, and the fun came through loud and clear from the first sketches.

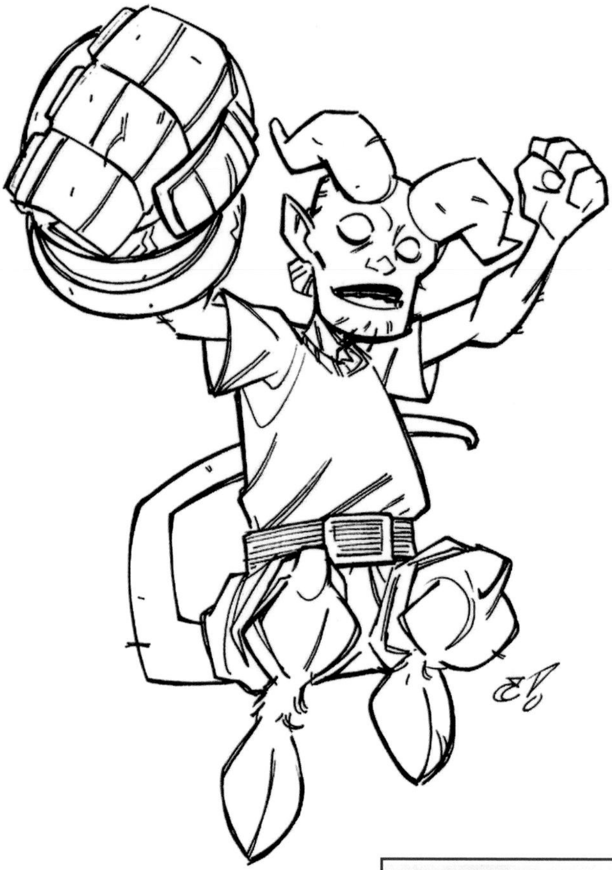

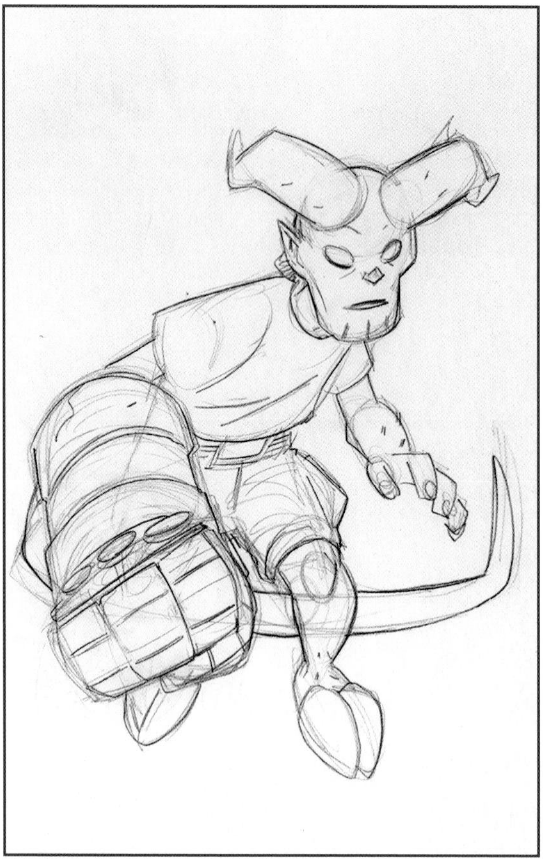

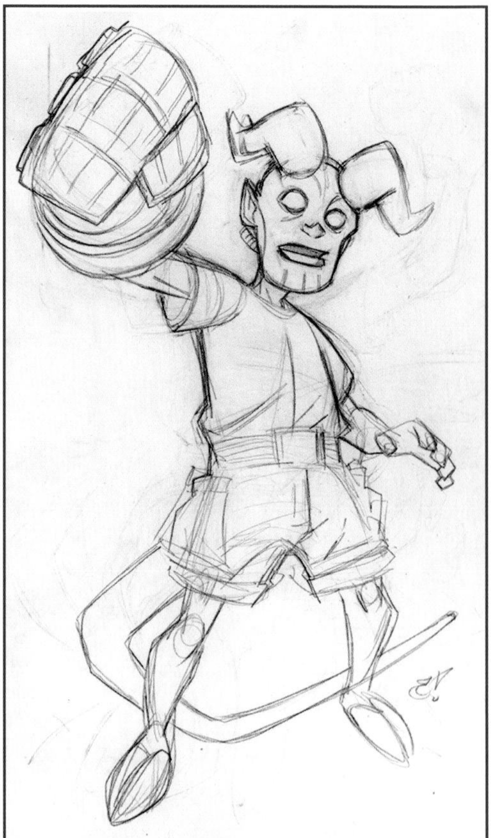

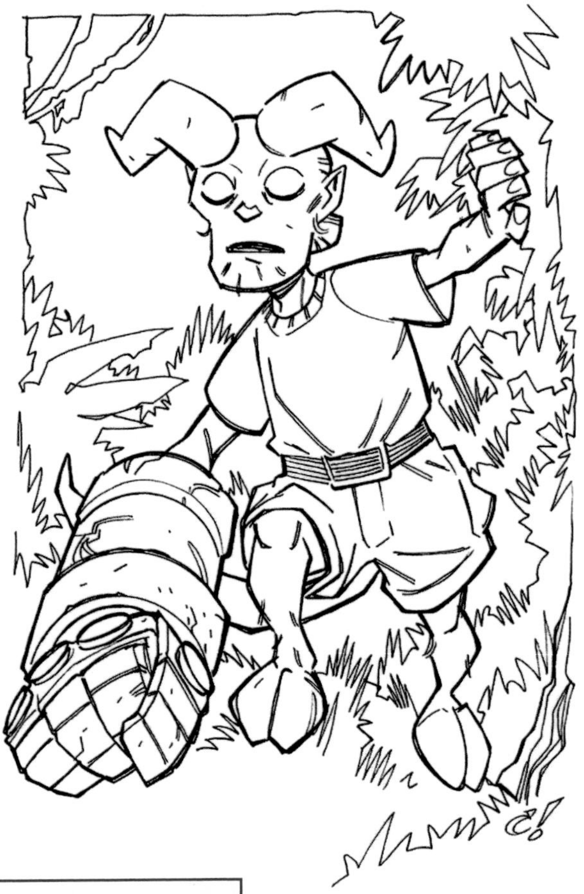

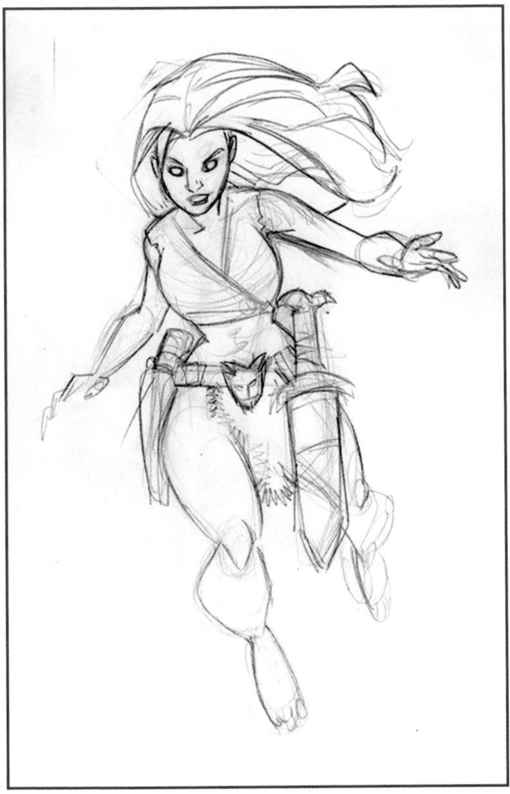

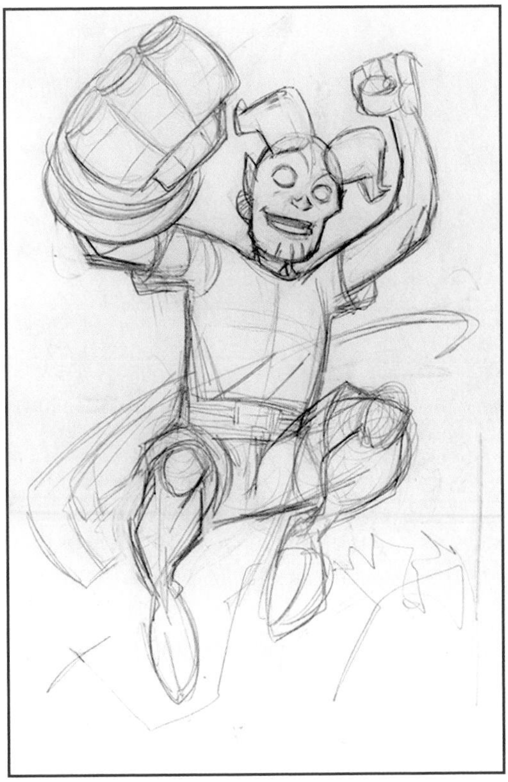

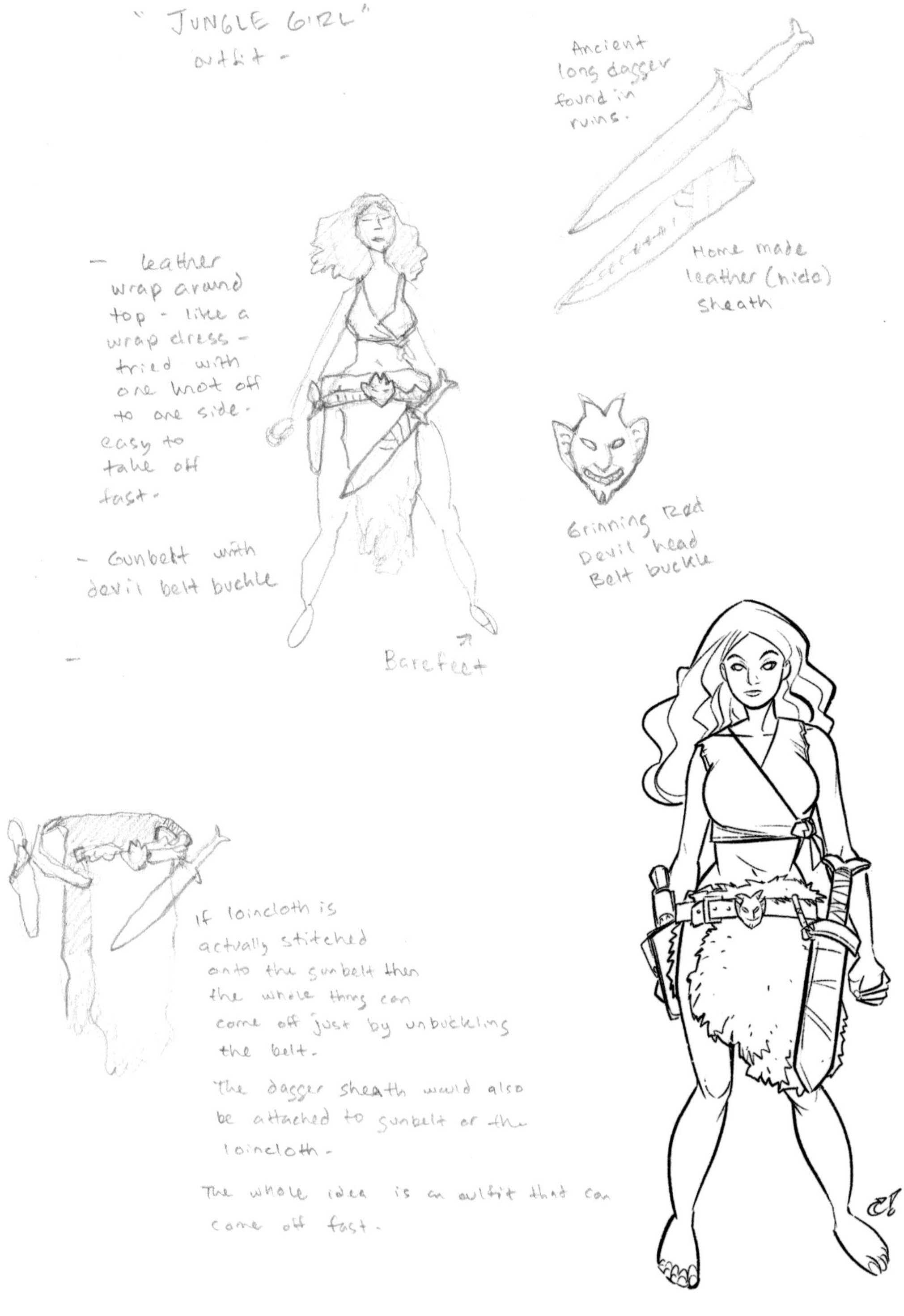
"JUNGLE GIRL" outfit -
Ancient long dagger found in ruins.
Home made leather (hide) sheath
- leather wrap around top - like a wrap dress - tied with one knot off to one side. easy to take off fast.
- Gunbelt with devil belt buckle
Grinning Red Devil head Belt buckle
Barefeet
If loincloth is actually stitched onto the gunbelt then the whole thing can come off just by unbuckling the belt.
The dagger sheath would also be attached to gunbelt or the loincloth.
The whole idea is an outfit that can come off fast.

From the beginning, Mike had a particular vision for our heroic jungle girl, Scarlett, so he did this sketch sheet with notes about her outfit, belt buckle, and dagger. Readers loved her as much as we hoped, so we may just see her again.

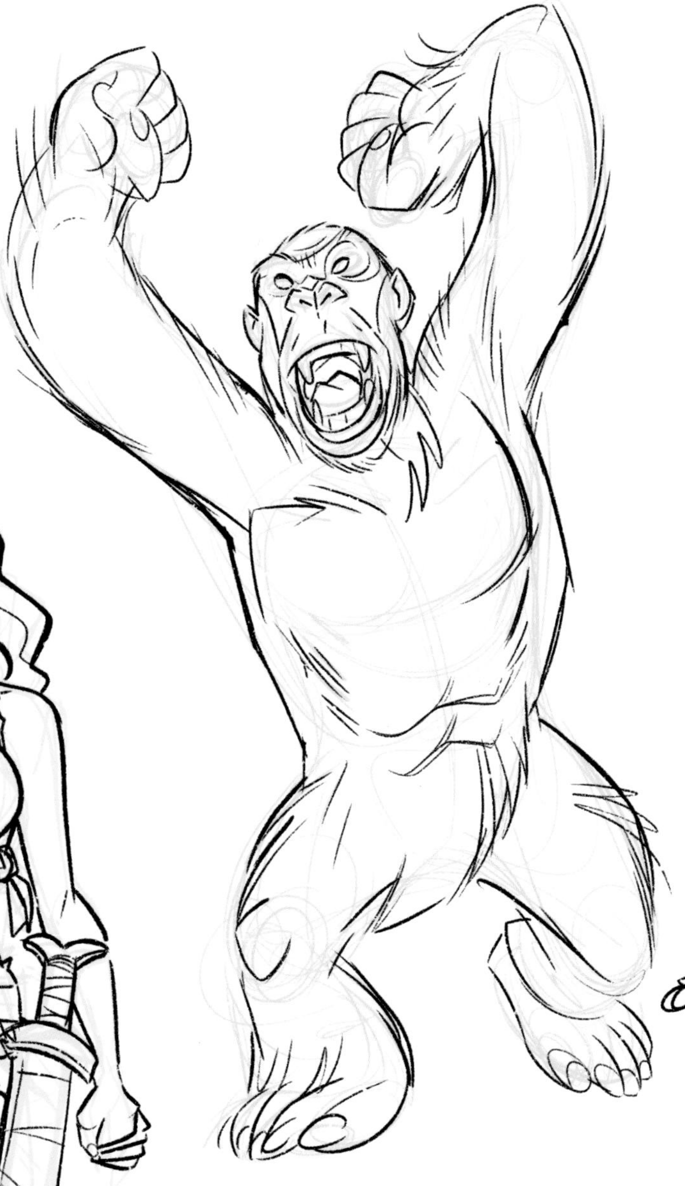

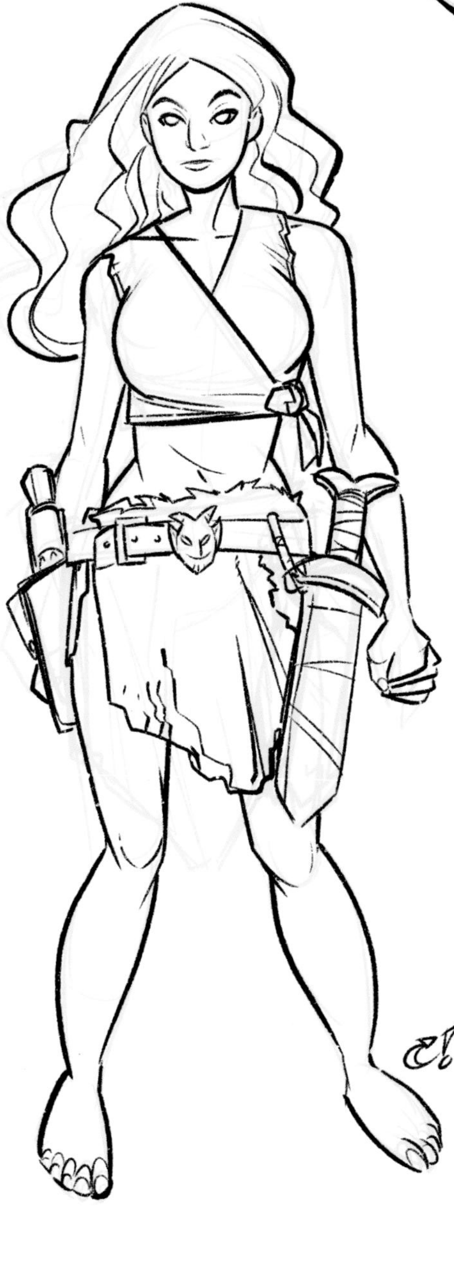

Craig's take on Scarlett in human and transformed ape form.

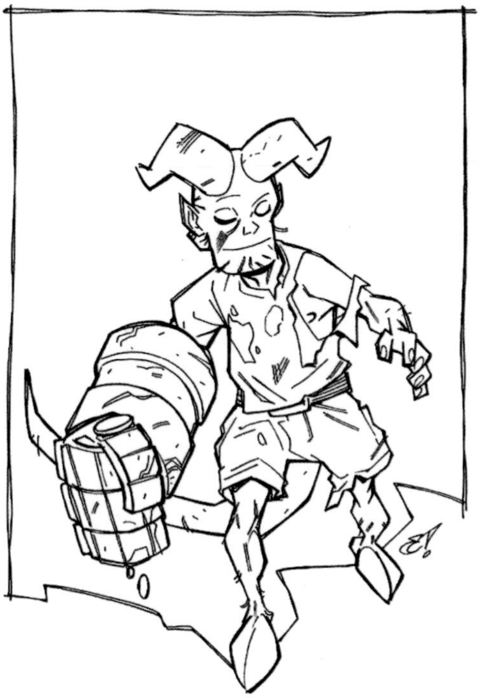

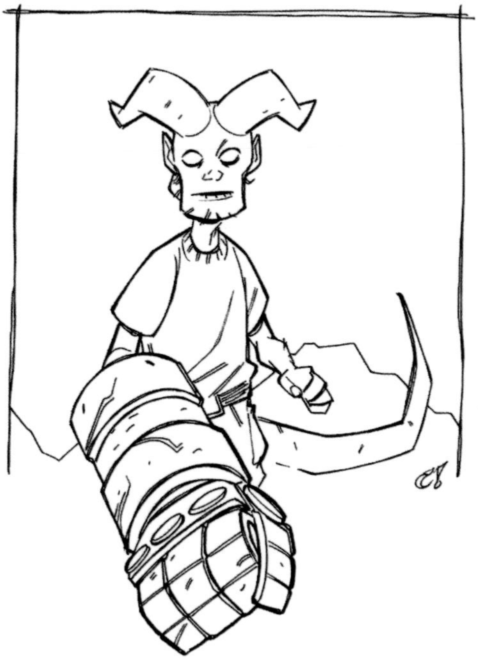

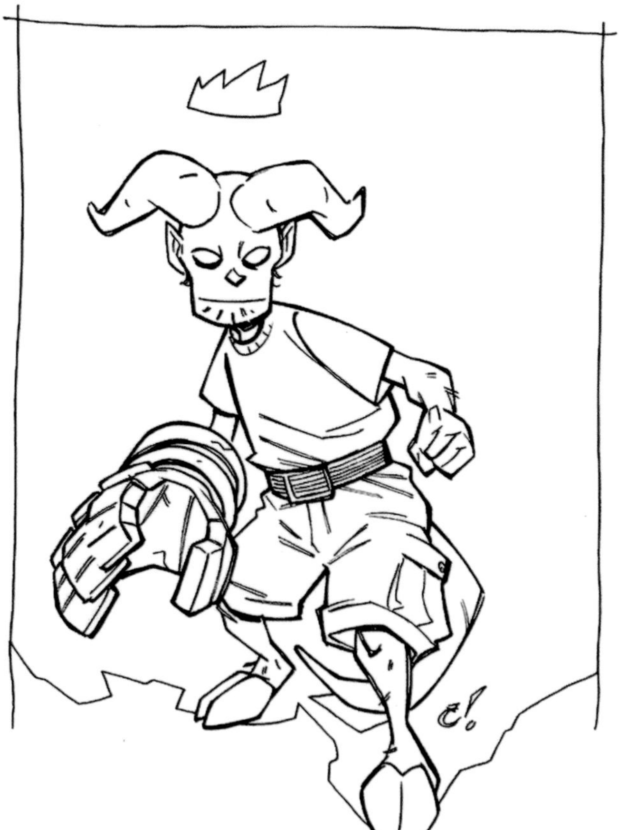

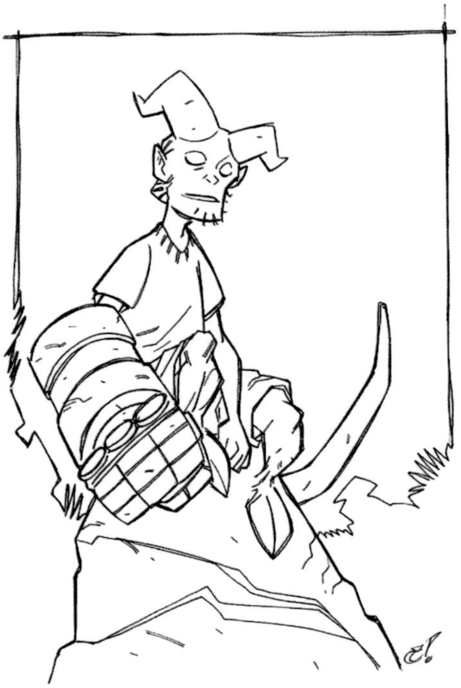

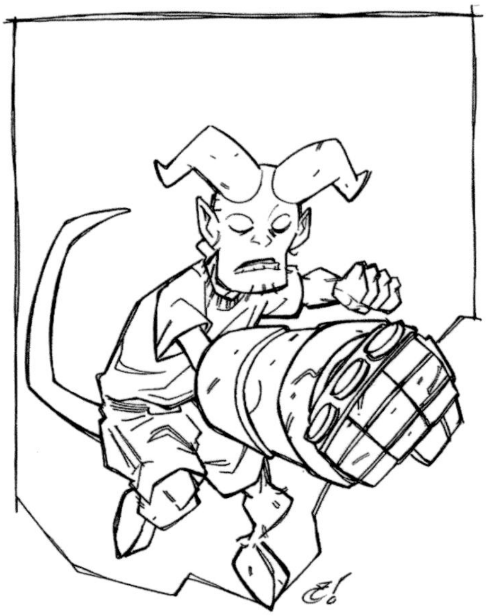

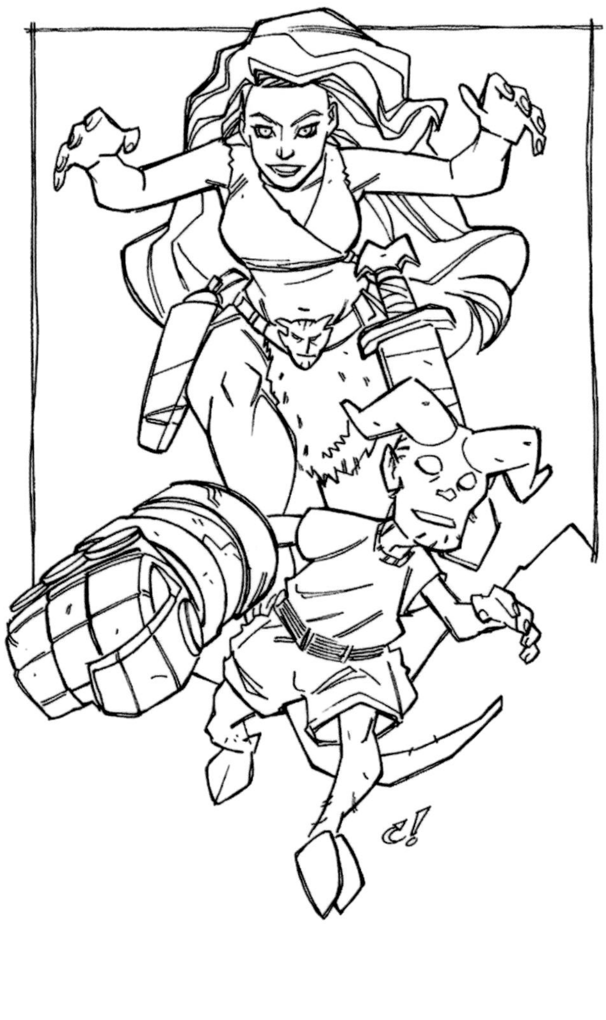

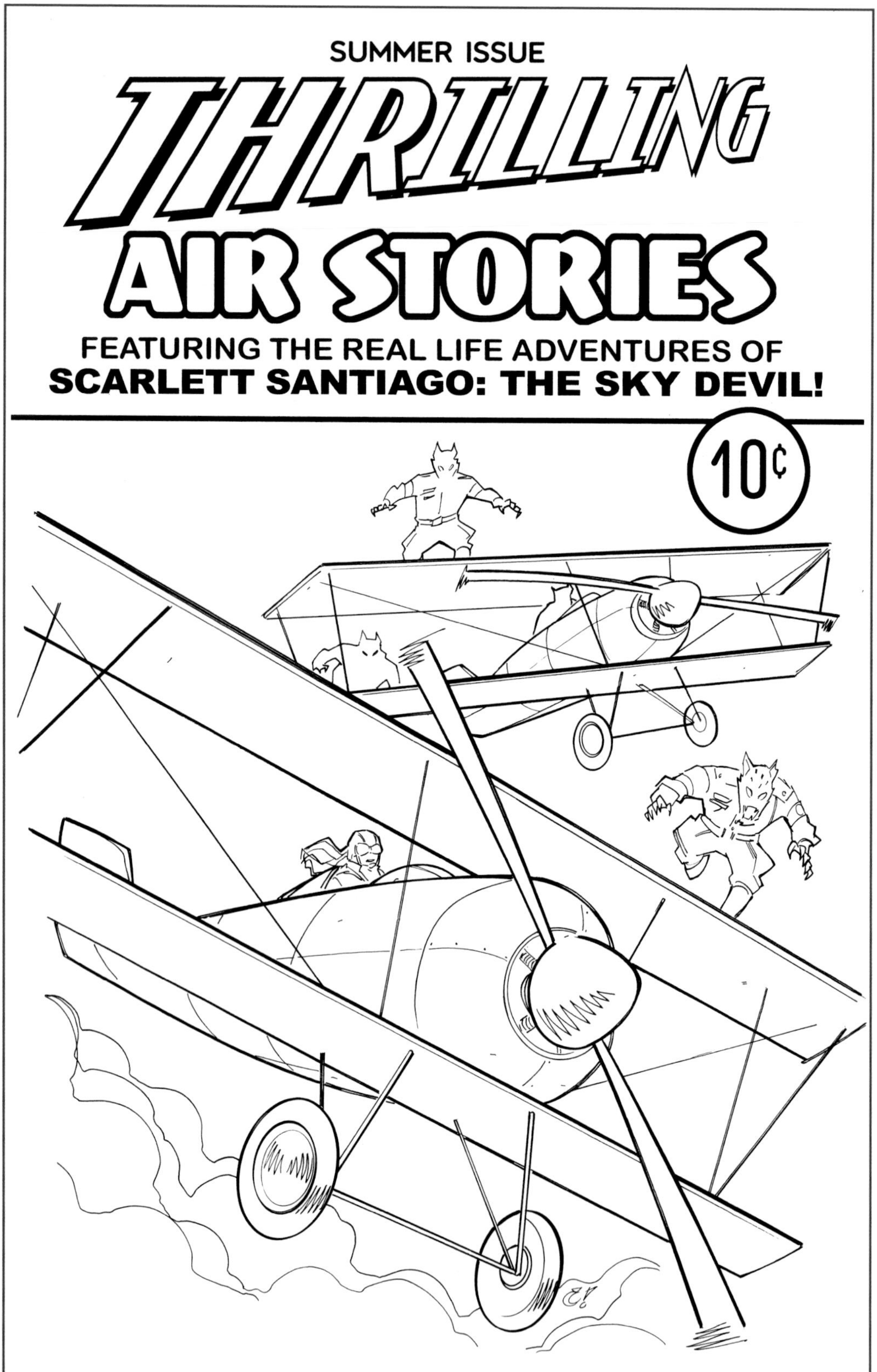
SUMMER ISSUE
THRILLING
AIR STORIES
FEATURING THE REAL LIFE ADVENTURES OF
SCARLETT SANTIAGO: THE SKY DEVIL!
10¢

Craig's cover to the pulp comic Hellboy reads in #2 and #4. This was drawn once at full-size and digitally merged into the line art for those pages later on.

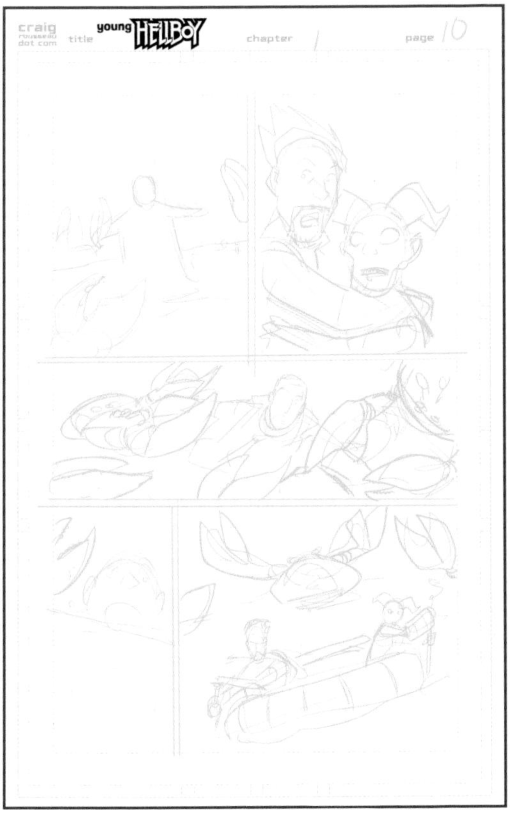
craig rousseau dot com
title
young HELLBOY
chapter 1
page 10

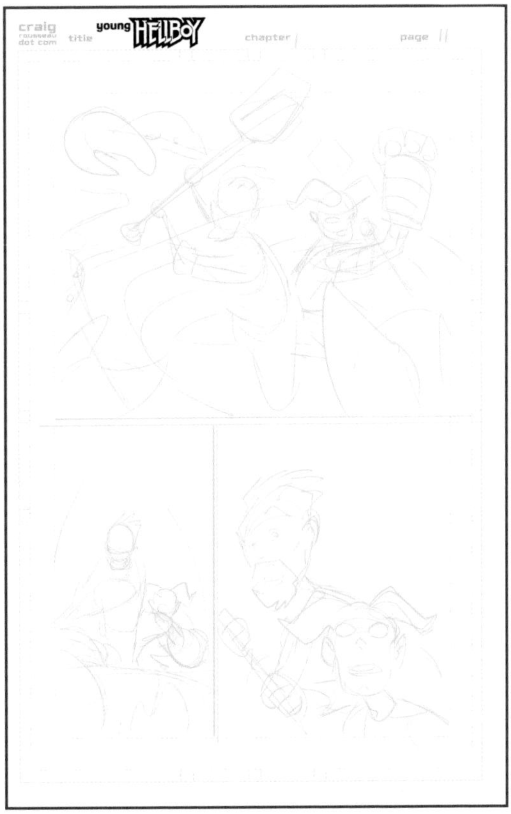
craig rousseau dot com
title
young HELLBOY
chapter 1
page 11

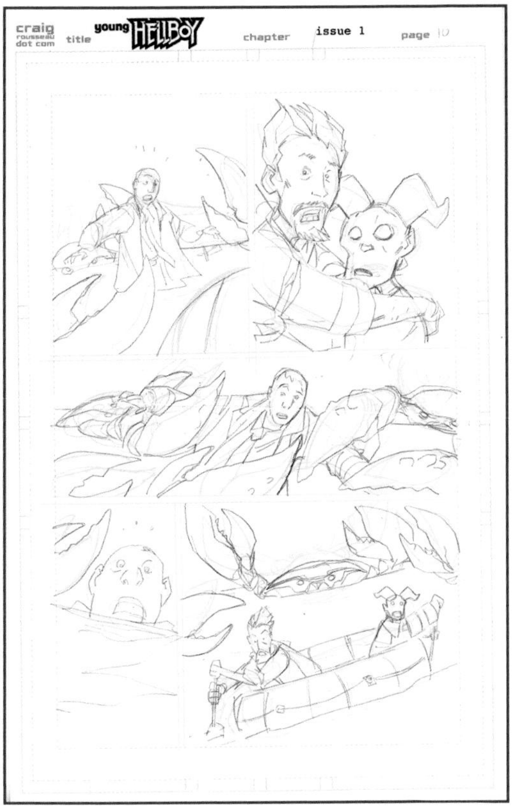
craig rousseau dot com
title
young HELLBOY
chapter
issue 1
page 10

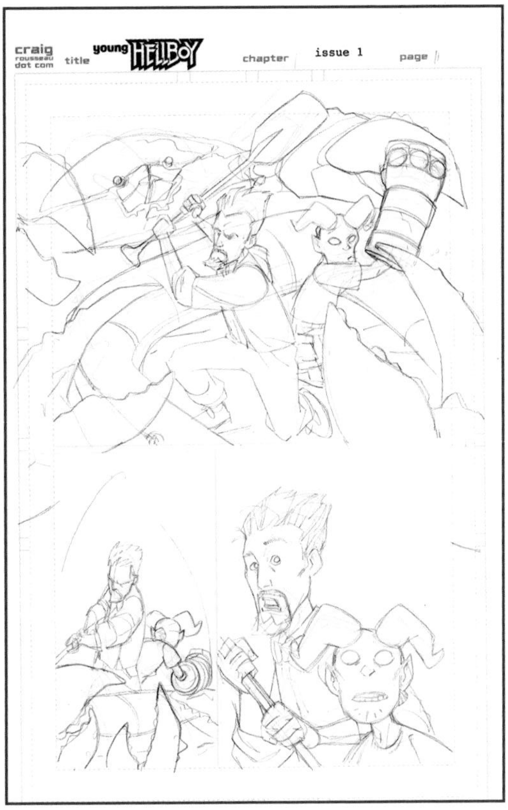
craig rousseau dot com
title
young HELLBOY
chapter
issue 1
page 11

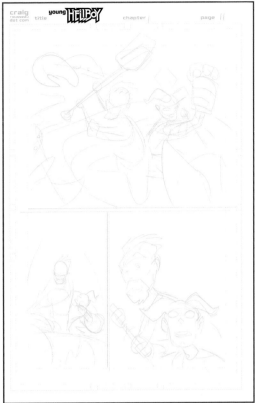

Layouts (top), pencils (bottom), and inks (following) for #1 pages 10-11, the big crab scene! You can see the finals on pages 16-17 of this volume.

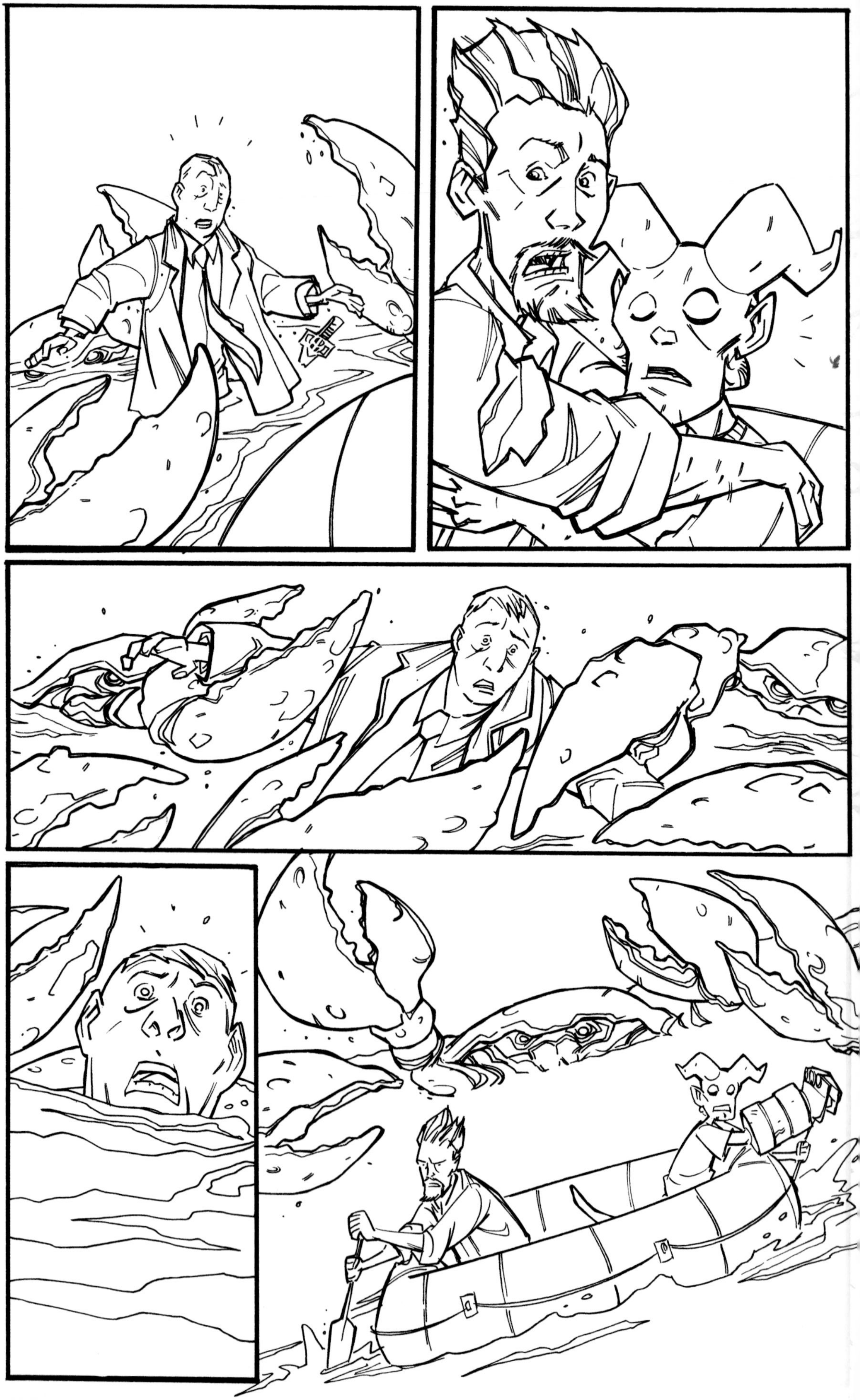

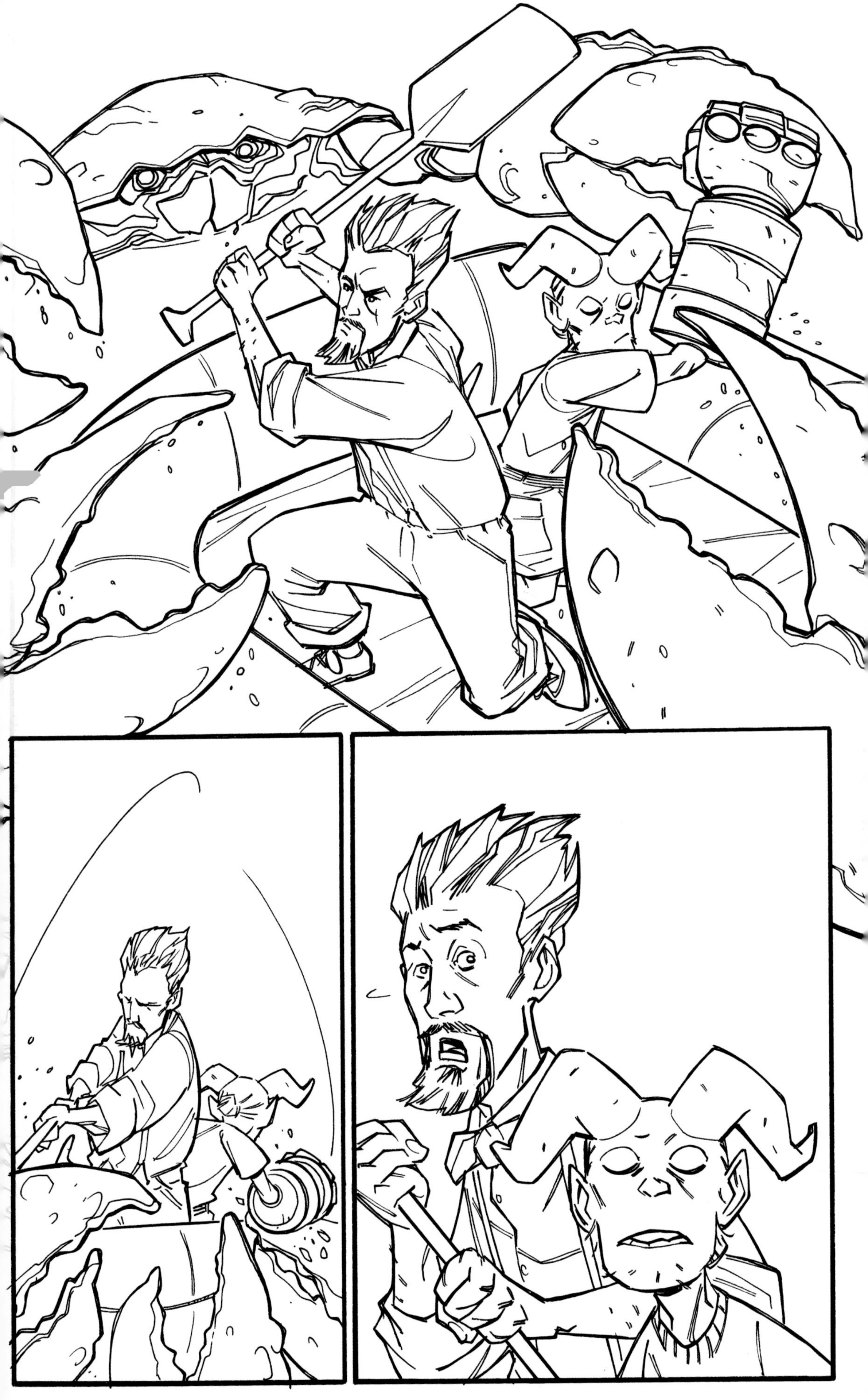

Vampire Queen.

shapes that suggest
bat wings but are
not realistic wing shapes.

← Hair .

Not ear rings —
They hang down from
the dress .

Mike's take on Vesperra.

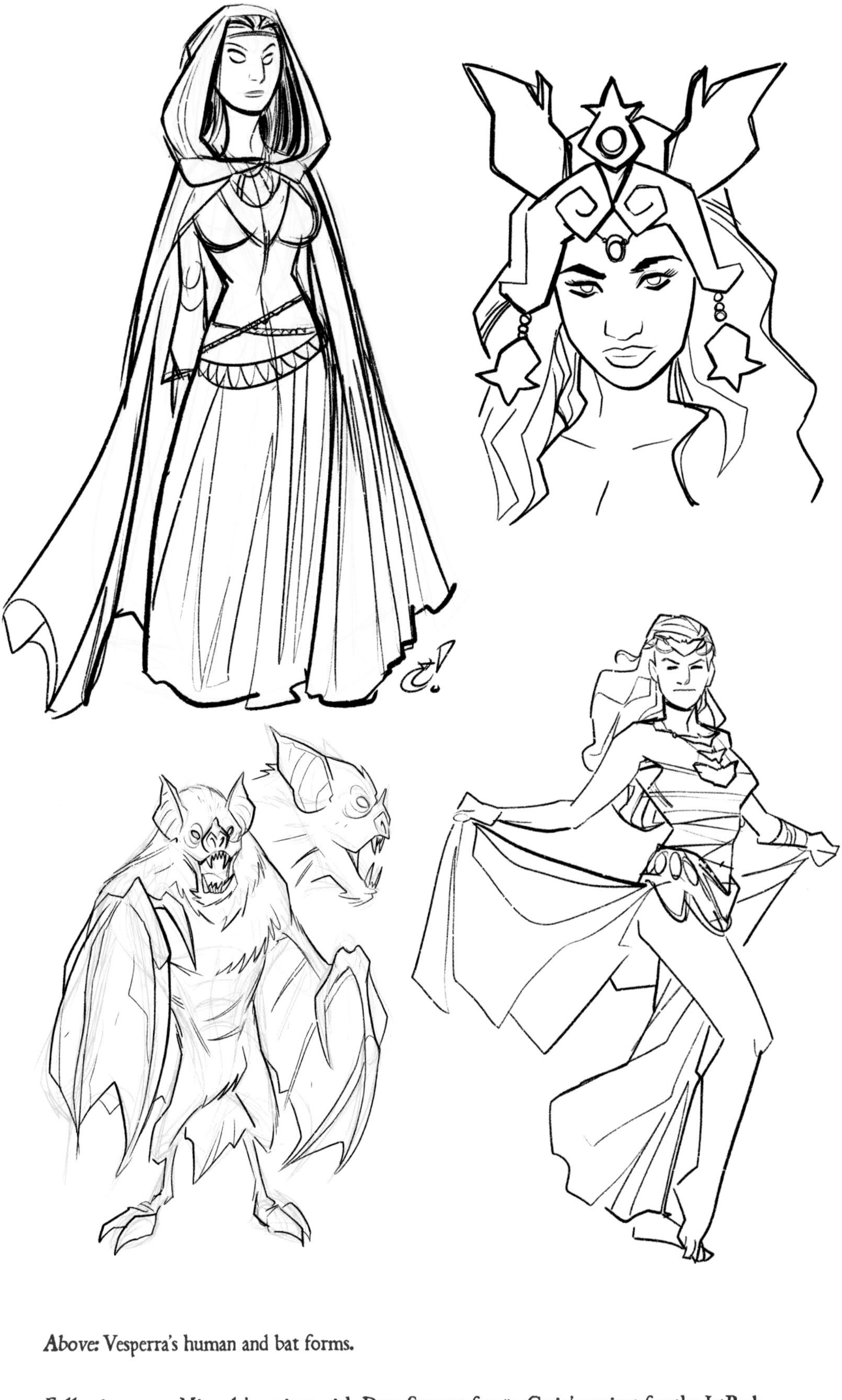

Above: Vesperra's human and bat forms.

Following pages: Mignola's variant with Dave Stewart for #1, Craig's variant for the JetPack Comics/Forbidden Planet edition for #1, Rachele Aragno's variant for #2, Wylie Beckert's variant for #3, and Anthony Carpenter's variant for #4

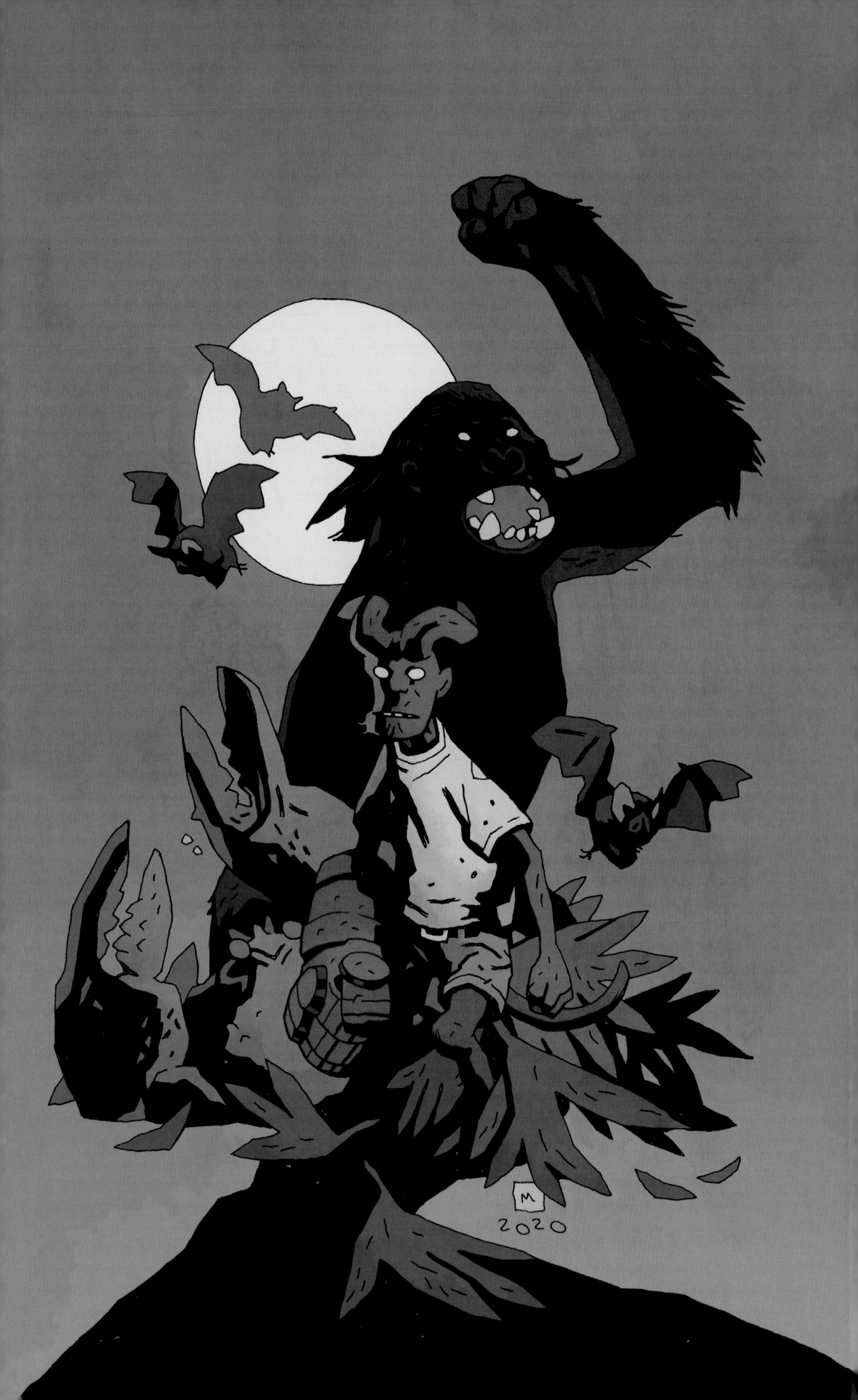
M
2020

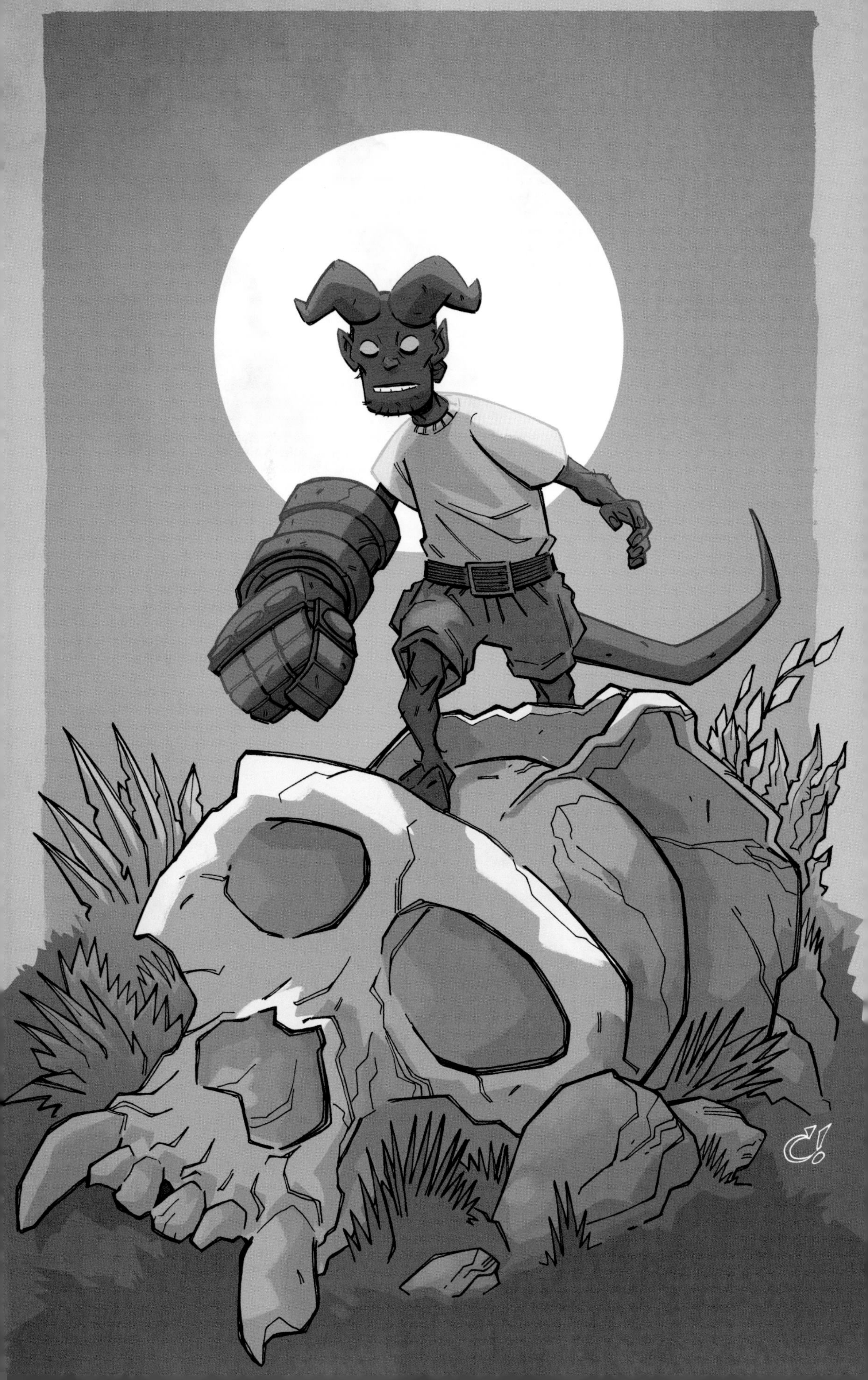

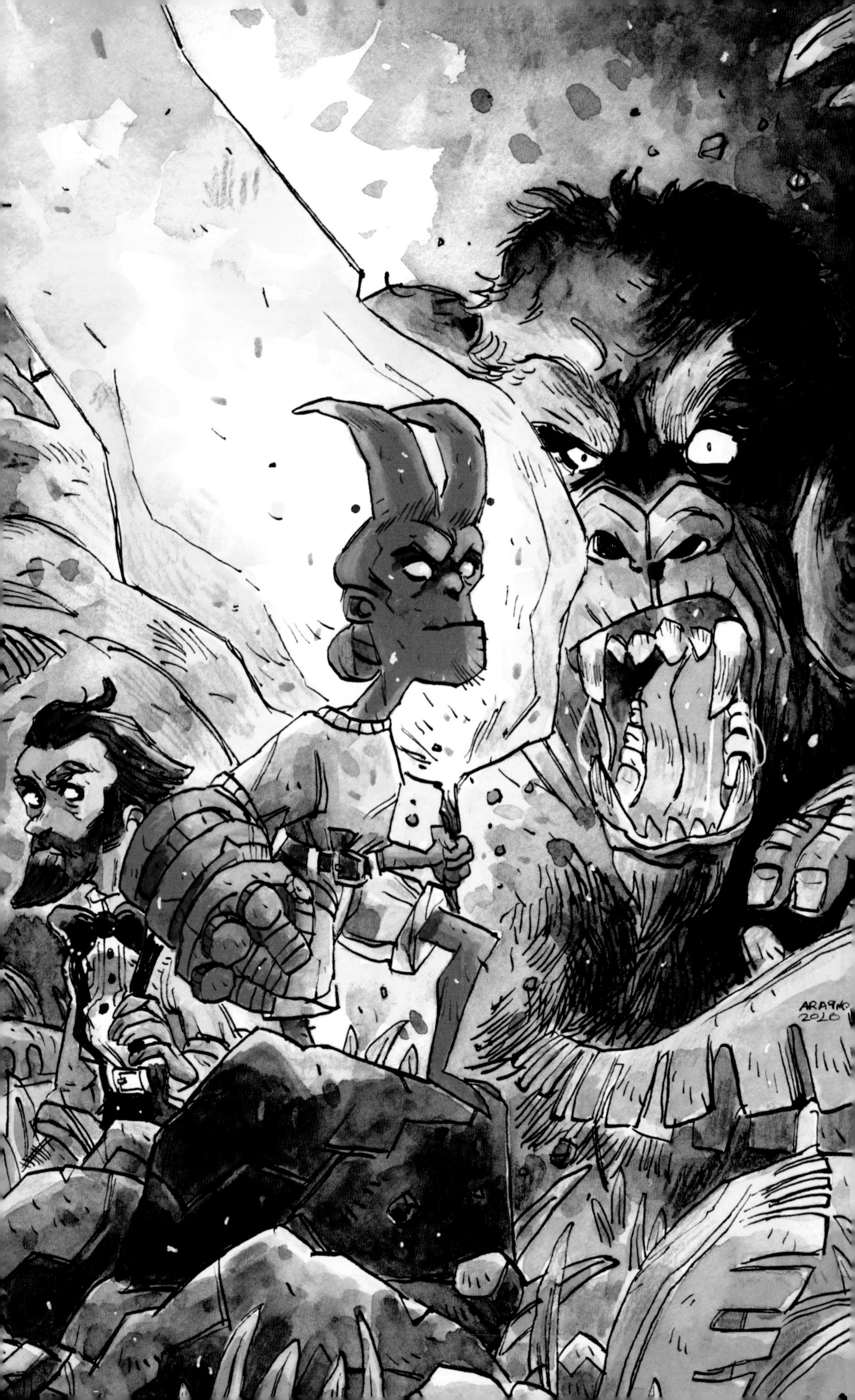

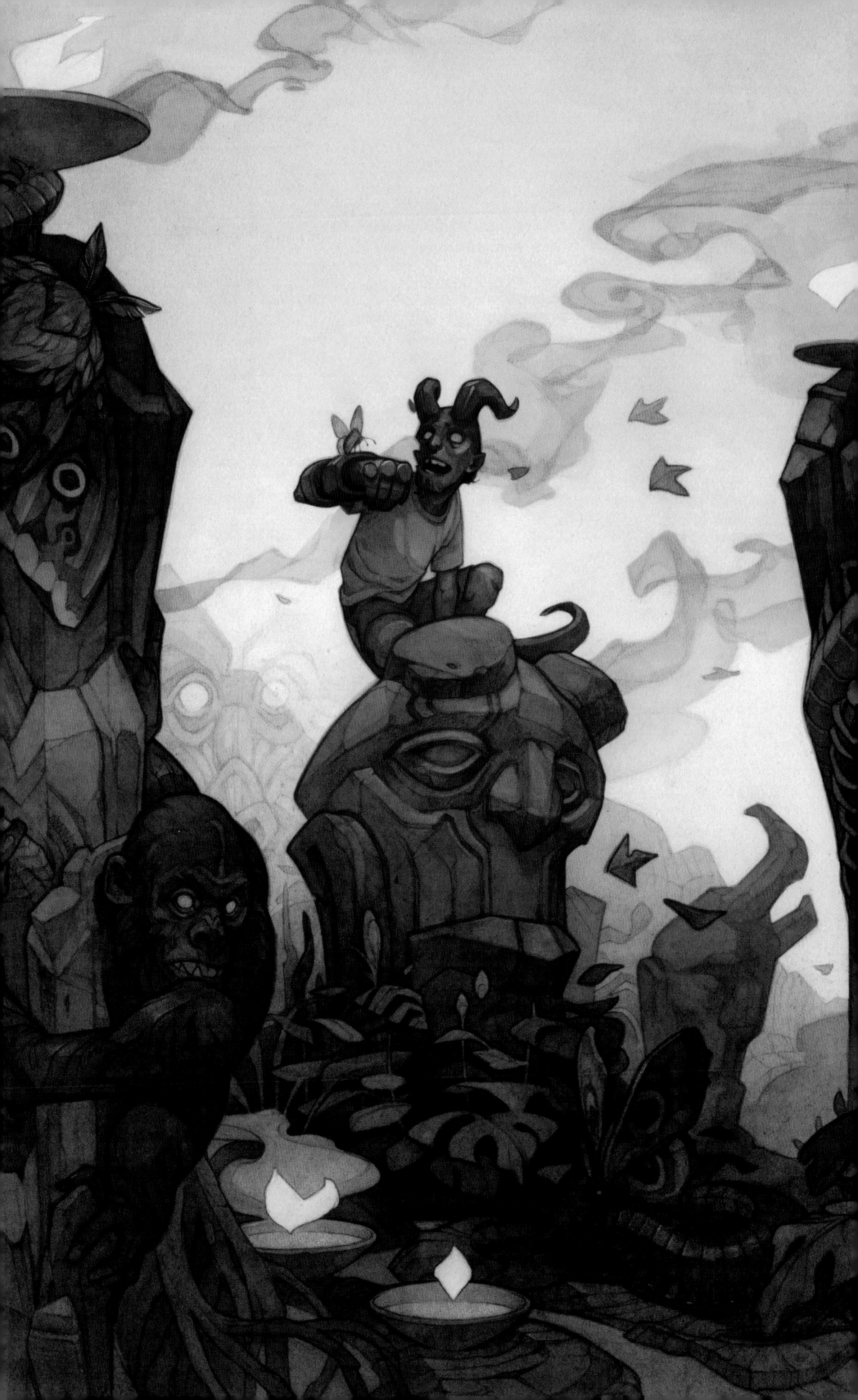

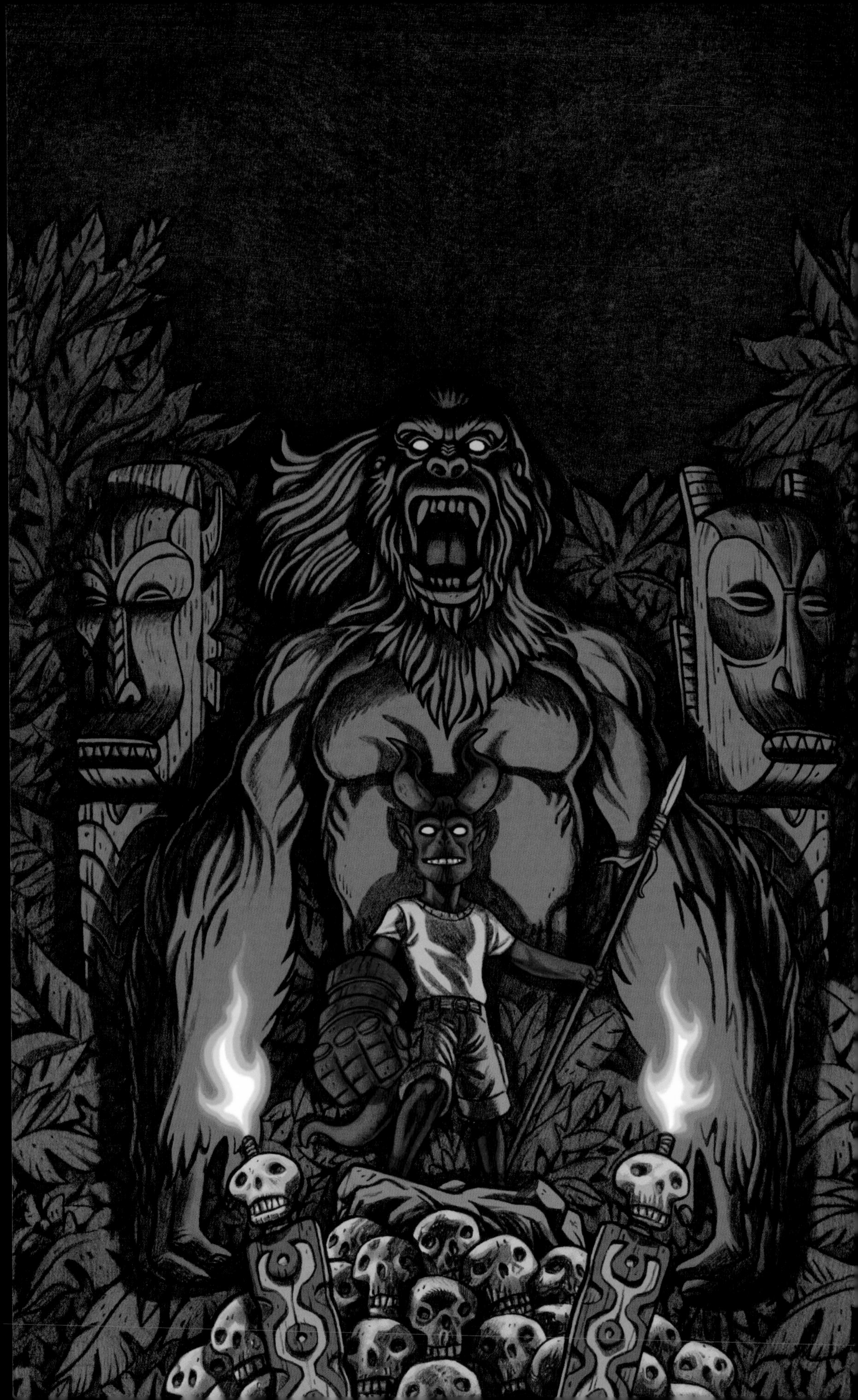

Also by MIKE MIGNOLA

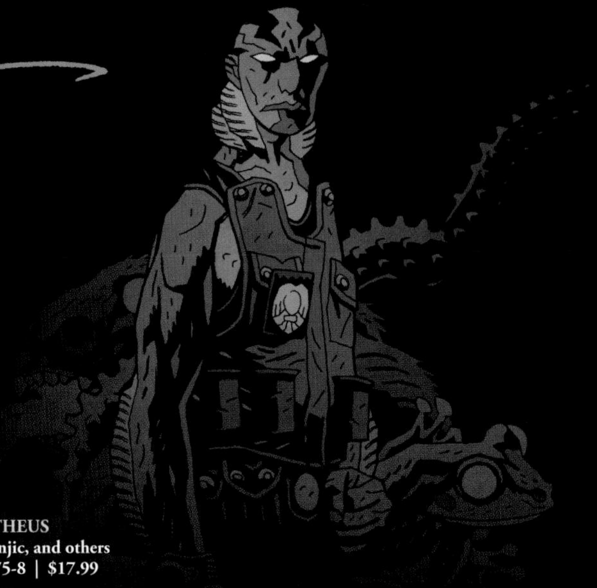

B.P.R.D. PLAGUE OF FROGS

VOLUME 1
with John Arcudi, Guy Davis, and others
TPB: ISBN 978-1-59582-675-6 | $19.99

VOLUME 2
ISBN 978-1-59582-676-3 | $24.99

VOLUME 3
ISBN 978-1-61655-622-8 | $24.99

VOLUME 4
ISBN 978-1-61655-641-9 | $24.99

1946–1948
with Joshua Dysart, Paul Azaceta, Fábio Moon, Gabriel Bá, Max Fiumara, and Arcudi
ISBN 978-1-50671-433-2 | $24.99

BEING HUMAN
with Scott Allie, Arcudi, Davis, and others
ISBN 978-1-59582-756-2 | $17.99

BPRD: VAMPIRE Second Edition
with Moon and Bá
ISBN 978-1-50671-189-8 | $19.99

B.P.R.D. HELL ON EARTH

VOLUME 1
with Allie, Arcudi, Davis, Tyler Crook, and others
HC: ISBN 978-1-50670-360-2 | $34.99
TPB: ISBN 978-1-50671-970-2 | $29.99

VOLUME 2
ISBN 978-1-50670-388-6 | $34.99

VOLUME 3
ISBN 978-1-50670-490-6 | $34.99

VOLUME 4
ISBN 978-1-50670-654-2 | $34.99

VOLUME 5
ISBN 978-1-50670-815-7 | $34.99

B.P.R.D. THE DEVIL YOU KNOW

with Laurence Campbell, Chris Mitten, and Sebastián Fiumara
OMNIBUS
ISBN 978-1-50671-971-9 | $24.99

VOLUME 1: MESSIAH
ISBN 978-1-50670-196-7 | $19.99

VOLUME 2: PANDEMONIUM
ISBN 978-1-50670-653-5 | $19.99

VOLUME 3: RAGNA ROK
ISBN 978-1-50670-814-0 | $19.99

MIKE MIGNOLA: THE QUARANTINE SKETCHBOOK

ISBN 978-1-50672-427-0 | $39.99

ABE SAPIEN

DARK AND TERRIBLE
VOLUME 1
with Allie, S. Fiumara, and M. Fiumara
ISBN 978-1-50670-538-5 | $34.99

VOLUME 2
ISBN 978-1-50670-385-5 | $34.99

LOST LIVES
AND OTHER STORIES
with Allie, Arcudi, Michael Avon Oeming, and others
ISBN 978-1-50670-220-9 | $19.99

LOBSTER JOHNSON

THE IRON PROMETHEUS
with Arcudi, Tonci Zonjic, and others
ISBN 978-1-59307-975-8 | $17.99

THE BURNING HAND
ISBN 978-1-61655-031-8 | $17.99

SATAN SMELLS A RAT
ISBN 978-1-61655-203-9 | $18.99

GET THE LOBSTER
ISBN 978-1-61655-505-4 | $19.99

THE PIRATE'S GHOST AND METAL MONSTERS OF MIDTOWN
ISBN 978-1-50670-206-3 | $19.99

A CHAIN FORGED IN LIFE
ISBN 978-1-50670-178-3 | $19.99

WITCHFINDER

OMNIBUS VOLUME 1
With Ben Stenbeck, John Arcudi, Tyler Crook, and others
ISBN 978-1-50671-442-4 | $34.99

CITY OF THE DEAD
with Roberson and Stenbeck
ISBN 978-1-50670-166-0 | $19.99

THE GATES OF HEAVEN
with Roberson, D'Israeli, and Clem Robins
ISBN 978-1-50670-683-2 | $19.99

THE REIGN OF DARKNESS
with Christopher Mitten and Chris Roberson
ISBN 978-1-50671-406-6 | $19.99

RISE OF THE BLACK FLAME

with Roberson and Christopher Mitten
ISBN 978-1-50670-155-4 | $19.99

THE VISITOR: HOW AND WHY HE STAYED

with Roberson, Paul Grist, and Bill Crabtree
ISBN 978-1-50670-345-9 | $19.99

FRANKENSTEIN UNDERGROUND

with Stenbeck
ISBN 978-1-61655-782-9 | $19.99

RASPUTIN: THE VOICE OF THE DRAGON

with Roberson and Mitten
ISBN 978-1-50670-498-2 | $19.99

KOSHCHEI THE DEATHLESS

with Ben Stenbeck
ISBN 978-1-50670-672-6 | $19.99

CRIMSON LOTUS

John Arcudi and Mindy Lee
ISBN 978-1-50670-822-5 | $19.99

JOE GOLEM: OCCULT DETECTIVE—

THE RAT CATCHER & THE SUNKEN DEAD
with Christopher Golden and Patric Reynolds
ISBN 978-1-61655-964-9 | $24.99

THE OUTER DARK
with Golden and Reynolds
ISBN 978-1-50670-395-4 | $24.99

THE DROWNING CITY
with Golden and Bergting
ISBN 978-1-50670-945-1 | $24.99

THE CONJURORS
With Golden and Bergting
ISBN 978-1-50671-413-4 | $24.99

BALTIMORE

OMNIBUS VOLUME 1
With Golden, Stenbeck, and Peter Bergting
ISBN 978-1-50671-246-8 | $34.99

OMNIBUS VOLUME 2
ISBN 978-1-50671-247-5 | $34.99

NOVELS

LOBSTER JOHNSON: THE SATAN FACTORY
with Thomas E. Sniegoski
ISBN 978-1-59582-203-1 | $12.95

JOE GOLEM AND THE DROWNING CITY
with Golden
ISBN 978-1-59582-971-9 | $99.99

BALTIMORE; OR, THE STEADFAST TIN SOLDIER & THE VAMPIRE
with Golden
ISBN 978-1-61655-803-1 | $12.99

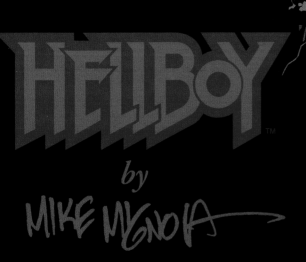

HELLBOY
by MIKE MIGNOLA